MR KEYNES' REVOLUTION

A NOVEL

E. J. BARNES

Greyfire Publishing

ISBN: 978-0-9935158-3-5

This book uses British English spellings/conventions.

1

———

P aris, 1919: three world leaders, determined to wrest a
new Europe from the wreckage of the old; a horde of
hangers-on, all out for what they can get; and a man
about to throw a promising career off a cliff.

THE FRENCH MINISTRY OF FINANCE, part of the old Louvre
Palace, stood upon the banks of the Seine, a fine specimen of
the grandeur and confidence of an age that was lost, buried in
the mud of the trenches, in the vicious, blood-stained battlefields of Flanders. Now the remnants of that world were being
fought over just as fiercely, but this time beneath chandeliers
and mirrors, in a thousand smoke-filled committee rooms. In
one of these, on an upper floor of the Ministry, a group of delegates were discussing the future of Austria. They came from
many countries, and spoke in varying accents, but all were
men, all wore the clothing of officialdom and all had piles of
paper in front of them.

One of those sitting at the long table was a man in his thir-
ties. He was extremely tall – well over six foot – and seemed

to have some difficulties with his limbs, which sprawled, and extended too far from the cuffs and trouser legs of his suit. His eyes were large, dark and intense; his mouth broad and rather sensual – only partly obscured by a luxuriant moustache, it hinted at a nature beyond officialdom. He had a peculiarly magnetic effect on those around him. Even when he was not speaking, they seemed to be waiting for what he had to say.

He was the British Treasury's representative at the Peace Conference, known to most as Mr Keynes, and by his friends as 'Maynard'.

The members of Committee 14(d) had many things to decide about the future of Austria, the former heart of the vast Habsburg Empire, ripped to pieces by the war. New borders, institutions, constitutions must be debated. For now they were addressing simply what the inhabitants had to eat.

'... and so, the majority of us are in agreement that cattle should be relocated from the area surrounding Vienna, in order to relieve shortages in the Prussian region ...'

The chairman spoke in a steady drone. Maynard raised a pen.

'Mr Keynes?'

The Chairman's tone was resigned.

'I object.'

'On what grounds?'

'On the grounds that the citizens of Vienna need their cattle for themselves.'

'But the problems in Prussia–'

'We have it on good evidence that in Vienna they are starving.'

The chairman flinched. He did not like the word, preferring to talk of 'shortages'. Besides, it had been a long and increasingly bad-tempered discussion, and he was hoping to wrap the matter up.

'I think we must remember that reports can be exaggerated–'

'*Starving*,' Maynard repeated. 'We have received credible reports of widespread starvation. I remind you that eye witnesses–'

A door opened onto the committee room. Maynard's attention shifted to the man who stood there, signalling discreetly. He rose hastily, gathering papers.

'I am called away. Please put on record that the British delegation can in no way agree to the confiscation of Austrian cattle.'

'Your objection is noted.'

The remaining delegates perked up as Maynard made for the door. The chances of the average Viennese citizen sitting down to a schnitzel in the near future might have declined, but the chances of the delegates making an earlier exit, to the hotels and restaurants of Paris, had just risen considerably.

In the corridor, Maynard set the pace.

'They don't seem to realize that Vienna is on the brink of revolution,' he told his bemused companion. 'Revolution or collapse. The average calorie intake is not half of what is needed to sustain life. How can a city which depends on manufactured goods and banking hope to feed itself after a war, when the things it produces are no longer in demand?'

'I'm sorry to–'

'Don't worry. I've argued myself hoarse but it makes no difference to them.' Maynard turned the corner into a wider corridor. 'So it's definitely on the agenda? My note? The Keynes Plan?'

'Not formally, but–'

'Have they finished lunch?'

'They – as I left–'

'And Lloyd George?'

'He's going to raise it, he says. He wants you there.'

Maynard stopped abruptly to stare at his companion – a very junior, bespectacled member not of the British, but the South-African, delegation, sent by command of General Smuts, who happened to be a friend of Maynard's. The young man, alarmed by the scrutiny, blinked and almost stepped into a passing trolley laden with patisserie. Around them the vast corridor heaved with conference minions going about their business: delegates clutching papers, journalists clutching notebooks, representatives from far-flung places, some in turbans or kaftans or versions of military dress; even a small group of women (members of the International Women's Conference) in long skirts and wide-brimmed hats. Among them too, industrialists, trade unionists, gun dealers, nationalists …

'I'd almost lost hope,' said Maynard. 'And now, suddenly, I'm not sure I can bear it.' He waved an arm. 'Or *this*. Look at them. Everyone on the make.' He did not wait for an answer but plunged back into the river of perspiring humanity.

Fifteen minutes later they got out of a taxi at the Crillon Hotel and entered a different world: the corridors deserted, the carpet muffling their footfalls, the riff-raff kept away. Yet this was the beating heart of everything: in the drawing room, amongst Ormolu clocks and silk fringes and far too much gilt, the Big Three – President Wilson, Prime Minister Clemenceau and Prime Minister Lloyd George – made the final decisions about Europe's borders, Europe's institutions and, crucially, how much a vanquished and humiliated Germany should be made to pay in atonement for the war.

Maynard paused in the entrance. The Big Three stood with their backs to the fireplace, about to take their seats. Gaggles of attendants stood about the room, and on one side a table was laid out with a map of Europe, adorned with red-inked lines and small flags.

A group of British officials looked at Maynard expectantly, but his attention was all for the Big Three.

Lloyd George was laughing at a joke Clemenceau had made; as his head turned, his eye caught Maynard's. He nodded a greeting, then looked back towards the French Prime Minister, said something – impossible for Maynard to make out what – then turned to a hovering official, snapped out an order, took a paper from him, turned back to the French Prime Minister, waved the paper, started to speak urgently–

My paper, thought Maynard, with a thud in his chest. The Keynes plan.

Clemenceau took it, sneered – there was no other word for it – then, with an emphatic shake of his head, cast it aside. *We've moved on. We're not interested. Don't waste our time.* Wilson nodded, mournful as a bloodhound. A French official picked up the discarded document and began to crumple it absently between his fingers: disposed of: discarded: forgotten. Lloyd George looked towards Maynard, gave a slight, apologetic shrug – *Well, I tried, but you see how it is* – and the discussion moved on.

The last hope, kindled so unexpectedly, had been snuffed out.

All those calculations, all those cunning proposals, all those persuasive passages … all those late nights.

Maynard sank into a chair. One of the British officials, a tall man with smooth, swept-back hair, gazed at him with concern, but Maynard did not notice.

His head was throbbing. Snatches of the discussion came to him as if through water: 'No more delays … German signature demanded … No further negotiations …' There was a rushing sound in his ears. He felt feverish and suddenly recalled that he had eaten nothing since a half slice of toast at breakfast. Around him, the babble of voices rose as raucous as ravens.

I've had enough.

He stood up, so abruptly that his chair crashed to the floor. The papers in his hand scattered. Maynard did not trouble to pick them up. He was aware of a sea of faces turned towards him, including those of the Big Three, now enthroned in their vast armchairs near the fireplace, and of a sudden, expectant silence.

'To hell with it,' he declared. 'To hell with all of it.' He lunged for the door and crashed out of the room.

The dust motes drifted in the streams of light from the windows. After a pause, the discussion resumed.

Only the smooth-haired British official was still staring at the door.

'There's a career consigned to oblivion,' his neighbour said.

'I wouldn't bank on it,' said Foxy Falk.

LONDON. His Majesty's Treasury was an altogether less imposing building than its French equivalent. A grey edifice wreathed in the grey remnants of a London fog, unadorned and rather squat, it sat stolidly looking out upon Whitehall. Power, and the appearance of power, are not the same thing, however: it was HM Treasury that held the purse strings, and consequently Treasury mandarins who told the rest of Whitehall what it could and could not do. Nor was the Treasury's influence any the less if at this particular moment in history, the purse was almost empty.

The office belonging to Mr Keynes, the head of B Division, was in keeping with the building: a utilitarian desk, some bookshelves and a long window hung with standard-issue government curtains of a peculiarly unappealing hue. In the midst of it was Maynard himself, still dressed in the grey suit of the bureaucrat, but stripping shelves and emptying papers with a frenzy seldom seen in Whitehall.

Finally, he pulled open the desk drawers, nearly

wrenching them onto the floor, and emptied the contents onto his desk. Among the papers were cigarettes, a lighter, a spare tie, a book of Marvell's poetry, cufflinks ... and a photograph. He picked it up, gazed at it, stroked it tenderly with a finger ...

There was a cough at the doorway. Hastily, he inserted the photo among the papers in his briefcase and turned to confront Otto Niemeyer.

Niemeyer stared around the ransacked room in unconcealed disapproval.

'What's going on?'

'Haven't you heard? I've resigned.'

'You've ...? I heard *something*. Naturally, I didn't believe it. I didn't think it possible that you would abandon your department ... your country.'

It was not clear which Niemeyer considered the greater crime.

'There was nothing more I could do for my department or my country. Paris has become a nightmare. They are determined to destroy Germany – and Europe with her. I had no choice.'

'Oh come. I hardly think–'

'They are intent on revenge ... Clemenceau, Wilson, Lloyd George ... All they are interested in is extracting their pound of flesh. And so pleasing the vultures at home. It's not the way to rebuild a continent.'

'That's one opinion. Personally, I think your judgement may be a little ... *clouded*. Of course, the war has been a great strain on all of us.'

'At least we survived it,' said Maynard flatly.

Niemeyer flinched, as if he found this distasteful. He continued standing in the doorway, his mouth pursed, as Maynard stowed his remaining things.

'I do hope–'

'Don't worry, Otto, I haven't taken anything that isn't mine.'

Niemeyer bristled. 'I didn't mean to suggest–'

'The boxes can be sent on. I've put the address. Have a look through, if you want. It's strange the amount of stuff you accumulate in four years–'

'You were never really a department man, were you? Although I'd almost come to think of you as one of us. I suppose it was inevitable really. After all, it's what you did before.' He paused, and then in case Maynard had not got the point, 'I mean, *walk out.*'

'Just a fly-by-night gadabout,' said Maynard politely.

'I never said that.'

'Anyhow, Otto, I wish you all the best for a long and distinguished career.'

Maynard picked up his bulging briefcase. He reached out a hand and after a pause, Niemeyer shook it.

'Likewise, of course. Your Cambridge fellowship will, I'm sure, give you plenty of time to recover your – ahem – equilibrium.'

But Maynard was already gone.

Soon afterwards, Oswald 'Foxy' Falk came in to find Niemeyer still in the same position, contemplating the bare room with, it seemed to Foxy, a look reminiscent of Napoleon on a victorious battlefield.

'I was looking for Keynes–'

'I'm afraid you just missed him.' (The smirk was not so much Napoleon as the cat that had got the cream, Foxy decided.) 'He's left – for good.'

'I was afraid of it. After they turned down his proposals in Paris.'

'A bit of an over-reaction to storm out, don't you think?

Having one's proposals turned down is an occupational hazard of life in the Civil Service.'

'He can't stomach what they've decided. That's the point.'

'Nervous strain, I expect. He wasn't looking well, I must say. Don't they feed you in Paris? I thought it was all wining and dining and dancing at the Majestic?'

Foxy said nothing. Dancing at the Majestic indeed! He stared at Otto curiously and recalled what he'd heard on the grapevine: that years ago, the young Otto Niemeyer and Maynard Keynes had sat the notoriously stiff Civil Service entrance exams together: Otto had come first by a whisker and Maynard second. Otto had gone to the Treasury and Maynard to the India Office, where he had soon decided the Civil Service was not for him. While Otto climbed steadily into the higher echelons of public service, Maynard lectured on economics at Cambridge – until war broke out, Maynard was unexpectedly summoned to the Treasury to help his country in its time of need, and Otto Niemeyer was forced to watch as his old rival ascended like a rocket through the Treasury ranks.

Foxy thought that Otto had always resented Maynard's influence, and his suspicions were confirmed by the look he saw on his face.

'Anyway, he'll have time to recover now,' Niemeyer went on. 'Fewer demands. He never really had the temperament for public service. Much better suited to life as a Cambridge don; far less taxing.'

And no longer a threat to you, Otto. Foxy, who was even taller than Maynard, stared down at the considerably shorter Otto.

'Well,' he said, rather distantly, 'I'd better be off. I'm going back to Paris tonight.'

'Don't overdo it, will you, Falk? We wouldn't want you to go the way of Maynard!' Niemeyer gave a bark of laughter, as Foxy left the room.

. . .

'KEYNES, WAIT!'

Maynard turned and paused as Foxy came legging it down the pavement towards him, his arm raised like somebody hailing a cab.

'Oh, it's you, Falk.'

'Foxy.'

'Yes, of course.'

They shook hands, eyeing each other appraisingly, as if the years at the Treasury and the Peace Conference now had to be reassessed entirely.

'Why aren't you in Paris?' Maynard asked.

'I was sent home on various errands at the behest of our political masters. One of them – well, Lloyd George actually – said to ask if you wouldn't reconsider. I take it …?'

'No.'

'I thought not. Well, I'm going back tonight. But not for long.'

'No, it won't be much longer. Once they've forced the Germans to sign…'

They began to walk along the pavement. A light rain started to fall.

'What will you do now? Cambridge?'

'I suppose so.' Maynard flinched. 'Only – not yet.'

Foxy thought Maynard looked jumpy and rundown: Niemeyer had been right about that much. There were deep shadows on his face, his clothes hung more loosely than even six weeks before and there was a twitch under his left eye. But he was also infused with a kind of nervous energy. 'I'm looking forward to academic life,' Maynard told Foxy. 'Admittedly, it will be a bit of a shock to return to an academic income.'

'Then don't.' And, as Maynard raised enquiring eyebrows, 'I mean it. I'm leaving the Treasury after the Peace Conference and I always meant to go back to the City–'

'Stockbroking, wasn't it?'

'That's right. You've a good nose for investments, I suspect. In fact, I know it from talking to you in Paris. Come and join me.'

'As a broker?' Maynard's tone was politely incredulous.

'No. As a private investor. We'll run a portfolio together, on our own account … for others too, if they'll join us. I reckon we'd make a packet. For a start, currencies are so volatile. Not like they were on the gold standard. It will still leave you plenty of time for your academic pursuits.'

'Financial speculators then?'

'Why not?'

'How d'you know I've anything to speculate with?'

Foxy laughed. 'I don't. Admittedly, it would help. But even if you can only lend your brains to the enterprise …'

'I don't know, Foxy.' Maynard, who had seemed intrigued momentarily by the idea, looked sceptical. 'It's not really what I had in mind.'

'Of course,' said Foxy, very casually, 'Otto would hate it.'

Maynard immediately bristled. 'What d'you mean?'

'I mean, he's delighted that you're burying yourself in Cambridge. He loves to think of you lecturing undergraduates on Elementary Theory in your patched tweed jacket, before heading back to a snoozing Senior Common Room. With no audience for your pen or your heretical ideas but the readers of the *Economic Journal*. Meanwhile, Otto will rule the roost at the Treasury. He certainly doesn't want you throwing your weight about with anyone that counts, or making a name for yourself in the City.'

'Damn him!' muttered Maynard. 'If he thinks I'm going to–' Then he stopped short and cast a sharp look at Foxy, who endeavoured to adopt an expression of innocence. 'All right. I'll think about it.'

'Do. Where are you off to now?'

'Sussex.'

'Oh yes? Country-house party?'

'Of a sort.'

Maynard's tone had become distant, and Foxy was intrigued, as he had been on other occasions, by what he might be trying to hide. A mistress? Or a secret meeting with the Asquiths? (Maynard was known to be a Liberal – could he be conspiring with the disenchanted former Prime Minister against the hated Lloyd George?) Or maybe (Foxy let fancy roam) Maynard was part of a hot-bed of Russian-backed Bolshevist conspirators? After all, he had been saying some pretty wild things towards the end in Paris ...

Foxy was still wondering as he made his farewells and set off for the Paris train.

2

Maynard also took a train south, heading deep into the English countryside, towards the rolling fields and hills of Sussex. Some of the other passengers cast sideways glances at him as he sat staring out of the window, perhaps, like Foxy, aware of his nervous tension, and wondering if it were the result of service at the front. Maynard was largely oblivious, as he had been during the war, when the starers had been wondering why a man his age was not in uniform.

He tried to focus on the view from the window – the falling sun and fresh green trees and hedgerows – but his mind kept harking back to Paris. The sick feeling, the sense of dread and dismay, was increasingly leavened by a growing anger. *The waste*, he thought. *The reckless, vindictive, unnecessary waste.* As scenes from the Conference ran through his mind, he found that he was gripping one knee so hard that his fingers hurt.

It was dusk when he arrived. The station master, professionally mournful, informed him there was no chance of a cab; no indeed, old Ned had trouble enough getting petrol these days, though of course if the gentleman was prepared to wait

... But Maynard, with a sudden burst of decision, interrupted his dirge to say there was no difficulty; he would walk. Maybe he would even hitch a ride on the way from some passing farm vehicle. The station master eyed his suit and leather brogues doubtfully, perhaps thinking that any farm worker would have been home for his supper long ago, but agreed to take custody of Maynard's suitcase until he could arrange to collect it. So Maynard set off down the deserted lane, swinging his briefcase and striding out bravely. It was, he thought, an absolute age since he had really walked anywhere.

And gradually, the stresses of the last months began to lift. He breathed in the untainted air and rejoiced in its freshness. No smog, no fog, no dust. No roaring traffic. No sweat from a hundred corralled delegates. Instead, there was a faint scent of ... Maynard was vague about plants. Could it be honeysuckle? There were rustlings from the hedge where birds were making ready for the night, and a cow's head emerged from the leaves, gazing at him with liquid eyes. In the growing darkness, bats flitted over a hayfield.

At the brow of a hill, he was forced to stop for breath. Suddenly he laughed aloud. There, in that hedgerow – yes, *that* was where he had hidden the Cezanne.

He leant against a stile. The Sussex Downs rose before him in shallow curves to meet the sky, where the moon hung like a Chinese lantern. As he stood watching, a barn owl floated out of the nearby wood; it sailed, ghost-like, over the field, then was gone. He stood a moment longer, feeling the quiet.

Perhaps, he thought, *not everything is lost.*

He set off again through the falling dark, and eventually, legs and feet distinctly weary – and with a slight yearning now for London taxis – he saw before him the glowing windows of Charleston.

. . .

'YOU REALLY WALKED OUT?' Duncan's voice was full of marvel, as he contemplated his friend from his end of the sofa. Bunny Garnett, sitting at Duncan's feet, turned to hear Maynard's reply.

'They can all go hang: Lloyd George, the Treasury, the whole damn lot of them.' Maynard stubbed out his cigarette. Relating the story to his friends had revived his anger.

'Well, you've burnt your bridges now,' Duncan said.

Vanessa was sitting in a low armchair, a heap of darning in her lap. 'Well done, Maynard,' she said fervently. 'Well done.'

'Better late than never,' said Bunny, and Maynard flinched.

They were in the sitting room at Charleston, gathered around the fireplace, although all it held on this summer night was a huge vase of wild flowers. The French windows were slightly open and the drapes fluttered in the breeze; an oil lamp glowed on the dresser, with moths fluttering about it, and there were candles on the mantel. In the dimness the rich colours of the walls and drapes – crimsons, golds and blues – glowed like the tent of some Eastern bazaar. Everywhere were the signs of Vanessa and Duncan's habitation; every surface that could be painted bore their decorations: repeated swirls and curlicues like reinvented fleurs-de-lys.

Maynard sprawled with his legs stretched out before him. The remains of a plate of bread and cheese was balanced on the arm of the sofa, as was a glass of whisky, and an ashtray painted by Vanessa to resemble a tortoise. Sustained by the food, his aching feet easing, he had been glad to unburden himself to his friends. But Bunny's words stung.

Duncan noticed. 'Now, now,' he told Bunny, but the look he gave him was more affectionate than reproachful, as he let his hand brush, oh so casually, against Bunny's hair. Vanessa picked up her mending and said quickly, 'So what drove you to it, Maynard? I mean, we knew from your letters you weren't happy.'

'It was just the final straw. I mean, I'd more or less given up hope, resigned myself, and then, over night almost, Lloyd George changed his mind, said he thought my proposals might work – said he'd give it a try. I told myself there was a chance; they aren't *wicked* men after all. Or maybe they are. I don't know. What's been done is pure wickedness.'

His friends waited. Maynard picked up the whisky and took a slug.

'Do you know there are people starving all over Europe? Women, children … there's simply not enough food. Or rather, it's in the wrong places. Markets, contracts, transport networks, they've all broken down. Everyone who has any food is hoarding it. But in Paris, none of that matters: there's nothing but endless bickering, debates about borders, who should take the blame, while everything is collapsing around our ears.'

'I suppose,' ventured Vanessa, 'it's a big job to clear up after a war. Especially *this* war.'

'All the more reason to get it right! It's the *irresponsibility* … At the end of the day, all they care about is trashing Germany. At least, that's all Clemenceau cares about. If Germany is on her knees then France is safe, that's his line of thought. And he brought the others with him. Lloyd George has sense enough to see the difficulties, at least when they are pointed out to him, but after all the promises he made at the last election – the rabble-rousing by the press, the cries for vengeance …'

'What about President Wilson? I thought you said he had principles. After all, the Americans aren't beholden to the French, are they?'

Maynard snorted. 'The French are beholden to *them*. We all are. That's one of the things most people don't realize yet: we survived the war on American loans and now we're up to our necks. I had a plan. I wanted … Well, I won't bore you with the details.'

'Bore us,' said Duncan kindly. 'You know you want to.'

Maynard sent him a fleeting smile. 'Well, it was about the debt really. The obsession of the Big Three is reparations – forcing the Germans to pay the costs of the war; an absolutely ridiculous figure, quite obscene. It came to me that instead of forcing on Germany a bill they couldn't pay, while we struggled to pay the Americans – and our allies struggled to pay *us*, because of course we lent to them part of what we were borrowing from the Americans -'

'It's all horribly complicated,' said Vanessa.

'That's why Maynard was so busy,' said Bunny. 'All through the war. Doling out the debt like a hand of bridge. And tapping the Yanks for the cash.'

Again, Maynard flinched. Duncan tapped Bunny reprovingly on the head.

'Well, anyway,' said Maynard more soberly, 'I'd tried originally to get them to reduce German reparations on humanitarian grounds - and practical ones, for the Germans simply *can't* pay, the figures won't add up. But the French, wouldn't have it. They don't care if the Germans starve. And of course our people too ... their only idea is to wring every last drop out of the Germans. Though you'd think after one Bolshevik Revolution ... Well, anyway, I had to give up on that.

'But then I had *another* idea: reassign the debt. Have the Americans write off what *we* owe, then we'd write off what *our* allies owe and we'd all of us *lend* to the Germans instead of milking them (especially the Americans). That way, the Germans won't starve but will rebuild their economy instead, so there's no collapse, no starvation, no revolution-'

'I don't really see what's in it for the Americans,' said Duncan.

'There's *everything* in it for the Americans! For a start, they can sell Europe their grain, and other things too, of course. But nobody can buy anything if they're bankrupt. That's the point that everyone keeps missing. The European economy depends on Germany. Cripple Germany, and you cripple the economy of Europe, which affects everyone – even the Americans. Far better for the Germans to get back on their feet – and for the Americans to get their export receipts – and for us all to be fed than ... And what's the alternative? We're obliged to pay the Americans back their loans, but we can't pay if the allies don't pay *us*. And they can't pay if Germany is impoverished, because they'll be impoverished too. The reparations they're obsessed with, these billions they're arguing over, they're just figures on the back of an envelope, phantoms floating in the air. They don't mean a thing if Germany can't pay. It's general impoverishment versus a bit of creative thinking, is what it comes down to.'

He took another slug of whisky.

'And you were doing the creative thinking?' Duncan twirled a lock of Bunny's hair, while Vanessa frowned at her sock.

'That's right. And I actually thought Lloyd George would buy it. He did up to a point. But it was too late.'

'The others vetoed it?'

'Wilson started off high-minded, but now, so long as he gets his League of Nations, he doesn't care about anything else. And the French – they can't conceive of any world in which what is good for Germany might be good for them – or what is bad for Germany could also be bad for them. It's – a failure of imagination.'

Maynard lit another cigarette while the others watched him.

'Carry on like this,' Maynard said at last, 'and we'll have another war.'

'Oh, no, Maynard,' Vanessa burst out. 'Don't say it!'

'There's nobody left to fight one,' said Bunny practically.

'Yes, well, tell that to all the new countries in Europe; the ones they're making out of the leftovers of Austria-Hungary and the rest. Their people may be starving but all their leaders think about is getting armaments.' He took a puff at his cigarette, then went on, 'It's dreadful to think, but it turns out our world is very fragile. Our food, our trade, our security – everything we took for granted – all rests on the most fragile foundations.'

His three friends watched him, all disturbed in different ways by his words and manner. His whole body was tense, his face set. Bunny thought, *He's on a knife-edge, it's the overwork and, I'm sure, the guilt.*

Vanessa thought, *Poor love. I'm glad he's away from all that.*

Duncan thought, *Maynard thinks too much. He's probably right, but it will drive him mad.*

'I expect there will be a Bolshevik Revolution in Europe,' said Maynard. 'And sometimes I really don't care.' He looked around at their familiar faces and smiled suddenly. 'I'm sorry. I talk too much.' His gaze fell on the picture above the fireplace. 'Look, the Cezanne. Do you know, I walked past the exact spot where I hid it in the hedge, when I brought it back from Paris, in 1918.'

'I couldn't believe it when you walked in and told us,' said Vanessa.

'It was I that tipped you off,' said Duncan. 'I mean about the sale.'

'And I fetched it from the hedge,' Bunny recalled.

They were silent, remembering how the magnificent collection of Edgar Degas had been put up for auction in Paris, and fears of a German invasion had kept potential bidders away. Maynard, ever resourceful, had persuaded the British Government that this would be an excellent opportunity to buy some pictures at cut price, especially as money spent on French soil counted as allied debt to be repaid. He had gone to the auction himself, alongside the Director of the National Gallery, and had been able to pick up a few things on his own account – notably the Cezanne, which, having hitched a lift only part of the way to Charleston, he had been forced to store temporarily under a hedge.

'Yes,' he said now, 'and thanks to us, the nation owns some rather fine paintings, which is some small gain to make up for the fact we are otherwise almost entirely in hock to the Americans.'

The lightness that had briefly entered him dissipated. Once more, he contemplated the wreck. 'You know, somebody should expose it; the scandal of this so-called *Peace*.'

'Perhaps they will,' said Duncan.

'But it's too late,' said Bunny. 'What difference can it make?'

'Oh, I don't know.' Some of Maynard's spirit seemed, his friends thought, to be returning; his old optimism reasserting itself. 'Is it ever too late to tell the truth?'

Vanessa looked at him over her mending. 'And what will *you* do now?'

'That's the question, isn't it? Well, I suppose I'll take up my old life. I've still got my fellowship at Cambridge. Though I wouldn't want to give up Gordon Square – even if money does get tight.'

His friends reacted with alarm.

'Surely it wouldn't come to that.' Bunny, who only stayed occasionally at Gordon Square, was the least perturbed. Vanessa and Duncan, who both had permanent quarters there, were shaken to silence.

'Oh, something will turn up,' said Maynard easily. He downed the rest of the whisky.

'What about this place?' Duncan asked.

Vanessa began, 'Maybe *we* should pay more ... '

'Don't worry about that.' Maynard sounded much more his old self. 'I just need to find a way to make some money.'

'Meanwhile,' said Duncan half-joking, 'I suppose we could always sell the Cezanne.'

'Over my dead body!'

They burst into laughter. Bunny leaned back against the sofa and Duncan reached to caress his hair, at which Bunny stopped laughing and pulled his head away. 'I'd better check the hens.' He left the room; Duncan looked after him and Vanessa bent her head over her mending.

Maynard had been pursuing his own thoughts. 'Maybe I'll write a book and make my fortune.'

'What about?'

'Economics, of course.'

'Dearest Maynard, I don't think those kinds of books make fortunes.' Vanessa smiled at him.

'No, but I might write one anyway. In fact, why shouldn't I write a book about the Peace Conference?'

They eyed him doubtfully.

'You'll create a lot of anger,' Duncan said.

'Will you sell enough for it to be worth it?' Vanessa asked.

'I don't care if it only sells six copies. Someone has to tell the truth.' Maynard commenced the task of unfolding his long limbs and levering himself out of the sofa. 'God, I ache! I'm done in. I'm going to sleep twelve hours. Then I want to see your paintings and what you've been doing. And then … well then, I'll think about this book. Maybe it will be a bestseller.'

They all laughed at the preposterousness of the notion.

3

'**O**of!'
Maynard was awoken by something landing heavily on his chest. He opened his eyes to sunlight and the beaming face of Quentin.

'Are you going to come and see our den?'

Another face loomed into view. Julian.

'We're going fishing. You can come too.'

'It's too early! Be off with you!'

'It's past ten o'clock!'

Maynard heaved at the bedclothes and Julian and Quentin fell onto the rug. Undaunted, they picked themselves up and sat beaming at him, like dogs begging for a walk.

'Go on!' said Quentin. 'It's a super den.'

'That was a very rude awakening,' said Maynard, pulling himself into a sitting position. 'Rude in the sense of unmannerly, and rude in the sense of unexpected. And then there is the additional meaning of something coarse, uncouth and lacking in refinement. Yes, I think you meet all those.'

'But we don't want you to miss anything.'

'How is Angelica?'

'Oh, who cares about her?'

'Well, she is my goddaughter. As well as your sister.'

'She's all right. Boring. *Do* come and see our den.'

Maynard inspected his watch. 'Not now. Tell you what. Bring me up the papers each morning, and you'll get sixpence.'

'Sixpence a day?'

'Do you think I'm made of money? Get off with you, rascals.'

They ran off laughing. Maynard shouted after them, 'And tell Grace to bring coffee!'

He reached for the old dressing gown that hung from the bed post, and slung it around his shoulders, then sat for a few moments staring at the window. Birds chattered in the Virginia creeper. Sunlight made elongated lozenges on the rug. Why was the light different here from London? More golden, just as the milk tasted creamier and the air smelled sweeter. He sighed with a deep content. Somewhere in the house was Duncan, probably wielding a charcoal stick, and Vanessa, in her painting smock, her hair tied back and a smudge of paint on her nose. He thought fondly of both.

Friendship was a marvellous thing. It had been good to talk to them last night. Certain things had gone back into place; the nightmare had receded.

He pulled out some papers from his briefcase. The photograph from his Treasury desk fell onto the bed cover.

Hoy. That enchanted Orcadian isle. It must have been the summer of 1911; he and Duncan, together in the heather. Duncan was wearing his flannel shirt, the one he'd always liked, that was fraying at collar and sleeves; he was brown as a gypsy – you could see that even in the sepia of the photo – with hair as black and shaggy as a wild pony. His sleeves were rolled up and – although this *was* impossible to detect on the print – Maynard could see the soft hair running along the line of his muscled arms. Art was no gentle profession: on Hoy,

Duncan had frequently lugged his easel over the moors for miles at a time. Next to him, the young Maynard was soft and slender, lanky even, very much the scholar: shoulders rounded, tweed jacket wrinkled, bushy moustache failing to hide the ridiculous mouth. But he was lit up with a sort of glow: how not, when it had been the happiest time of his life?

To Maynard, now, both looked bathed in innocence, even though they had been deep in what their society – what the law of the land – condemned as the reverse of innocence.

It felt like a lost age: Before the War. Then everything changed, and the worst of it was that *he* had changed and he did not know if he could ever feel so much again. He feared he had lost the capacity.

Quickly, he reached for the writing board which lay by the bed where he had left it months ago. With quick strokes, he wrote across a sheet of paper:

Peace and the Future of Europe
Paris: Europe Betrayed
The Paris Peace Conference and the Consequences
Thoughts on the Economic Foundations of Europe

Well, the exact title didn't matter. He began to scribble down sentences.

A CLOCK CHIMED SOMEWHERE in the house.

'Can I come in?'

Duncan looked up from his easel to see Maynard peering around the door. 'Come and tell me what you think of the current masterpiece. It's almost finished.' And, as Maynard approached: 'You're looking better. We've all been worried. Bunny thought we might have to send you off to a sanatorium with the Treasury equivalent of shell shock.'

Maynard snorted. He stood before the easel, which held a canvas of a naked man, painted entirely in shades of purple.

He looked bewildered, then said with great enthusiasm, as Duncan had known he would: 'Simply splendid!' And then, 'What's funny?'

'You. You're so predictable.'

'Me?' Maynard was slightly offended.

'Don't worry. It's good to be able to rely on appreciation from someone.'

'Meaning?'

'You're always encouraging, unlike the rest of the world. But the main thing is the work, not the sales one's making. Or not making.'

'We must see what we can do about that.' Once again, Duncan was struck by Maynard's new air of vigour. Although it had only been a week, Maynard was already slewing off Paris like a lizard discarding its skin. For a while, Maynard continued to gaze at the picture. Then, in a slightly melancholy tone he continued, 'I'm not an artist, sadly, but I've always felt that art is one of the things that makes life worth living.'

'I know. We've always been grateful for your support.'

'I don't want gratitude. It's enough to see the work you're doing – you and Vanessa.'

'Then consider yourself our patron.'

Maynard said seriously, 'I'm honoured.' He began to wander the room, picking up objects and putting them down, while Duncan reached for a sketch pad and began to sketch. Maynard lingered near a vaguely Degas-esque sculpture of a dancer. 'This is rather fine ... Are you happy, Duncan?'

'What? Oh yes, I suppose so. So long as I'm painting. And especially now the war is over.' He paused. 'But Bunny's getting restless.'

'Or you are?'

'Well ... you know how it is.'

Maynard *did* know; none better – unless it were Vanessa. His time with Duncan had been the most completely happy of his life, but Duncan had soon moved on to pastures new. Maynard held no grudges; he accepted Duncan as he was. When he hurt other people, this was simply because he could not help following his own desires (like a child, really) and, in following them, was bound to hurt those who found themselves discarded.

'I suppose Vanessa ...' He had been going to finish *will be relieved if Bunny goes*, but then he wondered if that were true. After Bunny, there would be somebody else.

'Oh, she's alright. I can't give her what she wants – not really – except for Angelica, but ...' He shrugged.

Maynard was startled by a sense of – was it actually annoyance? Impatience certainly. How very convenient for Duncan to have such an understanding partner! But he did not have to take it so much for granted. Maynard frowned. Was he being bourgeois, Victorian even? That's what Lytton would say, maybe most of his Bloomsbury friends. But he had become close to Vanessa these last years and felt her pain. Or was it that he was simply jealous of Duncan and his happiness with Bunny ... and with Bunny's likely replacement?

'My own life seems rather empty,' he said. 'I mean, one can always find someone to share a bed, but anything more ...'

'You'll soon be able to put that right.' Duncan was mischievous. 'Think of Cambridge – all those beautiful young men.'

Not as beautiful as you once were, thought Maynard. 'You wore that shirt on Hoy,' he said aloud.

Duncan, startled, replied, 'I don't think so.'

Maynard walked to the window. It probably had been a different shirt. He sighed. He did not wish himself back to that time, to any time. So then why was he so melancholy?

Duncan was also curious. 'Why so down in the mouth? Are you going to miss it after all? The hustle and bustle, and hobnobbing with the great and good?'

'Not at all. I'm looking forward to lecturing, sherry parties for the undergrads and some light gossip in the Senior Common Room. I might even take up golf again.'

His words sounded uncomfortably familiar. Who had said? ... Oh yes ... Foxy Falk.

'Sounds rather tame – for you.'

'Then I'll find a new hobby,' said Maynard gamely. 'Maybe collecting old books. Yes, that will do very well. I'll ask my brother for advice.'

Duncan laughed.

'ARE you part of this Bloomsbury Set?' an acquaintance had once enquired of Maynard. And then. 'What *is* this Bloomsbury Set anyway? And Maynard had shrugged, smiled a rather self-deprecating smile, and said that he did not know. He had friends, that was all. He liked to spend time with them. He had never signed up to any 'set'.

In fact, Maynard had become part of 'Bloomsbury' – so far as he *was* a part of Bloomsbury – through his lasting friendship, and brief love affair, with Lytton Strachey. He had first met Lytton during their student days at Cambridge, when the link between them was not 'Bloomsbury' but the 'Apostles'; a select and secretive discussion group to which both belonged. The Apostles were in rebellion against both organized religion and conventional morality – especially *sexual* morality – and their numbers included Leonard Woolf, Morgan Forster and Roger Fry. Lytton's wider circle also included two brothers called Thoby and Adrian Stephen, who just happened to have two sisters, Vanessa and Virginia. When, in 1905, the Stephen siblings set up house together in a rather shabby square in an unfashionable neighbourhood of London known as Bloomsbury, Thoby and Adrian's Cambridge friends soon came visiting. They sat up late conversing about literature, art and philosophy (with a generous sprinkling of gossip); they drank cocoa and ate buns; many of them, in time, chose to move to the same neighbourhood. The composition of the households, and the relations of the inhabitants, shuffled about regularly, but the network itself remained strong.

Maynard was, for some time, on the edge of Bloomsbury, but in 1911 he moved to its heart, taking up residence with Adrian and Virginia Stephen, and Leonard Woolf, while dividing his time between London and Cambridge. From then on Maynard was most definitely 'Bloomsbury', whether in London – where he now shared a house with Duncan and Vanessa, as well as Vanessa's husband, Clive – or the rural outpost of Charleston. He went to Bloomsbury parties. He wrote letters to other Bloomsberries and received interminable letters in return. He gossiped. He debated. He drank tea.

It was more than friendship that drew Maynard to Bloomsbury. It offered him something his own family, and conventional society, could not: it accepted him as a man who loved men. Furthermore, it shared the values to which he subscribed: art and friendship were their shared creed.

There had been strains, inevitably. The war had been one. But the friendships had held. Maynard hoped and believed that any fault lines were now deeply submerged.

It was not long before the rest of Bloomsbury learnt of Maynard's return and came calling.

4

The table was set out on the lawn, with a nearby tree to shade it from the sun. In essentials, it was not so different from the Victorian high teas of their childhoods, although there was no starched tablecloth, nor cucumber sandwiches. Nor was Grace expected to stay and pour the tea, any more than she was expected to wear a starched white apron or a cap with streamers and ribbons. There was an Indian tablecloth, cups of varied design and a jam jar filled with flowers from the meadow.

Vanessa sat as ramrod straight as any Victorian lady, although her dress was crumpled, with the inevitable paint on the collar. The hat she wore against the sun was a gardening one which had seen better days. Her sister Virginia had her hair loosely looped up behind her ears, and despite the heat wore a tweed skirt and, over her blouse, a cardigan. With her thin, clever face, she looked like the Mistress of a Cambridge women's college, which in another life she might well have become. Clive, Vanessa's husband, reclined in a deckchair, plump and raffish in a pastel shirt and striped blazer. He had left his current mistress in London, to everyone's relief.

Leonard Woolf, Virginia's husband, dark and reserved, sat next to his wife; Duncan, on the edge of the group, tipped back his chair and gazed upwards into the branches, as if he found the birds as interesting as the company.

Maynard had yet to appear.

'So the prodigal returns,' Virginia remarked, taking up a teaspoon to stir her tea.

'Yes.' Vanessa was handling the teapot. 'It would have been nice to have had *some* warning. But actually, now he *is* here, it's rather pleasant to have him.'

Clive said, 'Speak for yourself, my dear. And I hope he doesn't throw his weight around in London.'

'Well, it is his house.'

'What do you mean?'

Duncan said, 'He owns the lease.'

'And pays most of the rent,' Vanessa added.

'As he does here,' Duncan said, 'although he probably has less use of it than any of us.'

Clive snorted. Born to a wealthier family than the rest, he was thus able to affect more disdain for worldly things, though that disdain did not extend to letting his parents know that he and Vanessa were effectively separated, or that Angelica was not his daughter but Duncan's – information that might put future bequests at risk.

'You know you like Maynard more than you used to.' Vanessa looked coaxingly at her sister.

'I've always thought him extremely clever.' Virginia's tone was reserved.

'I think you and Leonard were turned against him by Lytton. Who wasn't very fair.'

Leonard said, 'I do admire the fact that Maynard has thrown over his Treasury post. It's an act of real sacrifice, for I doubt they will forgive him quickly, if ever. On the other hand,

I wonder if, when he realizes what he's done, he might yet recant, and try and get back in with–'

A discreet cough from Duncan alerted them to the approach of Maynard, accompanied by Bunny and a plate of scones. Bunny started putting up a parasol, while Maynard greeted the Woolfs.

'Sorry to be slow – Bunny and I have been discussing his idea for a new bookshop. In Bloomsbury, of course. I had a few ideas, and now I've time on my hands–'

Virginia, accepting his kiss, said, 'I hear you're no longer rendering to Caesar …?'

'No, I've seen the light. Mind you, if you spoke to some of my former colleagues, you'd think I'd sold them all down the river for thirty pieces of silver.'

'Well, I'm glad. Though won't you miss being so *terribly* important?'

If the tone was waspish, Maynard did not seem to notice.

'I wasn't terribly important, Virginia,' he said mildly, as he collapsed inelegantly into a deck chair. 'I realize that now.'

Clive said, 'Speaking of rendering to Caesar – have you thought about rendering up my house?'

'Your house?'

'Oh, come on, Maynard, you know what I mean. Gordon Square.'

'I don't follow. You asked me to take over the lease.'

'Yes, but I never meant– Anyway, now that everything's changed …'

'It's good of you, Clive, but I think I'll manage.'

Clive scowled. The rest of the party hid smiles. Virginia said to Maynard, 'Be honest, Maynard, won't you miss it? Rattling around Paris – and Europe, dining with Lloyd Georges and Asquiths and all the other muckety-mucks. Being solemn and wearing suits?'

'*Being solemn and ...*? You make me sound like an undertaker.'

'I *do* think you've enjoyed it. You've certainly enjoyed *telling* us about it.'

'Well, one has to give some account of oneself. Paris seemed more interesting than the details of Anglo-American debt-financing.'

This caused a general laughter. 'God save us!' said Clive.

Maynard was warmed. He looked around the circle of faces, all so familiar to him. 'I must say, I've missed you all.'

The atmosphere thawed noticeably then. As Virginia observed to Leonard later, it was a reminder of what they were sometimes inclined to forget: that for all his faults, Maynard had an affectionate heart.

'It's just a shame you couldn't have realized earlier,' said Bunny abruptly. 'That's what Lytton would say.'

His companions fell silent. Anything Maynard might have said in reply was pre-empted by the arrival of Quentin and Julian, who came running across the lawn and threw them-selves onto Maynard.

'What about our den?'

'You promised!'

'You said you'd look at it.'

Maynard said, 'Yes, I suppose I did.' Gamely, he levered himself out of the deckchair. 'Well, if it's up a tree, I just hope it can bear my weight.' He departed hand in hand with the chil-dren, leaving the company in silence.

'There was no need for that, Bunny,' Duncan observed after a pause.

'Yes,' Vanessa agreed. 'I really think he wants to make amends.'

Bunny shrugged. 'I think Maynard is addicted to power. I doubt he'll resist it for long.'

'He likes to be *useful*,' Duncan said. 'It's different.'

'Useful to warmongers.'

'He was useful to *us*,' Duncan pointed out. 'Without him and his ministry bag we'd both have been stuck in clink, miserable conchies that we were.'

This Bunny found unanswerable. They all helped themselves to more scones.

THE DEN WAS at the base of a tree, in the wild part of the garden. Maynard, having admired all the amenities to Julian and Quentin's satisfaction, crawled out again, with muddy knees and elbows, then gripped by a new idea for his book, stood staring at the leaves beneath his feet for a good five minutes. He was startled back into life by Quentin appearing above his head, dangling from a branch like an oversized monkey.

'The attic is upstairs,' he observed to the shrinking Maynard.

'Yes, well.' Maynard eyed the branches above him. 'I think I'll content myself with downstairs.'

'Come on! It's easy.'

'I'm afraid I've never been a great one for climbing. I remember once, as a student, going on holiday to the Alps. We were all roped together, with ice axes … at one point we had to rescue our leader from a crevasse. Everyone kept burbling about the view and the snow-capped peaks, but I was terribly relieved when I caught a cold and had an excuse to stay in bed with a book.'

'Quitter!' Julian came into view, a few feet further up the tree, his face streaked with mud according to his idea of a jungle-dweller. Then abruptly he said, 'You didn't fight in the war, did you?'

Maynard peered up at him through the leaves, but it was impossible to read his expression. 'That's so.'

'And Dad didn't and nor did Duncan.' There was bravado in his voice, but also perhaps an underlying anxiety. 'Why didn't you?'

'Well, I was working at the Treasury—'

'Why?'

'They asked me to, Julian.'

'So you were helping the war? Why didn't you *object*? Like Duncan, and Bunny? That's why we came to live here, you know.'

'Yes, I do know.'

'Why were you helping and not fighting?'

'It's all quite complicated—'

'If you're going to *help* the fighting, then why not fight yourself? It's hyp-*hypocrisy* otherwise, isn't it?'

'Who said that to you, Julian, about hypocrisy? No, don't tell me. I don't want to know. Listen, I was asked to help at the Treasury because I understand about finance – money – and there were lots of problems with money during the war. Money for the country, I mean. That doesn't mean I supported the war.'

'But wasn't the money for the fighting?'

'Well, in a manner of speaking. But if all the money went – all the country's money – then we'd be in an even worse position now. Now the war is over, I mean.'

'*Are* we in a bad position?'

'Pretty bad. And lots of men have come home injured and don't have jobs or homes either.'

'And the women.'

'What's that?'

'Some women don't have work or homes either,' replied Vanessa's son and Virginia's nephew.

'Yes. Quite so.'

'Anyway, I think I'd fight.' Julian scowled down at him. 'It's the best thing to do if your country needs you. Better than working at a desk.' He stared defiantly at Maynard, who thought, *I suppose this is how you rebel in Bloomsbury*.

'It's a difficult question, Julian,' he said aloud. 'My friends all believed different things. Some were pacifists, which means they thought war was wrong in all circumstances. Some thought fighting was right in some situations, but that didn't mean we should be fighting Germany. Still, at the start, everyone thought the war would be over quickly and we could choose – all of us – whether to fight or not. I decided to work at the Treasury, and I still don't know if that was the right decision. You're right that I was helping in a way, even though what I wanted was for the Government to stop fighting and actually *talk* to the Germans, and find some way of negotiating a settlement. I could never agree with Lloyd George, who thought we must fight it out until the end. And then they brought in conscription – that means that everyone had to fight, unless they were doing work that the Government considered more important–'

'Like you, at the Treasury?'

'Yes, like me, at the Treasury. So that was difficult, because I didn't agree with conscription *at all*, any more than I agreed with refusing to negotiate. But at least I was able to help my friends. You see, working at the Treasury, I could help support their cases when they said that they were conscientious objectors and wouldn't fight. That doesn't mean I did anything illegal,' he added quickly, 'just that my job gave my words more weight. There's really nothing like Treasury notepaper and a Treasury briefcase for impressing a tribunal! It made it seem worthwhile, that I could help Duncan and Bunny and others.'

What had happened to that letter? he thought suddenly. The one he had written claiming conscientious objector status for himself. He had never sent it in the end, had stayed at the Treasury, but he didn't remember destroying it either. Well, he was not a public servant any more. Still, if it ever got into the wrong hands ...

'Didn't *any* of your friends want to fight?'

'Yes, they did.'

'*I* think it would be exciting.'

'That's what Rupert thought, and Feri. And ... well, several more.'

'What happened to them?'

'They're dead,' said Maynard flatly.

Momentarily, Julian was taken aback. But then he shrugged it aside. Quentin had long lost interest in the conversation and gone to ground in the den, from whence came rootling noises – *Like a pig searching for truffles*, Maynard thought.

'Julian,' – he spoke gently – 'do people say things at school? Insulting things? About conscientious objectors – *conchies*?'

'Maybe.'

'There's no point laying aside your life for a war you think pointless carnage.'

Julian, shimmying up the tree again, said nothing. In the shadows it was impossible to see his face.

'It's a brave thing, really, to stand fast against what the world is saying; to refuse to fight.'

But as he said it, he experienced a twinge of doubt. Had it really been brave of Duncan and Bunny to tend apple trees in Sussex, or of Clive to raise pigs at Garsington? Nobody had thought the worse of them, or nobody whose opinion they respected. They had not suffered for their stand, or if they had, it was nothing to the trenches. No, Bloomsbury had experienced no self-doubt; and meanwhile, they had not troubled to disguise their disapproval of Maynard, who was working for the warmongers. Lytton had accused him ... What had he said? That he was sitting in an office, working out how to kill people in the most efficient way. Bunny too – he had written him a letter accusing him of selling his soul to savages. At the time, that letter had upset Maynard deeply … because he feared it might be true.

What should he have done? He had been all prepared to resign from the Treasury – that was why he'd written that letter – and yet somehow the moment had never come. He would have stepped down in an instant if any of his political masters, Reginald McKenna say, had made a stand. He had expected it, hoped for it, been ready for it. But the politicians kept patching things up, the cabinet held together – just – and there had seemed little point in one Treasury official falling on his sword.

It wasn't until Paris that he had finally snapped. Perhaps Bunny, Lytton – *all* his friends – would see that as opportunism, would claim that he had waited to take action until such a time as it would not cost him much.

And they would go on thinking it, unless he could find a way to show them otherwise.

5

_____

Slowly, Charleston worked its magic. Maynard's appetite returned, he was no longer jumpy and tense, and at night did not wake suddenly from dreams filled with a smirking Lloyd George or glowering Clemenceau – 'And thank God for that,' as he told Duncan over the breakfast table. 'They were making me bilious.' He ordered an armload of newspapers to be delivered each day, which he perused with only the occasional expletive; he wrote vast quantities of letters which he handed to Grace for posting; and he spent his mornings scribbling away, covering pages and pages in a dense scrawl. Sometime, during these weeks, Bunny departed in high dudgeon by taxi, and Clive removed himself to rejoin his mistress. The household breathed a sigh of relief, and although other friends visited at times, the pattern was set: there was no more discussion of Paris, no more disinterring of wartime choices or grievances, no more prickliness about house leases, and the only major altercation was when Julian and Quentin fell out over which one of them had dropped the jar of captured newts that smashed on the hall floor.

One summer morning, Maynard set out by train for

Cambridge, breaking his journey in London, where among other things he called on Oswald Falk. At King's Cross, he boarded the Cambridge train and was carried north and east through countryside so flat, featureless and, above all, familiar that he barely noticed it. Instead, he read an article which had been submitted to the *Economic Journal,* of which he was editor. It was on price indices, a nicely dry and technical subject. Occasionally he scribbled a note in the margins.

Finished, he replaced the article in his briefcase and stared unseeingly out of the window. He supposed he would have to talk to people about Paris. The Peace Treaty had been signed at last and, despite himself, he could not forget the images paraded across the front pages. The glittering halls of Versailles, where the signing had taken place, contrasted mightily with the German delegates, paraded like Roman captives, while across Europe, the hungry millions ...

Shades of Marie Antoinette, he thought, then giving himself a mental kick, forced his mind in other directions: as, for example, the Apostles. Was there any prospect of new embryos? He hoped the Fabian contingent had not grown in strength: it was not that there was anything *objectionable* in them, but it was all so *worthy*. He could feel himself drifting towards sleep whenever they started on about the peaceful evolution towards socialism ...

Think I'd rather be an outright Bolshie. Give me a good revolution any day.

He realized, from the shocked look on the face of the man opposite him, that he had spoken aloud. He grinned. His fellow passenger looked both respectable and disapproving, and as he buried himself in his newspaper, was probably meditating upon whether he should write first to the police or the Home Office – *Subject: Dangerous revolutionary met in railway carriage.*

Turning away, Maynard's eye was caught by that of a

young man across the aisle. Late twenties. A forelock of hair dipping over one eyebrow. He held open a copy of Goethe in the original: a brave choice, to be reading a German book in public in 1919, and intriguing. He stared at Maynard, and one eyelid drooped in an adroit wink.

Maynard felt his spirits rise.

'I'm so happy you have a place like Charleston to go to,' Florence said as she served up the apple tart. 'Sussex is such a beautiful county.'

Maynard's parents lived, as they had all their married life, in a solid, substantial Victorian villa on Harvey Road, not far from Emmanuel College, and every week they hosted a solid, substantial Sunday lunch for whichever family members were in Cambridge. This could mean a large gathering: today, the table held several of Florence's numerous Brown relatives, as well as Maynard's younger brother, Geoffrey, a surgeon, and his father, Neville. Margaret, their married sister, was in London. In between slices of roast beef and forkfuls of cabbage, Maynard responded to enquiries about the Versailles Treaty with relative patience ('It makes me sick,' he told his Uncle Walter, and when his Uncle protested, 'But it's peace, Maynard!', he replied, 'If you call that peace.') In between, he enquired politely about his parents' activities (Neville, golf and stamp-collecting; Florence, good works and local politics). He did not ask Neville about his work as University Registrar, for work, however routine and competently performed, preyed on his father's nerves. He forgot to ask Geoffrey about his work at Barts Hospital altogether.

'I'm lucky to have Charleston,' said Maynard in answer to his mother. 'It turns out it's a wonderful place to write.'

'I would have thought you'd need some rest first.'

'That too. I bask in the garden. And every day I weed the drive.'

'Well, you're looking much better for it. I'm so delighted to see you. Though I had thought you were coming yesterday. If I'd known it was today,' Florence glanced down the table, where Uncle Walter was holding forth on his bunions, 'I would have arranged a smaller gathering.'

'Well, it turns out I had things to attend to.'

'At King's?'

'At College,' said Maynard, which was not exactly a lie, it was just that the college was not King's, and the *things* were mainly a young man with a forelock falling over one eye.

'But what was so important?' Florence was not usually so persistent.

'I went to tea with Alfred Marshall,' he said, fastening on the one respectable part of the day's activities. 'Mary had written to London inviting me. She'd heard I was back, and I could hardly refuse.'

'Alfred is very poorly, dear man.'

'Yes, I think this time he really is.' Alfred Marshall, the former Professor of Political Economy at Cambridge, was a notorious hypochondriac. 'I was more moved to see him than I expected. Of course, I owe him my career.'

It was Marshall who had first taught Maynard economics, and who had later created the university post that enabled him to come back to Cambridge, at a time when the frustrated Maynard had feared being condemned to the India Office forever.

'He'll be delighted you are coming back. He'll be able to see a lot more of you.'

'Yes, although I won't be around for a while.'

'But your lectures?'

'I'm arranging for somebody else to give them. It won't be difficult. After all, nobody was expecting me back so soon.'

'But why, Maynard? Don't you have time?'

'No. You see, I'm writing a book.'

The words fell into an unexpected lull in the conversation. His father, distracted from his apple pie, said, 'A book?'

'Your book on probability?' Florence ventured. Maynard had been working on this topic, the subject of his fellowship thesis, on-and-off ever since graduation. He often joked that he had written more on probability during his time at the India Office than on anything actually connected with the subcontinent itself.

Maynard snorted derisively, dismissing years of toil. 'A book on the Paris Peace Conference.'

'Isn't that all over?' suggested Uncle Walter. 'What is there to say?'

'Plenty. I'm writing a book exposing the whole thing. The ... the *wickedness*,' said Maynard. 'Yes, the wicked recklessness and lust for vengeance and the disregard for the real needs of Europe.'

Wickedness was not a foreign concept to the older Browns or Keyneses: both were from long lines of Nonconformist Protestant stock. Florence's own father had been a minister. But it was not a term they often heard from Maynard.

'Isn't that rather strong?' asked Uncle Walter.

'No. What else is a lust for revenge?'

'If you'd seen what I'd seen ...' Geoffrey stuttered to a halt, aware of their eyes on him. 'I mean, Maynard, thank God you didn't. I've never seen such suffering. That young Highlander–' He stopped again. 'And ... and others. There was nothing I could do.'

'I know,' said Maynard, chastened. Geoffrey had served with the Royal Army Medical Corps at the front. 'I read your letters. But you can't pander to the ... the lust for vengeance. Or we'll never be free of it. The thing *is* to think in a hard-headed way about what Europe actually needs. And the only way to do *that* is to acknowledge that Germany is vital to Europe's economy. It's the engine. You can't take a hammer to it.'

'So many people can vote now,' his Aunt Etty observed unexpectedly from the end of the table. 'Oh, it seemed a good idea at the time, but it means the politicians can't ignore the multitudes. Or the press. And they want the Germans punished.'

Maynard was struck by this. 'That's very true. The press whipped them up into a frenzy of hatred, and the Goat found he could not resist–'

'I wish you would not call Lloyd George the Goat,' his mother murmured.

'– which is all the more reason to educate the voters!'

'And you think your book will do that?' his father asked. 'Will it have a wide readership?'

'No,' replied Maynard cheerfully, 'but wider than the *Economic Journal*. And opinions do percolate out eventually.' His face went blank suddenly, as if preoccupied with a new thought.

'But is it *proper*?' asked Uncle Walter, wiping custard from his beard with a handkerchief. 'I mean, for a public servant–'

'*Former* public servant. I resigned. Anyway, look at it this way – if at least I get it down on the page, it will save my inflicting it on you. And I've hogged the conversation long enough.' His eyes fell on his brother, and he said heartily, 'How is the hospital anyhow?'

As the maid, Gladys, cleared the plates and the others headed for coffee in the drawing room, Neville held Maynard back.

'This book, Maynard, is it really … *wise*?'

'Depends what you mean. It will make my name mud in the Treasury, but it's mud already.'

'But it's not just the Treasury. It'll be with a great many other people, I imagine.'

'True. But so what? Nobody can take my fellowship away. Anyway, it's the right thing to do.'

Neville was not comforted. He said fretfully, 'I wish you'd never given up your place at the India Office.'

'That was years ago, dear.' Florence hovered in the doorway.

'It had excellent prospects and security.'

'It wasn't right for Maynard.'

'It certainly wasn't,' said Maynard forcefully. 'The most I ever achieved there was securing an export licence for an English stud bull.'

'You never gave it a proper chance,' his father insisted, 'and when you entered the Treasury, I thought things had come right again. And now ... I'm not happy to see you destroy your prospects by offending so many important people.'

'I hope I do offend them if it means they read the book.'

'You'll be a pariah.'

'Good!'

'I'm sure Maynard will be diplomatic,' Florence said.

'Diplomatic!' said her son forcefully. 'I intend to expose them as the charlatans they are!'

His mother groaned slightly.

Neville said, 'You have your fellowship true, but it's modest. Our means are limited. If, say, you were to marry ...'

Maynard gave a bark of laughter. Then, seeing his father look genuinely confused, he said more gently, 'I've just come back from Paris, with a few trips to Germany on the side, and before that I was working seventeen hours a day at the Treasury. If I'm ready for anything new, it's a quiet nervous breakdown. I'm not about to introduce you to a wife.'

He had a sudden, disconcerting image of the young man with the forelock; a young man who had turned out to be a fellow of Jesus, whence they had gone to disport themselves. He smiled. It was strange how these images would recur: he could see those long limbs now, superimposed upon his parents' tablecloth.

Florence was watching him sharply. *She* did not expect a daughter-in-law to turn up any time soon, he would wager that.

'Listen,' he said, 'you mustn't worry. There are plenty of ways to make money, and as it happens, I've got a plan.'

'I hope not a post with a foreign bank. That would be exploiting your Treasury post in a most unacceptable way.'

'I'm not devoid of principle. On the contrary, my plan won't leave me beholden to anyone. I'm going to invest in currency markets.'

Neville blanched. Florence said uncertainly, 'I don't quite understand. We have some investments ourselves, in bonds, I believe. But currencies?'

'Yes, you can buy and sell currencies, just as you can buy and sell shares. At least, my friend Foxy can. He's a stockbroker. He'll look after the trading. But we're going to run the portfolio together. He's very sharp. I think it's going to be a great deal of fun.'

'Isn't it rather risky?'

'Riskier than bonds,' said Maynard airily. 'But then, you can't make *real* money from bonds. And it's only risky if you don't know what you're doing – which Foxy and I do.'

'I consider it most unwise,' said Neville. 'I never heard of anyone trading in currencies before–'

'Well, you couldn't before the war. We were on the gold standard.'

'And as for this notion of a book – I tell you, Maynard, you will regret it if you burn your bridges in that way. You will be forever an outcast. They won't forgive you. You will never have a voice again, and you won't like that.'

'Father–'

'That is my final word on the matter.'

Nevertheless, by the time they joined the others for coffee, Neville had pledged a sizeable sum to his son's venture. Florence who, unlike her husband, liked to play a bold hand in life, was amused. Only Maynard, she thought, could have persuaded Neville to put money into currency speculation, and in a mere ten minutes too. Maynard was so confident, so compelling in his arguments, that she was only astonished that the Big Three had managed to withstand him.

On Maynard's book, Neville was immovable however. If he must write it then it should be kept for private circulation only. Florence, reluctantly, was inclined to agree. She hoped Maynard had been swayed by their arguments: the idea of being side-lined was, she knew, anathema to him.

'Do be kind to Geoffrey,' she whispered as they entered the drawing room. Maynard sent her a puzzled glance. He didn't see what she did, that Geoffrey, supposedly deep in conversation with Uncle Walter, was already aware of them and speaking louder, desperate for Maynard's attention and approval.

'… and personally I think the idea of Russia is ridiculous. She would have to be mad to go there, White Russian general or no White Russian general, though that doesn't answer the question of where she actually *is* … Maynard, what do you think?'

'Think about what?' Maynard collapsed onto a sofa and stretched out his legs.

'You must have heard about Loppy.' And, when his brother looked blank: 'Lydia Lopokova, the star of the Ballets Russes.' Geoffrey sounded reproachful. 'I thought you *liked* ballet. I've seen her dance *many* times – she was especially good in *Firebird.*'

'Oh, Loppy. I think I met her once at a party.' *Although I couldn't get close, because Clive was salivating all over her.* 'I don't really remember.'

Geoffrey started to recall her performances, comparing them knowledgeably with those of Karsavina, Sokolova, even Pavlova (*Showing off*, thought Florence sadly, *for Maynard's benefit, and Maynard totally unaware*), while Maynard drank his coffee and finally interrupted the stream with, 'But what's all this about her going to Russia?'

'Well, you see, she's disappeared. Completely vanished.'

'Really?'

'I'm amazed you haven't heard. They were halfway through a run of *Boutique*, she was starring of course, and then – she was gone. Nobody knows where to. At least that's what the Ballets Russes are saying; left them high and dry.'

'How extraordinary.'

'There's all kinds of rumours flying round.' Geoffrey spoke importantly, not usually one-up on his brother for gossip. 'The whole of London is obsessed. She was last seen in the company of a Russian general. So, of course, everyone is saying they've gone to Russia.'

'I hope not. There's still a war going on there.'

'I know. But they say she was desperate to see her family. Or desperately in love with the general. Accounts differ. Of course, it may all be nonsense.'

Maynard recalled glimpses of a vivid face and expressive hands, and laughter rising like bubbles over the heads of an admiring crowd: a crowd that he, Maynard, had been unable to penetrate. 'Don't jostle me,' Clive had said, standing foursquare, holding his ground, 'there's Iddy-whatsit to keep *you* busy' – nodding in the direction of Lydia's dance partner, Idzikovsky, who was undeniably handsome. But Maynard had felt unreasonably aggrieved, and had abandoned his attempt to join the group only when he realised that their conversation was being conducted entirely in French. Irritated, Maynard contemplated his poor French. It had not held him back in Paris; it was annoying it should have handicapped him in London.

'I hope she's alright,' he said. Then he leaned forwards. 'Geoffrey, have you ever thought about investing?'

6

She sat very still, her hands in her lap, her face, rarely seen immobile, frozen as if in a photograph. She had wide-spaced eyes, a round face, an upturned nose. *A gorgeous pixie. A naughty schoolgirl. An ingénue.* These were the epithets that attached themselves to Lydia Lopokova. She was never going to be the Swan Princess, but she could make the crowds laugh with her, as she pirouetted across the stage.

There was no laughter now.

It was a utilitarian space: a bed, with the sheets and blankets pulled neat and square; faded linoleum on the floor and a small, hooked rug; curtains of army blue; a table holding a chipped ash tray and a vase of bulging pink that looked vaguely obscene; and one picture on the wall, of a stag at bay. There was no mirror, as if personal vanity – or self examination – were not allowed. There were also two wooden chairs, in one of which Lydia sat, with her bag at her feet.

The door behind her opened and a woman in nurse's clothing peered around the door. 'Just twenty minutes, then doctor will be with you.'

It was a hushed voice, almost a whisper, suitable for a

surreptitious enterprise. Lydia looked round, nodded briefly, looked back at her hands, wound her fingers tightly around each other.

'You should really be in bed, Miss Smith,' said the nurse. 'You need to regain your strength.'

'I am strong,' said Lydia. 'I don't need rest.'

The nurse hesitated, then quietly closed the door behind her.

Lydia went on sitting in the hard-backed chair, in her grey serge travel clothes, straight-backed and demure, her hands neatly folded, as once, long ago, she had sat waiting on the bench outside the office of the senior mistress at the Mariinsky School, about to be reproved for some misdemeanour or other. Only then that indefinable quality – the twinkle, the spark, the bounce – had still been present underneath, irrepressible, which now seemed gone forever.

Beyond the curtains, it was raining slightly. It was a quiet residential area, with only the occasional passer-by. Lydia watched a delivery man go past, then, after a long interlude, a young woman leading a toddler by the hand. Abruptly, she looked away, then bent and pulled three envelopes from her bag. She fingered them in her lap. One was a fat, unmarked, brown envelope which crinkled under her hand. Another was of cream paper, sealed, and bore the inscription *Gen. Martynov*, followed by a London address, written in Lydia's own handwriting. The third was a flimsy telegram. She turned it over and studied the sender's details – New York – with some satisfaction. Then she smiled.

She peered through the window again. What were they doing at home? she wondered suddenly. She tried to picture them, seeing their faces through the inevitable haze of time and distance, because it was such a long time since she had received a photograph: Mama, Evgenia, Feodor, Vasily. *I send you kisses. I thought I would see you very soon. But it is not to be.*

So many years. Half the time, she did not even think in Russian anymore.

On the street, the rain had cleared. A dog was being walked by its owner, when a ginger cat appeared in front of it, almost nose to nose. The cat arched and spat. The dog – a rather refined looking creature, with a clipped coat – leapt back, yapping wildly; its owner (a very large, fat man) began to shout, and the cat spat and made off. The dog ran wildly at the end of its lead, spinning the owner round. Lydia, who had leapt up and glued her nose to the window, began to laugh. It bubbled out of her, a cascade of sound, and she flung her head back and held her sides as she went on laughing.

There was a tap on the door, then it opened and a man peered in at her. His face – arranged into a solemn expression, like that of an undertaker – registered surprise and then reproof.

'Miss Smith? Are you all right?'

'What's that? Oh, I think we can do better than Miss Smith!' Lydia wiped her eyes.

'Can I ask you to sit down? Better yet, get into bed. Rest is important.'

Lydia gave a loud snort. 'I can't rest.'

'My advice, as your doctor–'

He advanced upon her and she thrust the fat brown envelope at his chest.

'Here. For you. It cover everything.'

'But Miss Lop ... Miss Smith: this is somewhat premature!'

Lydia snapped her fingers. 'No. My mind is made up. I go to New York.'

'New York?'

'Yes. Third-class cabin, it is come down in world, but no matter. I do that before. It's not so bad. You will post this for me, please.' She held out the cream envelope. He reached for it, almost without thinking, but she snatched it away from him, held it against her cheek a moment, then returned it. 'There,' she said, her voice rather muffled, 'you take it.'

He glared at the letter, then at her. 'Most unwise. If you do this, it will be on your own head. And, well, there could be *complications*, which could rebound on all of us. In fact,' he drew himself up, 'I'm not sure I can allow it.'

Lydia laughed. Then she kissed her fingertips and pressed them to his cheek. He stared at her, outraged and dumb-founded.

'Do you think,' she asked, 'that I let you lock me up? In Russia, prisons are bursting. I will not let you make me pris-oner here!'

She waved merrily and positively skipped towards the door. He reached out, but she was too nimble and dodged around him. When he made a more determined effort to grip her arm, she twisted away, bracing her legs – those strong, dancer's legs – and he found his hands empty, and she was off down the corridor, leaving him puffing in indignation.

'Good bye!' she called over her shoulder. 'I hope we shall not meet again!'

FINALLY, Maynard could put it off no longer: he returned to King's.

Jack Sheppard, entering the college from King's Parade with a bag of plums in one hand and a bunch of flowers in the other, saw the tall figure standing on the grass, contemplating the Perpendicular Gothic magnificence that was the Chapel as if he had never seen it before. Shephard exclaimed, 'Maynard!' and set off to meet him.

Maynard turned as the plump, middle-aged don came puffing across the grass.

'You're *back*, Maynard, and you never even told me you were coming. I reproach you, I really do. Back for good, I believe? Yes, I know all about it, no thanks to you … Virginia wrote Lytton, and Lytton wrote me … But what are you doing? Contemplating the eternal verities? That's not like you. You're always in such a *hurry*.'

Maynard gestured towards the Chapel. 'I was just thinking – can you imagine being the man who designed *that*? What a thing to leave behind!'

'And it's only just struck you?' Jack eyed him sceptically. 'Anyway, he'd never have seen it. They would still have been putting in the foundations when he was on his death bed. Medieval churches took a while, you know.'

'He'd have had the intellectual satisfaction.'

'Oh, that– True. But why the sudden interest?' Jack, who wanted to get his flowers into water, made some tentative steps across the grass but Maynard didn't budge.

'I went to see Alfred Marshall, you know. He's in a bad way.'

'And doesn't he enjoy it,' Jack murmured.

Maynard ignored this. 'He told me he took up economics when he lost his belief in God.'

'Well!' Jack was intrigued. 'Economics … that's a rather curious deity to elect in the Almighty's place.'

'I think it hit him hard, his loss of faith. He read Darwin, and found the foundations of his world shaking.'

'It was the same for all that generation. Sidgwick, for example … ever meet Sidgwick?'

'My father and I sometimes played golf with him.'

'He was the same. Shaken to the core. Spent the rest of his life fretting about metaphysics and ethics and all that business!'

'Well, he was the University's Professor of Moral Philosophy,' said Maynard, straight-faced. Jack sent him a reproachful look.

'Now, now Maynard. That's no excuse. Still I expect your

parents were the same, weren't they? Left stranded by Arnold's outgoing tide?'

'Actually I don't think my mother is given to crises of faith, and my father finds too much to fret about in this world, to worry about the next.'

'So why did Marshall pick economics for his idol?'

'He got off the train by mistake in Manchester – I'm not sure why – and found himself wandering the slums. Saw all manner of horrors. Decided there and then that the vice and iniquity all around him was nothing to do with Christian sin, but poverty plain and simply. And how to tackle poverty? The principles of economics would put people on the path to right-eousness, he reckoned, not the Ten Commandments. He hopes that I'll follow in his footsteps.'

'And …? Will you take up the mission?'

'I'm no do-gooder. And I have a life philosophy – remember? G.E. Moore. In his *Principia Ethica* he says that by far the most valuable things in life are "the pleasures of human inter-course and the enjoyment of beautiful objects". Which I take to mean: art and friendship.'

'Well, I hope you didn't tell old Alfred *that*.'

They both laughed, and Maynard finally, to Jack's relief, began to move across the grass.

'How was dear Mary?' asked Jack with real warmth, steering them in the direction of his own rooms.

Maynard smiled. 'Delightful. She thinks I should get married. Asked what kind of person would be my perfect wife.'

'My word! What did you say? Not the truth, obviously.'

Maynard laughed and saw in his mind's eye the Marshalls' garden, where he had been invited after his interview with the old man, and Mary Marshall sitting at the table under the chestnut tree and pouring out their tea. She was an old friend of his mother, like Florence one of the first women students at Cambridge; she had met her husband when attending his lectures on economics. The books Alfred had written during their long marriage, which had done so much to establish economics as a serious academic discipline, were their joint progeny.

He had looked at her gentle, intelligent face and considered her question as if it were a serious possibility. His perfect wife … Not, he found to his surprise, someone like Mary herself, however much he liked her. He didn't want another clever, intellectual companion: he had enough of those. No … he craved something else: a nature different from his own: intuitive, instinctive …

He had said something of this to Mary and she said reproachfully, 'I hope you aren't looking for a little woman to warm your slippers,' to which Maynard gave a shout of laughter and replied, 'The Angel in the House? No, not that. I couldn't bear it. I suppose I had better just remain unmarried then,' and Mary smiled and shook her head.

He said to Jack, 'We decided my perfect wife is too rarefied a creature to be found in this world.'

Jack gave a bark of laughter. Maynard, smiling, said, 'I'll let you know if I decide otherwise.'

Their conversation had lasted to Shephard's rooms, where he had stopped to deposit flowers and plums, and then half way to Maynard's quarters. Jack said, 'Well, before you embark on any matrimonial ventures, there's a perfectly *delectable* young man I want you to meet. He came to audition for the Greek Play–'

But Maynard was no longer listening. He had stopped and was staring at the entrance to one of the staircases, with an expression of – what was it? – *as if he were seeing it all crumble around him*, thought Jack, mentally describing the scene for a letter to his dear friend, Cecil Taylor. But why? It was only a perfectly ordinary staircase where undergraduates lived. And yet Maynard had gone completely white.

I really did think he was having a Road to Damascus experience, he told Cecil. *Like old Alfred in Manchester. Either that, or he'd eaten some dodgy seafood at lunch.*

'How long, Jack?' asked Maynard very quietly.

'How long …?'

'Before one stops seeing ghosts round every corner?'

Jack followed his gaze, and his levity died. Freddy had lived on that staircase, he remembered, and Rupert had come visiting: he could see them in his mind's eye, dressed in white flannels, without a care in the world, setting off for the tennis courts or river.

'Not so long, Maynard,' said Jack gently. 'Not so long.'

7

1920
In the smoke-filled bar of a West End theatre, Otto Niemeyer sipped champagne. He shared the mood around him, which was complacent. The hardships of war were finally receding: Germany lurched from failed coup to failed uprising, but did seem to be *trying* to pay its reparation bill; the League of Nations had been launched (although the Americans, whose idea it had been, were still wrangling about whether or not to join); and in Britain, Lloyd George had commanded there must be "Homes for Heroes" and the peace-time economy was suddenly booming, as people went out to spend the cash they had not been able to spend during the war. Nevertheless, Otto would not naturally have indulged in anything so ostentatious as champagne, except that he would never have turned down a suggestion from the Governor of the Bank of England.

Sir Montagu Norman, the Governor, had a debonair appearance for the ruler of Britain's most important, long-standing and stuffy financial institution – a position which also made him, in most people's eyes, the ruler of the City of

London itself. His beard had a touch of Van Dyke; his moustache a continental curl; and his caped evening dress was on the flamboyant side for a banker. But appearances can be deceiving. The soberly dressed Otto Niemeyer had never had reason to doubt Sir Montagu's character for a moment, or that he was the right person to lead that most staid institution, the Bank of England. Norman was sound, even if, instead of golf or billiards at his club, he preferred to meet at the ballet.

Tonight, Sir Montagu dealt only briefly with the performance, before moving on to the obligatory remarks about the bloodshed in Ireland ('well, but what else can one expect') and his hopes that Lloyd George's economic policies would not get out of hand. 'That fellow Keynes was in *The Sunday Times* again,' he then remarked with apparent casualness. 'Opining about something or other.'

Niemeyer's feeling of complacency evaporated. He grimaced then replied, not casually at all, 'It's that wretched book. Nobody would ever have heard of him otherwise.'

'*The Economic Consequences of the Peace*. For such a dry title, it does seem to have caused rather a storm. I even saw it on display at Harrods.'

'The treachery!' Outrage radiated from Niemeyer, like waves of heat. 'Do you know he had the effrontery to send me a copy? And I was so sure it would sink without trace.'

'I'm afraid that horse has bolted.'

'I know. I even had the Chancellor wanting to discuss it. The Chancellor! When I thought we would never hear of Keynes again – except, perhaps, for the occasional, obscure article in the *Economic Journal*.'

Niemeyer brooded on this lost vision. Sir Montagu sipped delicately at his champagne.

'I do hope he won't cause us any problems.'

'How can he? He won't be coming back to the Treasury, of that I can assure you.'

'No, but he seems to be a man who makes himself heard. And a man of ideas.'

'Utterly unorthodox ideas!'

'There are people who might listen. Even the Chancellor.'

'Oh, surely not! Keynes is nothing but a gadfly! And as for the press …'

Niemeyer's voice had risen in his indignation, and Sir Montagu raised a hand in warning. Too late. A tall man in evening dress, making his way across the crowded bar, had turned at the sound of his voice.

'Otto! Well, fancy seeing you.'

'What? Oh … Foxy.' And then, with obvious reluctance, as Foxy came towards them and stood, waiting expectantly, 'Sir Montagu, do you know Oswald Falk? Foxy, this is …'

'I recognize the Guvnor, of course. It's an honour, sir.'

The two men shook hands. Sir Montagu said, 'You're at Buckmasters, I believe?'

'That's right.'

Otto said, 'Foxy was at the Treasury during the War.'

'Really? How interesting. Then I expect you also know Mr Keynes.'

Foxy was startled. His eyes flickered towards Niemeyer. But he replied with aplomb, 'That's right. It was a great privilege to work with him.'

Niemeyer snorted. Sir Montagu raised an enquiring eyebrow.

'A brilliant man,' continued Foxy. 'I don't think we would have made it through the war without him.'

'I wouldn't say that!' Niemeyer spluttered champagne.

'Well, I would.'

While Niemeyer was still huffing, Sir Montagu intervened smoothly: 'You're still in regular contact with Mr Keynes?'

'Very much so.'

'Even after he wrote that book?' Niemeyer's voice

squeaked with indignation. Clearly, in his view, Foxy was guilty of nothing less than fraternizing with the enemy.

Foxy said equably, 'Yes, even after that book.' Under his urbane surface, however, alarm was flickering. *They can't have heard about–? Well, no point worrying.* 'I hope you're enjoying the evening's entertainment? I always love the Ballets Russes, although I must say I miss Lopokova. She had so much vitality. Did you hear she's on Broadway now?' Foxy chattered manfully and was relieved when the interval bell rang. 'Excuse me, I'd better get back to my companions–'

'A moment.' It was Sir Montagu's voice, and Foxy turned back in surprise. 'I have a private dining club that meets monthly. Otto here is a member, along with some other men of influence. We discuss high policy. Perhaps you and Mr Keynes might care to join us?'

My jaw just about hit the floor, Foxy imagined telling Maynard later. *An invitation from Sir Monty! To his private dining club! As for Otto, he was ready to burst. It was a joy to witness.*

'We'd be delighted,' Foxy said, recovering himself.

'I'll be in touch.'

Foxy took his leave. *What the hell was that about?* he wondered. He reckoned Otto Niemeyer was probably thinking the same thing. But what a feather in their caps – if only he could persuade Maynard to see sense and accept.

There was a certain irony, of course, that he and Maynard should receive this invitation now. He wondered if Sir Montagu Norman would be so keen to welcome them to his inner circle if and when their names appeared in the bankruptcy listings.

8

1921
   Lydia Lopokova had been back in London some months when received a summons to which she responded with unusual promptness. After all, when you have become famous for vanishing without warning, it is a good idea to show those who provide your bread and butter that you can turn up on time.

The Alhambra Theatre was almost empty. Lydia entered and stood in the auditorium unnoticed, watching the two men pacing back and forth on the stage. They were deep in discussion, at one moment gesturing towards the wings, then examining the backdrop, then pointing out towards an imaginary audience: they were *planning* something. Big Serge looked extremely animated, as he always did when in the grip of a new idea, stabbing with his walking cane to make his point, even his black moustache bouncing in sympathy. His companion was cooler, more reserved ... *English*, thought Lydia. She could not recall his name, although she recognized him as the owner of several London theatres, including the Alhambra.

She cupped her hands together. 'Cooee,' she called, like a schoolboy she had seen on the street two days before. She ran lightly down the central aisle, and arriving just below the stage, made a flourishing curtsey.

'You ask for me, and here I am.'

Big Serge said, 'Come up here, Lydia.'

'Pronto!'

A few moments later she was standing before him beaming. Big Serge, she thought, looked unusually forbidding. 'You don't have smile for me?' she asked cheekily.

Sergei Diaghilev, the great impresario, looked severely upon his diminutive ballerina, with her round face and upturned nose. Her dancer's grace was evident, even in her street clothes: it was not the ethereal, swan-like grace of a dancer like Pavlova, more that of a compact and sturdy pony. But he sometimes felt she lacked dignity.

'You are well rested? You are enjoying day off?'

'Yes. My feet ache so I bathe them in mustard Sokolova give me. I long for summer.'

'You dancers. You plan holiday while I plan future. You are going to France, I hear, up to who knows what?'

A guilty colour rose in Lydia's cheeks. She said rather defensively, 'All dancers need holiday. We work hard. This season was big success.' Diaghilev's companion, the theatre owner, nodded. Perhaps he was remembering, as Lydia wanted both men to remember, the rapturous applause and gushing reviews she'd received as she'd reprised her most famous roles in *Boutique, Petrushka* and *Les Femmes de Bonne Humeur*.

Diaghilev said sharply, 'As to that, we cannot dance the same things forever. Do you agree?'

Lydia said nothing, but her expression showed her puzzlement. This was Big Serge's business, not hers: *he* chose the ballets and commissioned their creators –Fokine, Massine or

Bronislava Nijinksa for the choreography; Igor for the music; Picasso or Bakst for the sets and costumes.

Diaghilev asked, 'Before you left Russia, did you ever see *The Sleeping Beauty*?'

'Yes, I saw it.'

'We are thinking to perform it here.'

Lydia's mouth fell open in unconcealed astonishment. 'We can do that?' she asked at last.

Big Serge did not like her question. 'Of course we can do it! It will be a marvel, a masterpiece of a time that is lost; a jewel of Imperial Russia. It will run for months, perhaps years. London will talk of nothing else.' He looked across at the theatre owner, who was frowning slightly. His name was Stoll, Lydia recalled suddenly.

'It will *have* to run for many months if it is to recoup the costs,' Stoll observed in a dry voice.

Big Serge dismissed this with a wave of the hand. 'Do not doubt it.' He beckoned Lydia to the centre of the stage. 'Here, my Lydia, imagine that you are standing in the spotlight, in costume as Lilac Fairy. Behind you a tableau of roses ... The *corps de ballet* enter dressed as peasant dancers ... Aurora, to dance the Rose Adagio. The castle rises up behind. You wave your wand. The thorns spring up about the walls ...'

But all Lydia could see in her mind's eye was the Mariinsky Theatre in St Petersburg – the Mariinsky of her childhood: the gilt-encrusted interior; the audience stuffed with jewel-clad aristocrats; the vast stage brimming with row upon row of classically trained ballerinas, in layers of floating tulle, all moving in perfect unison. It seemed extraordinary that Big Serge could even *think* to recreate such a thing. 'Maybe we find some Archdukes to come watch,' she joked. 'If any left.'

Diaghilev ignored this. '*Sleeping Beauty* will be magnificent. But its success ask much of everybody. Much work.'

'We all know how to work.'

'*You*, Lydia, work hard, but you also become … *distracted*.'

Lydia was silent.

'You will have important role in new production. No, not Aurora. That is not right for you.' Stoll gave a cough of dissent, and Diaghilev said quickly, 'Except for a few performances, *a very few*, to please your most special fans. But mostly, more classical ballerina will take that role. Karsavina perhaps. We will see. *Your* part, for you perfect, is Lilac Fairy.'

Lydia nodded. She was beginning to understand. She was the company's most popular dancer, an important asset in drawing the crowds. Big Serge was mounting an ambitious and expensive new production: *The Sleeping Beauty* would be on a scale far beyond anything the Ballets Russes had attempted before. This Mr Stoll was no doubt advancing the money, and he must have made it a condition that she, Lydia, take an important part in the production – and that she be given a stern talking-to first.

The greater mystery was why Big Serge should have chosen *The Sleeping Beauty* in the first place. It represented, surely, everything he had reacted against: the Ballets Russes had always been about the daringly modern, the avant-garde. *Maybe three years after Revolution*, she thought, *even Big Serge feel nostalgic*.

'You know I will be slave to part – I always am.'

'When you are *here*,' Diaghilev replied. 'It is if you are *not* here that troubles me.' There was an uncomfortable pause.

'That … there were circumstances not my fault.'

'So take care that no such circumstances arise again.'

'They were not my fault,' she repeated.

'Miss Lopokova.' Stoll leaned forward gravely, the tips of his fingers pressed together. 'Two years ago you vanished in the middle of a run. It was a hugely successful production and suddenly you weren't there: all London was talking about your disappearance, the press was full of it and your colleagues were left high and dry. Nothing was known of your whereabouts until you reappeared months later in New York, performing in a rather bad Broadway musical.'

Lydia flushed deeply. She was angry, but it was not in her nature to show anger. *What do they know of these things?* she thought. *How can they understand?* She laughed and threw up her hands. 'I am like rabbit in hat, Mr Stoll: I vanish and then I pop out again.'

'It's *Sir* actually,' he said. '*Sir* Oswald Stoll.' He reached out his hand and she shook it ceremoniously. 'Remember then, Miss Lopokova, this time ... no *popping*.' He turned to Diaghilev. 'We will just have to hope that the public is in the mood for this new offering. It will, at least, be a distraction from newspapers full of the unemployed. I will be in touch.' They heard him bid farewell to the stage manager on his way out.

When he had gone, Diaghilev let out a sigh. He leant upon his cane and beckoned Lydia closer.

'This production,' he said in Russian, 'it could be a very good thing. For all of us. But Lydia, there must be no more ... *circumstances*. How old are you?'

'Twenty-seven,' she said after a pause to do the sums. With most people she would have knocked off some more, especially if she thought they'd read about her in the newspapers; but Big Serge had known her since she was eighteen, and was the one who had started knocking off the years for the newspapers in the first place.

'You turn twenty-nine in October,' he said, surprising her. 'A dancer grows old. She has to think about the future. I do not see you as a teacher or choreographer. So ...'

'So?'

'You must choose a partner wisely.'

'Like Barrocchi?' she asked, a hint of bitterness in her voice.

'Barrocchi is no good, so forget him.' Big Serge waved a

hand, dismissing Barrocchi. 'Also that Martynov ... And what is this I hear of Igor?'

Again, Lydia flushed. 'I don't know what you hear.'

'I hear you were both in Paris in the spring. And I know what I know: that he is married, even if his wife is sick. Also, that he has the roving eye. My *Lydochka*, I tell you this for your own good: you must take care. Above all, do not think if you run away again, that I will take you back.'

So easy to say and yet how little he understood, thought Lydia wistfully, of what it meant to be a woman on the stage. Of how easy it was to be betrayed by your own body, the body you relied on for your bread and butter, as well as by the men who wanted to possess you. Then she looked at him again and saw a softness there: perhaps he *did* understand after all. He understood, but he would not always forgive and forget.

In her most emphatic Russian, she swore to devote herself to the Lilac Fairy. They kissed farewell and she left him contemplating the empty stage, while she went back out to the street. She was unusually pensive. In Russia's Imperial Ballet, there had been pensions for dancers when they retired – although even so, plenty had been glad to hook an archduke to help with the bills – but in the Ballets Russes there were no pensions, and so she should find a man to take care of her: that was what Big Serge was really saying. But who? Not another sleazy conman like Barrocchi; nor a weak-willed Russian exile, with nothing to offer but a box full of medals, like General Martynov. A dancer? *But often they are like you, Big Serge; they prefer men to women.* Besides, male dancers faced early retirement also. An English aristocrat, hooked at a fashionable party? It was not inconceivable, but the idea made her laugh. She could not imagine herself as 'Your Ladyship'. Or maybe somebody like Sam, who she'd met recently at a party and immediately felt was interested in her: a kind and gentle man, possessed of a thriving business and a Rolls-Royce, but also, married.

Oah! she thought, dismissing the topic. *Maybe I don't want to be looked after. I prefer to look after myself.*

THAT EVENING she put on an evening dress, some minimal make-up – offstage, she could rarely be bothered; in fact, she did not always bother onstage – and left her room at the Waldorf Hotel, carrying her bag and evening slippers under one arm. On the way down the stairs, she met Barrocchi going up. They nodded to each other and were almost past, when Barrocchi stopped: 'Ah, Lydia–?'

'What is it?'

'You look *bellisima, amore.*'

Lydia favoured him with a scowl and he took a step back. 'I hope you have a good evening, my dear,' he said hastily and turned back to the stairs.

Lydia went on, shaking her head and muttering to herself in Russian. *Big Serge was right. It's no good.*

By the time she reached the lobby, she had recovered herself. She greeted Frank behind the desk with her usual sunniness and handed him her key, refusing his offer to fetch a cab: 'It is not far. I like to walk. I have been lazy today. It is good for lazy ballerina legs to do the walking.'

She was almost out of the door, when she remembered something, and turned back to the desk.

'Frank–?'

'Yes, Miss Lopokova?'

'If Mr Barrocchi ask for key to my room …'

'Yes?'

'Please don't give it him.'

Frank blinked, then nodded. 'Yes, Miss Lopokova.'

Lydia made to leave again then turned back once more.

'Oh, and Frank. I am wondering ...'

'Yes, Miss Lopokova?'

'Maybe if I give you my money, in future you can look after it for me? I am not happy just to leave it in room.'

'Yes, of course. I can put it in the safe.'

'And if Mr– I mean to say, if *anyone* ask for it ...'

'Of course I will only ever give it to you.'

Lydia beamed, threw him a kiss and tripped out into the evening.

9

G ordon Square, Bloomsbury
Mrs Harland sat at the kitchen table drinking her morning cup of tea and watching the new maid, Lottie, rushing back and forth gathering the things for Mr Keynes' breakfast tray: cup, saucer, napkin, plate ... put the kettle on ... small pot of jam, small pat of butter on a saucer, knife, fork ... There was the smell of burning.

'Move a leg, Lottie,' said Mrs Harland, as with an exclamation Lottie leapt, too late, to save the toast.

Mrs Harland refrained from comment while Lottie inspected the blackened slices hopefully, as if they might magically revert to gold. Finally Lottie threw them aside and began to cut more bread, just as the kettle began to whistle.

'I think I told you before that Mr Keynes prefers coffee in the mornings.' Lottie, who had been spooning tea leaves (best Assam) into the teapot, exclaimed again, and the tea leaves went flying like confetti.

Gates laughed. Mrs Harland had forgotten about him, kneeling on the floor in the passageway. Like Lottie, he was new to Gordon Square and was currently cleaning the boots and shoes: not an onerous task, with only half of the family in residence. Mrs Harland still tended to think in terms of 'family', even though it was not a family that resided at 46 Gordon Square. Well, Mr and Mrs Bell were married, of course, but in a way that just made the whole situation even odder, given that while Mrs Bell took all her meals at 46, her bedroom and her children's were at Number 50, whereas Mr Bell's was here at Number 46. Gates had been hired by the James Stracheys on the other side of the Square but they were off somewhere on the Continent – Vienna, or was it Venice? – and their house shut up for the summer, so their housemaid had been sent to another Strachey sibling, and Gates had come here to replace Mr Harland, who had gone for a week's stay with his old mother.

Gordon Square – Bloomsbury – was like that. Its residents, and consequently its servants, were always revolving like a game of musical chairs, so that you never knew who you would be left with when the music stopped.

It made life interesting, thought Mrs Harland. More varied than a family; less impersonal than a boarding house. Now *that* was something she could never have stood. Some people might think Number 46 *was* like a boarding house, with so many grown people all living their separate lives under one roof, coming and going, with their own quarters, their own friends, their own work. (Even the ladies had their own work, something Mrs Harland found extraordinary: Mrs Bell had a studio at Number 50; and when Mrs Woolf came to stay, she was given a study – a strange thing indeed, to give a visiting lady her own study.) But the inhabitants of a boarding house did not share their lives, were not in and out of each other's rooms, talking, arguing, debating – and doing other things too, although Mrs Harland did not care to think on that – entertaining their (shared) friends to tea or supper or large, noisy parties. All these comings and goings could be chaotic, but it meant they were less likely to monitor the servants' quarters, and to be too exacting about hours worked – or days off – or if say, some whisky happened to go missing.

'Wish I could have breakfast on a tray at ten o'clock o' the morning!'

Lottie spoke cheerfully, her hair flapping like a spaniel's ears as she leapt across the kitchen once more – this time to fetch the tomatoes. Watching her hairpins pinging onto the floor, Mrs Harland almost regretted that the liberal Bloomsberries, unlike most of London Society, did not insist that their servants wear uniforms. Lottie would have benefitted from a maid's cap.

Lottie was still only fifteen and looked younger. She had grown up in an orphanage in deepest Sussex, destined always for a life in service. Gawky, black-haired, always smiling, she had no gift for domestic order, but she lifted the spirits all the same. When Mr Bell and Mr Keynes had held a dinner party, and the servants had got merry upon the leftovers – Mr Harland had managed to procure a half-full carafe of wine when Mr Bell was too busy telling anecdotes to his guests to notice – Lottie had disguised herself as an Irish washing lady and sung 'Goosey-Goosey Gander' to general applause.

'You'd not want to be lolling around in bed that late,' said Mrs Harland. 'You wouldn't know what to do with yourself.'

'She might,' said Gates from the passageway, with a sideways grin.

Mrs Harland ignored this. Lottie was busy trying to get a fried egg off the pan and onto the plate without breaking it.

'Will Mr Keynes be going to France too?' asked Lottie when, with a sigh of relief, she had everything on the plate and a bowl over the top to keep it warm.

'I doubt it. He hasn't said anything.' (And he'd seemed worried lately, Mrs Harland thought, and very twitchy about the telephone, which was odd, because Mr Keynes was generally in such good spirits.)

'Oh, he won't want to be stuck in Lunnon – any more than they do,' said Gates, as if he knew all about it: an attitude that grated with Mrs Harland. *They* were Vanessa and Duncan, who had been in Saint-Tropez for weeks.

'Mr Keynes works, you see,' she said rather sharply. 'That's the difference.'

'Nice work if you can get it … in bed until ten o'clock!'

'No, you're wrong: he works before breakfast. Every morning he's on the telephone, for hours sometimes, or writing. Of course, half the week he's away in Cambridge. But that's work too. You'll see. He never stops scribbling.'

'Past midnight last night,' said Lottie, on her way towards the door, moving carefully, the tray gripped tight.

'How do you know that?' Gates sat back on his heels, one of Clive's brogues in his hand.

'Got up, didn't I? Heard a noise. Or thought I did. Went out onto the landing, peeked down the stairs, could see the light from his study. Didn't hear nothing else, so I went back to bed.'

'Now, Lottie, you shouldn't be up at that hour.' Mrs Harland got up to hold the door open for her. 'You need your sleep – up at six and working all day.'

'Thought maybe there was a burglar.'

'And if there was, better you stay snug in bed. You don't want to be tangling with no burglar.'

'Yes, I'm here now,' Gates agreed. 'I'll sort 'em!'

'Or there's Mr Keynes,' said Mrs Harland repressively.

'What's he going to do – sock 'em over the head with one of his books?'

Mrs Harland could not help smiling. 'Well, he might. They're heavy enough.'

'Good that they're useful for something!'

Lottie had gone. Gates rubbed at a shoe thoughtfully while

glancing sideways at Mrs Harland, who was now making notes for the grocery order on the back of an old envelope.

"Course it's not burglars that do the intruding round here, is it?'

Mrs Harland, muttering to herself – 'Rice ... flour ... dried peas' – did not respond.

'I mean,' he added helpfully, 'when you meet strangers on the stairs, in the middle of night, it's not the *silver* they're after.'

'There's no silver to speak of anyhow,' said Mrs Harland, for once slow on the uptake. So Gates felt obliged to spell it out.

'They don't head for the silver cabinet – if there were any – because they're heading for the *bedrooms*. Ain't that the truth of it?'

Mrs Harland looked up into eyes that gazed back, blandly innocent. After a pause she said, 'They have their ways. They're good employers; fair-minded. If you're a Salvation Army type, this might not be the best place for you.'

Gates grinned wolfishly. 'Do I look like a Salvation Army type?'

'No gossip in front of Lottie. She's only a child.'

'Don't it worry you, her working in a place like this?'

'No. Why should it? She'll see nothing. She's too young to understand.'

'But is she safe?'

'Of course she's safe! Safer than any house in London!'

And that was the honest truth. Even Mr Bell, who had a wandering eye if ever a man did, would not prey on a scrap like Lottie. None of them would. They could find plenty in their own circle who would willingly hop between the covers. They wouldn't take advantage of a servant – not like some households she had known, where the paterfamilias, so solemn at morning prayers, could not be trusted on encountering a young maid in an empty corridor.

'But that Mr Keynes is a single man, and she taking him his food while he's still abed ...'

Though irritated, Mrs Harland was amused too. 'She's safe enough from Mr Keynes, believe me.'

'You're saying he never has ladies slipping into his room to join him?'

'Not la–' She broke off. Did Gates not listen to the gossip? And had he not, only the other week, noticed ... (her imagination skittered away from it). Maybe he had not been here long enough to observe the frequent visits of a certain young man from Cambridge, or to wonder where he slept.

After a pause she said, 'He won't trouble her, believe me. Anyhow, he's a gentleman.'

'There's many a gentleman in this square has company slipping into his room at night – company that's not his wife.'

Mrs Harland had had enough. 'Well, there's no law against it,' she observed, and determinedly turned back to her shopping list. Though Gates, had he known more, might have retorted that there certainly *was* – and the penalty was disgrace and prison, as Oscar Wilde had discovered.

MAYNARD hardly noticed Lottie when she tottered in, all baby steps, her attention fixed on balancing the tray. He was in bed, in a kind of nest of dressing gown and manuscript and morning paper, his attention riveted on the telephone.

'Five per cent!' he declared suddenly and so loudly that Lottie, lowering her tray towards a chair (the bedside table being piled high with books and manuscripts) at the very last moment let go, so that it landed with the most enormous clatter.

'By God!' said Maynard, and into the phone, 'No, just crocks – must have been in sympathy with the mark. Yes, I'll be there, Foxy. See you next week.'

Maynard hung up and rested a sympathetic eye on the plainly mortified Lottie.

'Oh, there's milk slopped over your toast, Mr Keynes–'

'Bread and milk, always my favourite as a child,' he said promptly. 'Had it for supper every night. Don't see that toast and milk is much different.'

'It was just that you made me jump–'

'Well, you see, the German mark has plummeted. Do you know what that means?'

Mutely, Lottie shook her head.

'It means – well, for one thing, I could have lost a hundred pounds.'

Lottie, whose yearly salary was less, gasped. Maynard nodded solemnly. Horror-struck, Lottie put her fingers to her mouth.

'Or, I could have gained a hundred, had I sold the mark short, as I would have been inclined to do.'

'But … how can you do both, Mr Keynes?'

'Well, there would not be much point in doing both. A balanced portfolio is one thing, but being long and short in the same currency … now that hardly makes sense, does it?'

Lottie, totally befuddled, shook her head.

'As it happens, I did have some holdings in marks, but I chose to close my account. You see, Lettie, I am not without influence. Last week I published my opinion on reparations, the repayment on German debt, you know – in the newspaper, and I gave my opinion that a German default next year was highly likely. Since when, the mark has crashed. It would be hardly ethical, would it, to publish such an opinion in *The Sunday Times*, if I were speculating in marks myself? It is for that reason that I closed my account temporarily, before the article appeared.'

Lottie's head was spinning. A hundred-pound loss was something she could barely imagine possible: she was envisaging him evicted onto the street (did such things happen to gentlemen?) and she and Mr and Mrs Harland homeless. And somehow (she was hazy about this) the Germans were to blame.

During this interlude the phone rang again and Maynard answered. 'What's that? … Oh yes, very well, Foxy. I can come this afternoon, if you think it best. Have you heard any more about–? Well, it can wait.' He hung up looking preoccupied.

'What will happen now?' Lottie whispered. She had hardly noticed the phone call, being still caught up in a vision of financial ruin and homelessness.

'What? Oh, you mean about the mark? Well, I expect it will recover somewhat. That is the way with markets. If it does, there is a point at which I will choose to buy short, in expectation of future profits.'

Lottie heaved a sigh of relief.

'But there is always the possibility it will fall further.'

'What then?' asked Lottie. A loss *beyond* one hundred pounds was too awful to contemplate.

'*Then* it might actually be advantageous to get *into* the mark; to buy while the price is low. It's not something to be done without consideration, though, Lettie – it is Lettie, isn't it?'

'Lottie.'

'Well, Lottie, don't look so worried. Should you ever want to indulge in currency speculation, come to me, and I'll explain the principles. But until then – I shouldn't trouble yourself too much.'

'I never had a head for figures, Mr Keynes.'

'Well, I'm no good at anything domestic.' And as she looked blank, 'Cooking, and – so forth.'

Not that Lottie had much of a talent for it either, as Maynard discovered when Lottie had left and he took the bowl off his breakfast plate: overcooked egg, undercooked tomato, cold sausage and the milk-soaked toast. He must remind Mrs Harland how much the household needed a full-time cook, he decided. Although with the house half-empty just now, they could hardly justify the expense. If only Vanessa and Duncan were here ... The place felt wretchedly quiet without them. He contemplated potential months of a silent house and tepid breakfasts, and his mood – which had not been shaken by the imagined loss of one hundred pounds – dimmed slightly.

FIVE HOURS LATER, he walked down a crowded street in the City of London, surrounded by dark-suited men in bowler hats and the occasional woman (most likely somebody's secretary) clutching a business-like handbag in one hand. Maynard reached his destination and ascended some steps. The gold plaque next to the doorbell announced: *Buckmaster and Moore, Stockbrokers*.

He was ushered upstairs and into an inner office, where Foxy, dressed in his stockbroker's uniform of suit and waist-coat, his dark hair as shiny and polished as his leather shoes, rose to greet him. They shook hands vigorously.

'Maynard! Glad to see you. I hope I didn't put you out?'

'Not at all.'

'Well, shall we get down to things?'

With sudden gravity, Foxy began to open up the files for their portfolio. Maynard unclipped his fountain pen from his jacket pocket. For a while the talk was all of rates of return; of francs, dollars, marks and rupees; of the allocation of risk and portfolio diversification; of bond markets, railways and steel. Eventually, Foxy sat back in his chair and grinned.

'So, I think we can say ...'

'We're finally back in the black,' Maynard concluded. 'And not a moment too soon.'

'No, time was almost up. We're actually in profit – despite your high-minded principles–'

'No bankruptcy declaration on the horizon?'

'All debts repaid. And if we go on this way, well … Mind you, markets are funny things.'

'We won't be caught out again,' Maynard said firmly. 'Dammit, Foxy, you had me worried this morning.'

'Oh, you mean, because I changed the time? No, I have plans for next week, that's all.' He chuckled at the expression on Maynard's face. 'How about a drink?'

He rose. Maynard laughed. Accepting a glass of sherry he said, 'We've been on the brink at times. I'm grateful to you, Foxy, for not pulling the plug.'

'Oh, I never doubted we'd get it back!'

They raised their glasses. In truth, it had been a tumultuous year. At one point, due to unexpected movements of the dollar, they had owed far more than they possessed, and had been kept clear of formal bankruptcy only by Foxy's flexibility with Buckmasters' cash account, and by the fortunate fact that neither Maynard's parents nor his friends (several of whom had invested their savings with him) had insisted on getting their money back. All the same, it was a rather deflating prospect, as Maynard admitted to Foxy, to have lost every penny entrusted in one by one's nearest and dearest, and although he was sure he could get it back in time, that required more capital to invest – capital he did not have.

And then, when everything was looking at its most bleak – round about the time he was due to attend his first meeting of Montagu Norman's private dining club, in a threadbare evening suit he could not afford to replace – an envelope had arrived from America. Opening it without much interest over breakfast at Gordon Square, Maynard had found himself contemplating a cheque for royalties that just about made his eyes drop out of his head. He'd been saved. And more cheques followed: *Economic Consequences of the Peace* was an international sensation, and Maynard's pen in continual demand with the press.

Of course Maynard had no hesitation putting the proceeds straight into the market and soon they were speculating again.

Foxy leaned back in his chair, the business of the day over and now in a comfortably philosophic mood. 'It's been hair-raising ... no good for my blood pressure ... but then I suppose that's why we do it really.'

'What do you mean?'

'The joy of the gamble. Otherwise, why speculate?'

'*I* do it because I'm an impoverished Cambridge don with no private wealth and inclinations that run beyond my means.'

'Nonsense! It's because you're a born gambler.'

'Well, I admit I do find it intriguing – the psychology of the investor. It's not something that's been studied much in economic theory. The *theory* assumes everyone is rational and that was my mistake: to assume that the theory was right. But in fact, speculators are completely *irrational* half the time and it makes pricing stocks and currencies very difficult, because instead of deciding what something is worth, the way I thought, it's about working out what all the *other* blighters in the market think it's worth.'

Foxy gave an exclamation, and to Maynard's great surprise leapt up and started fishing around in the wastepaper bin.

'What *are* you doing?'

'What you said. It's like this, isn't it?'

Foxy unfolded the morning paper and Maynard found himself surveying a page of smirking, blonde beauties. *Divine Doris. Enchanting Esme ... Pick the Winner for £200.*

'Err ... I'm not sure I follow?'

'It's a newspaper beauty competition, don't you see, but you're not picking the one with the prettiest face, but trying to work out who everyone *else* will pick. That's how you win the prize. And they're in the same boat, of course.'

'That's *exactly* right,' said Maynard, pleased. He peered at the paper. 'I think I'll go for *Glad-Eyed Gladys*.'

'We must tell Monty about our new theory,' said Foxy, amused. 'How financial markets really work. According to Keynes and Falk. Maybe we could write a book ... I take it you're going along next week?'

'Yes, and I might even buy a new evening suit for the occasion.'

'I'm fond of your suit. It reminds me of my great-aunt's crochet.'

Maynard laughed. 'Then you can have it as a souvenir. But I've been the down-at-heel don for too long. A new suit is worth every penny if it will make them take my opinions seriously.'

'I think they do take them seriously. They just don't *like* them much.'

'No. Well ... I don't mind that, but I wish Otto wasn't always giving us his Medusa's stare. Do you think he'll ever forgive us for leaving the Treasury?'

'Actually, I think it's the only thing we ever did that he *really* approved of.'

Maynard laughed. Foxy said, 'You know, I had the devil persuading you to join Monty's merry band, and now here you are, buying a new suit for it. But you can't bear it for long, can you – I mean, not having a finger in the pie?'

There was a long pause. Then Maynard said: 'For the longest time I thought I was well rid of them. But it turns out I can't bear watching them cock up, and not saying anything.'

'No, you really can't, can you? It's funny, sometimes, just watching your face while Otto's talking.'

'In truth, I'm worried, Foxy. The post-war boom ... it's been and gone. They mismanaged it, of course, and what do we see now: *over one million unemployed.*' Maynard paused, as if to give the dread statistic more weight. 'It's ... unprecedented.'

'Yet for a while it all seemed to be going so well: Jobs for the Boys and Homes for Heroes–'

'Yet it all came to nothing: precious few homes and now unemployment too.'

'Still, the numbers *must* fall eventually. Employment *will* rise again. It's the nature of the beast. We just need to wait out the economic cycle.'

Rather to Foxy's surprise, Maynard did not immediately agree. 'That would have been true before the war,' he said slowly, 'but now, all bets are off. I don't think Monty and friends realize yet. The devastated export industries – the industrial wastelands – they're all in the north: out of sight and out of mind, if you work at the Bank of England.'

'The coal strike wasn't out of sight and mind: the King called back to London, and troops in Kensington Gardens and the whole City talking about how it was the start of the revolution–'

'And when the transport workers failed to join in, they promptly forgot about it again. But the underlying problem remains. And things could get worse. What if there's some kind of shock – say, a stock market crash?'

'We've just got back into the black,' protested Foxy.

'Oh, I know. I'm not expecting it. But it's a risk. Meanwhile, this slump ... the Bank of England should lower interest rates, but Monty is dead against it ...'

They were interrupted by Foxy's new secretary, a Miss Trenton, coming in with some letters to sign. 'Excuse me for disturbing you, but I think you wanted these before the week-end, Mr Falk,' she said, as she leant to place them on his desk. Foxy, watching appreciatively, thought that she beat Enchanting Esme and Divine Doris into a cocked hat. He disapproved of workplace dalliances, but there was no harm, he told himself, in admiring the view.

'Rather fine,' he observed to Maynard, when the door had shut, 'don't you think?'

Maynard, his mind elsewhere, was startled. 'What is?'

Foxy smiled. 'Never mind, old boy.'

THEY LEFT Foxy's office together, joining a surge of City workers heading out at the end of the working day. Foxy paused at the newsstand to buy an evening paper.

'As we were saying,' he said, low-voiced, indicating the headline which read UNEMPLOYMENT RISES. 'And there's the human evidence.' He jerked his head towards a man sitting on the pavement. Dressed in a shabby overcoat, he had a sign next to him that read WAR VETERAN, and a cap holding a few coins.

Maynard and Foxy dug out their change. The man, slumped in apathy, barely acknowledged the stream of silver.

'Poor blighter,' Foxy observed as they walked on. 'No job, no health, no house … I daresay, no family.' He glanced sideways at Maynard, and added, knowing he was playing with fire, 'Expect he'd like to see the Germans in the gutter, just as much as the French do. And can you blame him?'

'Punishing the Germans won't help. What *he* needs is a job.'

'Ah, but who is going to find him one?'

'You know, sometimes I think we should.'

'We? You mean *us*, personally?' Foxy raised an eyebrow.

'We, the tax-paying citizens of this country; we, the Government. It would make more sense to pay him to build roads say, than to pay him the dole for doing nothing.'

Foxy took a long look at Maynard who, he was well aware, often enjoyed advancing an outrageous opinion for the sake of it, sometimes one that had sprung into his head on the spur of the moment, then vanquishing his opponent in argument, before completely reversing his view the next time they met. He thought he detected a playful look in his friend's eye.

'The Government won't pay men to work if it does not have the money,' he countered.

'But why shouldn't it have the money? Every business borrows to invest. It is exactly the same with governments.'

'Ah, but the Government cannot go cap in hand to the bank!'

Maynard tutted. 'You are aware that the Government has been borrowing money since ... well, pretty much the dawn of time? I wouldn't be surprised if Adam wasn't after credit to improve his fruit trees just before he was thrown out of Eden.' Foxy gave an appreciative snort. Maynard, getting into his stride, continued: 'In 1802 they introduced income tax as a temporary expedient to pay off the National Debt, and strangely enough both debt and tax are still with us.'

'Ah, 1802. The Napoleonic wars. That's a rather different kettle of fish. You have to pay for a war. Well, we know that – having been at the Treasury for the last one.'

Maynard waved an arm, almost knocking the hat off a passer-by.

'Exactly! During the war we put the entire population to work, increasing production beyond anything the Treasury had thought possible. Now we've peace and we leave our people to moulder. Why can we take on a debt for a war, to destroy assets and poor devils like that one, but not to invest and make ourselves richer?'

He became aware of the woman with the hat glowering at him, and swept her an apologetic bow, at which she decided not, after all, to take umbrage, but to alight on to a passing bus instead.

'You put it well,' said Foxy smiling, 'but common sense says otherwise. Everyone knows economic downturns are a time for belt-tightening.'

'Ah, common sense. Have I ever mentioned how much I detest common sense?'

Foxy laughed. 'I'm beginning to think some champagne is what you need. Shall we go to my club? Or how about here?'

They were passing a City watering hole. Several City gents were descending the steps: stout, sleek, prosperous, with complacent expressions and braying voices. A snatch of conversation floated towards them: 'The trouble is the working classes don't understand that they have to *work* for their wages …'

Maynard wrinkled his nose then inspected his watch. 'No, I don't think so. I'm going out this evening.'

'Where to?' asked Foxy, always curious about Maynard's other life.

'The ballet.'

'Really? Which one?'

'*The Sleeping Beauty*, though they've renamed it apparently: *The Sleeping Princess*. The Ballets Russes. Care to join us?'

'I can't,' said Foxy regretfully. 'Ah well, you must let me know how you find it.'

BACKSTAGE AT THE ALHAMBRA THEATRE, all were getting ready, a process with its own elaborate choreography, in which each member of the company played its part. Lydia Sokolova was applying greasepaint, peering into the mirror of her dressing table, when Lydia Lopokova appeared: 'I am afraid I have been taken by surprise, you know what I mean' – and Sokolova, reaching for her bottom drawer, thought that her friend looked in surprisingly good spirits, for such times usually found her loud in expression of her sufferings.

There was one obvious explanation, of course.

'You were worried?' she murmured, handing over the necessary supplies.

'Of course I was worried. I might bleed all over stage! Luckily, I find out in time.' Lydia took a napkin, and without any self-consciousness, proceeded to tuck it into her knickers. Sokolova glanced away embarrassed. She was Russian only in name, having been born the very English Hilda Munnings and rechristened by Diaghilev when she joined the Ballets Russes; she sometimes struggled with the free-and-easy ways of her Russian colleagues, Lydia in particular.

'I thought you were regular as clockwork.'

'It is so.' Lydia sat down beside her. 'How we women suffer!' She pulled back her hair and examined her face in the mirror. 'Sometimes I get the spots ... but not now, thank God!'

Sokolova thought Lydia's relief excessive for a lack of spots. But if she had really feared ... well, then who could it be? Randolfo Barrocchi? They were still married, but Lydia barely addressed a word to him, and in fact, he had left recently for Italy, some said permanently. Or there was Igor Stravinsky ... Sometimes Sokolova had harboured suspicions about Igor ... but he had left for France, and his wife, Katya. Of course, he had been here in London until only a week ago, and without the long-suffering Katya, who was said to be very sick.

She laid a hand on her friend's arm. 'Be careful.'

Their eyes met in the glass. 'I *am* careful.' Suddenly Lydia grew angry, although not, Sokolova felt, with her. 'You sound like Big Serge ... I am almost thirty, a married woman, a dancer ... Does all this require that I live my life as nun?'

Sokolova squeezed her arm.

'You are lucky.' Lydia's voice was rough.

'I know.' Sokolova followed Lydia's gaze to the photograph on her dressing table. Natasha was almost four. In a carefully casual tone she asked, 'Did you hear all the fuss about this new clinic?'

'What new clinic?'

'A birth-control clinic for married women.'

'What does that mean?'

'It helps women not to become pregnant ... by medical ways, modern ways.'

Lydia's eyes opened wide. 'You have been to this clinic?'

Sokolova said simply, 'I'm married and I need to dance.'

There was a pause while Sokolova carefully filled in her lips with red lipstick, and Lydia frowned into the mirror, caged in her own thoughts.

Sokolova blotted her mouth. 'Of course some people say it is scandalous and should be closed down. I'm sure they aren't dancers. Others say it's all about preventing degenerate types having so many children ...'

Lydia laughed, one of her bubbling, champagne laughs. 'Russian ballerinas are always degenerate!'

It was then that a backstage boy arrived with a note for Lydia. She opened it casually, scanned the contents and remarked, 'It is from a Mr Clive Bell. He say we met at Lady Colebox party.' She narrowed her eyes.

'And what does he want?'

'To look at my breasts most likely. Most of them did there.'

Sokolova laughed. 'What does he *say* he wants?'

'He comes tonight and wants to come backstage. What is it to me if he come backstage?' She shrugged.

'He should have sent flowers. That's the polite thing to do.' A new thought came to her. '*Sam* always sends you roses. I've seen them on your dressing table.'

'Yes,' said Lydia. 'Did you notice they are also from his wife?'

Her expression was hard to read and Sokolova decided not to push further. Lydia stretched, said, 'Now I finish my getting ready', and went towards the door.

Sokolova watched her in the mirror.

'The clinic is in Holloway,' she said.

10

M aynard had no inkling of the significance of the evening; indeed, he would not have agreed to go in the first place, only Clive had goaded him into it. 'Let me guess!' he had declared theatrically, when Maynard had murmured that he was actually rather busy. 'A paper to write. A journal to edit. A lecture to give. Advice for the Treasury. Dinner with Lloyd George, the old Welsh Wizard, or bridge with Lord Asquith himself. The clever Mr Keynes: so vital, so important, so in demand!'

Stung, Maynard had agreed to go, and had then scribbled a note to his brother Geoffrey inviting him to come too. Geoffrey was always talking about ballet and a joint outing would please Florence.

Still, as he ran up the steps of the Alhambra Theatre, empty except for a few stragglers, he felt that he would much rather have been in the warm, smoky surroundings of Foxy's club, sipping whisky and pondering events in the City; or else scribbling that article *The Times* was calling out for, which he was determined to finish by the weekend. Still, at the least, he comforted himself, it would give him something to write about

to Vanessa and Duncan, to remind them that there were other
joys than those offered by Saint-Tropez, and that he, Maynard,
had other facets besides work. And then, he entered the
dimness of the auditorium and the overture came billowing
forth in a great wave to greet him, and he was genuinely glad
to be there.

'I made it,' he whispered to Clive, as he took his seat.

'By the skin of your teeth!'

From beyond Clive, Geoffrey raised his eyebrows, then
turned his attention back to the orchestra. The music
surrounded them, as the heavy, red velvet curtain began to rise
revealing a lushness of white silk and tumbling flowers, like a
Fragonard painting.

'I thought it would be one of those modern things,'
Maynard whispered to Clive, already charmed. 'Fairies in
bathing suits.'

'It's certainly not what you expect from the Ballets Russes,'
Clive replied. His eyes swept over the set. '*Hideously* old-fashioned,' he remarked.

Maynard did not reply. He was watching the courtiers, in
their glorious finery, revolving about the stage like the bright
patterns of a kaleidoscope, and he felt both thrilled and
soothed. He had always paid his respects to the Ballets Russes,
but this was like being offered a box of mouth-watering choco-
lates – so enticing – so much colour. How sad Duncan would
be to miss it – so innocent and yet so gorgeous, like a child's
book of fairy tales –

And then Lydia entered.

She arrived with a jump – one of her famous jumps – her
lilac costume trembling from the movement, like the petals of a
flower. She paused for a moment, her arms graceful, her hands
and feet elegantly turned out, her eyes gazing out at the audience, a smile hovering at her mouth. There was something
conspiratorial about that smile; almost, she might have

winked. There was a crown on her head – a tall, delicate, fairy-tale crown. And then she launched herself across the stage with that peculiarly vivid energy that she brought to every role and that expressed pure joy.

The audience sighed its happiness.

LYDIA'S DRESSING room was crammed with flowers. A huge bunch of orchids, with a card inscribed 'From Sam and Lil' took pride of place on the dressing table, while sumptuous white roses ('All my love, Vera') balanced precariously on the window ledge and three more bunches were piled on the sofa. They bloomed amongst a motley collection of objects: scattered tubes of greasepaint, hair nets, old ballet shoes, a string bag full of oranges, a postcard of the South of France jammed into the frame of the mirror, *The Complete Works of William Shakespeare* and an apple on a chair, a towel scrunched up on the window sill, *War and Peace* on the floor, and assorted clothing – her costumes hanging, gauzy and irides-cent from a rail, but also an ancient tweed coat, a woolly jumper, sturdy lace-up shoes and items of underwear – at which her visitors might perhaps choose not to look too closely.

In the midst of it all, Lydia held court, seated at her dressing table, still dressed in her Lilac Fairy outfit of shim-mering gold and purple, although now with a rather shapeless shawl pulled over the top. She had removed her crown and was intermittently dabbing cold cream on her face – presum-ably, to remove the remnants of greasepaint. A middle-aged couple and their bachelor friend were on their way out, Lydia blowing them kisses as they went, but another man lingered, clutching a notebook.

'Now, Cyril, you will write a wonderful review for your paper, will you not? Otherwise Big Serge will be sad.' Lydia put her head to one side and gazed at the man who was watching her laconically in her dressing-table mirror.

'I will certainly write wonderful things about *you*.'

'About me? No much more than me! I am only Lilac Fairy.' Lydia tried to hide her alarm. She wagged a chiding finger. 'Do you know how much Big Serge has spent on this production?'

'No, how much?'

'I don't know exactly, but I know it is enormous, bigger than Grand Duke's fortune, so very important everyone come and buy ticket.'

'It was rather unfortunate that the enchanted wood collapsed in Act Three.'

'Oah! What does that matter? Audience love it when thing go wrong. It gives them story for their friends.'

As she spoke, she dabbed on more cream, so that there were now random dots intermingled with patches of greasepaint.

Her companion's mouth twitched. Lydia followed his gaze towards her reflection and laughed. 'I look like chessboard! Or Dalmatian dog. Really, I prefer no paint, but Big Serge say different. But what is the point? No paint or powder ever hide this ridiculous nose.' She wrinkled it at him, and although she certainly did look ridiculous, all he could think was that she reminded him of a delightful rabbit.

'You were wonderful, my dear, and I will certainly say so.' He bent to kiss her forehead then took his leave.

Lydia, left alone at last, reached for an apple and took a large bite. Munching thoughtfully, she became aware of voices on the stairs. More visitors, and the stage manager trying to prevent them.

'But I tell you, I am a very good friend of Madame Loppy–'

'But, sir, I have strict instructions–'

'I assure you, we won't stay a moment–'

A second later, the door was pushed open and Clive swept in.

'*Ma chérie!*' he declared theatrically. '*Tu étais vraiment magnifique. Une princesse magique et mystérieuse ...*' He went to Lydia and made a show of kissing her hand. For a moment, she looked blank.

'My dear ... Clive Bell. You remember.' Clive was visibly put out. 'Along with Mr Keynes – the two Mr Keynes.' He gestured to his companions who were hovering behind him in the doorway.

'How very nice to see you again. Of course I remember. You must excuse me, I am all covered in paint.' She beckoned. 'Come in, you look like schoolboys waiting for cross governess. I am not Carabosse! I will not throw curse on you. Sit down ... Not there, Mr Keynes, or you get a prickly bottom. Oh, now you sit on Mr Shakespeare!'

Geoffrey, attaining a clear space on the sofa next to his brother, said shyly, 'We enjoyed the evening very much.'

Lydia beamed. 'Did you see the little avalanche?' She mimed the collapse of the set.

Clive said, 'We did notice that ... tiny *mishap.*'

'But there was nearly a greater mishap for me – more of a *catastroff.*'

'What was that?'

'I thought something else was going to fall down – my panties.'

'My word.'

'It happen, you know. Sometimes I am not very attentive when I am putting on my under things, I forget to do the hooks, and when I do the big jump ... oah!' This time her eyes caught Maynard's. She had been going to go on to say that she had been afraid her napkin might fall out, but she was distracted by the intensity of his steady gaze.

For the first time, he spoke. 'So what do you do then?'

'It is no good to pretend so I pick them up and I throw them into the crowd. They are delighted. If you come again, Mr Keynes,' her eyes were smiling, 'who knows what you see?'

Geoffrey, embarrassed, remarked, 'Well, they are certainly splendid big jumps.' And then, as Lydia turned and looked at him with raised eyebrows, 'I mean, even when your underwear ... your underwear ...'

'Behave itself?'

Geoffrey swallowed. 'You must have wonderfully developed calf muscles,' he managed, his voice hoarse.

Clive, who was leaning on the edge of the dressing table, said to Lydia, 'He's a doctor – professional interest, you know.'

Lydia at once pulled up her skirt. 'Feel it!' And to their astonishment, she thrust her left leg towards the two Keynes brothers.

'Excuse me?'

'See the muscles? I am like little horse ... That is why I can do the big jump. Feel!'

Clive, very willingly, came forward and gave her calf a quick squeeze. Lydia looked at Maynard, who hesitated. Geoffrey grabbed his arm. 'I really think we must go.'

Maynard rose reluctantly. Lydia, not at all put out, smiled at him. 'Maybe another time, Mr Keynes.'

Leading the way down the stairs, Clive vented his feelings with no concern for who might overhear.

'... to think the Ballets Russes was once the cutting edge of the avant-garde ... and now they produce this backward-looking twaddle. Tchaikovsky indeed! I predict it will close within the month ... '

Maynard stopped suddenly and slapped his pockets. 'I've dropped something. Back in a moment.'

He did not wait for a reply, but turned and took the stairs three at a time. Below him he could hear Clive being supercilious to the stage manager. Lydia's door was open and Maynard plunged right in.

'Oh, excuse me!'

Lydia, in the centre of the room, was bent over, undoing the ribbons on one shoe. She was now dressed only in her underwear, her silk-covered bottom being the first thing that caught his eye. At his voice she peered round, straightened up and laughed at his blushing face.

'Have you come to feel my muscles, Mr Keynes?'

'No – certainly not – I mean, it would be an honour, of course–'

Lydia reached slowly for a dressing gown. She was not at all disconcerted.

Maynard said abruptly, 'You remind me of a statue. By Degas. One of his bronze ballerinas.'

'Ah yes, but they cannot jump like me!'

She demonstrated, and they both started laughing. Maynard said, 'I wanted to ask if you would have supper with me one night.'

She raised an eyebrow. The briefest of pauses then: 'I should like that. Where will we go?'

'The Savoy?'

She considered, then nodded. 'Tomorrow?'

'Yes,' said Maynard immediately, unconcerned for all the plans that would need changing. 'I will collect you after the performance, if that's convenient?'

Lydia nodded again. She was smiling. Maynard backed out and shut the door quietly behind him.

'I've found it,' he called to Clive and Geoffrey breezily, as he galloped down the stairs.

11

T he following night, Maynard stood outside the theatre, watching the people emerging onto the street and trying to gauge their mood: satisfied, he felt, but not as ecstatic as they should be. Didn't they understand the full value of what they had been privileged to watch? Then he turned away, only to be arrested by a poster on the wall which declared in bold capitals (under a picture of Tamara Karsavina as the Princess Aurora) AND LYDIA LOPOKOVA AS THE LILAC FAIRY. As he gazed at the words, he felt a tremor pass through him.

'Growing out of the pavement, guv?' enquired the usher who was moving to shut the doors, and Maynard came to himself and hastened round to the side alley and through the stage door. He had hardly started up the staircase, however, when the stage manager appeared and this time he was in no mood to be overridden or cajoled. Perhaps he *had* seen the gentleman before, he could not say, but that did not mean that he would allow him entry to the dressing rooms; Miss Lopokova was in no mood for visitors, whoever they might be. Strict orders had been given. No, he would not go upstairs to check. Even the offer of a sizeable tip made no difference, except to cause affront.

Fuming, Maynard found himself banished to the alley. He walked up and down for a bit, slapping his arms against the cold, then sat on a doorstep, but the stone was icy. From time to time other cast members left, but each time the door shut firmly behind them. Maynard thought about Lydia dancing to Tchaikovsky, and his mood relaxed, but finally, even the charm of this faded. He tried to reconstruct the discussion from earlier that day at the meeting of the Editorial Board of the *Economic Journal*, and was mortified to find he could hardly remember a word. The same for the King's College Council minutes he had reviewed that afternoon. What was the matter with him? Had he spent the whole day mooning about Lydia? What a waste of energy, especially as it was now crystal clear that she was not coming.

He checked his watch. There was no doubt that he had been stood up.

'All for the best,' he said aloud, trying to convince himself. Then he started off down the alley. He would take the train to Cambridge, where he would have been today, had it not been for this temporary madness. He would be able to go to that College Council meeting first thing tomorrow after all, then there was his Keynes Club to plan for – oh yes, and of course Cambridge meant Sebastian. It was odd how he kept forgetting.

He could not help taking one last look back but the stage door was still shut, the alley empty.

Dammit, I'm not giving up that easily, he thought suddenly, and he changed direction and made his way to the front of the theatre where a crisp note slipped to the usher ensured his entry. But when he finally reached the dressing rooms, he found Lydia's was empty.

. . .

'I THOUGHT you'd given up on the whole idea,' Jack Sheppard said, 'when I got your note yesterday.'

'Yes, well, there was a temporary hitch. But here I am, and about to beard the Council in their lair.'

Maynard was walking rapidly across the icy court. It was one of those wintry days when the inhabitants of Cambridge recalled that there was nothing between them and Siberia in terms of high ground to prevent the chill winds from rushing in. Even sheltered by the bulk of the College Chapel, the cold air cut like a knife. Sheppard, though well-padded with fat, was suffering.

'I don't understand why you want the job,' he grumbled. 'You hardly have a free moment as it is.'

'You remember we were talking about art and friendship and all that? That time I came back from Paris?'

'You tax my memory!'

'The point of life is "the pleasures of human intercourse and the enjoyment of beautiful objects".'

'Oh, G.E. Moore. He always seemed a bit touched to me. Anyway I really don't see what that's got to do with—'

'I came to a realization. I'm not an artist. I'm an economist. And economics doesn't exist for its own sake — like King's College Chapel.' Maynard waved an arm at the Gothic pile. 'No, it has to engage with the world. I've realized lately that to do that I need *freedom*, to go to London, to form opinions. It's no good staying here, lurking in my rooms like some mad old professor.'

Sheppard recoiled as if hit. 'Maynard!'

'Oh, not you! You'll make a wonderful mad professor. Besides, you're a classicist, not an economist.'

His friend, who was hoping that the University's Greek Professorship was finally within his grasp, was mollified. 'Well, with your help ... but none of this tells me why you want to be Bursar.'

'I'm explaining why I want to be *rich*. You see, it's the only way to talk sense and have people pay attention. The power brokers, if you will – the people who get things done – they only listen to their own type. You have to wear the right clothes, belong to the right clubs, go to the right places. Montagu Norman invited me to join his inner circle – but nothing I said there would count for anything if my invest-ments – well, anyway, that didn't happen, but if it had–'

'You do realize that being Bursar won't make *you* rich? Not personally – not unless you're planning a spot of embez-zlement.'

'Of course I know that. But I reckon with all I'm learning, managing my portfolio … well, I might as well make the College rich too.'

'Very good of you, old boy,' said Sheppard drily. 'I still don't pretend to understand. There's port in the cellar. You've got some of the best rooms in College. Who wants to be rich?'

'Life is not about money, Jack, and yet with it we can create a world where art and love can prosper!'

Maynard was in an oddly fey mood, Sheppard decided. Almost *too* cheerful. As if something was troubling him, which he was trying to hide in this whirl of words. But he was plan-ning to vote for Sheppard's election to the Greek Professorship, and if he really wanted this other thing …

'I hope when you do become Bursar you'll increase the wine budget.'

'Certainly!' said Maynard promptly. 'What could be more conducive to love and friendship? Other people's anyway, because I don't think I'm much good at either.'

Sheppard laughed, although again with the slight sense that something was awry. They had reached their destination. Maynard glanced at his watch, then absently smoothed down his jacket. Sheppard straightened his tie.

'I wouldn't mention all this to the Council, you know,'

counselled Sheppard *sotto voce*. 'Art and love ... not really their thing.'

'I won't,' Maynard promised.

Sheppard knocked on the door.

IT WAS DARK WHEN, some hours later, Maynard flitted along a path, passed through an archway and positively skipped into the entrance to his own stairway. He took the stairs two at a time.

He reached the landing and passed through the door to his own rooms. A few more steps and he flung open the door to the sitting room and stood framed in the entrance.

Heads turned. Voices ceased. Somebody – Robinson of Christ's College – was standing on the hearth rug, the paper he'd been reading in his hand. Young Frank Ramsey was sprawled on the rug, while the undergraduate contingent, four second and third years still rather in awe at their inclusion in such distinguished company, sat wedged on the sofa, glasses of red wine in their hands, as upright as ladies at a vicar's tea party. Others of various ages lounged in armchairs or, like Sebastian Sprott, perched on chairs turned around from the dining table; one colleague of Maynard's was bent over the cheese tray.

This was Maynard's discussion group: his Keynes Club. Sir Montagu Norman offered dinner once a fortnight at the Café Royal; Maynard burgundy and cheese once a week from the College buttery, and economic discussion that was equally incisive – in fact, perhaps more so.

'I'm sorry I'm late!' Maynard waved a hand in greeting. He felt slightly drunk, although he hadn't touched a drop. 'The College Council went on, but you see before you the new Junior Bursar!'

A ripple of congratulation. Rather theatrically, Maynard bowed.

'The assets of our beloved College, you will be delighted to hear – those of you who belong to our College, and those who don't … well, we don't care a toss for your opinion – those assets are now to be steered into new waters by yours truly, and let us hope they are prosperous waters. May our burgundy never run dry!'

A clamour of voices. He took two long steps to the sideboard and poured himself a glass of wine, then picked up a plate and began to load it with cheese.

'Forgive me, I haven't eaten.' One of the young men got up to offer him his chair. 'Thank you. Do fetch another from my study. Right, let me just balance myself, we want no red wine on the rug–'

'Did they take *so* long to agree to it?' Dennis Robertson, an economist from Trinity, sipped a glass of water in an armchair on the other side of the room.

'What? No, they almost bit my hand off. I don't think the College is bursting with fellows desperate for the job, quite the contrary. But once it was in the bag, I thought I'd strike while the iron is hot, and see if we could agree some changes I want to make to the College's portfolio. *That* took a bit more persuasion.'

'I hope Kings knows what it's doing.' Dennis smiled. 'Choosing a bursar with a gambling streak.'

'Nonsense! You're confusing me with Jack Sheppard. He's the one who lost his shirt this summer in Monte Carlo.'

'Nevertheless, there is something of the gambler in you, Maynard.'

'And if I didn't know better, I'd say there was something of the parson's son about *you*, Dennis.'

As Dennis was, in fact, the son of a Scottish minister, this was greeted as a time-worn joke, not least by Dennis himself, who observed smiling, 'I'll watch with interest, Maynard, and sleep more easily at night because Trinity keeps its wealth in land.'

More laughter. Maynard waved a piece of cheese in the direction of their speaker. 'Commence!'

Young Austen Robinson began to read. Maynard listened intently, but as he followed the argument of the paper – 'Regarding Changes in the Level of Real Wages since the War' – he was also aware of Sebastian's eyes upon him. Sebastian was not deeply interested in economics; his subject was Psychology, and he might not have received an invitation to the Keynes Club were it not for his interest in the club's founder, and the club founder's interest in him. It was a soft gaze, Maynard thought, with a melting quality, like a faithful dog.

THE LAST OF the guests were leaving.

'So, until next week … A *good* paper, an excellent paper … You must not take my criticisms too seriously, Austen … Watch the turning of the stair, the steps are quite uneven …' Maynard, standing on the landing, acting the part of good host, waved a hand in farewell, then, as the lower door shut with a clang, stepped back into his own rooms.

The flush of the lavatory sounded, the WC door opened and Sebastian stepped out. 'I thought we'd be contemplating real wage changes forever.'

'It *is* a fascinating topic.'

'I'll take your word for it. I think it's lucky the wine you serve is so good, otherwise they wouldn't be half so keen to come.'

'Does that go for you?'

'I don't need wine to make me keen.'

He reached out his arms, but Maynard had already stepped

away into the sitting room. He collapsed onto the sofa and stretched out his feet towards the fire. The energy seemed to have gone from him.

'I'm fagged. What a day. Light me a cigarette.'

'A cigarette *now*?'

'Now,' said Maynard.

Sebastian passed him one silently, then lay at his feet upon the rug. Behind him, the Muses skipped hand in hand across a landscape of gold and purple, painted by Duncan and Vanessa one weekend before the war. Skipping ... dancing ... in gold and purple, the colours of spring crocuses ... or of a ballerina dressed as a lilac fairy ...

Maynard shook himself. It had been a temporary insanity, and anyway, he had been rebuffed. Sebastian, on the other hand, was very much *here* and deserved his attention. There was no doubt he was handsome, sprawled upon the rug. Maynard considered Sebastian objectively. He was pleasant, agreeable, everyone thought so. Nice-looking, suitable, well-educated ... Duncan had once sprawled on the same rug, and Duncan was *not* well educated, not remotely, and yet it had never mattered. Maynard had never sat and made lists of Duncan's good qualities, reminding himself to be grateful: he had not needed to. Maynard shook himself. He did not *want* Duncan. If he had the power, he would give Duncan completely to Vanessa, to make her happy, but Duncan was not his to give. So if it was not Duncan he wanted, other than his friendship, then why was he thinking about Duncan? It was because he wanted ... he wanted to feel as he had once felt for Duncan.

As he had felt since seeing Lydia on the stage.

You're in love with an illusion, he thought, *a fairy tale*. But his mind immediately presented an image of her bent over, all round, satin-covered rump, and be-ruffled hair – then turning round to show a greasepaint and cold cream-dabbed face.

Lydia was no illusion: she was extraordinarily, naturally herself. Like few people were … like Duncan, in fact.

'So have you solved it?' Sebastian asked.

'Solved what?'

'The question of what is causing the rise in real wages since the war? I assume that's what you're wrestling with?'

'It *is* an interesting question' – Maynard struggled to refocus – 'especially as many people feel high wages are to blame for the current high levels of unemployment. And especially as prices have actually been rising – which ought to bring the real wage down.'

'Myself, I think Austen neglected the psychological issue.'

'Which is?'

'That wages are paid to human beings with perception and understanding, and if they see their wages fall, they will resist it.'

'No economist would deny that.'

'I'm not convinced. Economists have a tendency to treat workers – any human agent – as automata; rational automata, but automata all the same: calculating machines clad in flesh and blood.'

'Go on.'

'Well, I mean to say that the British worker can tell that his wage is declining, even if it is doing so because prices are rising rather than because his employer is cutting his weekly pay. And so he decides to resist.'

'But that has always been true.' Interested now, Maynard leant sideways for the ash tray. 'The question is why things have changed these last few years. Why is the worker able to maintain higher wages *now*, when he could not before?'

'Because of a change in power relations. He has the power to resist now, which he did not before.' Sebastian's expression was earnest.

'Because the Trade Unions are stronger? We discussed that this evening and–'

'Because of Socialism! For the first time, the Government is afraid to go against the workers. Look at Lloyd George and his *Homes for Heroes*. What was that about but fear?'

'Well …'

'The politicians look at Russia and rightly so. What happened in 1917 to the Tsar can happen here. Revolution is in the air. It's the fear of Bolshevism that makes them all bow down to the workers. That is why wages are rising, despite unemployment, despite the slump.'

Sebastian was excited as he had not been during the discussion earlier in the evening, in which he had hardly spoken a word. Maybe he was more confident when only Maynard was there.

'It's not exactly new, what you are saying.' Maynard spoke mildly. 'When I speak to financiers, Government officials, I hear them say what you have just said – in rather different language. But *they* take from it that if wages *are* to fall – as they believe they must, if unemployment is ever to fall from the current disastrous high – then the power of the unions must be broken. That was why they were so delighted when the miners failed to spark off a general strike.'

'Yes!' Sebastian sat up, eyes blazing.

'Yes?' Maynard was startled.

'Yes, of course the capitalists must break the power of organized labour: how can they do anything else? It is the logic of the situation, and the Lloyd Georges of this world, who are desperate to avoid such a confrontation, they cannot prevent it forever. And when they succeed – and wages fall further, and hardship takes hold and misery spreads: well, then revolution is inevitable!'

'Like Russia?'

'Of course! There's a Communist Party now in England. We will have Bolshevism here too.'

Maynard took a puff on his cigarette. Was it really the case, he wondered, that Sebastian and the bankers saw clearly, in their different ways, what he was still struggling to see through a glass darkly? And he did struggle. This was why he had suggested to Austen that he might look at the subject in the first place.

He said, 'After the Paris Conference I had moments of thinking Bolshevism was the answer – yes, you may well stare – but in reality, I'm not sure it's the Utopia you believe it.'

'It's the only way to bring about a just society.'

'Then maybe I'm not so concerned about justice.'

'What are you concerned about?'

Art and friendship, thought Maynard, and wondered if it were true. 'Avoiding waste,' he said aloud. 'Wasted lives more than anything. And wrong-headedness, and wrong-headed decisions that waste lives. Wasted potential – lives that do not fulfil their purpose. And ensuring possibility for individual flourishing, which is what we mean by civilization: that at least the possibility is preserved.'

Sebastian made a sound of exasperation. 'Your mindset is too individualistic. You need to look beyond that.'

'*You* were the one who just told me off for treating people as automata.'

'Not you – other economists.'

'Isn't your theory of revolution also treating them as automata? Subjugating them to a system, predicting their reactions as if they are inevitable? As if they have no individual powers of choice or reflection?'

'Individualism is a dead end.'

'That's rich, coming from a psychologist!'

Sebastian laughed. Then he smiled, and reached up his arms and pulled a reluctant Maynard down towards him on the rug. And Maynard, throwing his cigarette into the fire in a shower of sparks, reflected that after all one could be too hard on *pleasantness*. It was pleasant to embrace, here upon the rug, and slowly to undress and be undressed, and to see the flames dancing in his lover's eyes. Nevertheless, however agreeable, he had a sense of questions left unanswered. On none of the issues raised that evening, he thought, had any of those present reached a satisfying conclusion: there must, at some point, still be more to say.

12

————

Dressed in a heavy overcoat against the chill, and clutching a bulging briefcase, Maynard entered the hall at Gordon Square from the front door as Clive came sauntering down the stairs. They converged upon the hall table, Clive just in front so that he was able to inspect his mail, forcing Maynard to wait to do the same.

'Good weekend in Cambridge?' Clive leafed through the pile of letters. 'You look industrious.'

'I've just got in from the station. I'm in a rush. I need to pick up some papers before I go to my insurance company.'

'Didn't know you owned an insurance company.'

'I don't *own* it. I've been elected Chairman of the Board.' Maynard reached around Clive and swiped his post.

'Actually, I'm in a rush too. Got a mistress to meet.'

'Have you heard from Vanessa?' Maynard was now inspecting his own letters.

'Yesterday. Just more raptures about bloody Saint-Tropez. No scruples it seems about abandoning the children in order to quaff absinthe and stuff langoustine. Or that it's rather rough on Grace – or me.'

Maynard grunted and continued flicking through his post, of which, as usual, he had plenty. Then he commenced ripping open the envelopes. Clive marked the moment when he suddenly froze. There didn't seem any reason for the reaction. It was a very ordinary looking handwritten note in a similarly unremarkable envelope.

'What did you say?' Maynard asked, after a long moment.

'I *said*, you missed an excellent evening. I'm a good host, if I say so myself. Do you know, I really think all civilization can be summed up in the form of a good dinner party?'

'You should write an essay on it.'

'Perhaps I will. Want to come to dinner with Mary and me tonight? We've found a new place in Soho – excellent retsina.'

Maynard was still holding the letter in one hand. However hard Clive tried to peer at it, he could not make it out.

'Not tonight, thank you, Clive,' said Maynard with decision. 'I have other plans.'

IT WAS one thing to be stood up once, but twice …

He had purchased himself a solitary seat in the stalls. As he watched it all unfold again, just as marvellous as before (and this time the enchanted wood did not collapse) he had known that this would be just one of many visits. While *The Sleeping Princess* still ran, he would want to come and have a little taste of paradise each evening, and everything else – well, most things else – would have to take second place. He was still walking on air when he left the auditorium and made for the alleyway. He had sent Lydia a note via the stage manager – she would know where to find him. And all the time her letter was safe in his inner pocket, over his heart. It was written in a slanting hand on the notepaper of the Waldorf Hotel.

• • •

Dear Mr Keynes,

I am very sorry about the other evening. If you were to overlook it, perhaps we try again.

Sincerely, L. Lopokova

MEMBERS OF THE CAST, leaving in twos and threes, glanced curiously in his direction, before making off, chattering, towards the bright lights of the street. Maynard, at first, barely noticed, but eventually the growing quiet, and the hardness of the stone step he was sitting on, broke through his distraction, bringing the grim awareness that the trickle of departures had slowed to nothing. He inspected his watch. A sense of outrage bubbled up.

Dammit, she's done it again.

He stood up and brushed down the seat of his trousers. *So there you go. You should be relieved really. After all, by most standards, you're a lucky man.* So why this coldness in his stomach, like a lumpish toad had jumped in and taken residence?

And then, the stage door swung open behind him.

'Mr Keynes! What are you doing here?'

Lydia stood there smiling at him. She was dressed in a shapeless tweed coat that made her look a great deal more like a cottage loaf than a ballerina had any business to look, with sturdy boots on her feet and a knitted bobble hat on her head. Altogether, it was the kind of get-up his mother might have worn when setting off by bicycle for one of her committee meetings. Anything less like the Lilac Fairy was hard to imagine.

'If you remember, we were supposed to be having supper.' He sounded grumpy; it was not at all the way he had imagined greeting her.

'I meant why are you waiting out here in the cold?'

'Because your stage manager seems determined to guard

you like a fiery dragon and I did not expect you to take so long.' He paused a moment. 'You'd forgotten, hadn't you? Again?'

'Not at all. But I am Russian, Mr Keynes, and so time is a concept a bit vague for me. I warn you of this, because it will most likely drive you mad – if we see much of each other.'

She had a charm which was hard to resist: hard, certainly, for Maynard to resist. He smiled down at her face, shiny in places and with remnants of stage make-up, and was reminded of a flower.

'I still think you forgot.'

Lydia shook her head. 'No. Look.' She held open her coat to reveal a glittering cocktail dress. 'See? Tonight we are going to the Savoy.'

A BAND WAS PLAYING. A wave of chatter, laughter and clinking glasses washed over them, as the waiter led the way deftly through the crowds of fashionable diners to a table laid for two, lit by its own hanging lamp of rose-pink glass, then waved Lydia into her seat with the same graciousness he had shown earlier on taking possession of her tweed coat, as if it were the equal of all the ermine cloaks and cashmere wraps. In any case, if her coat looked shabby, Lydia did not. The pink light glowed on her skin, and gave a rosy tinge to her silver dress; her face, if not classically beautiful, had character, and the remnants of stage paint, which had looked slightly mawkish under the street lamp, made her eyes seem larger, her cheekbones more Russian.

Now she turned those eyes upon Maynard, as the waiter, having taken their drinks orders, left them together.

'Tell me again what you do, Mr Keynes.' Her accent was strongly Russian. 'I remember it had a complicated name ... pharmacist, psychiatrist, chiropodist?'

'Economist.'

'That is impressive and important-sounding. So much that I don't understand what it means. A bit like your friend when he speak French.'

They both laughed.

'He believes he speaks it like a native,' said Maynard, with a pleasurably guilty twinge.

'He believes lot of things,' said Lydia enigmatically. 'It's funny, I understand when they speak in Paris, but don't understand him.'

'You've lived in Paris?'

'Oh, yes. Everywhere. France. Spain. America – yes, I cross America side to back to front to side. South America. Then Big Serge say, 'We open in Italy!' So off again. That is dancer's life.'

'You forgot Russia.'

'Russia!' Her face clouded momentarily. 'No, I don't forget Russia. I never forget Russia.' For a moment a light had dimmed. Then she said, 'But tell me about your work, Mr Keynes. Economist – it is *like* chiropodist maybe? I show you bump on my toe?'

'No, it's nothing like that.'

'Pity. We dancers have big problem with foot. I find good chiropodist, I kiss *his* foot. So? Don't be man of mystery, Mr Keynes.'

Maynard was troubled by a strong desire to touch Lydia's feet. Bump or no bump, he should like to see them and hold them in his hands. At that moment – or was he imagining it? – her foot brushed his under the table.

He said, 'It probably wouldn't interest you. It's to do with money … resources.'

'Why wouldn't that interest me?'

'Because artists aren't interested in understanding money – at least in my experience. They look down on it.'

'You mean your friends, the ones they call *Bloomsbury*? If

they don't care for money that is because they have plenty of it.'

Maynard could not help smiling. 'I'm not sure they would agree.'

Lydia wagged a finger at him. 'Do they have to do other work besides their art? Do they have to do their own wash-up?'

'Never.'

'Well then. You see? Now at the moment, I work. I have money. And so I do not wash up. I live in the Waldorf Hotel, I drink champagne and buy new hats. But tomorrow, who knows? That is dancer's life. Now, Big Serge …'

'Big Serge?'

'Mr Diaghilev. He is very interested in money: no money, no Ballets Russes. And so we, his dancers, just have to hope he can produce it, like big fish from hat.'

Maynard was amused. 'Big fish from hat … My work is about understanding bank rates, Government debt, unemployment, investment.'

'Unemployment, that's something every dancer fear. When I look out at the audience, I hope and beg I do not see seats too many empty. Especially now. These are hard times for artists, Mr Keynes.'

'You're right.'

'It better in America.'

'Yes, it's booming there. On the other hand, things are considerably worse in Germany, where they are up to their ears in debt and political assassinations. But let's not talk about that.' The waiter had filled their glasses earlier and retired discreetly. Maynard raised a glass. 'To the success of *The Sleeping Princess.*'

Lydia held hers up towards him. 'To your health, Mr Keynes.'

'Why don't you call me Maynard?'

'Lydia.'

She reached out a hand to him across the table. They linked fingers.

'Here's to you, Lydia. And to a theatre packed to the rafters.'

'And to you, Maynard.' She pronounced it *Maynar*. His name had never sounded so endearing.

THEY ATE and they talked and they talked and they ate. 'I am Miss Talky,' said Lydia at one point. 'If too much, then just pretend I am magpie. Chatter, chatter, chatter, no words. Then you can ignore me.' They scarcely noticed the waiter who refilled their glasses or brought the dishes – crab paté on toast, peach melba – and carried them away again. They did not notice that it was past midnight.

'Why did you stand me up the other night?' he asked abruptly.

'Ah. You see …' She looked at him thoughtfully, as if pondering what to say. Then she seemed to reach a decision. 'The truth is, I got what you call the cold foot.'

'I see. Well, that's honest.'

She shrugged. 'Of course, it is only supper, but you see, I have the luggage, Mr Keynes. Maynard.'

'Luggage?' He was totally baffled. 'Ah … you mean *baggage*. Well, we all have that.' Fleetingly, an image of Sebastian crossed his mind.

'I am tired of men; they only make me unhappy. So I decide, *No, Lydia, you will live henceforth as nun* …' She began to laugh.

'I am very glad you changed your mind.'

'Let's dance, Maynard.' She held out her hand towards him.

'I'm not really a dancer.'

'But I am dancer enough for both.'

Maynard was reluctant, but she was already taking his hands, pulling him to his feet. Still protesting, he found himself being propelled towards the band. With a reluctance born of the submerged memories of a thousand school games lessons (rugby, cricket, athletics, tennis … he was awful at all of them, and had become convinced he had no physical grace) he shambled onto the dance floor. He felt enormous. She looked up at him and perceived his fear.

'Be brave!'

They began to dance, her eyes laughing at him, daring him not to give up. Maynard felt awkward, as if all his limbs were determined to move in opposition to each other. He had some vague notion he was supposed to be leading Lydia, and no notion how to, but then he realized, with great relief, that she was guiding him expertly and joyfully, and that all he really had to do was move where she took him. And she was enjoying herself. Whatever his inadequacies as a partner, she really was enjoying herself: she was humming as she revolved around the floor, her feet springing beneath her as if they had not already danced a three-hour ballet with some of the most difficult choreography of the entire classical repertoire …

'Relax, Maynard!'

So Maynard did.

13

'**G**ood evening, sir. Watch the steps, they're slippy. It was the rain earlier.'

'Thank you.' Maynard headed up towards the entrance of the magnificently understated Georgian building in Piccadilly, and the stout, overdressed figure who had just expressed concern for his welfare, and whose epaulettes and gold cord suggested more a general of the lately imploded Austrian-Hungarian Empire than someone whose job it was to open and shut a door.

He passed under a stained-glass fanlight and stepped into a hallway of panelled mahogany. He looked around him, and before he could decide in which direction to head, he was arrested by the sight of Otto Niemeyer gliding towards him across the shining parquet floor, managing to look strangely puritanical even in full evening dress and by the glittering light of a chandelier. It was those pursed, *governessy* lips.

'Ah, Maynard. How delightful you were free.'

He did not sound it.

'I'm delighted to be here,' Maynard replied with careful geniality.

'Come this way. Montagu will be so pleased you were able to meet. I suppose Foxy was not able to join us. What a pity–'

Only there, at that moment, was Foxy, his long overcoat glittering with raindrops, shaking off his umbrella before handing it to a porter to take and store in the luggage room. 'Am I late?' he asked. 'Oh, good, you're here, Maynard. And I can't be late if Otto is here too.'

Otto looked as if his cup of happiness were completely failing to flow over.

FOUR HOURS LATER, dinner was finished and only the silver bowls of nuts and candied fruits were left to occupy the diners, along with the cigars and liqueurs. As the after-dinner smoke drifted around the room – rather as if the London fog had penetrated through the long windows and their shrouding velvet curtains – Foxy became aware of a change in Maynard. He had been his usual self during dinner, making short work of four courses *and* the arguments of various opponents. But now, although discussion still bounced back and forth like the candlelight off the crystal glasses, Maynard had withdrawn and was as silent as the racehorses and bewigged judges in their gilt frames. In fact, he seemed to be taking rather less interest, if possible.

Foxy could not understand it.

Around the table sat all the usual suspects. Sir Montagu Norman, of course, presided as by right. Otto Niemeyer sat on his left. Below them were the usual variety of figures, all men, all clad in evening dress, all prominent in their own worlds of high finance, politics, journalism, academia or officialdom.

Maynard and Foxy sat towards the middle of the table, and every now and then Foxy would cast a sideways glance at his friend. He was well used to Maynard appearing to be almost asleep in a discussion, until he came in with a sharp comment that would turn the whole topic on its head, leaving the rest of the company struggling for a response. But this time the inter-jection never came. It was hard to credit … Foxy could hardly believe it … but he began to feel that Maynard *was not paying attention.*

And the subject was of particular interest to him: whether interest rates should be lowered due to the sluggish state of the economy (a position Foxy knew Maynard supported) or should be kept high to support the pound (a position he knew Maynard vehemently opposed).

'Without certainty on the foreign exchanges, there will be a fall in investment. How will people choose to invest through London markets, if they can have no confidence in the future value of the pound?'

The speaker was a banker. Foxy rubbed his nose. He considered speaking, only Maynard would do it so much better, dammit, and now the chance was gone!

'… there is an issue here of property rights.' This was surely a Bank of England man: one of Montagu's minions. A regular bean-counter he looked too, Foxy thought, with his pince-nez and his thinning hair neatly arranged over his dome-like head. Which basement desk had they unshackled him from to bring him here tonight? He could not prevent a contemptuous snort.

It was a louder snort than he intended; he felt Montagu Norman's eyes upon him and the whole company – except for Maynard, who was still oblivious – waited for him to speak.

Foxy took a breath. 'I think the issue about property is balderdash,' he said loudly.

'What *do* you mean?' Otto Niemeyer was staring at him from the head of the table.

'Well, what do *you* all mean?'

'I mean, and I think I speak for Sir Ernest too …' he nodded at the bean-counter (who was not, after all, a bean-counter but,

Foxy suddenly remembered, rather abashed, the partner in a medium-sized merchant bank), 'that those who bought Government War Bonds did so in expectation of a certain return; a legitimate expectation on their part. If sterling is not returned to its pre-war parity, then bond holders are being repaid in a *devalued* currency, and in effect the value of their property has been reduced. We have *stolen* it from them. A promise has been broken.'

What a lot of words to say that the income of their friends and families should be guaranteed!

'Not so.' Foxy glanced sideways at Maynard to see if he were listening to any of this, but could see no sign that he was. 'You are proposing that the value of sterling should be raised against the dollar, back towards the rate which pertained *before* the war, when the gold standard was in operation. But when were most War Bonds taken out? Was it when sterling was high? Not so! Most were taken out towards the *end* of the war, when we had already left the gold standard and the value of sterling had depreciated substantially. So, by proposing an *increase* in sterling, you are therefore proposing to repay these holders of War Bonds at a *higher* rate than that at which they lent – therefore you are proposing a substantial *windfall* to these borrowers!'

Halfway through this speech, Maynard's head jerked: something seemed to have got through to him at last. Meanwhile Otto Niemeyer wanted to speak, as did Sir Josiah Black, a banker sitting further down the table, but Foxy, feeling more confident now, ploughed on.

'Furthermore, the truth is that any change in the value of sterling – or any changes in the domestic price level designed to effect the level of sterling – must have redistributionary effects. So, for example, if you deliberately deflate the domestic economy, raising interest rates and so reducing domestic prices, in order to allow sterling to rise in value on the foreign exchanges, you will inevitably reduce the wealth of debtors to the benefit of creditors, to take but one example. Debtors will pay higher interest payments, and creditors will receive them – that is a redistributionary effect. And the resulting fall in trade will also, of course, have all manner of redistributionary effects – in particular, it will lighten the pockets of both business men and workers – certainly those that work in the export indus- tries. It therefore makes no sense to talk as if the property rights of one particular group – viz. the holders of War Bonds, had priority over the rest.'

And I hope I've got that right, dammit, Maynard, because it all made perfect sense when you put it to me over dinner the other night, but I had drunk rather a lot of champagne.

At any rate, he seemed to have silenced Otto Niemeyer for the moment. So much for the vaunted intelligence that had beaten Maynard in the Civil Service entry competition! Foxy had always suspected that this said more about the Civil Service exams than it did about the relative intellects of Keynes and Niemeyer, which was not to say that Otto was stupid – most emphatically he was not – but he was, in Foxy's opinion, a pedant who lacked all the playfulness and creativity that Maynard brought to a subject. No doubt this explained his supremacy at the Treasury.

'After all,' Foxy continued, making the most of things, 'who will suffer if interest rates and sterling go up? The workers, that's who – and those who would prefer to be workers than be forced onto the dole. So why are you choosing to privilege those fortunate enough to own bonds over the working class?'

'Beside the point.' The head of a Merchant Banking house that Foxy knew only vaguely was spluttering with indigna- tion. 'The important thing is a *promise* was made to bond holders. They were *promised* a return. The whole City works on it, don't you know. Our word is our bond. I keep my promises, don't you see, and the Government must do the same.'

You sound like a child, thought Foxy. *But you promised! Wah, wah!*

'Well,' he said aloud, 'after all, the buyers of War Bonds were also interested in winning the war. And they got that much. So really why should they complain, even if they don't get handed a great big bonus at everybody else's expense?'

His adversary was not pleased. 'It's the principle of the thing,' he insisted. 'And as for all these other so-called *redistributionary effects*,' – he spoke the words as if he did not like the taste of them, and as he did so glowered at Maynard, as if he knew perfectly well where they originated – 'what are they? You can draw all manner of pretty pictures and show that I'm buying the pound at one level, and somehow the working man in some shipyard somewhere has less butter for his bread, but I say let's stick to the basics and my–'

Word is my bond, Foxy finished mentally for him. *And the working man doesn't eat butter, he eats margarine; a substance you've probably never encountered.*

He looked sideways at Keynes, who seemed to have lapsed into a dreamworld once again: his eyes distant and his lips moving as if he were … what? Reciting? Or was he *humming*? Yes, his foot was actually moving in time beneath the table, Foxy could feel its vibrations against the table leg.

'… ingenious arguments can always be made,' the merchant banker was still in full flow, 'showing left is right and right is left. I know our friend Mr Keynes is the master of it. No doubt he would be providing us with such an argument now were it not that he seems to be asleep.' Laughter. 'Let me say that the City of London has thrived over the centuries and served us well, without indulging in such mental acrobatics as are required by our modern so-called *economists*.'

During this speech, Maynard stirred again. He leant back in

his chair and stared at the merchant banker through narrowed eyes. He said nothing, however, and the discussion moved on without any further contributions from Foxy either. He had shot his bolt.

He leant over towards his friend and said very softly, 'Penny for them.'

Maynard, to Foxy's great surprise, blushed.

MAYNARD HAD, indeed, been largely oblivious to the discussion. In his own head, he had been in the Alhambra Theatre, absorbed by the rhythms of Tchaikovsky and the tale of *The Sleeping Princess*, although in truth the princess herself, so pale and ethereal, played little part in this vision, which instead revolved around the sprightly, vivacious Lilac Fairy. In a flower-like bell of purple skirts, a crown upon her head, Lydia leapt lightly across the stage; with delicate flicks of her hands she communicated her thoughts and feelings: at times playful, at others mocking, and then, for a moment, elusive, pensive, strangely melancholy ...

He wished he were in the front row of the stalls again.

But he also wished he had listened more closely to the discussion. A new suspicion had entered his head. *Could they be planning ...? No, surely not. Surely they could see the insanity ...?*

It was too late for regrets. The gathering was breaking up, the participants were beginning to leave. 'We didn't hear much from *you* today,' said Montagu Norman, leaning forward in his chair towards Maynard. 'I hope you're not sickening for something.'

'Just sickening, I expect,' said Maynard, an uneasy attempt at a joke.

Montagu did not smile. 'Your deputy did well,' he said, his eyes flickering towards Foxy. 'But better if you say your own lines, Keynes.'

Foxy looked offended. Maynard said, 'It's rather a new experience for me, to be asked to speak up.'

Those within hearing laughed. Foxy, watching, thought that Montagu was not amused, although he replied, courteously enough, 'Yes, perhaps I should be thanking Mr Keynes for allowing the others the chance to get a word in for once. I look forward to seeing you at the opera, Mr Falk.'

'I'll certainly be there.'

As Maynard and Foxy waited for the porter to collect their coats: 'The opera?' Maynard enquired.

'Yes, we've got a mutual friend with a country pile who likes to put on private productions. Baroque stuff usually. This time it's Purcell, King Arthur.'

'See if he lets drop any hint about what he's really up to.'

'What d'you mean?'

Maynard was silent, wrapping his scarf around him. 'All this business about War Bond holders,' he said at last. 'It came to me, while you were saying your piece – which you did very well, by the way – that what they *really* want is to take us back onto gold.'

Foxy glanced over his shoulder, but there was nobody listening. The two men closest were loudly discussing hunting conditions in Warwickshire.

'Well, what if they do?' he demanded, rather pugnaciously. After Maynard's apathy that evening, he felt he deserved it. 'Gold did well enough before the war. Why not go back to it now?'

'You know perfectly well why not: restoring the gold standard is no less than a declaration of war on the working classes.'

'Depends how it's done.'

'It will hit *somebody* hard, that's inevitable. A massive hike in interest rates means nothing less. As you were explaining so lucidly before. That lot in there … if they have to choose between the City of London and the working man, who will they choose?'

'Some pain is worth the gain.'

'This particular pain brings no gain and is utterly avoidable. Come on, Foxy! You must agree with me. It's lunacy. I wonder if that's why Otto and Montagu invited me back in: to try and make me party to it? I bet that was it!'

'Neither of us will ever be party to it,' said Foxy firmly, giving up his attempt at playing devil's advocate. 'And if you don't like it … these days you have a line straight to the press.'

'I can't make the papers print what they don't want to. And who knows what their proprietors will think? They are all rich men.'

'Try the *Daily Herald*,' said Foxy light-heartedly. 'Read by dockers and other Bolshie types … and the Secret Service, of course, to keep an eye on them.'

Wrapped in overcoats and mufflers they proceeded into the fog. Maynard stood for a moment on the steps, looking at the street lamps throwing their columns of light into the murk: like … like spotlights on a stage.

'Have you ever seen Lydia Lopokova dance?' he asked Foxy suddenly.

'Yes, of course I have. In fact, I saw her with you, back before she disappeared – *The Good Natured Ladies*, I think it was.'

'With me? Surely not with me.'

'I remember distinctly. You said she had a stiff bottom.'

Maynard harrumphed, plainly put out. Foxy shook his head. 'What is it with you this evening? You're not yourself. And now we're leaving early, when you could be staying to grill Monty about the gold standard, if you wanted to. It's none of it *like* you.'

'I have an engagement, you see,' Maynard said carefully, after a moment. And then, as if this were supposed to explain everything, with a wave of his hand, he set off into the fog.

Foxy shook his head, mildly baffled by the whole affair, then dug his hands deeper into his pockets and went to find a cab.

In the early hours of the morning, unable to sleep, Maynard sat in bed with his writing pad propped on his knee. He wrote to Vanessa in Saint-Tropez, trying to explain his feelings (in so far as he understood them): the disturbing new feelings that had overcome him since first seeing *The Sleeping Princess*. 'I'm in turmoil. I never expected it. I was sure I was too old ever to feel this way again, and to be honest, maybe I was glad of it. Better to save one's time and energy for other things. And then out of nowhere, this has hit me like an express train – if that doesn't sound ridiculous when talking about a trained dancer!' He added a note of affection for Duncan, reread the letter, thought how very inadequately he had expressed himself … then took the sheets of paper and ripped them into small pieces.

How far away they seemed, and although he wanted a confidante, at this moment he also prized his solitude. They would all know soon enough – Maynard and a ballerina! – and then they would dissect, examine, discuss, as was the Bloomsbury way. At this moment, he rather prized not being under their scrutiny.

But – what was he to do? Maybe it was not too late to step back. After all, what had really happened? Just a couple of suppers at the Savoy. It was surely not too late … if he steeled himself … but what did he actually *want*?

He turned off the lamp, pulled the covers over him and drifted at last towards sleep. In those last moments of wakefulness, he thought he heard footsteps on the landing, footsteps that trod softly, so as not to disturb. They stopped, surely, just outside his door.

He struggled to wake himself … or to consider whether to wake himself … but it was altogether too much trouble. Besides, most likely he had imagined it.

14

1922

Lydia awoke in her bedroom at the Waldorf Hotel and lay for a moment watching the light moving on the ceiling and listening to the sounds from the street. Then she closed her eyes, as she sometimes did, and tried to remember how it had been, waking up in her family's apartment in St Petersburg. The light had a different quality for one thing, colder and paler; there were delivery men below her windows, as there sometimes were here, but shouting in Russian, not English; and her sister, Evgenia, would be in the next bed, just a hump of blanket and a little bit of hair poking out, for she was even worse at getting up than Lydia. She heard in imagination her brothers' voices from the hall, then her mother calling ... Lydia turned and buried her face in the pillow. *Thirteen years*, she thought. *And what is happening there now? In the newspapers, only war and starvation.* To distract herself, she tried to remember the dormitory at the Mariinsky Ballet School, which was easy, for she had spent the greatest part of her childhood there, and besides, the emotions were less painful.

Sitting up at last, she stretched, cat-like, and reached for her dressing gown, then for the book on her bedside table. She considered it thoughtfully.

The Economic Consequences of the Peace by J.M. Keynes.

'Funny,' said Lydia aloud. 'Yes, funny.'

Maynard had sent it to her after their second meeting. He had told her it had been a bestseller, not only here but in America and worldwide, which was funny indeed, for it did not look like her idea of a bestseller. *But I like you*, thought Lydia, stroking the cover with her finger. *Yes, I like you.* She opened the cover and read the inscription:

To Lydia Lopokova, this book is presented with most affectionate wishes, from the author. And his signature.

'Yes,' she said aloud, 'I like it.'

She opened the cover and studiously read four more pages on the subject of the pre-war economy. There was some dry stuff in it, Maynard had told her when, tentatively, he had presented it, and he did not wish to bore her, but she would perhaps enjoy the descriptions of the statesmen at Versailles. Lydia, however, was determined to read every page. If she did not understand it – well, she could always question the author himself when she saw him. And she was curious.

When she had finished, she sat for a moment thinking. Then she replaced the book, and with one easy gesture, thrust aside blankets and dressing gown and slid gracefully out of bed. She stood for a moment on the floor, stark naked, then did a quick pirouette. *How you joggle,* she thought, cupping her breasts. *Your bosom not so big, but still … in ballet, best maybe to have no breast at all. Certainly Big Serge would like that. Or poor Nijinsky* (this was how she usually thought of her former partner and adversary, now confined to a lunatic asylum). *They prefer woman not to have breast because really they like best the young man.*

She stood on one leg, arm extended: *arabesque en attitude.* She could see herself in the mirror, graceful yet also slightly comic, with her round breasts and dimpled thighs, her upturned nose, her hair still sleep-mussed and sticking out on one side of her head. *It is good thing I do not take myself seriously,* she thought. *Anna Pavlova – no, that is not me. I don't make audience weep as dying swan, but I make them laugh, and maybe they like that more. Maynard certainly like to laugh.*

She came out of her pose into a jump, then quickly began to dress. It was cold in the room and Lydia hated the cold, despite having grown up with the long winters of St Petersburg. She pulled on tights and tunic, and topped them with a tweed skirt, a woollen jumper, and the same coat and hat in which she had met Maynard at the theatre. Finally she wound a large shawl round her shoulders. She picked up her bag and left the room.

At the hotel reception, she asked for her post and examined it eagerly. Nothing from Russia. But there was a note in the now familiar writing of Maynard Keynes.

'Maybe you'll get something from home tomorrow,' said Frank, watching her frown as she read the note.

'Home?' she asked, looking up at him blankly.

'Russia.'

'If home is somewhere you have not been for thirteen years that is very sad. Russia not my home.'

'I know. Sorry, Miss Loppy. It's them Bolshies. It's all their fault. Cheer up, miss.'

Lydia favoured him with a glorious smile. 'I am cheerful. Just this note, is all.'

'An admirer, is it? You don't want to let him worry you. Not a beautiful young lady like yourself.'

Lydia beamed, accepting the compliment as by right, even if, pushing thirty, she did not exactly consider herself young, and had never considered herself beautiful.

'You need any money, Miss Lopokova?'

'No. You keep it all safe for me, Frank.'

''Course I will.'

Lydia blew him a kiss and made for the door. At the last moment she turned back. 'Oh, Frank, if Mr Keynes calls … No, don't worry. You don't need to say anything.'

LYDIA STOPPED for breakfast in a small café near the hotel, where she ate toast and eggs, and drank strong coffee. Thus fortified, she braved the street, walking briskly and congratulating herself that she had worn so many layers. She dug her hands into her coat pockets, and kept away from the pavement edge and the arcs of spray sent up from the wheels of passing cars and buses. January was a horrible month, cold and wet. Was that why the audience was dwindling? Night after night she looked out beyond the lights and saw more and more empty seats. Was it that people couldn't face the cold? Or simply that they did not care for *The Sleeping Princess*? Or maybe they did not have the money for tickets?

Maynard had told her that even though unemployment was well over one million, and inflation (which was, he explained, the increase in the level of prices) zero, the Government was not moving to reduce interest rates. This was pushing the country into a dangerous deflation. 'High interest rates keep the price of credit high, so businesses do not invest, which means that jobs are not created.' Lydia was a little hazy about the exact meaning of this, but the practical outcome, that people did not feel prosperous enough to pay for theatre tickets, was painfully clear.

Maynard himself was deterred by neither weather nor deflation: when he did not have a prior engagement – such as meeting and arguing with the foolish men who set the interest rates – he came to the Alhambra. He tried to persuade his friends to come too, but Lydia suspected that they did not greatly care for *The Sleeping Princess*. Clive Bell had been almost rude about it in her hearing, and that tall, thin, bearded man (Littun?) that Maynard had brought backstage one evening: 'It makes me sick,' she had heard him say, when he believed her to be talking too hard to someone else to notice, and though she could not be sure, she suspected it was *The Sleeping Princess* he meant. She had comforted herself that Maynard's friends probably did not have the same tastes as most people. After all, many of Lydia's own friends had adored it – or so they had assured her. Sam Courtauld in particular had been overflowing with praise. But very few of them had come back again. Except Maynard.

He is loyal, she thought. Not like Barrocchi, who had taken off for Italy, with the excuse that he was scouting out opportunities for Big Serge. (He had tried to get her room key before he left: what a good thing she had her money safe with Frank!) Or Igor, now in France with his wife and a new mistress. Lydia shrugged, and did not dwell on them: she had learnt to let go of her troubles in the course of an up-and-down career. But Maynard … that was different. What did she think of him?

He was completely unlike any other man she'd ever met. They inhabited completely different worlds. That first time that he'd invited her to supper, she had thought of that and panicked. How could such difference lead anywhere? He thought she was something from a fairy tale … she was not. He spent his time at a university and she had no education. He was so English and she was a wanderer, who belonged nowhere. And yet … and yet … So, he was not from the theatre, he was nothing like Barrocchi, he was not Russian. Well, what of it? Those were good things perhaps. They found they had much to say to each other. He reminded her sometimes of Big Serge: he had that strength and vision. She might wish he had more money. He did not have a house of his own, or a car, or any other trappings of wealth; certainly his appearance did not suggest somebody with much spare cash. Well, one could not have everything. (She recalled Big Serge's advice on this point with a mix of guilt and defiance: *Big nose out, Big Serge!*) Maynard was a thinker and she liked that. How wonderful to gain excitement from something that happened purely in the head! And although she, Lydia, was so ignorant, he was always happy to discuss his ideas ... and to listen, really listen, to what she had to say.

Still meditating on all of this, she crossed a main thoroughfare and entered the maze of Soho. Although some people found it drab by day, even squalid, and miserably dank in this weather, she liked the tiny restaurants, even when they were shut (there were still vegetables being delivered, and people mopping floors) and she also liked to wonder what kind of people lived up the stairways (though sometimes it was all too clear, from the cards posted next to their doors). She skipped over a gutter running with water, turned into an alleyway, and made for a door of battered green paint, with a sign, slightly askew, above the door knocker. It read *M. Cecchetti*.

Inside, a tiny hallway led almost immediately to another door, which opened onto a large studio, with mirrors along one wall, a piano and a wooden barre.

Lydia hurried inside and began to divest herself of her layers in a corner. A couple of dancers were already there, also getting changed, and Lydia smiled and waved.

When Signor Cecchetti appeared, they were already waiting for him. As they swept into a curtsey, he walked along the line, tiny, neat, imperious, and stopped opposite Lydia.

'Ah, my little Lydia! Today you have no performance, that is right?'

'That is right, Maestro.'

'So we will work – work – ah no, already your hair is falling down!'

With a broad smile, she stuck the pins in more firmly, while Signor Cecchetti shook his head at her and greeted his other dancers. The pianist, who had arrived almost unnoticed, a middle-aged lady with a perpetually bored expression, began to thump away on the keys. Lydia took her position and began.

When she danced for Cecchetti it was impossible to think of anything else. Years ago, in the practice rooms of the Mariinsky Imperial Ballet School, she had learnt to concentrate completely on the movements of her body and the instructions of her teacher. How else could a dancer learn? How else could she perform with immaculate control? Now they were a thousand miles from the old St Petersburg, yet still, when the music began, everything else receded: the sounds from the street, the damp in the air, and her own thoughts, whether of dwindling audiences, her mother's last letter – or Maynard. Reality narrowed, satisfyingly and convincingly, to the beat of the piano, the tap of Maestro's cane upon the barre, and her own body: the turn of her hips, the lift of her feet, the flex and hold of each muscle.

'I JUST THOUGHT YOU WOULD COME.' Maynard was reproachful. 'When you got my note. And not make me kick my heels for more than an hour.'

They were walking through St James's Park. Water was dripping from the leaves, although it was not actually raining. Nevertheless, everything was sodden and the leaves were dank; ribbons of mist hung beneath the trees. The park was almost empty.

They walked a little apart, at a quick pace. Lydia did not say anything, but energy flew off her in sparks.

'I mean, I understand about Russians always being late …'

'I was not late.'

'All right, I understand about Russians and time, but I thought you would want to see me.'

'Because *you* were unexpectedly free. But I had things

to do.'

'But you aren't performing today.' His voice was puzzled. And irritated.

'I had a class.'

'A class! What kind of class? Flower-arranging?'

'My ballet class.'

'Your ballet class?'

Lydia stopped suddenly and, humming, began to demonstrate ballet exercises. 'First position. *Demi-plié. Bras en bas.* Second position–'

Befuddled, Maynard asked, 'You do that every day?'

'Every morning if I do not have rehearsal or performance, for three hours. You think I am not going to class, because my *petit ami* sends me a note? You think I am going to walk out early? On Maestro? Unthinkable!'

'I see.'

She stopped, her arms still extended over her head, and glared at him. 'I am glad that you see. But I don't think you do. You think little Lydia, sometimes she dresses up as a fairy, but the rest of the time she stays in bed and drinks champagne? Or comes trotting when Maynard clicks his fingers? I don't think so.'

She turned away and headed off the main path onto the grass.

'Where are you going?'

'To see the ducks!' she shouted over her shoulder. 'They are less annoying than you are at this moment!'

Maynard gaped. Then he gingerly rolled up his trousers and squelched after her. Drawing close to where she stood next to the lake, he called, 'I'm sorry. I was so looking forward to seeing you, that's all.' He came to a stop beside her. 'Believe me, I have the greatest respect for hard work.'

A brief pause, then she looked at him sideways. 'I think we are both the hard workers, Maynard?'

'We certainly are ... and I think I've just ruined these trousers.'

She looked down; the bottoms were heavy with water and pond slime. 'I think so too.'

They both burst out laughing.

'I wonder,' said Maynard, after a while, 'without making any kind of presumptions at all ... whether you have any plans for this afternoon? And if not, whether you could be persuaded to spend it with me?'

'That would be delightful,' she said at once. 'I could perhaps accompany you to the tailor for the new trousers. Or ...'

'Or?'

'We might lie in bed and drink champagne.'

There was a pause then Maynard reached out and touched her cheek. He said, 'I only buy my clothes in Cambridge anyhow.'

As FRANK HANDED Lydia her bedroom key he could hardly avoid noticing Maynard hovering sheepishly in the background, but he obligingly kept his eyes fixed on Lydia, who smiled at him with her usual aplomb. He watched unobtrusively as she went towards the stairs, and Maynard emerged out of the shelter of the banisters to join her. They walked up the first few steps in single file, then drew level, and Lydia took Maynard's extended arm.

A strange-looking cove, Frank thought, to be accompanying Miss Lopokova. Not a dancer, that was certain. Not somebody in the entertainment business at all. The suit said 'businessman', or maybe 'government official', yet he didn't look quite like either, and then there was the peculiar fact that, judging from his trousers, he seemed to be have been wading in a duck pond, which was surely impossible.

Frank felt a little wistful. He hoped this man, whoever he was, would be good to Miss Loppy. She had seen the world, of that he had no doubt, but that did not mean she could not be hurt. He was not entirely sure that she could look after herself. Still, something about this man, the rather shy way he had accompanied her up the stairs, suggested that he was not a user. Lydia was not the first glamorous female celebrity to stay at the Waldorf, and Frank had a feel for the kind of men they attracted; this one, whoever he was, seemed different.

Upstairs, Maynard and Lydia stood in the corridor while Lydia unlocked her bedroom door. As usual, the key stuck a little as Lydia turned it the wrong way, and she muttered as she wriggled it in the lock. Then the door opened, Lydia said, 'Ah!' and they went in together. Immediately, they embraced, kissing long and passionately. When they came apart, Maynard said, 'I should tell you that this is, in some ways, quite a new thing for me. I mean, with a woman.'

Lydia looked up at him. Her nose crinkled and her eyes laughed. 'And for me,' she said, 'with an economist.'

IN A PAVEMENT CAFÉ IN SAINT-TROPEZ, Vanessa lowered the sheet of paper she was holding and stared over it at Duncan, who was peering out to sea and alternately sipping coffee and sketching the scene on a napkin.

'My goodness,' Vanessa said.

'What is it?'

Vanessa did not immediately answer. She seemed shocked, turning over the sheets of writing paper to reread what was written there. Duncan eyed her dubiously, then said, 'It's not … Virginia? She's not …?'

'It's Maynard.'

'Maynard!'

'He writes that he's in love.'

'In love?' Duncan digested this. 'Do you mean with Sebastian? It's taken him a long time to discover it. Still, I suppose we should be pleased for him–'

'Not Sebastian. With a *woman*.'

There was a note of outrage in Vanessa's voice

'Well!' Duncan leant back in his chair, dumbfounded.

'I know. It's hard to believe, isn't it?' She breathed slowly. 'A bit of a case of while the cat's away–'

'Is it Barbara whats-her-name? They were always dining out at one time.'

'No. I wouldn't mind if it were. She's terribly suitable – married of course, but that doesn't really matter.'

'So is this person *not* suitable?'

'Not remotely.'

Duncan, now recovering from his surprise, was intrigued. And playful. 'A shop girl? A jam-making member of the Women's Institute?'

'No. Try again.'

'Mrs Harland.'

Vanessa snorted.

'Virginia – Lottie – Lady Ottoline Morrell–'

'Lydia Lopokova. The Russian ballerina.'

Duncan gave a low whistle.

'I know. And I know she's famous and the Ballets Russes is a bit more exalted than a Music Hall revue, but *still*.'

'Picasso designs for the Ballets Russes,' Duncan protested.

'Maybe, but Clive said their new production was *awful*, really retrograde and clichéd. He mentioned Lydia – "Loppy", he always calls her. He said she wasn't anything like as charming as she used to be, and has no conversation except dancing.'

'I expect that's because she won't flirt with him,' said Duncan shrewdly.

'Well maybe – but can you imagine *Maynard* with someone who only talks about dancing?'

'It doesn't sound very likely.'

'I wonder what Sebastian thinks?'

'Oh, he'll just sit back and bide his time.'

'Do you think so?' She considered the letter again, with the same air of disbelief. 'It can't be … well, it can't be *more* than a fling, can it? I think Maynard is rather horrified himself. *Head over heels*, he says. *He doesn't know what's hit him*. I shall write and tell him he must keep his head. There's no harm in an affair, even a mistress, *but …*' There was a long pause.

Duncan looked at her bent head, rereading the letter, and her shoulders stiff and tense.

'He's not yours though, Nessa,' he said at last, and immediately wished he hadn't. Vanessa said nothing. 'Anyway, I'm sure it will soon blow itself out.'

'Do you really think so?'

'Oh yes,' said Duncan, with the confidence of long experience, 'these things always do.'

It would have surprised them to know that Lydia, to some extent, shared their scepticism. 'Of course, most like it goes nowhere,' she told her friend Vera Bowen, a fellow émigré now married to an Englishman, in the interval of an afternoon concert. 'Economist and ballerina is too strange. Do you know, until I meet him, I don't know what economist is?' She did not mention other doubts: hints and intimations that, until he met her, Maynard's preferences had been like those of Diaghilev and Nijinsky. It was rather enjoyable to be the one to introduce him to … but in the long run … although, of course, Nijinsky himself had gone on to make a happy marriage. 'Happy anyway, until he lose his mind,' said Lydia, accidentally aloud, to the great astonishment of Vera.

The thing was, Vera said, not to rush things. Vera, like Big Serge, thought wealth and established position would be great advantages in any prospective partner for Lydia, and it was far from clear that Maynard possessed either. Vera, who dabbled in choreography, was well aware of the precariousness of the arts. She did not spell any of this out, but it was what she meant when she said that Lydia should proceed *prudently*. Lydia, as she left the concert hall, rolled the word over her tongue. Lydia's life so far had not been much marked by prudence. Was it time to begin?

She made a start by visiting the clinic in Holloway, having borrowed a wedding ring from Sokolova. Emerging, she felt well-satisfied. Whatever else happened, she would not go through all that again ... she thought of that dreadful place in Marylebone and shivered. Furthermore, this way she could be certain of keeping her promise to Big Serge. In buoyant mood, therefore, she set off for the evening's performance at the Alhambra, totally unprepared for what she was to find there.

The whole place was in uproar. Dancers in states of semi-nudity were shouting at each other; half of the younger ones (male and female) were in tears; the two stage managers (employed by the theatre) were holding on tightly to a box of props and costumes, claiming it belonged to the management and refusing to divest its contents to the cast; and Massine, the company's choreographer and favourite of Diaghilev, was standing in the middle of a crowd of dancers, gesticulating wildly and declaring, 'But I know nothing! Nothing!'

Lydia grabbed the arm of the ballerina Lydia Sokolova.

'What is happening?'

'My ring?'

'Yes, yes, I have it here. But what is going on?'

'*The Sleeping Princess* is closing.'

'What?' Lydia looked around wildly. 'Where is Big Serge?'

'Everyone says he has run away.'

15

Maynard, climbing off the Cambridge train that evening, was greeted by the woebegone face of Lydia. When told the earth-shattering news, he responded initially with strongly expressed indignation: for the failings of the British theatre-going public, for the derelictions of Big Serge, who appeared to have run to Paris to evade his debts; and for the shortsightedness of Oswald Stoll and the Alhambra Theatre, who had provoked the crisis by cancelling the rest of the run. But as his temper cooled he showed a disappointing tendency to view the whole debacle from a more analytical perspective. Was it the economic climate that was to blame, with the current deflationary regime of falling prices and wages dampening the inclination of theatre-goers to spend? In which case, the demise of *The Sleeping Princess* could be laid at the door of the Bank of England and the Treasury – adding to the list of calumnies for which Maynard already held them responsible? Or was it rather the result of a change in aesthetic tastes generally? Perhaps the Ballets Russes had inadvertently sown the seeds of its own destruction by pioneering over so many years an avant-garde style of performance, which in its disregard for traditional conventions, had perhaps served to destroy the appetite for the older – and, Maynard himself felt, more richly rewarding – parts of the repertoire, such as *The Sleeping Princess*? It was a paradox he sometimes wrestled with himself, in his own work. How could you create but not destroy? How could you present a radical critique which did totally undermine that which it was critiquing? In short, how could you ensure you did not throw the baby out with the bath water?

'Maynard,' said Lydia, 'Big Serge has not paid the company. I have some savings, but young dancers – no. I lend them, Sokolova lend them, some other principals lend them, but we don't have much to lend.'

They were in the Waldorf Hotel, where they were sitting in the downstairs lounge drinking port in an attempt to 'warm the blood', as Maynard put it.

'That is a concern. You need to speak to Big Serge.'

'But he's in Paris. Everyone say he borrow too much for *Sleeping Princess*. Now it close early, he cannot pay. I write to him, but …' Lydia shrugged her most theatrical shrug. 'Now I fear, no more Ballets Russes.'

'That is the problem with a deflationary environment, such as the one we are in now. A great deal of attention is always paid to the unjust effects of *inflation*. And rightly so, but deflation can be equally unjust, by penalizing those debtors, like Big Serge, who are the entrepreneurial motor of the economy. Without them, how can we expect to see any growth in prosperity?'

'Maynard!' Lydia banged down her glass, slopping port across the table. 'I am sorry for Big Serge, but still, he stays with rich friends in Paris while his dancers cannot buy food to eat. Soon there is no more money for all this!' She gestured at the hotel.

'Don't worry, Lydochka. You are the jewel of the Ballets

Russes. Whatever their difficulties, you will find a new setting in which to shine. And don't throw away the port, even if it isn't High Table standard.'

Lydia's voice rose in a wail. 'But how do I *live*?'

'Oh, as to that, you come to Gordon Square and live with me.'

There was an astonished silence. 'With you?' she echoed. 'But it is only weeks we have been … not even two months …'

'What does that matter? It's the obvious answer, and I want you to come.'

Lydia gazed hard at Maynard, as if trying to read him. Then her mouth tightened.

'No. Absolutely not possible.'

WHEN VANESSA and Duncan had departed for Saint-Tropez, they left Quentin and Angelica at Gordon Square under the care of their nursemaid, Grace. ('So much less disruptive for them,' Vanessa had said firmly, and with rather less confidence, 'besides, they'll have Clive.') Julian was away at boarding school, and with Angelica so young, and Clive and Maynard both busy about their own affairs, Quentin got most of his companionship from the servants. It was rather fascinating, he found, to observe a downstairs world which ran so entirely in parallel with that of the upstairs inhabitants.

He listened to the afternoon gossip, took part in the evening card games and knew all about the fruitcake that was kept hidden away behind the tea caddy – and the even more secret bottle of whisky, which was regularly replenished by Mr Harland from the drinks cabinet upstairs and kept hidden in a sack of pudding rice. Lottie was only allowed a nip (Quentin none at all) but after she had drunk her thimbleful she would become surprisingly noisy and sing 'Ta-ra-ra Boom-de-ay!' to which Mr Gates would respond with 'Daisy, Daisy' sung in a light tenor voice.

These kitchen gatherings could be quite large. There were not only the servants from Number 46 and Number 50, but also from the households of the various Woolfs, Stephens, Stracheys and the rest, who were scattered across the neighbouring squares.

The only one Quentin was uncertain of was Gates, who seemed to move between all these residences according to no principle that Quentin could understand. He was friendly and often gave Quentin a humbug from his pocket, but he asked so many questions. Why should Gates care who came to visit, or where they slept? But then, Quentin reminded himself, if he, Quentin, were fascinated by *downstairs*, it was perhaps only natural that Gates should feel the same about *upstairs*. Still, there was no need to be so touchy if Quentin asked a question in turn. 'That's how they do it in the army,' Gates had said, showing him the correct way to shine shoes, but when Quentin asked, 'Were you in the army then, Mr Gates?' his face had gone pale, and he had refused to answer. Of course, some people thought serving in the army a bad thing – his father did, and so did Duncan, even though his own father was a major – but somehow he hadn't expected servants to feel the same.

Most fascinating was to glimpse what the servants really thought of their employers. When Clive came into the kitchen to explain that the devilled kidneys he had been served at breakfast were unacceptably overcooked, Quentin had seen Mrs Harland grimace as soon as Clive's back was turned: 'Mr Hoity Toity,' she murmured to Lottie in passing. He had overheard, too, Mrs Harland's remarks to Mr Harland about Vanessa, made while Quentin, unknown to her, was helping himself to raisins in the scullery: 'Positively unnatural for a lady to spend all her time *daubing*. And to leave her own kiddies at home too, while she goes gallivanting in foreign parts.'

About Maynard, they were more respectful, mainly because of the highly mysterious nature of what he did: 'Look at *this* he's been scribbling on his napkin, like necromancy or summat.' (Gates had even been seen to pocket such cryptic notes; he seemed to be keeping a collection.) They were proud of the constant stream of articles in the press, even if they never tried to read them, and loved taking his messages and hearing about the people he met: 'He's dining with the German Ambassador tonight' (or the Duke of Connaught or the Princess of Romania) 'he was arranging it on the telephone.'

Winter wore on, and Duncan and Vanessa's return kept being put off. It felt quite natural to be spending a dark, February afternoon in the kitchen making toffee with Grace. The only surprise was when he heard the front door bang, then a shout from the hall. 'Anybody there?'

It was Maynard's voice. Grace rose and went upstairs and Quentin, left with the toffee, stirred the pan once, twice, three times then, overcome by curiosity, went to see for himself.

The hall was empty and the front door open. Quentin peered out onto the square and saw a taxi parked a little further down, outside Number 50, and a small knot of people next to it; he picked out Gates and somebody else (presumably the driver) humping suitcases, Grace standing by, and Maynard, directing operations.

'Just put the luggage in the hall! Gates will take it up later – won't you, Gates? Ah, it's you, Quentin. Good. Come here a moment. There's someone I want you to meet. Lydia, this is Quentin. Quentin, Miss Lopokova. But you can call her Lydia, I expect, can't he, Lydochka?'

Quentin found himself staring at a small, smiling lady with a snub nose, who he could not help feeling he recognized from somewhere. She was oddly dressed, with an elegant, brimmed hat at one end and clumpy boots at the other, and a shapeless, tweed coat in between. But it was with immense poise that she extended her hand and shook his solemnly.

'I am delighted to meet you.'

'Quentin is Vanessa and Clive's son.' Maynard was paying the cab driver. 'Now, we will need the room aired and the bed made up – Grace, you must take care of that – and Gates will sort out the luggage later. For now, I want to show Miss Lopokova around.'

Maynard went striding towards Number 50, Grace and Gates followed, and Lydia beamed at Quentin, who asked, 'Why are you looking round our house?'

'She's going to live here,' declared Maynard over his shoulder.

'Is she?' Quentin turned back to Lydia. 'Do you know Mummy and Duncan?'

'No, but I look forward to it very much. I meet your father several times.'

Of course! She had once come to one of Clive's lunch parties, and he had watched his father ogle her all through the meal. She had been much more smartly dressed then, which was perhaps why Quentin had not immediately recognized her.

Maynard was urging them into the house and up the stairs. Quentin, trotting behind, enquired, 'If you don't know Mummy but you *do* know Daddy and Maynard, why aren't you staying with them? You could have Duncan's room.'

'Proprieties!' Maynard declared from above them. 'Lydia is very keen on the proprieties being kept!'

'What's prop-proprieties?'

Lydia turned and smiled conspiratorially. 'You see, it is not really respectable for me to move in with two gentlemen. But to move into your mother's house – that is different. And Maynard assures me she will not mind.'

'Oh, she won't,' Quentin said confidently. He decided he liked Lydia. He liked the way she spoke. Her words sounded funny – and it wasn't French, he knew that much. She must come from somewhere else.

He was going to ask where, but then something else occurred to him. 'What about Lottie?'

'Who is Lottie?'

'She cleans and carries and washes up–'

'That's different,' said Lydia. 'Hard to explain, but it is so.'

Maynard intervened. 'What I say is: who gives a hang for proprieties? But she would not be moved.'

'You see, I have reputation to think of.' Lydia's mouth twitched. 'Not very *good* reputation – but then, all the more reason to think of it.'

'In any case, it doesn't make that much difference, Number 46 or 50.' Maynard had reached the upper landing and was waiting for them. 'Just a hop and a skip. And we all eat together. One big family really. That's always been the idea.'

Lydia nodded. 'I am social person,' she told Quentin. 'For me, stage has always been family.'

Maynard flung open a door. 'This will be your room! Wonderful afternoon light.'

Lydia looked around with approval. 'There is space I can do my exercises.'

'What exercises?' Quentin asked.

'I show you.' Still in her outdoor clothes, Lydia pointed a toe and began. 'And one, and two, and three – extend the arm – now full *plié* …'

Quentin imitated her and fell over. Lydia and Maynard hauled him to his feet.

'Vanessa and the children have the rooms right below you,' Maynard said. 'You will have plenty of opportunity to turn

Quentin into a Swan Prince. Now come and see 46. You must have the full tour.'

Their arrival at Number 46 was, in Quentin's eyes, somewhat marred by the recriminations of Mrs Harland regarding the abandoned toffee. Maynard, however, was unmoved by the news that a perfectly good saucepan had been ruined. In fact, he was in a terribly good mood altogether, Quentin thought. He had rarely seen him so bouncy.

Lydia approved the dining room where they would all eat together – 'very nice, like school days' – but her response to Vanessa and Duncan's murals of grape pickers in the drawing room was less favourable. She scrutinized them silently for several moments, then announced, '*These* are not so good. My friend Picasso's better.'

Maynard burst out laughing. Quentin said, 'Mummy and Duncan painted them.' Then, in case this should be taken as a reproach, he added, '*I* don't like them either.'

Maynard and Lydia found this even funnier, although Quentin could not understand why. Their mirth was interrupted by Mrs Harland summoning Maynard to the telephone. He departed, leaving housekeeper, ballerina and boy all gazing at each other.

'I'm sure I hope you will enjoy your stay, ma'am,' said Mrs Harland at last. She was finding it hard not to stare; after all, it was not every day that a living, breathing ballerina (and Russian to boot) moved in.

'Thank you. And don't worry. I am messy, but I am friendly!'

Mrs Harland was still searching for a response when Maynard's head appeared around the door. 'It's damnable, but there are things I must attend to. I will be dining out, Mrs Harland. Quentin, you take care of Lydia.' He vanished.

Quentin reached out to take Lydia's hand. 'Come on, I'll

show you everything. The cellar is the best. I saw a rat there once.'

Lydia followed, quite ready, it seemed, to brave whatever the cellar might offer. Gates, who had appeared almost unnoticed, waited until they had disappeared, then murmured to Mrs Harland, who was passing him on her way to the back stairs: 'Well, this'll be interesting, won't it?'

'I daresay. She's an interesting lady – and pleasant too, I'll be bound.' Mrs Harland, as usual with Gates, aimed to repress, but also as usual, could not entirely conceal her interest in whatever he might be going to say next.

'Let's see what she says when young Mr Sprott shows up.' Gates leered at her. 'Oh, didn't you know? He's in London. He left a telephone message for Mr Keynes earlier.'

IN HER NEW quarters at Gordon Square, Lydia was explaining her situation to Quentin, who was lolling against her bed, and to Grace, who was helping to unpack.

'You see, I have no work. Problem is: people not come to *Sleeping Princess*. Maybe it not for them. Or maybe they have no money. Maynard say it is bad now. Even in London, which is richer than other places. People who used to buy ticket, instead they put it in little box.'

'What little box?' asked Quentin.

'For birthday present – and gas meter – and new handkerchief.'

'You mean a savings box,' said Quentin inspired.

'Yes, save-it-up box. I had one once with picture of London Bridge. Only then it was gone.' Her face darkened. 'So then Frank look after my money, at Waldorf Hotel. But Maynard says no good – I must have own account, that Maynard organize. Very fancy. I am dancer with bank account – only unfortunately, nothing to put in it.' Lydia laughed.

146

Grace removed a pile of clothes from a suitcase, uncovering some photographs. Quentin leaned forward at once to look. He was intrigued by Lydia's possessions; not the rather bedraggled finery which fascinated Grace, but the oddments she had gathered over her peripatetic life: the battered *Shakespeare*, the Russian copy of *War and Peace* (she translated the title for him), the crisp new *Economic Consequences of the Peace*, the baby shawl, the model Statue of Liberty (four inches high), the ancient ballet shoe, the handwritten musical score and the bundles of letters, tied with pink ribbon.

'Who's that?' Quentin picked up a photo.

'Igor Stravinsky, who write music for *Firebird*. I don't want to look at picture of Igor, even though he make beautiful music. No place on dresser for *him*.' She tossed Igor casually back in the case. 'And *this* is Big Serge – I don't want to look at *him* either, and remember how much money he owe me!' Diaghilev joined Igor, and others followed. Quentin reached forward and picked up a picture of a dark, foreign-looking man from the reject pile. 'Who's this?'

'Never mind. Look at this one. Maybe I give it to Maynard.'

Aware that he was being distracted, Quentin nevertheless took the picture. 'Who is it?'

'Me, drawn by Picasso.'

'Oh.' Quentin thought the image hardly did Lydia justice, but was too polite to say so.

'And look at these.' She shuffled through a pile of loose photos. 'Me as *Firebird*, me as *Good-Humoured Lady*, me as *Petrushka*–' Grace abandoned Lydia's toiletries and bent over them, exclaiming with delight. Quentin noticed that among the posed stage photographs, there were two that looked completely different: a stout, soberly dressed woman with her hair pulled back tight, and the same woman at the centre of what looked like a family group. But Lydia put these away in a drawer and before Quentin could enquire further, there was a knock at the open door and Gates came in with a coal scuttle.

'For the fire, miss. I'll build it up, shall I? You'll catch your death in here.'

'Thank you. I hate cold.'

'Mr Harland, he reckons it's going to snow.'

Gates knelt by the grate – although generally, Quentin knew, he despised fires as women's work – and deftly handled poker and coals, turning the feeble glow into radiant warmth. 'That's better, ain't it, miss?' Gates brushed off his trousers. As he did, his eyes fell on the photographs, lying on the bed.

'Very handsome,' he said softly.

Lydia, talking to Grace, did not hear him. Grace had suggested hot muffins as a fireside supper; and Lydia had immediately flown into a rhapsodic speech about muffins she had known: muffins served with asparagus and hollandaise sauce at the Savoy; muffins served with real black-cherry jam in her friend's drawing room; thin, stale muffins served with margarine in inferior boarding houses ('What good is thin muffin? Muffin is like baby, should be plump always'); muffins toasted in old-fashioned tearooms … Grace listened in rapt attention, her eyes fixed on Lydia.

It was only Quentin, therefore, who noticed the peculiar expression on Gates' face – somewhere between hunger and pleasure, almost as if he were licking his lips – and the way he looked from Lydia to the photos and back to Lydia again.

Clive put his head around the door. 'Well, well,' he declared, 'what a merry gathering. My dear Loppy, I gather from Harland we are to welcome you as a permanent resident.'

Gates quietly withdrew. Lydia said, 'Permanent? Who knows? But I am grateful to have bed and roof for now.'

'My dear, it is our privilege. I think you should come over to Number 46 and have a drink before dinner. Maynard has abandoned you, so I will be your host.'

Framed by the door, he gazed down at Lydia with an expression strangely similar to that of Gates before – or so it struck his son, watching. *Hungry,* thought Quentin: but hungry for what?

'No,' said Lydia quite casually, 'you see, first I unpack and then I have my bath, and then I tell Grace and Quentin a story, a story from Russia, while we eat muffins by kitchen fire.'

Clive started to protest, then thought better of it. 'I see you have it all planned. I won't interfere then. After all, there will be plenty of opportunities.'

It sounded curiously like a threat.

16

I t was the start of a war. And the commencement of hostilities was marked, most incongruously, by the clinking of a teaspoon against a crystal glass in a private dining room at the Café Royal. Montagu Norman, the holder of the teaspoon, waited until all eyes were turned towards him, then began to speak.

'I'd like to stress the confidential nature of these discussions. Of course, the conversations of this group are always private, but it does no harm to remind everyone that whatever is said within this room must remain within this room. Tonight is an opportunity for both Government and the Bank of England to take informal soundings regarding a proposed return to the gold standard ...'

Foxy entered and slid into the seat next to Maynard.

'... as you know, Britain's membership of the gold standard was suspended at the outbreak of the war, but it has always been a policy objective that sterling should return to it when possible. This was clearly stated in the Cunliffe Report of 1918, and I quote: "it is imperative that after the war, the conditions necessary for the maintenance of an effective gold standard should be restored without delay". The question now is when Britain can re-enter the system, and what this means in the short and medium term for our interest rate policy…'

Maynard was shaking his head.

Foxy whispered, 'Hold your horses, old boy.'

'They're planning to raise interest rates,' Maynard whispered back, 'due to some insane notion that we can scrub out the war and return to 1914.'

'Don't make it so clear what you think.'

' … I will now ask Mr Niemeyer of the Treasury to make a few remarks …'

Niemeyer began to enumerate, in school-master style, the many advantages he perceived in a return to gold, and soon Maynard could hardly conceal his frustration.

'… so finally we see that a return to the gold standard is the only way to ensure the stability of the international financial system, and the pre-eminence of the City of London. We should raise interest rates *now* as a first step towards returning sterling to its pre-war dollar value.' Otto Niemeyer permitted himself a small smirk.

Maynard coughed.

Sir Montagu Norman stared at him over his spectacles. 'Mr Keynes, you wish to address us?'

All eyes were upon him. Maynard leaned back in his chair, enjoying the attention.

'First of all, I'd like to point out that we are in a situation of large-scale unemployment. We have approximately ten per cent of the workforce unemployed; an unprecedentedly high level.'

Norman said, 'What is your point, Mr Keynes?'

'What is his point?' muttered Foxy beneath his breath. 'What is his point indeed?'

'My point is that this is not the Victorian hey-day, nor the long Edwardian summer. It is not even 1918, when the Cunliffe

Report was written. We are in a place we have never been before. It seems to me that returning to the gold standard at this time would most likely be disastrous, for the old prescriptions of fixed currencies no longer apply.'

Otto Niemeyer said, 'I disagree. Returning to pre-war stability is exactly what we seek to achieve.'

'Fixing the exchange rate at an arbitrary level is the last way to ensure stability.' Niemeyer wanted to object, but Maynard held up a hand. 'My second point is, we are a trading economy. Our prosperity has always depended on exports. Before the war we were the largest trading economy in the world, and the third largest manufacturer, but during the war, inevitably, our trade relationships suffered. There were disruptions, and countries who had once bought our textiles, coal, ships and other industrial goods searched out supplies elsewhere. Since the war ended, our exporters have struggled to recover these markets, or to find new ones. Now, if you go back onto gold at the pre-war rate, that means an increase in the value of sterling: our exports become uncompetitive. The only means to compensate for that will be by forcing workers to accept lower wages.'

'But lower wages are precisely what we need! You mention unemployment. If unemployment is too high, then wages are too high. For unemployment to fall, wages must fall – when this happens, supply and demand will come back into line, the labour market will clear and full employment will be restored. Standard undergraduate economic theory, Mr Keynes – and, of course, plain common sense.'

There was a murmur of assent from those around him. Maynard observed their faces. Reginald McKenna, his old boss from the wartime Treasury, sitting across the table, looked vaguely sympathetic, but the other bankers supported Niemeyer, of course. So, he reckoned, did the sprinkling of academics and officials. Only Foxy was securely on side.

So be it. *Into the Valley of Death*, he thought … and they don't have machine guns, after all. Nor even sabres.

He said quietly, 'Yet in point of fact we do have widespread, large-scale unemployment that shows no sign of falling, contrary to standard undergraduate economic theory. How do you explain that?'

'The problem was introducing the dole for the unemployed,' Niemeyer replied glibly. 'Without that, wages would fall.'

Foxy muttered, 'Fall too far and the buggers won't be able to eat.'

'That may, or may not, be true,' Maynard addressed Niemeyer, 'personally, I doubt it, but abolish the dole and you could have a revolution on your hands.'

'You are a socialist, Mr Keynes?'

A ripple of alarm among his listeners.

'Certainly not. My aim is to save capitalism, not destroy it.'

Montagu Norman said, 'I'm most glad to hear it.'

There was laughter around the table. *Sycophants*, thought Maynard. *Foot soldiers*. He glanced around, searching out McKenna's eye again, and that of Sir Josiah Black, who could usually be trusted to look a little further than the rest. But Black was not present and McKenna was doodling on his napkin.

Maynard took breath. 'We won't save capitalism by clinging to a few Victorian shibboleths about free markets and laissez-faire, nor by restoring the gold standard just because it suited our grandparents. And in any case, a drop in wages purely due to a change in sterling won't increase employment. How can it, when the price of our goods abroad remains the same? You'd need to enforce still further wage drops. How much do you think the British worker can take?'

Norman said, 'You are getting a little heated, Mr Keynes.'

'My point is,' Maynard deliberately leant back, letting the

tips of his fingers come together in don-like manner, 'that you cannot abolish the dole and let wages drop without risking major social upheaval. We have seen revolution rage across Europe: would you have that here? Besides, even if we could enforce lower wages, I am not convinced that it would work. It seems to me, that wages might fall indefinitely, and we still might still have a downward-cycling economy, where production falls – prices fall – and only unemployment rises.'

'Not according to orthodox economic theory.' Niemeyer's tone was snippy. 'If you have devised a new model, I would be interested to hear it.'

'Classical economics omits the psychological issue of people's expectations. As it happens, some of my own work has been in that area, in the mathematical field of probability. I won't bore you with it–'

'That's a relief,' said Norman, to widespread laughter.

'– but the point *is*, people's expectations are based on their assessment of the future. If confidence is low, then they will not invest, they will not spend, nor will they employ new labour, however cheap it is. Markets will not clear, for the price mechanism alone will not restore optimum outcomes. To put it another way, wage falls will not restore employment. So instead, we must increase spending, investment, confidence through every means in our power.'

As he spoke, Maynard felt that he was running ahead of himself. *Where has all that come from?* he wondered. *There's something there, but I need to think about it.*

Niemeyer was smiling triumphantly. 'But the gold standard is required precisely to *provide* certainty and hence *build* confidence. So, on that ground alone you should support it. Nobody can interfere with sterling once it is pegged to gold. It is a promise to the businessman, if you like.'

'But a promise set at too high a rate is the wrong promise.'

Sir Montagu coughed. 'Mr Keynes, I take note of what you

say. All bankers understand the importance of confidence. Now I would like to invite some more opinions.'

As a new speaker began their say – a banker, and so naturally in favour of a return to gold – Foxy leant over to Maynard.

'Well, I do think you may actually have achieved something.'

'You like a gamble. Would you bet on it?'

'In this case, I'm not a betting man.'

FLURRIES OF SNOW flew into their faces as they made their way down the steps towards the pavement. Maynard hunched himself further into his coat and buried his chin in his muffler. He turned to Foxy.

'Of course, this is only the first salvo. It feels like it's going to be a long and bloody fight.'

'Ah well, when the proletariat rises up and hangs us all from the lamp posts, we can comfort ourselves we did our best.'

'I didn't notice you saying much.'

'I'm just a stockbroker, old boy. I'm no good with clever theories, though I was tempted to point out that however much Otto and company may detest the dole, it's not within their remit to get rid of it. Not unless they are thinking of flinging in their jobs and going into politics.'

'I can see Otto at the stump, can't you?'

'Oh yes, he'd give Lloyd George a run for his money.' Foxy snorted with laughter, entertained by the notion. 'He'd send his audience to sleep. They'd promise to vote for him just to get away.'

There were no taxis. They gave up looking and together turned north and began trudging through the snow. Foxy said meditatively, 'Old Otto may be right about one thing though.

It's the *theory* you need to work at. Give them something new to chew on, instead of "orthodox economics says blah-de-blah". Every time anyone questions anything, they trot it out.'

'I *do* work on it. Time is the problem; too many things to do. D'you know I'm supposed to be going to India?'

'India?'

'Yes, for the Royal Commission on Indian Tariffs and Currency.' There was a touch of pride in Maynard's voice that he could not quite conceal. Once, he had flung over the establishment in disgust; but they had been forced to invite him back.

'Well, that will be exciting, old boy, but I rather feel you're needed here.'

They walked on. The snow was falling more heavily every moment and settling on the ground; the streets were empty of traffic and pedestrians alike.

'This is rather how I imagine Russia,' said Foxy suddenly, 'just before the Revolution. The lull before the storm; the Imperial Family locked away in their winter palace, with no idea what might be unleashed. Just like Montagu Norman in fact – he rules like a bloody autocrat. He ought to think about Tsar Nicholas and what happened to *him*.'

'I thought Montagu was your new friend?'

'We both enjoy the opera. Our paths sometimes cross. But as Governor of the Bank, he's a positive menace. For one thing, he's too much in the pocket of the Americans – holidays in the South of France, they say, with Benjamin Strong. And of course the Americans want us back on gold, they own most of it these days. If we're on gold, they'll call the shots.'

'Maybe you can point that out, in between arias.'

'I can try. Speaking of opera, I hear *you've* developed an interest in the ballet.'

His tone was clearly insinuating. Maynard's head jerked.

'How did you hear? Well, you must keep it to yourself. She doesn't want everyone to know.'

It was Foxy's turn to look startled. '*She* doesn't …? I'll be dammed. Who is she?'

'Didn't your sources tell you?'

'All I know is that you've been seen regularly in the stalls during performances of the Ballets Russes. You've even got your own seat.'

'It's Lydia Lopokova. Only now the ballet's folded and Diaghilev's done a runner, so I've made some arrangements for her accommodation … near me in Gordon Square. But Lydia's very concerned as to how it might appear.'

'Well, I'll be dammed,' said Foxy again. He gave Maynard a sideways smile. 'Lydia Lopokova. Not such a stiff bottom after all, eh?'

'First impressions can be mistaken.'

'You'll both have dinner with me one evening?'

'We'd be delighted.'

'I'll look forward to it. Meanwhile, don't be downhearted.' He saw a solitary cab coming towards them and stuck out his arm. 'If you can conquer a Russian ballerina, Maynard, then anything is possible!'

MAYNARD ALSO TOOK A CAB. As it headed north, he drummed his fingers on the door. *So it's started. The troops are being marched into place. Time to prepare for hostilities.* Or maybe not. Maybe it was a war that could yet be aborted. But they had sounded very determined. And why had he been informed of the gathering only at the last minute? Had they hoped he would already be engaged and kept away?

He stared out at the dark streets, cold and dismal as any abandoned battlefield. A very few people struggled past, hunched against the falling snow, mere bundles in their winter coats: soldiers on a long march. What would it mean to impose yet more misery? Why did they do it? Was it because they hated the working class? But why hate them? You didn't need to be a socialist to concede that they were owed a decent living for what they did ... and, anyway, what was the alternative? What would happen if people were pressed too far? Bolshevism was on the tongue of every Tory, every City gentleman – 'Load of bloody Bolshies'. If they took the threat seriously, then their current policies were reckless in the extreme.

Of course, some people he knew – Sebastian, say – would argue that it was all to the good, if Monty, Otto and their like pushed the proletariat beyond the edge of its endurance. They *wanted* to pass the point of no return. For a while, after Paris, Maynard had been sympathetic to that view: but not anymore. He thought of Lydia, waiting day after day for a letter from her family; and when it came, however much they'd tried to spare her, it was clear enough what they were suffering in a country wracked by the aftermath of revolution. *Try living it, before preaching its virtues*, he imagined telling Sebastian.

(Sebastian. Dammit! What was he going to do about Sebastian?)

No, if Montagu was declaring open war, then he would not hold back. He was confident that he had as much fire power as anybody else. And at least however bloody the fight, there would be no trenches, no barbed wire.

'THIS IT, GUVNOR?'

The cabby stopped at the end of a narrow row of stone terraced houses: two storeys, with no basements or gardens, just a step down onto the cobbled street. Maynard peered doubtfully through the snow. 'Yes, I think it must be.'

He climbed out and was immediately bedaubed with snowflakes, which he brushed ineffectively from the knees of his evening suit. He hesitated, peering at the dark buildings. There were no signs to guide him, but the end house had a slight glow at the edge of the window, and a burst of raucous laughter, penetrating the night, confirmed his suspicions.

He set off towards it. As he reached the door it burst open, letting out a din of voices, and a man, dressed in cloth suit and cap, staggered out and almost collapsed onto the pavement.

Maynard stuck out an arm and caught him. 'Easy now.'

'Thank you, good sir.' The man spoke in a formal manner at odds with his appearance. He swayed, steadied himself on a lamppost, then set off along the pavement, charting a zigzag route that reminded Maynard of recent movements in the stock market. He hoped he would not crash to earth.

He turned and entered the building, and found himself in what might have been somebody's front room, except that it was devoid of furniture and there was a counter across the back. This served to transform it into a pub: a very small one for the dozen or so bodies that were in it, with shutters at the window, bare floorboards and the air full of smoke. Everyone was dressed plainly, many in working men's' suits and flat caps, and Maynard, still in evening dress and scarf, and a head taller than most, felt undeniably conspicuous. It would have been hard to find a greater contrast with Sir Montagu's dining club.

In the middle of it all, happy as a sand boy, was Sebastian.

'Maynard!' He waved and beamed broadly, as Maynard came the short distance required to join him.

'I'm glad I found the right place.'

'So colourful, isn't it? I do enjoy a touch of the lowlife!' Maynard grunted. Sebastian, flushed with drink, had made no effort to lower his voice.

'What will you have?'

'Actually, I've already been drinking. I don't think ...' *that beer would go down well after champagne*, but Sebastian was already ordering from the bar.

'Sebastian–'

'I'll tell you, Maynard, this beats the West End any day. There's some lads here I want you to–'

'Sebastian! We need to talk. The thing is–'

'I know. You don't want to me to stay at Gordon Square. You said already, on the phone. That's all right. I've made other arrangements.' He grinned.

'Yes, but not just tonight. The thing is ...'

I've met this woman. Yes, a woman. It's not what I expected, she's *not what I expected, and I've been knocked sideways – bouleversé – everything's turned upside down. I don't know how to explain it or what it means but I want to be honest with you ...* It occurred to Maynard that they could hardly have found a less suitable place to attempt this conversation.

Thankfully, it seemed he did not have to. 'It's all right,' Sebastian said. You don't need to say anything. I'm not going to stand in your way.'

'You aren't?'

'Of course not.'

'I mean, what I'm trying to say ...'

'Don't say anything. And don't look so terribly worried. I'm not about to throw myself off Westminster Bridge. You haven't broken my heart.'

'Oh. That's a relief. I'm glad that you ...'

Sebastian was no longer listening. He thrust a brimming pint of beer into Maynard's hands and said, 'Look, have you met these fellows? They're road builders,' and was immediately pulled into a different conversation, leaving Maynard contemplating the two men, both of them drably dressed and clutching half pints.

'How do,' they murmured, and 'All right then.'

'You sound as if you're a long way from home,' said Maynard pleasantly.

'Aye,' they said, and a rather halting conversation followed, in which both sides sometimes struggled at times to understand the accents and expressions of the other, but from which Maynard gathered that the two were from the industrial parts of County Durham, almost three hundred miles north, and had come to London looking for work.

'Aren't there roads that need building closer to home?'

'What for?' said one, grimly. 'Pits closed, docks closed, steelworks on half time. Where's need for roads?'

'Ent no carts enough to make pot holes,' added his companion.

As he listened, Maynard's sympathies kindled. The two men were, he noted, painfully scrawny and underfed, and it was hard to imagine them having the strength for their trade, although their hands, cracked and swollen with black, broken fingernails, spoke of many hours of hard, manual work. Their tales of life in a small pit village seemed both more alien to him, and more bleak, than the devastated German cities he had visited since the war. *But what can I do for them? The only work I could offer would be cleaning shoes at Gordon Square, but they wouldn't want that. Besides, what about Gates?*

In lieu of anything more practical, he bought them a drink, and was wondering if it would cause offence to offer money, when Sebastian declared, 'Maynard! Look here, this is Joe and Billy. They're sailors, can you imagine? They want us to go with them. What do you say?'

His companions, two strapping youths, were grinning suggestively, and Maynard discovered that not only had he no intention of joining them, but also that the idea was not even tempting.

'Actually,' he said, 'I'm ready to get home.'

He turned back to the two northerners, whose names, he

realized suddenly, he did not know; but their faces had become closed. They had just understood what kind of place they had stumbled into. They responded only with mumbles to Maynard's cordial wishes of good luck.

'Goodnight,' said Maynard to Sebastian. 'And thank you.'

'Thank me? Whatever for?'

'For your understanding.'

'What? Oh – well, what did you expect?' Sebastian was surprised. 'After all, I'm Bloomsbury too.' And as Maynard made to leave: 'I'll be waiting for you in Cambridge!'

Maynard hesitated, abruptly aware that a situation he had thought resolved was actually anything but. However, Sebastian was now wholly engrossed in Billy and Joe, and after a brief pause he went out into the night.

17

A grey February melted into spring and a green haze appeared under the trees in Gordon Square. Quentin enjoyed himself, for as well as the servants, he now had the bonus of Lydia as a companion. She often joined Grace and him for nursery suppers, and on evenings when Maynard had to go out, played gin rummy with the servants in the basement and entertained them all with tales of places she had been and people she had met (they heard the name Picasso with indifference, but were impressed by the King of Spain).

Not that Maynard went out as much as usual, nor did he go to Cambridge: he was taking a break from lecturing in order to write a huge series of supplements on the post-war economic order for the *Manchester Guardian*, and spent much of his time in the house writing. He did go out with Lydia to the cinema, and when Lydia took Grace and Quentin to see *Alice in Wonderland* in the West End, he met them afterwards and treated them to a slap-up meal at a Lyon's Corner House, complete with enormous ice-cream sundaes. Yet wonderful as that was, nothing could top the morning in late March when Maynard led Quentin out of 46 Gordon Square to reveal, at the kerbside, a car longer and shinier and altogether more beautiful than anything Quentin had seen before.

'Is it yours?' he asked Maynard breathlessly, unable to tear his eyes away from it. He was already writing a detailed description of its magnificence in his head for Julian.

'Borrowed, but I shall drive it, assuming I can remember how.'

'It's beautiful,' said Quentin reverently.

'I'm glad you approve. Lydia's seen very little of London, and even less of England, despite living here, on and off, for years. So now that she has some free time, it's a good opportunity for us to show her round.'

Quentin appreciated that *for us*.

'What about you?' he asked.

'What do you mean, what about me?'

'What about *your* work?' In Quentin's experience, Maynard was nearly always working. True, he had been more available of late, but an evening off was a different thing from going on an excursion.

'Oh, work,' said Maynard, as if this were not an especially important concept to him. (*Curiouser and curiouser*, thought Quentin, who could not get *Alice* out of his head.) And as Lydia came to join them, in a flurry of scarves and bags and shawls, Maynard asked, 'Where shall we go first? The Tower of London or Richmond Park?'

They chose the Tower of London, and had an excellent time. To Quentin's pleased surprise, it turned out to be the first trip of many, and by April, they were venturing beyond London: Maynard driving rather erratically and easily distracted by Lydia next to him, overflowing with laughter, and looking both charming and ridiculous in a leather coat and enormous gloves, finished with a ludicrous feather-topped hat.

They chose Windsor, and had a most satisfactory morning. Quentin was still besotted by the car, but had enthusiasm to spare for the tea and muffins that Maynard bought them in a roadside inn. Lydia exclaimed over the castle and Maynard was in his element, delivering reams of information on the English Monarchy, the history of Royal hunting parks and the architecture of St George's Chapel (including a brief digression on the origins of the Order of the Garter). 'Maynard can't help lecturing people,' Vanessa had once observed in Quentin's hearing. 'I suppose all dons are the same.' Quentin could see what she meant, but neither he, nor so far as he could tell Lydia, minded in the slightest.

They had lunch in a hotel, roast chicken and trifle – *a most excellent meal*, thought Quentin – and afterwards strolled out to explore shops and river, until eventually Maynard pointed at brick walls and said, 'That's my old school.'

Lydia was immediately interested. 'How old were you? You like it there? Why you not go to school in Cambridge?'

'I *did* go to school in Cambridge until I was fourteen, then I came here to board.'

Quentin watched as an Eton schoolboy, clad in starched collar and tails, emerged from a gateway. 'It's a school for toffs,' he announced scathingly.

Maynard chuckled. 'I was a scholar, Quentin, a member of College. We were the intellectuals, who won the prizes; the Oppidans were the toffs.'

'And you like it?' asked Lydia again.

'Yes. It was an important part of my life, not least because it meant I went on to King's. It was the start of everything really.'

Maynard gazed bemusedly at the medieval brickwork. *The start of everything.* His own room. The break from Harvey Road and the oppressive hovering and fussing of his father. Freedom. The intellectual cut and thrust of College. Theatricals. Prizes. Dilly Knox ('It's all just a game, Maynard, so why not? Let's explore everything. I mean *everything*'). All his life since had been a natural continuation ... until Lydia. Yes, until Lydia.

'I, too, go to boarding school.'

He looked his enquiry.

'The Mariinsky. In St Petersburg.'

'And did you like it?' asked Quentin.

'Like it?' She shrugged. 'Like or not like ... what does it matter? I learn to dance, I learn to act, I dance for Tsar, I meet Pavlova, I meet Big Serge, I run away to join Ballets Russes. It too start everything.'

As HE SNUGGLED DOWN under the rugs on the back seat for the journey back to Gordon Square, Quentin said, 'Mummy's been gone a long time.'

Lydia turned round to look at him from the passenger seat in front.

'I am looking forward to meeting her much of a muchness!'

'I expect she's looking forward to meeting you too.'

Maynard said nothing, but eased out onto the London road. After a pause he said, 'Tell me more about your boarding school, Lydochka.'

So Lydia told him, while Quentin half-dozed and half-listened to her tales: of sleeping in a vast dormitory with fifty other girls; of being supervised by strict and unrelenting governesses ('The toads, we call them. Now I am sorry for them, poor things'); of the hours of practice at the barre each morning and being shouted at by her beloved maestro, Cecchetti ('If he shout, you know you are good'); of running to the bathhouse through the freezing winter air; of riding through the streets of St Petersburg in a horse-drawn carriage in order to perform at the Mariinsky Theatre or even the Tsar's private theatre at the Hermitage. All this merged in his head with stories Lydia had spun for him and Grace – of samovars and wolves and bears roaming in deep forests – so that the whole began to seem like some rich, exotic dream.

Maynard listened, his eyes flicking every now and then from the road to Lydia, and when she paused he would say, 'Go on'.

'Enough,' she said at last. 'Lady Talky needs rest. Tell me about your school.'

'Too dull. Far too dull and English.'

'Did you ever wear those stupid collars?' asked Quentin, sitting up.

Maynard laughed. 'I've probably got a photo somewhere.'

And then they were turning into Gordon Square and pulling up in front of Number 46, which was lit up like a Christmas tree.

They had scarcely time to wonder why this was, or why the front door was standing open, when Vanessa came running to the car, her face drained of colour beneath her suntan, like a white, angry ghost.

SAINT-TROPEZ HAD BEEN A SUCCESS. It was something, Vanessa told Duncan, that they must definitely do again: the warmth, the food, the landscape, the quality of the light. Lovely though Charleston was, even in the depths of an English winter, it could not compete with the Mediterranean. Duncan had agreed: they should go south every winter from now on, he said. They were artists, after all. They were not tied down to workaday routine. They should go where they wanted, when they wanted, as the spirit moved them. 'Maynard misses us,' said Vanessa, a trifle guiltily. 'He thinks of us as family.' Duncan said that they could not be tied down by Maynard.

Nevertheless, Vanessa was looking forward to seeing him again. As the train carried them north and the landscape grew steadily greener and the air colder, or they stood on the ferry, staring at the distant smudge that was the English coast, or they sat on a station platform eating stale sandwiches and drinking tepid tea, she pictured how his face would light up as he set eyes on her again.

At last, drooping with fatigue, they climbed out of their taxi at Gordon Square. Grace came to the door to meet them, Angelica beside her. 'But where's Quentin?' asked Vanessa. None of the servants knew.

It was reasonable to assume he had gone out with Maynard and Miss Lopokova, or so Mrs Harland suggested. Vanessa, exhausted from her journey, was not inclined to be reasonable. The hours ticked by, Vanessa's anxiety increased and Duncan did not help ('If we were still in France, we shouldn't know where he was, so why worry?'). And then there came the sound of the car pulling up and Vanessa ran to meet it. In those first moments, she found it impossible to conceal her alarm and anger.

The fault was all Quentin's: told by Maynard to inform the servants where he was going, he had simply yelled the information down the back stairs ('I thought *someone* would hear. They must have been gossiping too hard to pay attention'). Vanessa, rather stiffly, apologized to Maynard, then with more warmth ticked off Quentin, who yawned and said, 'Oh well, I was fine. Anyway you haven't properly met Lydia.'

So Vanessa turned at last to Lydia, feeling completely wrong-footed, aware that she was bedraggled, crumpled, dusty, smut-covered from the journey and, worst of all, in the wrong. (Duncan, by her side, might be equally crumpled, but it made no difference: he was destined always to be one of the beautiful people.) She felt enormously tired, her shoulders and feet ached, and all she really wanted was to dissolve into a hot bath. But basic civility forbade it.

'I am delighted to meet you, Miss Lopokova.'

'Ah, but it is Lydia and you are Nessa, I know. Maynard

speak of you many time and I most happy to be your friend. Your lovely son, Quentin, and me, we are best of friends.'

'Is that so?' She could not make herself sound pleased.

'We are all one merry gang,' Maynard interjected. 'We've been here, there and everywhere – eh, Quentin?'

Maynard seemed entirely happy: straightforwardly delighted that his dearest friends were finally meeting his beloved Lydia. Lydia, too, was beaming, bouncing on the balls of her feet. Any attempt to reciprocate could only look anaemic by comparison: so really, Vanessa asked herself, was there any point in bothering?

'It's really very good of you both to take an interest.'

Maynard said, 'My God, Nessa, what's happened to you in France? You sound like a Victorian governess,' and then Lydia leapt in again, shaking hands with Duncan, saying that she had recognized him at once from the photo on Maynard's desk, 'Such handsome man. You remind me of Nijinsky.' She sounded very Russian, as she pumped his hand vigorously.

Quentin said, 'Lydia and me went to the cinema, Mummy. And to *Alice*. And she's given me and Grace tickets for her new show. Today Maynard drove us to Windsor Castle–'

'That's wonderful. I've missed you so much, you must tell me all about it.' She said to Lydia, 'How very sweet of you, to give him such a good time.'

'I am just happy you lend me your son!'

'For God's sake,' Maynard said, 'let's stop hanging about and go and get some drinks. And ask Mrs Harland about dinner, or if we should all eat out.'

They trailed after him into the drawing room. Quentin felt that his mother was not being as warm as he had imagined: it was as if she did not quite get the point of Lydia. The sight of the murals on the wall prompted a train of thought. 'Do you know Lydia knows Picasso? He's drawn her lots of times and her costumes too. Lydia says Picasso is a *great* artist.'

Vanessa said nothing, but a slight flush spread up her neck, while her throat puffed out a little, like a lizard Quentin had once seen at the zoo at Regent's Park.

'Of course not all can be Picasso,' said Lydia. 'I am not Pavlova! No, compared to her I am just music hall turn!'

'I should like to paint you, Lydia,' Duncan said, 'even if I can't compare with Picasso. Maybe I'll design a costume for your next ballet.'

Vanessa said, 'I really must go and take a bath.'

18

There was a canopy of green in the garden at the centre of Gordon Square, and through the open window of Vanessa's studio came the sound of the soft thud of the tennis balls from the nearby courts. Virginia sat in dappled sunlight in front of the window, with a cigarette dangling from one hand. Vanessa, at her easel, was simultaneously painting her sister's portrait and complaining to her.

'She will keep *talking* at me.'

'I thought you said things weren't so bad.'

'Not when she's dancing. She's too busy then. And she can be charming in small doses. But now her show is finished – it only ran a few weeks, unfortunately–'

'That's when she did the Scottish dance that Duncan painted? All whirling plaid, and arms and legs?'

'Yes, I didn't think much of it.'

'I rather liked it.'

'Anyhow, so now *that's* finished she's *always* here, and she talks and talks, sometimes for *hours*.'

'I do feel for you.'

'And meals ... Maynard finds her amusing when he's here,

but half the time he's in Germany; hush-hush meetings about reparations apparently. Nobody else can bear her. Well, Duncan doesn't mind her *so* much, but Clive's totally turned against her for some reason. And really, she is relentless.'

'She reminds me of a sparrow. Hopping and fluttering. After a while that incessant chirping must get irritating.'

'Oh, it does.'

A rhythmic thumping began above their head. Vanessa winced. Virginia looked quizzically at the ceiling.

'My word, is that the happy couple? Well, at least they won't be long. I've always heard that Maynard had no stamina … with women.' She thought about this a moment. 'Though how does anyone know, when Maynard only ever liked men before?'

Vanessa said, 'She's practising her ballet. It can go on for *hours*.'

'Well, don't worry. If they get married, she'll give *that* up straight away.' Vanessa winced again, while Virginia drew reflectively on her cigarette. 'I see her as a fat, society hostess; the overstuffed wife of an eminent man, devoting herself entirely to Maynard and whatever grim progeny they produce.'

'You don't *really* think he would, do you?'

Startled by the panic in her sister's eyes, Virginia felt obliged to backpedal. 'Oh, Nessa, I'm sure he'll be bored of her soon enough.'

There was an especially loud thump from above. Vanessa put down her paintbrush. Her hands shook.

'Right. That's *just* about enough.'

She abandoned her easel and headed for the door. Virginia raised her eyebrows, took one last puff at her cigarette then ground it into the ashtray, rose to her feet and followed her sister.

Ascending the stairs, she was in time to see Vanessa fling

open the door on the landing above. There she froze, a picture of mute astonishment. Virginia hastened up the last few steps and peered over her sister's shoulder.

Lydia, stark naked, stood in the middle of the floor, her body twisted around with one arm raised above her head. She looked like – what was it? – that picture by Delacroix, *Liberty Leading the People*; it was the same posture, anyhow. She must have been in the middle of her exercises. For a brief moment the three women stood there, unnaturally still, like mannequins in a shop window.

Lydia moved first. She swept them both a curtsy. 'Ah, Vanessa, Virginia. You would like to take some tea?'

Vanessa could find no words. Lydia laughed – *What a laugh she has*, thought Virginia. *Surely no English person ever laughs like that?* – and after a moment, humming, she began to dance again, little sideways steps, elevated on her toes. *How strong she is*, thought Virginia in unwilling admiration. The legs were muscular, yet the curve of her arms was soft; the slight wobble of breast and thigh did not detract from the overall impression of strength and grace. Virginia found herself unable to avert her eyes, as Lydia launched herself into the air, and everything shook, like some delightful blancmange–

'You are surprised.' Lydia had landed, knees bent and one arm extended, breathing quickly. 'You see, it is warm day, I sweat, and I don't expect visitors.'

Vanessa's neck was flushed. 'Well, there's one thing about it, we can at least see that you're female.' She spoke crisply. 'With Maynard's tastes, we were rather wondering.'

She stepped back and slammed the door.

She did not meet her sister's eye, as with head held high, she marched past her down the stairs. Lips twitching with amusement, Virginia followed.

Left alone, Lydia remained in the middle of the floor; with her left hand on her hip, her right foot extended, she looked like one of the Degas figures that Maynard so admired. Her expression was detached, thoughtful. Then she continued with her exercises.

MAYNARD SAT at his desk in Gordon Square, writing. The curtains were half closed, but in between he could see a slice of dark sky and wagging branches. Smoke drifted from his cigarette, lodged on the rim of the ashtray; an amber paper-weight winked in the glow of the desk lamp. It was very quiet, although every now and then there came a distant sound from the square: the yowl of a cat, the slam of a car door. From somewhere in the house, high-pitched laughter – Lottie's – and a distant thud.

Maynard went on writing at full pelt.

'*The purpose of monetary policy should be to make the price level subservient to the level of activity in the economy as a whole ...*' He finished the paragraph and began to sketch out a diagram.

The door opened behind him and Lydia slipped into the room. She closed the door soundlessly and advanced in stockinged feet over the rug, paused just behind Maynard, and grabbed his shoulders. He jumped, they both laughed and he embraced her.

'Are you a woman or a cat?'

'Miaow! But I have dancer feet.'

'If you get tired of being a dancer you can always find work as an assassin.' He squeezed her tighter.

'It will be good to have something to do when I am fat and middle-aged – or, I *should* say, even more fat and middle-aged. Or maybe now. Perhaps assassin has more work than dancer.'

Maynard had turned back to his manuscript. 'Look, I've just smudged this: thanks to you, the rate of interest is now doing something entirely unexpected.' He considered his diagram. 'No, however idiotic they are, the Bank of England couldn't make interest rates do *that*.'

'The Bank of England are idiots?'

'Not exactly. Well, yes, sometimes.'

'What is it they are doing?'

'They are determined to push up interest rates in a time of economic downturn, which can only worsen an already bad situation.'

'Why do they do this?'

'Because they want to raise the value of sterling against the dollar, so that they can put us back on the wretched gold standard – but the result is that capital becomes more expensive, because of high interest rates, and so do exports in foreign markets.' He looked at her and saw that she was struggling to follow. 'Think of interest rates like a corset. The kind of thing you wear sometimes on the stage. If you lace it too tight, it stops the blood circulating and you collapse – you certainly can't dance. Well, in the economy, investment is like the blood circulating, and if you raise interest rates and reduce the flow … well, economic activity collapses.'

Lydia leant against the back of his chair, considering. 'Is this why my show closed? Because of downturn?'

'Most likely.'

'Not because everyone hate me, and think I have an ugly nose?'

'Nobody hates you. You were marvellous.'

She sighed. 'Always, always I get work before.'

'The same with the economy; always it recovered before. But now … Still, don't give up.'

'Since *Sleeping Princess* I only have short engagements in bad theatres. Nothing run for long. Will there be other shows?'

Maynard put his arm around her waist. 'Of course there will! Very soon.'

She gazed into his face, mock-accusing. 'Ah, you want to get rid of me!'

'No, I want to come and gaze at you adoringly from the stalls.'

'I would like that too.' She stroked his hair. 'It is true, I prefer to work.'

She released him and began drifting around the room, picking up books and objects, examining them and putting them down again. She stared for a while at a landscape, a swirling purplish representation of what might be sea and heather. Next to it was a portrait of Duncan as a young man, painted by Vanessa.

'I think Vanessa also prefers it if I work.'

Maynard was writing again and only half-listening. Lydia glanced towards him.

'I don't think they like me so much, the *Bloomsberries*. But you, Maynard, you do like *them*?'

Maynard paused. 'Well, of course. They are my very old friends.'

'You are loyal, which is good. Tell me what good friends they've been and then I will like them too.'

'They've supported me through difficult times. For example, when I ditched the Civil Service and wrote my book.'

'The one I read? *The Economic Consequences*? They helped you how? Maybe Virginia wrote some chapters?'

Maynard was amused. 'No. It's not her sort of book. But I went to stay at Charleston with Vanessa and Duncan and ... they gave me the strength to do it. Moral support, I suppose you could say. You see, I had to give up a lot to write it, and I wrote some very rude things about some very important people, and I knew a lot of them would be angry ... which they were.'

Lydia had begun to do dance stretches. Bent down over one

ankle, her hair covering her face, she remarked, 'Vanessa doesn't mind the being rude. And it was worth it?'

'Yes. No. I hoped it would change things, but nothing's really changed. Still,' he added, 'at least I tried.'

'Like when you go to Germany?'

'Yes. I tried then too. But they won't listen.' He stared out of the window thinking of the clandestine meetings of the last few weeks, the secret trip to Germany at the request of his old friend Carl Melchior, the correspondence, the devising of a new plan which he'd hoped might finally lead Europe out of the log jam of debt and recrimination. But the political will was not there.

He looked so sad momentarily that Lydia felt eager to offer comfort.

'Still, lots of people read your book!'

'True. And I made money from it. That's another thing about Duncan and Vanessa. I lost some of their money once, investing in currencies, and they never uttered a word of reproach.'

'Ah!' said Lydia tragically. 'They give you money and I only take.'

'Oh, don't worry. They've taken plenty too.'

He spoke a little absently, his attention back on the page in front of him. Lydia straightened up and came to join him. She patted the manuscript on the desk. '*This* time I will provide the … *morality support.*'

Maynard laughed. 'I'm sure I need it. Actually, it's amazing how much work I've done since I've met you.'

'Really?' Lydia was transparently pleased. 'Despite Windsor Castle and Tower of London? Despite times I entrance you away to bedroom?'

'Yes. You inspire me.'

'Me?'

'Stand like that … with your arm curved like that. You see,

you most perfectly represent my notion of rate of interest against money supply.'

Lydia began to laugh. She bent over and kissed his head. Face buried in his hair, she said, 'Maybe we go next door now and I demonstrate something else for your book.'

'I like that idea.'

He laid down his fountain pen and let her pull him towards the bedroom.

THE SERVANTS OF GORDON SQUARE, from their subterranean basement, were used to observing the changes in the constellations formed by their employers. Even so, the arrival of a Russian ballerina, one whose photograph they had seen in the evening paper only a couple of weeks before, had been something new: the Bloomsbury firmament had not, hitherto, included any stars of the stage. Lydia's friends, wardrobe, eating habits and exercise routines – Vanessa and Virginia were not the only ones to have been taken by surprise on that count – were the subject of scrutiny and discussion. Generally speaking, they approved. Lydia's informality, her jokes, her irrepressible laughter, her willingness to share gossip about backstage life, all endeared her downstairs. Lottie and Grace adored her; Mr Harland was indulgent; and Gates avidly curious. Only Mrs Harland reserved judgment: Lydia was a nice enough lady, she acknowledged, but *still*. She was not sure she liked all these foreigners about the place: Russians seemed to have very peculiar notions of entertaining, and when Mr Keynes was away, Lydia's friends would sometimes stay for hours. The noise they made! No wonder Mrs Bell was sometimes so put out.

Lydia's presence marked a change in their perception of Mr Keynes. Mr Bell, now, had always had plenty of lady friends, the main one being Mrs Hutchinson (who they struggled to like), but then he flirted with everyone female, even including Mrs Cotton, the gnarled old creature who came in to help with 'the rough'. Mr Keynes, on the other hand … none of them had ever expected *him* to develop an 'understanding' with a woman, and yet here she was, a famous ballerina to boot, and actually living at Number 50, and sitting down with everyone at Number 46 for meals. It 'fair took the wind out of you', as Mr Harland said. They could not help noticing, however, that the new arrangements were not entirely free of tension.

'She was in late again last night. I heard her coming up the stairs at midnight when I was seeing to Angelica.' Grace was sitting at the kitchen table drinking tea with Mrs Harland, in the interlude before Mrs Harland had to deal with the laundry delivery and Grace make the children's tea.

'Is the poor little thing still coughing?'

'Just at night. Some honey in hot water settles it. Anyhow, Miss Loppy came upstairs just as Mrs Bell was heading to her own bedroom–'

'Had Miss Loppy been dancing?'

'Yes, but it were only a one-night thing. Mrs Bell, she says to me before, if only Miss Loppy would get a good long *run* of performances. So sad for her not being able to dance, and if she went on tour that would be even better, because Miss Loppy would love to travel about and see the country.'

The two women looked at each other and could not help smiling, even Mrs Harland who was struggling not to. 'That's very kind of Mrs Bell,' said Mrs Harland. 'Very thoughtful.'

'Oh yes, Mrs Bell is very concerned about Miss Loppy,' said Grace solemnly. 'She thinks she doesn't have enough space at Number 50, did you know that? She thinks she deserves something nicer and bigger *somewhere else*.'

'Do you mean here at 46?' asked Lottie, her head poking unexpectedly around the scullery door.

'Oh, no, she don't mean *here*. I think she means another

street entirely. Actually, I heard her say that she thought *Kensington* might suit Miss Loppy better than Bloomsbury.'

Grace stirred her tea and Mrs Harland looked gnomic.

'But Kensington's a long way,' ventured Lottie. 'I never even went there. Besides, here are her *friends*.'

Mrs Harland said to Lottie, 'Don't just stand there. You're letting in a draught. Why aren't you peeling the potatoes anyhow? You surely haven't finished them?'

'It's the laundry, Mrs Harland,' said Lottie guiltily. 'The man's here. I said I'd let you know.'

Mrs Harland tutted. 'Then don't dawdle, go and tell them to bring it in.'

There followed a general commotion, at the end of which the big laundry baskets stood on the kitchen floor, while Mrs Harland sat ready to check the lists against the contents. Lottie had been sent back to her potatoes and Grace remained, ready to help with the laundry or entertain with more gossip as the case might be.

'Tea towels, six,' Mrs Harland murmured, then glanced at Grace. 'So what *did* happen last night?'

'Oh, well, Miss Loppy comes up the stairs, just as Mrs Bell is crossing into her bedroom. They meet on the landing, and I can see Mrs Bell do *this*.' Grace imitated Vanessa's slumping shoulders. 'Disappointed, you see, she hasn't escaped.'

'Why don't she like Miss Loppy? They used to get along well enough.'

'Miss Loppy will *talk* at her, Mrs Bell says. She says to Mrs Woolf, as to how Miss Loppy follows her, and talks and talks, and Miss Loppy don't seem to see that Mrs Bell just wants her to go away. I don't know why she doesn't,' Grace added frankly. '*I* can see it well enough.'

'Miss Lopokova's too full of excitement after a performance. Giddy. I've seen it myself.'

'You're right. It's like she can't help herself. She followed poor Mrs Bell into her bedroom, and sat on the bed, and then on the dressing table, and then cross-legged on the rug, and she never stopped talking, not once, and she were even doing bits from her show. She were still at it when I'd settled Angelica and was going up to bed. Even when I were trying to drop off I could hear their voices coming up the stairs. Miss Loppy was saying all about what the stage manager said, and what flowers she got, and what Mr Keynes thought, and how they went to a party after, only then Mr Keynes had to catch a train to Cambridge, and how she'd better put some olive oil on her feet, and maybe Mrs Bell would rub it in for her.'

'She never asked that!'

'She did.'

'Well, she don't mean no harm.'

'She'd have had more chance asking *Mr* Bell to rub it in.'

Mrs Harland snorted.

'Only,' Grace went on, 'she don't care for Mr Bell. And now he's taken against *her*, because he's saying he don't want Miss Loppy down at Charleston this summer.'

'And what does Mr Keynes say about that?'

'He don't know yet. Mr Bell tells Mrs Bell *she's* got to tell him.'

'Huh! I'd let him do his own dirty work.'

'But Mrs Bell don't want her there neither. She says she'll have her there over her dead body!'

'Well!' Mrs Harland contemplated the joy of incipient fireworks, none of which posed any risk to her. 'Well!' she said again. 'And what about Mr Grant? What does he say?'

'Not much. He likes drawing Miss Loppy, I do know. She looks nicer in his pictures than the ones Mrs Bell does.'

Lottie came into the room carrying the pan of peeled potatoes. She took them over to the range, then joined the two, now silent, women at the kitchen table. Mrs Harland went on steadily counting laundry. Lottie began to giggle.

'What is it, child?'

'They're full of holes!'

'Yes, well, those are Mr Keynes' vests, and it's not our fault they're past mending. It's up to him to buy some more, but I don't reckon he ever thinks about it.'

Her hands moved methodically, putting all of his clothes on one pile. Suddenly Lottie gave a squeak. 'Oh, Mrs H., what's he doing with *those*?'

Hastily, Mrs Harland pushed the silky cami-knickers to one side, half-covering them with some hand towels. 'There must have been a mix-up at the laundry.'

'They belong to Miss Loppy, those do,' went on Lottie, indefatigable.

'Nonsense!'

'They do. I've seen her doing exercises in them. I'd recognize them anywhere.'

'Then the laundry got muddled, like I said.'

'But our laundry don't go with Number 50's—'

'Lottie,' said Mrs Harland, 'go find Mr Harland and ask him if he'll help me with these baskets. And no chatter!'

Lottie did as she was bidden. Mrs Harland's gaze met Grace's.

'Don't Lottie have eyes in her head?' Grace wondered.

Mrs Harland sighed. 'She's one of the world's innocents, is Lottie. Even when that Gates more or less spells everything out right in front of her, she don't get it. I'm trying to keep her that way.'

Grace's mouth twitched. 'Good luck in this house.'

'You can't ruin innocence. But,' Mrs Harland shook her head, 'it makes for hard work at times, so it does.'

She was thankful that Gates had not been there. He had an unwholesome interest in the habits of upstairs, in her opinion (as compared to the wholly normal gossip that all servants indulged in) and she had noticed that he had a particular interest in Mr Keynes. She had come across him once standing outside Mr Keynes' bedroom door, in the middle of the night, for no reason that she could see. Another time, she had caught him searching through his wastepaper basket. He had said that he was looking for a train ticket that Mr Keynes had lost, but Mrs Harland did not believe that for a moment. He had also been strangely curious about the times and destinations of Mr Keynes' recent trip to Germany. Gave her the creeps, Gates did. Of course, they all (save Lottie) understood what Miss Loppy was to Mr Keynes (even in her thoughts, Mrs Harland shied away from the word 'mistress'), but at least she hadn't had to watch Gates gloating over Miss Loppy's underwear.

19

Rain. Rain. Rain.

It came down in torrents from a sky the colour of slate, promising yet more rain to come. Raindrops bounced off the window sill and Lydia could hardly see through the swirls of water on the glass. Not that there was much to look out at: a street, identical to all the others, without so much as a leaf of green, still less a park, should she have the inclination to go and squelch around one. Maynard, before she left, had talked enthusiastically about Manchester's role in the Anti-Corn Law Crusade, and with real concern about the current-day state of its textile industry; he had even suggested she might like to tour a mill while she was there and report back. Lydia found that her urge to explore any part of Manchester was currently notable by its absence.

She was sitting on her narrow hotel bed, wearing two jumpers and a cardigan over her pyjamas, and a winter coat over the lot, and still feeling cold. Rain, rain, rain. It was August, and yet the room was like an ice box. It was a grim place altogether: a bed that shook at the slightest movement; a framed biblical text upon the walls ('Ask, and it shall be given'

– *not my experience*, thought Lydia of her encounters with the hatchet-faced housekeeper). There was a smell of damp and suspicious dark patches on the wallpaper; a wardrobe with one door and a mousetrap underneath; and finally, a tiny dressing table at which it was impossible to write because there was not enough space to wedge her knees underneath, which was why she was perched on the bed with her writing pad on her knee.

Lodging rooms of my life, she thought, peering back in memory at a succession of French *pensions* and South-American *posadas* and rooming houses in the American Midwest: but none (so it seemed at this moment) had felt as depressing as this. This tour of provincial towns, organized by the Ballets Russes' one-time choreographer, Massine, had achieved no moments of lift-off, those brief interludes of exhilaration and rhapsody that made everything else worthwhile. Instead, it had been made up of half-empty variety halls, shabby theatres, decrepit hotels, lack-lustre reviews and endless quarrels among the cast, not least between Massine and Lydia. Massine, also the lead male dancer, was bitterly jealous of the way audiences loved her; he deliberately cut short her curtain calls and was now even leaving her name off the publicity posters, with the result that ticket sales were falling. Massine was a talented choreographer, perhaps even a genius, but he was also mean-spirited, small-minded, vain and penny-pinching; completely lacking in all the qualities required for an artistic impresario – the opposite in every way of Big Serge.

It is no good, she thought despondently. *And I am getting older.*

She had, when the weather was better, tried to get away from the cast by exploring the towns they were visiting; expecting that she would enjoy meeting the inhabitants and seeing the sights. But she had been shocked by the grinding poverty she had found in the northern towns. Although Maynard often spoke passionately of unemployment, nothing had prepared her for these streets: the ragged children, the careworn women clutching babies, the men queuing for work with bent shoulders and empty faces; the misery and the squalor.

She longed for Gordon Square where, even if Maynard was not there, she could spend a rainy afternoon in the kitchen gossiping with Grace and Lottie, or drawing and telling stories to Quentin and Angelica. Then she picked up Maynard's letter, sent from Hamburg where he was currently lecturing to local luminaries and hatching yet more new plans for achieving German economic revival and stability: 'I really believe,' he had written, 'that Germany can become the foundation of a peaceful and prosperous Europe, if only we get the economic principles right.' She kissed the letter. If Maynard could try to bring about a new order in Europe, then she could withstand a gloomy hotel and the horrors of the Manchester Hippodrome. She finished her own letter of reply, breathing not a word of her disappointments (except to laugh at them) and sealed the envelope. Then she glanced at her watch, saw that she still had time before the afternoon performance, and took up her pen once more.

My dearest Vera,

How I wish that you were here.

I won't tell you about pain and suffering of working with Massine, because you can imagine. I wish some time we work together, you and me. It is not good to work with someone when there is no respect. (And if you are not as good a choreographer as Massine, she thought, well, genius is not everything.) *Sometimes I feel I would like to push him off the stage, and that would have benefit also that audience would finally wake up.*

I am most happy that you and Garia invite me to stay with you this summer. I crave quiet away from city streets. I have told

Maynard I will spend next weekend at country place with him, and watch seals and puffin birds. (And meet his friend who invited us and I fear will look down on me, but I will not tell Maynard that). *But I will not go to Charleston. I tell Maynard I visit you instead.*

BECAUSE THE SAD truth was that Vanessa did not want her at Charleston. She knew it perfectly well. She was not a fool. Though come to think of it, Vanessa *had* been kinder recently, most helpful and encouraging about this tour, wanting to lend Lydia money and help her pack and saying she must not worry about anything at Gordon Square. Strange. Maybe she was thawing at last. Yet still, Lydia dared not risk Charleston.

Lydia sucked her pen. Then suddenly inspired, she wrote:

WHY SHOULD we not work together? I know you make ballet for Marie Rambert so why not for me? Big Serge is gone, alas, but we will do as well – no better – than the rest. Think and we will discuss.

With my kisses to Garia also,
Your very loving
Lydia

THE CAR MOVED SLOWLY NORTH, and Lydia sat curled up on the back seat next to Maynard feeling warm and cherished as she had not done for weeks. He had been so obviously pleased to see her, beaming at her from the platform at Newcastle Station as her train pulled in, and taking her arm as he led her out to where the car was waiting, the porter following with her case. He was obviously in an immensely good mood. He felt more optimistic about Germany than he had for months, he told her, and moreover had greatly enjoyed seeing his old friend, Carl

Melchior. It seemed as if the effects of the war might be consigned to history at last, even in Germany. And the few days he had spent so far in Northumberland had been delightful: he and Foxy had thrashed out a whole new strategy for American equities; he had read the mountains of English newspapers that he had missed while he was in Hamburg; and the air had been wonderful, so fresh after London. He was sure the break would be good for both of them.

The car glided onto the road towards the coast, expertly driven by the chauffeur. Lydia rested her head on Maynard's shoulder.

'I miss you so much, my Maynarochka.'

'I've missed you too. If I don't get a letter from you in the morning, I feel low all day. They send their love from Gordon Square,' he added, almost as an afterthought.

'That is nice.'

'Are you sure you won't come to Charleston?'

'I am sure. You are all happy there. Maybe it spoil things if I come.'

He glanced at her uncertainly. 'I think Nessa did wonder – not because she doesn't like *you*, but she's a bit funny about Charleston. She thinks new people can disturb the dynamics.'

'Won't it just adjust to a new equilibrium, like model of demand and supply?'

Maynard laughed. 'Very good. Yes. It's a shame Nessa's not an economist. But actually she did ask me most specially to invite you.'

'That is nice. But I have already told Vera I visit her,' and she told him her idea that she and Vera might form a dance company. As she had hoped, he kindled instantly: indeed, his enthusiasm and suggestions were such that anyone would think he had hidden ambitions himself to be a theatrical impresario. Hesitantly, she voiced her doubt as to whether she had the necessary skills – she had danced all her life, but that was a different thing from running a company – but he dismissed this out of hand, and Lydia felt her sense of optimism grow. Maynard made all things seem possible; it was one of his qualities. Manchester became hazy, a mirage – failure did not exist in Maynard's ambit.

'This Mr Falk,' she said, changing the subject at last.

'Foxy.'

'You are sure it is all right? I only meet him once, and I don't wish to be here just as … as your *friend*.'

'Oh, nonsense. Foxy's a balletomane. He's dying to entertain the famous Lopokova. In fact, he's having a grand dinner party tomorrow, I think to show you off. You and his new place.'

'Oh? Show me off who to?'

'Friends of Foxy's, anyone he could lure north: from the City' – he registered her expression – 'and maybe even the theatre. He's a friend of Pavlova, I believe.'

'Pavlova in America.' But Lydia was reassured.

The car left the main road, and suddenly there was sea stretching out in front of them, a dazzling expanse of light. 'But there is only water!' protested Lydia as the car stopped, and Maynard replied, opening the door, 'See there – that's the causeway, where the old monks crossed. But the tide's in, and we'd be up to our necks, so we're taking a boat. That's where we're going: Lindisfarne.' With sudden doubt he said, 'You may get a little wet – I hope you don't mind. It's rather … unusual. Lytton came here once, and hated it.'

But Lydia was enchanted, even as the wind came whipping in from the North Sea, bringing the wheeling gulls with it. She sat in the prow of the boat, arcs of spray coming up on either side, wrapped only in an old mackintosh and her hair tossed around her so that she resembled some wild maenad, while Maynard sat wedged next to her case, and old Jack Lilburn (who had taken one contemptuous look at Maynard and dismissed his help with the oars) guided the boat onwards, until they reached the island at last: the cluster of houses clinging to the rock, the monastic ruins, and beyond them, perched on an outcrop above the sea, the castle that Foxy had bought on a whim with his stock market winnings.

Lydia breathed in deeply and felt all the burdens and petty humiliations of the last few weeks dissolve into salt-filled air.

Foxy's other guests arrived the following day and were decanted onto the stone cobbles, where Foxy stood waiting to greet them, his clothes billowing in the wind, and to lead them up the steep ramp to the castle itself. They were shown their rooms (those who were staying over) and issued with gaiters (those who were prepared to brave the elements) so that they could make the walk with Foxy to the headland in order to admire the cliffs, the sea, and with luck, a seal or puffin or two. The less intrepid remained in the castle to be entertained by Maynard and Lydia, who had already visited the headland. 'I'm afraid it's a rather male gathering,' Foxy had apologized earlier to Lydia. 'You will be the leaven in the bread so to speak. Mostly financial types that I thought Maynard should meet – or who should certainly meet *him* – some of them on their way to Scotland for the shooting and fishing, you know; the womenfolk thought it all sounded a bit primitive, I'm afraid.' Lydia replied graciously that she had no objection to male company. She had taken to Foxy who, as Maynard had said, was a keen balletomane, but not one of those who therefore felt entitled to explain ballet to her.

So Maynard and Lydia played host and hostess, Maynard pointing out the architectural features (Edwardian but with Tudor remnants), while Lydia gave a comical account of her recent tour and its tribulations. Foxy and his party returned, gaiters were discarded and evening attire donned, the gong sounded, and they all went through for dinner.

Sitting at the long dining table, Maynard found his eyes frequently drawn to Lydia opposite: the candlelight falling on her brocade dress and her strong, dancer's arms. She was engaged in lively conversation with her neighbour, a diplomat who had apparently seen her perform with the Ballets Russes in Lisbon, in 1919, just before that city had been caught up in an attempted coup. Snatches of their talk reached him across the table.

'It lasted a full five days as I recall–'

'– when bullets start flying, we dancers dare not step outside the door–'

'– we were all under our desks at the Embassy, waiting for news–'

'– we hide under bed at hotel. I drink tea out of my shoe–'

'The ambassador was cool as a cucumber, dictating telegrams to London–'

'Big Serge, he go crazy. He run out of cream for his moustache!'

'*Definitely* one of the most interesting episodes of my career. I doubt I'll ever be lucky enough to witness *another* revolution, even a failed one ...'

The diplomat spoke with an amused detachment. Maynard saw Lydia go very still. She was not exactly angry, he felt, but as sombre as he had ever known her as she replied, 'You are lucky you see only one.'

Her companion merely smiled amiably and poured her some more wine. 'Now, you said you'd been to South America. Which countries did you visit? Argentina is my favourite–'

'Keynes?' Maynard's attention was claimed from his left by Reginald McKenna, Chancellor of the Exchequer during Maynard and Foxy's own time at the Treasury, and now the head of a bank. Maynard had always liked McKenna, now an investor in his and Foxy's syndicate, even if he could not help remembering some of McKenna's failures during the war. 'Quite a lot in what you said the other day at the Tuesday Club. Old Montagu didn't care for it. But still, quite a lot in what you said.'

'You think so?' Maynard was immediately attentive.

'Yes. Mind you, it's a difficult subject, very difficult, the gold standard; a lot to consider. But what about these latest talks with Germany, eh?' McKenna pressed on determinedly, as if he knew that if he weren't careful Maynard would be explaining to him how it really wasn't difficult at all.

So matters of international finance were discussed, wine was drunk and glasses and conversation glittered – or seemed to glitter under the influence of the wine. Dessert eaten, some of the guests drifted outside to smoke and watch the sea; others departed to see the pictures in the gallery. Lydia murmured in Maynard's ear, 'I have been asked to play piano', and disappeared.

Foxy said, 'Let's go upstairs for drinks. It's wonderfully *faux* medieval', and so he found himself sitting with Foxy and an assortment of Foxy's guests, all male, on dark oak furniture with thick velvet cushions, surrounded by lances, pikes, halberds and other assorted weaponry, in front of a vast and roaring fire. It was all rather feudal, thought Maynard, and no doubt Vanessa and Duncan would have disapproved horribly. But it was so *comfortable*.

Across the room, an old school friend of Foxy, now a banker, said in a low voice, 'What d'you really make of that fellow – Keynes, isn't it?'

'Cleverest man I've ever known,' said Foxy instantly. 'Was at the Treasury with me, during the war. Stopped the Exchequer going off a cliff.'

His companion snorted. 'Wrote that book; the one that caused all the fuss. Saying we were beastly to Germany over reparations, kicking her when she was down.' He wagged his cigar at Foxy. '*I* say we should have kicked her a whole lot harder, bled her for every penny she's got.'

Foxy tapped Maynard on the arm. 'Old George here doesn't agree with you about reparations, old boy. Reckons we were too soft on the Germans.'

'Old George' harrumphed. 'Well, the blighters did start the war in the first place.'

Maynard gazed at the large, round face, shiny with sweat, which he dimly recognized as having seen around the City: George Fotheringill-Whyte, or was it Feathersgill-Whyte? He said abruptly, 'I suppose we should have let their children starve.'

'The Kaiser should have thought of that before he started the whole damn shooting match.'

'Yes, but it's not the Kaiser who has to pay, is it?'

Another of the group intervened: 'This business of reparations is getting stale. Every few months they seem to have another conference.'

'What's your feeling?' Foxy asked Maynard. 'Can we find a deal that works? We need to for everyone's sake – the mark has fallen off a cliff.'

'Oh, I think we can come up with something. I think the Government are prepared to see sense.'

'Only it doesn't depend on you,' said a drawling, American voice. 'It depends on the Americans.'

A lean man with deep-set eyes was smiling sardonically down at them. 'Keynes' friend Walter,' murmured Foxy, for the information of those around him.

Maynard narrowed his eyes. 'Why do you say that?' he asked.

'Because they – *we* – are the paymasters now. Washington will call the shots.'

The rest of the gathering stared back at him, with varying

degrees of hostility. 'Because we're so deep in hock to them, I suppose he means,' said somebody.

'The point I keep making,' Maynard said, 'is that *we* bore the brunt of funding the war, *we* bankrolled the allies – France and Italy, and so if *we* are prepared to forgive *their* debts, then the Americans should do the same by *us*. It's the only way out of this mess.'

Walter said, grinning: 'I thought you were an economist, not an ethics professor.'

'I don't see economics as excluding ethics.'

'Well, that's not how they see it on Wall Street. Or in Washington.'

'We still have the Empire.' George had puffed out like an indignant adder.

'Oh for sure – you have *that*.'

'He's right you know,' Foxy murmured to Maynard, as the conversation around them fragmented. 'Why *should* the Americans forgive our debts, just because it suits us?'

'Because it is in their interests to have us prosperous and buying their goods. Just as it's in *our* interests for Germany to prosper.'

'I think they'd rather move in while we're struggling, and grab as much of our business, financial and otherwise, as they can.'

Foxy rose to replenish his guests' glasses and the American slid into his place. 'Good to see you, Keynes. I often think about our time in Paris.'

'That terrible hotel full of decrepit generals – at least we did well at poker.'

'And you got a good book out of it.'

'Thank you. You wrote an excellent introduction.'

'Why don't you come to the States? I'll arrange you a speaking tour.'

'I'll think about it.'

'Meaning: no. You're smarter than your friends, but you still don't entirely see it. America's where it's all happening.' He grinned, while Maynard tried to conceal irritation. 'Montagu Norman does, he's thick as thieves with Benjamin Strong. Knows he needs to keep in with the Fed.'

Maynard frowned. He said in a low voice, 'I suppose the Fed are dead set on us joining the gold standard?'

'They think everyone should – since they acquired all the gold!'

They talked a while longer until the sound of the piano, which had been drifting through from the music room during the conversation, stopped, and everyone clapped politely. After a pause, it began again, very fast and showy: Rachmaninoff perhaps: definitely not Lydia at the keyboard this time. Besides, Maynard could see her though an open doorway, in conversation with Reginald McKenna.

'She's charming,' said Foxy, reclaiming his seat. 'Lights up the room. Imagine her taking up with a dry economist like you!'

'Tell me,' said Maynard, 'what's this really all about? Most of these people are from the City, aren't they?'

Foxy grinned wickedly. 'You're waging a campaign. Or will be soon. You need to sound out opinion, hopefully win some converts.'

The piano sounded close to combustion, and they were awed into silence for a moment. Then it relaxed into a quieter interlude. Almost as if he had heard Foxy's comments, one of the bankers remarked, '*One* thing the Americans have right anyway. *Their* currency is on gold. We need to do the same.'

Foxy nudged Maynard. From around them came a chorus of agreement.

'Quite right.'

'Sound money.'

'Hear, hear.'

'Do we have to do a thing because the Americans do it?' inquired Maynard, seemingly of the ceiling.

'Point is, that if we don't get back on the gold standard soon, the Americans will take the lead. Like that chap was just saying–'

'They'll take the lead anyway,' interrupted Maynard. 'They've got all the gold. *As* that chap was just saying, in fact. Since the war they've cornered all the reserves.'

'It doesn't matter,' said his opponent stubbornly. 'If the City of London is to be on top again, then we need a strong pound sterling, backed by gold.'

'And I suppose what is good for the City is always good for the country?' enquired Maynard, into the chorus of agreement.

They turned and stared at him, incredulous.

'Well, of course it is, old boy–'

'The country needs the City–'

'It's the City that built the British Empire, don't you know.'

A stockbroker, Jock, poured everyone another drink. He pushed a glass solicitously towards Maynard, in the manner of a nanny offering a tonic to her sickly charge. Only Foxy was smiling, detached and amused, awaiting Maynard's next move.

'What about the miners?'

Even more astonishment.

'Who?'

'What miners?'

'Don't know what you're on about, old boy.'

'Much of our coal is exported.' Maynard spoke patiently, as if to some particularly slow undergraduates. 'If our currency strengthens, our coal exports become more expensive. It's inevitable. Therefore, the only way to sell coal abroad is to reduce costs, which means miners' wages fall.'

'So?'

'The miners may not like that. Or the road builders,' he

added, thinking of the two Durham men in the Kentish Town pub.

'Who cares what they like?' George's eyebrows rose like startled spiders. 'That's life, old boy. They'll just have to accept what the market can pay. And maybe work a bit harder.'

There were murmurs of agreement and glasses were raised. Jock commented, 'Anyway, from what *I* hear, Montagu Norman himself wants us back on gold. And I doubt he'll be too worried about the grievances of a few coal grubbers from … where is it they do the mining?'

'Amongst other places, not far from here.'

'There you go then. He won't care about a few whiners in the north. Now let me tell you, *I've* just done a deal which will see a fortune worth five times one of these little northern towns invested in Canadian lumber. Would have been a lot easier to tie together if everyone knew the value of sterling, and where it would be six months from now. *Stability*, that's what we need.'

He was like some kind of grotesque parody, thought Maynard, and he didn't even know it. 'I'm not opposed to stability. But a stable exchange rate will not guarantee a stable domestic economy: quite the opposite. And if you peg sterling too high, exports *must* suffer.'

He argued the case a little longer. But they were soon bored with the topic. The conversation turned to other deals they had been involved in – South African mines, South American ranches, South Asian plantations – and then to grouse-shooting and the state of the ground in Aberdeenshire. When it came to grouse, Maynard noted, they seemed to have the intimate knowledge of Britain's geography that was so lacking for its heavy industry. Or was it simply that their knowledge ceased a certain distance north of London, and did not resume again until north of Perth?

Foxy said *sotto voce* to Maynard, 'Well, you see how it is.'

'Do they not care at all about industry?'

Foxy shrugged. 'They just think the miners will have less butter for their bread. When in fact, they don't even eat butter.'

'Don't they?' Maynard was genuinely surprised.

Foxy chuckled. 'You don't know the first thing about the working classes, do you? You're as ignorant as *them*.' He waved his hand at their companions. 'We should go and visit a pit village. As you say, there are plenty not far from here. A lot more educational than the puffins and the monkish ruins – for this lot, anyway.'

Maynard laughed.

'Though you're not really that interested, are you?' added Foxy curiously.

'Interested in what?'

'The working classes. And yet you're prepared to do battle on their behalf.'

'I know I couldn't live off what they get paid. And I know if they cut my wages, I'd be bloody angry.'

'Angry … and dangerous.'

'Yes. Both situations best avoided.'

'Now the socialists, they like 'em angry. They *want* 'em dangerous. Dare say they'd even like the idea of gold, for just for that reason. Makes the workers more likely to rise up. You're no socialist anyhow.'

'Certainly not.' Maynard thought suddenly of Sebastian.

'I hate socialists,' said Foxy simply. 'I hate 'em as much as fools like Montagu, who would stamp all over the workers out of pure stupidity.'

Maynard was squinting at the amber glow in his glass. 'Here's a thing: how is it that a group of people that invest the nation's wealth as their profession, know so little of their country's industries that they don't even know where to find its coal mines?'

'Oh, that's standard. They invest in Indian rubber, or South-

American coffee plantations, or if it *is* mining, then in South Africa. Anywhere but *here*.'

'So all this blather about Empire: they really believe it?'

'I suppose they must.' Foxy sipped brandy. 'I'll tell you another thing, my diplomatic friend, the one your Lydia was sitting next to at dinner, he agrees with them.'

'About Empire?'

'And gold. The way he sees it, we have to go back on gold, so we can compete with the Americans.'

'But–'

'Oh, not economically. Just so we can lord it over the other nations, kind of thing.'

Foxy was once again diverted into his role as host, and Maynard sat and watched Lydia. She was demonstrating dance steps now, looking flushed and animated.

'Wonderful treat, seeing Lydia again.' Jock spoke with more warmth than he had shown all evening – and, indeed, surely a tinge of envy. 'Last time I met her was after her big success in *Boutique.*'

'Oh?'

'Yes, Sam Courtauld threw her a party. You know, the owner of the viscose company.' And as Maynard still looked blank. 'Great lover of the arts; ballet particularly. They say he gave a cool £50,000 to the Tate.' And he turned back to the grouse-shooting conversation, leaving Maynard to digest this.

Later, he was smoking a cigarette on the Upper Battery, gazing out towards the dim shapes of the Farne Islands, when he heard an American voice behind him.

'That's a wonderful view out over the sea. Thanks for getting me this invitation. It's a wild coast, though. I can't imagine what it's like in winter.'

'Ferocious, I should think.'

'Think about what I said before. If Sir Montagu thinks it's

worth coming over, maybe you should too. I can introduce you to some people.'

'Thank you.'

Walter looked at Maynard and laughed. 'You don't want to, though, do you? You've invited me to pump me about Wall Street and the Fed, and as a thanks for your American book contract, but–'

'I enjoy our conversations!'

'But at the end of the day you'd rather visit Russia. Well, you have good reason, I guess. And some think that's where the future lies. I remember when we were in Paris–'

'I was young and hot-headed and I said some foolish things. A lot has changed since then.'

'It's not that long ago.'

'It feels like it.' And it really does, thought Maynard, surprised. My life has gone in directions I never guessed. 'I would be interested to visit Russia,' he said aloud. 'But from curiosity.'

'Well, I'd say the future is with us, in America, whatever the leftists think – or the people here, with their dreams of imperial glory.'

'Tell me, would *your* top bankers know where your coal-mining industry was to be found?'

His friend's eyes crinkled in surprise. 'Well, I can't answer for every stuffed shirt who ever drank too much at a Wall Street lunch – but yes, I expect they would. Why?'

'I just wondered. You know, you might be right. Perhaps America is the future after all.'

20

1923

Mrs Harland and Lottie were preparing afternoon tea when the door from the back hall opened and Gates entered, his eyes curiously avid. *Makes my skin crawl, so he does,* thought Mrs Harland, bracing herself for whatever had produced that gloating expression. Gates divided his time now between various Bloomsbury residences, making him a conduit for news and information. Of course all Bloomsbury servants gossiped, forming a network of talk that in some ways mirrored their employers', but Mrs Harland could not shake herself of the feeling that there was something different about the harmless chit-chat of herself or Grace (or Lottie, or Nellie, or Mr Harland or … well, Bloomsbury was a well-populated place) and the salacious way that Gates conveyed his insinuations. She always had the uncomfortable sense that Gates knew far more than he ever revealed.

Now Gates said, 'Young gentleman visiting, so there is. Come to see Mr Keynes.'

'How do you know?' asked Mrs Harland sharply.

'Met him just now on the pavement.'

Mrs Harland brushed off her hands on her apron. 'I'd better go get the front door.'

'No need. Mr Keynes came out himself and let him in.' Gates' eyes gleamed. 'Must have been expecting him. Quite a handsome feller he is too.'

Mrs Harland became aware of Lottie, her brown eyes round and interested. 'Lottie, fill the kettle, why don't you. I'm surprised the bell hasn't rung yet.'

'Might be they don't want tea,' said Gates, all innocence. Mrs Harland shot him a killing look.

'But it's almost four o'clock,' said Lottie. 'Mr Keynes always likes some tea at four. Miss Loppy does too.'

Mrs Harland, who was arranging muffins on a plate, fumbled and almost dropped one. Gates' nostrils flared, like a horse detecting a new scent in the air. Grace, who was sitting by the stove mending one of Angelica's smocks, shook her head. Only Lottie hummed, entirely unaware, as she turned and filled the kettle noisily and slammed it on the range.

'Maybe I should warn her,' murmured Grace.

'Warn her about what?' asked Gates, smiling.

'It's always good to know there's company,' returned Mrs Harland smartly, as Grace flushed a deep, becoming pink. She was a pretty girl, thought Mrs Harland, her thoughts skittering, helter-skelter, she was surprised really that she wasn't married. Of course there was still time. In the pause that followed, Gates watched Grace, while Mrs Harland hoped the topic was closed.

'I just don't want Miss Loppy upset,' said Grace abruptly. Mrs Harland drew in her breath. 'After all, things are different now.'

Gates grinned wolfishly. 'A leopard don't change its spots.'

If it hadn't been for Lottie hovering, Mrs Harland thought, she'd have given him a piece of her mind, oh yes, she would! Although quite what she would have found to say, given that she had never admitted (even in her own mind) the existence of … well, there were certain unspeakable things in this world, and in her view was it was better not even to *think* of them. Doors were made for shutting and keeping shut, in her opinion.

Best if Lottie stayed down here, while she or Grace took up the tea.

Her eyes met Gates' across the kitchen table. Greedy, he was, she thought. And – and *revelling* in it; the very thought of it … whatever *it* might be.

He stared back at her boldly and winked suddenly. It transformed him. His grin became attractive again: schoolboy, not wolf. Maybe she had misjudged him after all.

'Never mind, Mrs H. I say, let everyone take pleasure in their own way. That's my philosophy.' He spoke with sincerity, but she wished that he would not put these things into words … or *almost* into words. And 'pleasure' was a word she could have done without. Still, she relaxed enough to nod briefly at him.

'What pleasure?' asked Lottie. And then: 'Miss Loppy likes Ceylon tea best, but Mr Keynes prefers Assam.'

'*Ass*am, eh? Well fancy that.' Gates' chuckle left Lottie mystified. Mrs Harland fortunately was distracted by a bell ringing: the drawing-room bell.

'That will be them,' said Mrs Harland. 'Shake a leg, Lottie. They'll want their tea.'

'So, Sebastian thought he would drop by,' Maynard was explaining. 'As he was in the area anyway.'

'Visiting the London Library,' said Sebastian. He had already mentioned this, but seemed eager to stress the point. 'Usually I can find everything I want in Cambridge, but I needed to consult a book in the London Library.'

They both looked at Lydia. She was sitting on the sofa next to Sebastian, with her legs curled around to one side, her left hand holding her ankle. 'Ah, the London Library!' She beamed. 'Someday I go to the London Library! I love books.' Her eyes fastened on Sebastian's. 'I have read *all* of Maynard's.'

'You haven't read my *Treatise on Probability*.' Maynard leant back on his chair. 'I wouldn't wish it on you, either. Years of my life it took to write ... and now I can't remember the first thing about it.'

'Oh, come, Maynard.' Sebastian was smiling, 'I'm sure it's very fine – for those that can understand it.'

'Frank Ramsey understood it. Young fellow at King's, very clever,' he added for the benefit of Lydia. 'Unfortunately, he understood that it was wrong.'

'I will tell him *he* was wrong!' Lydia sounded unexpectedly fierce.

'No, no, he was perfectly right. It was all founded on a misconception, the whole thing. Anyway, he did me a favour. I learnt from it. For one thing, I'll never again touch philosophy. It's not my field. I'll leave it to Frank and that fellow Wittgenstein. Also, things that look clever aren't always right. Finally, I will keep away from unnecessary mathematics. It just obscures errors of thought half the time. My whole aim *now* is to convey everything as simply and plainly as possible.'

'*Oah*, so that is why you like *me* to read what you write!'

Maynard smiled. 'Only if you enjoy it.'

Sebastian said to Lydia, 'But you must find it very hard to make *any* sense of Maynard's writings. I mean, not being an economist.'

'No, that I do not always understand. But there is a sort of poetry in it. It makes me moved, and above myself, like listening to Tchaikovsky.'

Sebastian blinked. Maynard said cheerfully, 'Not a comparison I've heard made before – Tchaikovsky – but I'll settle for it. Ah, tea.'

Grace came in with the tea things, including a plate piled high with crumpets which she arranged on a table.

'Where's Lottie?' Lydia asked immediately. 'Isn't she well?'

Grace replied evasively, 'Mrs Harland needed her.'

Maynard said, with evident pleasure, 'Crumpets! No don't worry, Grace, we can manage,' and after Grace had left, reached for the butter.

Sebastian took a slice of Mrs Harland's fruit cake, and balanced his full teacup on his knee.

'*I* should like more tea, please.' Lydia held out her cup and waited while Maynard filled it. Then she turned to Sebastian. 'It very nice to meet you, Mr Sprott–'

'Please, call me Sebastian.'

'– you see, I not know many of Maynard's Cambridge friends and so I wonder sometimes what they are like. And now I find out: most agreeable young man.'

Sebastian stared back, wordless.

'I expect you have wondered about *me*,' Lydia went on. 'And here I am. You see? So now, tell me about London Library. Very fortunate,' she added, 'you have errand there. Very fortunate. For me, I mean. And Maynard. We like when people come to tea. What is it like, this library?'

Sebastian found himself unable, at that moment, to describe the London Library.

Maynard said, 'Lydia will have to come to Cambridge, won't she, Sebastian? I was thinking she must come for the Greek Play, if not before. It's unfortunate that, being a woman, it's rather hard to know where to put her up.'

'Ah, Cambridge is a world of men,' Lydia announced. She dunked a biscuit in her tea. 'Virginia told me this.'

'Not entirely,' said Sebastian, coughing slightly. 'Lytton's sister is the Principal of Newnham. Lytton Strachey,' he added. 'I don't know if you've met.'

'Ah, this Lytton; *another* old friend of Maynard.'

'Yes, indeed.'

'Maynard once spend Christmas at his house.'

'*I* was there too.' Sebastian spoke a trifle defiantly.

'I remember, because Maynard wrote me. One of our first letters. I remember he address me most properly as Miss Lopokova.' Lydia put back her head and laughed. '*That* not last long.'

Sebastian stared at her as if mesmerized. 'Maybe you'll come too and visit at Tidmarsh,' he said at last, wondering even as he spoke why he was saying it.

'Tidmarsh is Lytton's house? No, I not go there.' Lydia leaned forward confidingly and lowered her voice. 'It is because of *immorality*. He live with young lady and she is not married to him. True?'

'Carrington,' returned Sebastian, still hypnotized. 'Dora Carrington, but everyone calls her Carrington. She's a painter. Actually, she's married to somebody else. It's ... *complicated*.'

'Life always complicated.' She beamed broadly at Sebastian. 'You must have muffin, Mr Sprott.'

'What's that?' He was startled by the change of topic.

'Muff-in. With butt-er.' She spoke slowly, as if to a child. 'I fetch you one.'

She got up and Sebastian found his eyes turning helplessly to Maynard, who shrugged, smiling.

'Anyway, we must and shall get Lydia to Cambridge,' Maynard said. 'And to Charleston – yes, Charleston above all. Are you coming to Vanessa's party?'

'Well, yes. I thought I would.'

'Wonderful! It's going to be a real blowout she says. The first really big party since the war.'

A little later, Maynard was called away to the telephone.

Lydia sat watching attentively as Sebastian ate the crumpet that she had buttered for him herself. The sight seemed to give her a great deal of pleasure.

'Yes, yes, you need warm food … This is what I tell Maynard also. Bread or cake only is not good … "Man not live by bread alone." Who said that? No, nor woman neither … We don't have muffin in Russia, but I like it … Maynard calls me his muffin sometimes … Toasting on fire, sometimes I pretend I'm caveman – or cavewoman! … English food very strange … Me, I show Grace how to make the beetroot soup, though I admit, I am no cook …'

Her stream of chatter ran on, her hands gesturing wildly and on one occasion nearly upsetting Sebastian's teacup. Sebastian felt the situation was increasingly surreal. He was not sure what he had expected, turning up unannounced on the spur of the moment. To see for himself? To remind Maynard of his existence? Or more than that: to have it out with him, or at the very least stir things up a little? But sitting on a sofa, being fed crumpets by Maynard's Russian mistress while she enveloped him in warm, inconsequential chat, was not it.

Lydia sat looking at him with her head on one side, like an alert and expectant sparrow. 'We are going to be friends, Mr Sprott. *Sebastian*. Yes, you are friends with Maynard and so you will be friends with me. You will call me Lydia.' Her face was open and guileless, her tone firm.

'Yes Lydia,' said Sebastian huskily. 'I'm sure we will be.'

Lydia nodded. She reached over and patted his hand.

'I'm very interested in Russia, you know,' said Sebastian suddenly. 'The changes there … very exciting. I would be interested to discuss them with you.'

'Ah!' Lydia's expression was for the first time enigmatic, difficult to read. 'Yes,' she said at last, her tone distinctly more reserved, 'I like that.'

Why the change? thought Sebastian. But there was no chance to pursue it, for Maynard came in the door and Lydia rose, brushing the crumbs from her lap. Once again her expression was open and friendly as she announced she had some things to do, they must excuse her. She was sorry to say goodbye, but it had been truly *very magnificent*. She held out her hand to Sebastian, very charming, blew a flirtatious kiss to Maynard and was gone.

Left alone, Maynard and Sebastian sipped tea in silence. Sebastian could find nothing to say. Maynard appeared distracted: his eyes drifted to the windows; he was humming – Tchaikovsky, Sebastian realized, after a few moments. A little later, Sebastian remarked that it was time he was going. He needed to be back in Cambridge for High Table.

'Good to see you,' said Maynard, getting up with alacrity. 'You must come again.' He paused. 'You'll let us know, next time, won't you?'

Sebastian did not in fact take the Cambridge train. Instead of King's Cross Station he went to Paddington, where he boarded the west-bound line. As it left the city behind, the countryside darkened and he gazed out onto low hills, patches of woodland and tiny country stations. Eventually, he alighted onto the platform at a small village in the Wiltshire Downs.

THE FOLLOWING DAY, after a good breakfast, Sebastian walked out with Lytton Strachey from Lytton's home of Tidmarsh into the surrounding countryside. After passing a long time in silence, the two men eventually stopped at a gate and stood staring out at a quintessentially English scene of ploughed field, circling birds and straggling hedgerows receding into the distant hills.

'I don't think you have any cause to worry,' drawled Lytton at last, his voice rising and falling in the peculiar, exaggerated manner habitual to all his family. 'I could see at Christmas that he was *deeply* fond of you.'

'I can see that he's deeply fond of *her*.'

'It's not impossible to be both. As you well know,' Lytton coughed, 'that's been rather the case *here*.'

A pair of pigeons rose up from the field in a flurry of feathers and launched themselves over the hedge.

'It's all so sudden.'

'Exactly. I think these dramatic *coups de foudre* are rather to be distrusted, don't you? And Maynard's always had a most *loyal* nature, whatever his other faults.'

'It's not that I don't feel he's fond of me—'

'He's never cared for a woman before. Never. Never even been in lust, never mind anything more elevated. In fact, I can think of nobody less likely to—' He came to a halt. 'I ask you, is it credible that a man who for twenty years pursues only men, should suddenly fall in love with a woman? And *such* a woman? Maynard is the last man to be dished by a pair of pretty legs. I mean, it's about as likely as Queen Victoria having it off with Gladstone.' He leant forward confidentially, although there was nobody who could conceivably overhear. 'I doubt he can *do* it with her, you know. I really doubt it.'

'She's an odd choice.' Sebastian ran his hand along the top of the gate. 'Not educated. Though not stupid, either, I don't think. Not remotely beautiful; a kind of *jolie laide*. And with no knowledge of *anything* that matters to Maynard. Unworldly, I think, despite everything—' A splinter of wood pierced his skin and he broke off, sucking his finger.

'Of course, Duncan wasn't educated either. *And* he's unworldly. That charms Maynard oddly, given that he's so worldly himself. He does so love to look after people.' Lytton snorted disparagingly. And Sebastian, watching the sunlight winking on Lytton's spectacles, and the expression of malice behind them, recalled various stories he had heard over the years: as for example, how Maynard had helped Lytton settle the terms of a publishing contract, and that Lytton then blamed Maynard for making £20,000 less from his American sales than he should – although the Woolfs had commented that hindsight was a fine thing, and nobody, least of all Lytton, had ever expected *Queen Victoria* to sell as it did. Or how Lytton and Maynard had vied bitterly for possession of Duncan many years ago, resulting in the spreading of poisonous rumours about the triumphant Maynard by the vanquished Lytton, some of which still reverberated around Bloomsbury to this day. Finally, he recalled the well-worn tale that Duncan had been the great love of Maynard's life.

'She *is* possibly the same type as Duncan,' he ventured. 'A kind of wise fool.'

'Artistic, not cerebral.'

'But she's *female*.'

'And there's your answer,' said Lytton at once. 'For that reason, you will always maintain your place. It's a temporary madness. For you, it's just a matter of playing the waiting game.'

As if the subject had been conclusively settled, Lytton turned and led the way back towards the house. Smoke was rising in columns from distant fields, where farmers were burning off the couch grass. 'Like funeral pyres,' thought Sebastian in melancholy mode, building on this to further meandering fancies of Maynard and Troy, which he decided not to share with Lytton. But still: *what a Helen!* And who would *he* be in this scenario? Patroclus surely, to Maynard's Achilles … which would demote Lydia from Helen to the lowly Briseis – a much more satisfying notion, even if he could not picture Maynard as Achilles: he could not imagine him raging on the shore among the ships. No, Maynard was surely the canny Odysseus, if he was anyone … but then was Lydia the faithful Penelope? Or was she only the seductive Circe, spinning her enchantments? He shook his head at his foolish-ness, and walked more quickly to catch up with Lytton.

'Of course, if you wanted to, you could *push* things a little, provoke a showdown.' Lytton threw the words over his shoulder.

'I thought you said I should wait.'

'Yes, but it might be wearing on the nerves. Why not push Maynard into a corner: *force* him to choose?'

'And what if she–?'

'Well?'

'Fights back?'

'We'll see, won't we.' Lytton's eyes glittered. Sebastian thought uneasily of single combat before the Gates of Troy. Strangely, it was easier to picture Lydia with sword and armour than Maynard. She would make an agile and formidable opponent.

'I don't know, Lytton. It's not in my nature.'

'Even to stir the embers a little?'

'It's hard now he spends so much time in London.'

'Then lure him elsewhere, further away than Cambridge. Somewhere male company will be *so* much more enticing.'

'We always said we'd go to North Africa.'

'Perfect! Remind him of it. Maynard hates to disappoint.'

Above them, on the terrace of the house, a small figure appeared, her short hair flying in the wind, a tweed jacket hugged around her: Carrington, who loved Lytton dearly, and did not seem to care that much of his time was spent in pursuit of men.

'But remember, you are one of us,' Lytton shouted over his shoulder, his stride lengthening. 'And so is Ponzo. He's always valued friendship above everything else. It's his credo. His raison d'être. He won't go against his friends.'

For a moment, Sebastian felt displeased, even insulted, both by the use of Maynard's old nickname, invented by Lytton and designating a sewer, and by the suggestion that Maynard would choose Sebastian simply to please old friends. But he was not given to taking offence, and besides, the most important thing was that Lytton thought he would win. He walked on, the columns of smoke transformed into beacons of hope: for after all, pyres were lit by the victors, weren't they?

21

Lydia, walking towards Victoria Station, could tell to the second the moment when Maynard's mood changed. Until then, he had been remarkably jaunty. He had worked enormously hard all week and was now (he declared) undoubtedly in need of diversion, and what better diversion could there be than a party? And what better party than a Bloomsbury party? And what better Bloomsbury party than a party hosted by Vanessa, at Charleston, with his dearest Loppy in attendance?

Dear Bloomsberry, echoed Lydia, *Dear Vanessa, Dear Charleston*. But not aloud, because then Maynard would have been able to hear her tone of voice, which was not affectionate. But it was something of a comfort to say it inside her head. And luckily, Maynard took it for granted that she was looking forward to the party just as much as he was, and had not seemed to find anything lacking in her spirits.

She had packed the night before with Lottie's help. 'Here you are, Miss Loppy.' Lottie had handed over the silk petticoat and glittering dress. 'No, look, you don't want to cram it in like that. Let me do it.' Lottie shook out the dress then folded it painstakingly length and crossways, before placing it gently in Lydia's suitcase.

'Very nice. In the theatre, my dresser tell me off too. I crumple up my clothes.'

'But you don't want to spoil them. Not when you have such lovely things.'

'They aren't really.' Lydia spoke absently. 'On the stage yes, my clothes are chosen for me. But when I choose myself I have difficulty, and so I end up looking, my friend Vera tell me, like Irish washing lady.'

'Not *this* frock,' said Lottie reverently. Lydia was silent. She had in fact put unusual effort into the selection of this particular dress, and while it was gratifying, in a way, to have her success acknowledged – even by one as naive as Lottie – she also felt strangely exposed. She hoped that others would not recognize what it meant, the unusual elegance, especially Vanessa, who had an acute, artist's eye.

'Mr Keynes will think it looks wonderful too,' added Lottie.

'No, he will say he like me best in Russian peasant smock … Men very strange.' Lydia heaved a sigh. 'It shame you not be there.'

'Oh, but I will. I'm going down with Grace. To help out, you know. I wouldn't miss it for the world.' And Lydia had felt her mood lift, and told Lottie warmly that she was so glad that she would have *some* friends there – and then, seeing Lottie's pleased but startled expression, thanked heaven that it was only Lottie, who would not wonder too much about this statement and what it implied.

Gates had carried down her bag (he was always so agreeable, she thought, and yet there was something disagreeable about him all the same) and there was Maynard, waiting by the taxi, full of pleased anticipation and not suspecting her of anything but pleased anticipation too, which meant she had to act as if that really were the case. Not that it was Lydia's nature to do anything else. If you were going to do something, why make a martyrdom of it? And by the time they arrived at the station, she really had convinced herself that it might be quite an enjoyable weekend after all – until, following Maynard towards the entrance, distracted momentarily by petting a passing dog, she had looked up and seen his shoulders stiffen. And known that something was wrong.

'What is it?' She drew level with him.

'Foxy phoned earlier but I forgot to return his call. Now I see why.' The initial disappointment was turning quickly to anger. The shoulders had a set look, as did his mouth beneath its moustache. 'Dammit all! I knew it, but still–'

'But what *is* it, Maynard?'

She took his arm, then followed his gaze to where a newspaper hoarding displayed the headline: BANK RATE RISES TO 4%.

'Oh.'

'Such stupidity. Maybe when my book comes out–'

'You told them and even I understand it. Raise interest rate no good.'

'Not in a stagnating economy. Not with so many unemployed.'

'They say wages must fall. I read it in paper.'

'They do indeed. "Frictionless adjustment," they call it, and we all sail merrily on. It's a bit different for the poor bugger who's taking home half the wage. More to the point, wages don't fall until unemployment rises and *forces* them down. But either way – lower wages or higher unemployment, whatever combination of the two – it won't affect the gentlemen of high finance, sat in their citadel, quaffing their champagne. Do go ahead.' A rather large gentleman, dressed in a business suit, glared and walked around Maynard, who made no effort to move out of his way. 'It makes me so – so –'

'Let's go to France!'

'What?'

'Paris. We get on train for Paris. *There* you forget beastly bank and interest rate.'

Maynard laughed. 'I do adore you, my own Lydochka.'

'So we go?'

'We don't have our passports with us. More importantly, Vanessa would be desperately disappointed. I know she's been looking forward to hosting your first Charleston house party. And it will cheer me up: a bit of frivolity and your company.'

He beamed at her and Lydia shrugged, and accepted defeat. They were about to move on, when a voice said, 'Maynard?' and they turned to see the blinking, startled face of Geoffrey Keynes.

Beneath her hand, she felt Maynard's arm stiffen. He muttered something.

'It *so* very nice to see you.' Lydia tried to make up for Maynard's coolness.

'And you too, Lydia. I'm sorry I haven't seen you dance lately. I wish the Ballets Russes were back in London.'

'Maybe one day. For now, I make my own dance.'

His face lit up. 'Choreographer as well as dancer!'

'Yes. Unfortunately I am not good business woman. And now I have problem with big toe.' She held out her foot and waggled it at him. 'You know foot doctor?'

'Come and see me and I'll take a look.'

'Ah, that will be magnificent.'

'Very obliging.' Maynard's voice was over-hearty. 'But we are getting in everyone's way.'

They had been in everyone's way for some time, but Lydia allowed him to guide her into the station. Geoffrey, however, followed them, determined to continue the conversation.

'I'm off to Cambridge tomorrow,' he announced, as they stepped into a quiet spot behind a pile of luggage, and found themselves able to speak.

'Harvey Road?'

'That's right.'

'Give my love to the parents. I'll be down soon.'

'They've been rather wondering why you spend so much time in London.'

'I've been very busy. These supplements for the *Guardian* …'

'I thought those were finished now. Still, I know you always have a lot on. Where are you off to now?'

'Charleston.'

'It's a party,' interjected Lydia. 'A big outdoor party that Vanessa host.'

'Oh … *Bloomsbury*.'

'I know you don't much care for them,' said Maynard stiffly.

'No?' Lydia looked at Geoffrey, then Maynard, then back again. 'You don't like the Bloomsberries?'

'I wouldn't say that. They are just not my … not at all my … though I did once save Virginia's life.'

'*Wonderful!*' cried Lydia effusively, leaving them to guess whether she meant his saving of Virginia or his opinion of Maynard's friends. Soon after Maynard said, 'Is that the time?' and Geoffrey glanced at his watch and departed.

'You not happy to see him?' asked Lydia, when they had reached their own platform.

'Geoffrey? He's always been a little … dull.'

Lydia shook her finger at him. 'He is different from you, that is all. I have three brothers I never see. You have good brother who like ballet and say sensible things about it. He is sad, would like to be your friend, I can see it.'

'If you think so–'

'I know so.'

'Then we will invite him to dinner.'

'Good.'

'It's just he will run straight to our parents and ...'

'And?'

'Well, gossip. He won't be able to resist it.' Maynard had a sudden vivid image of Harvey Road, so solid, so respectable, and the faces of his parents, so earnest and well-meaning. 'They might even ask to meet you.'

'That would be so terrible? I am horrible monster to be hidden away?'

'No!' He looked at her rather crossly. 'And after all, it's *you* that always stands on proprieties, that insists on separate lodgings, separate bedrooms–'

'You are foolish, Maynard. Geoffrey will say nothing.'

'Oh, I expect you're right. That's our train.' He stepped forward, then paused and looked round at her. 'Next week, I'll send that invite.'

LANTERNS BOBBED AMONG THE TREES, their coloured shades turning the quietness of a rural garden into a kind of Eastern paradise, an impression heightened by the costumes of some of those who wandered beneath the branches. Vanessa had announced that the theme of the party was Ancient Greece and Rome, but this seemed to have been interpreted rather widely: a lady passed in billowing silk, like something from a Persian harem; another leant against an apple tree, in a tunic and turban, with a long cigarette holder dangling from one hand, while her companion, a very thin, monocled young man, was wearing yellow pyjamas; an older man, one of the writers for the Hogarth Press, appeared to have come dressed as an Indian Maharajah.

Entertainment had been provided, including a poetry recitation in the orchard (young Tom Eliot, determinedly *not* wearing fancy dress, tried to escape unnoticed into the bushes but was frogmarched back again); a masque by the pond, with

Roman costumes designed by Duncan; and games on the lawn, directed by Clive, the shrieks and collisions of Blind Man's Buff increasing in proportion to the wine consumed by the participants. The less energetic reclined in deckchairs drinking cocktails, or else just stood around chattering, the smoke from their cigarettes rising to mingle with the leaves. And through these scattered constellations, like a comet, flashed Julian and Quentin, pursued by a boisterous and undistinguished-looking dog who had turned up from a neighbouring farm. They circled three times, then rushed away, drawn by the golden light of the bonfire that glowed in the wilderness beyond the shed.

Anyone observing Lydia would have had difficulty believing she was only present under duress. She had appeared in the first run-through of Duncan's masque, donning a toga over her cocktail dress, to rapturous applause ('Really,' drawled Lytton to Virginia, 'the dear little thing, she'd make the perfect Roman Matron,'); had delighted Quentin and Julian by teaching them 'bad words' in Russian; and had pleased their father by conversing in French, followed by a game of Blind Man's Buff. She had smiled sweetly when asked by various Bloomsberries why she wasn't wearing costume ('Vanessa told us you were coming as Messalina') and sweeter still when various artistic types deigned to explain the nature of ballet to her. Her Russian shrug came in very useful, although one persistent young man kept demanding: 'But you see what I mean about Nijinsky, don't you?' to which Lydia replied: 'I see only that there should be more champagne!'

She had always enjoyed parties, yet she had a sensation at times as if everyone was laughing at her. As she did not generally mind being laughed at – in fact, invited it – it was hard to say why this should be disturbing. *They all look down on me,* she thought, and immediately pushed it away, throwing herself giddily into new conversation. Yet she had a peculiar feeling at times that she was watching herself, and that what she saw was not Lydia but somebody else, wearing an elegant dress she did not recognize, with an air of brittle pertness which did not reflect what lay beneath. It was a performance only: *And not one of my best.*

Maynard was induced to join a group touring Duncan's studio. When the last picture and sketch had been exclaimed over, the rest of the group drifted onto the lawn, tottering slightly and clutching hard to glasses and cigarettes. Maynard remained to help Duncan lift some canvases, which he had brought out for the guests to see, back on top of a cupboard.

'You've produced a lot of new work,' he said, puffing rather, as he manhandled a painting. 'It makes me realize how seldom I've been down lately.'

Duncan said nothing. *And we've hardly spoken, just the two of us,* thought Maynard. *We've not had a proper conversation in a long while.*

'Listen,' he said, seizing the moment. 'Can't you talk to Vanessa? About Lydia and Charleston? Can't you persuade her to take a more rational view?'

'I never argue with Vanessa.'

'But – it's as if she's prepared to put everything we've created here at risk.'

Duncan said nothing. Maynard felt a sense of exasperation. *You're both so damned uncompromising,* he thought. *At least, she is, and you won't go against her because … well, because that's the deal you've made, I suppose.*

'It's such a haven,' he said aloud. 'I can't take Lydia to Cambridge for obvious reasons, and anyway, it's not the same–'

'Maybe you could sneak her into your rooms,' suggested Duncan, 'and scandalize the porters. A woman! In King's! That really would set them all by the ears.'

Maynard did not trouble to answer this. 'And in London,

life has so many stresses. I'd just like to be able to escape from time to time – a week here, a weekend there – without having to rent a place – and to bring Lydia with me.'

'Something will come up.' Duncan picked up another canvas. 'Anyhow, it's much easier at Gordon Square now that Nessa and Lydia aren't sharing a roof.' For Vanessa had instituted another round of musical chairs, and moved her bedroom and studio to 46.

'Yes, but in London I've always got a thousand obligations. Since I took on *The Nation*–'

'How is all that going anyway?'

Maynard was aware that he was being distracted, but it was a relief to vent to Duncan, who had always been a good listener about work.

'Damnably. At least, I'm glad that I've bought out *The Nation* – I'm Chairman now – and it's worth all the time and trouble because it means I've always got a guaranteed outlet for whatever I want to say. The other papers don't always like to criticise the government line. Of course keeping it afloat will be a challenge, but then I like a challenge. I'm hoping Leonard will do the arts pages – did I mention that? Then I'm writing a new book, but it's going slowly … the worst of it is this business of the gold standard.'

'You've mentioned it before, but nothing happened, did it?'

'Sterling was too far from parity. They couldn't bring themselves to make the leap. But the gap's been narrowing.' He frowned. 'The whole problem is unemployment. It hasn't fallen the way it should. That's the great puzzle … of our time really. Nobody can explain it; nobody can solve it. I see glimpses, but … Yesterday the Bank of England raised interest rates by a whole percentage point. It's a clear indication they're readying to take us back on gold. It's criminal; absolutely criminal. It's putting the interest of the financiers ahead of the whole damn country.' He became aware of

Duncan's expression and said stiffly, 'Sorry if I'm boring you.'

'You didn't used to be so concerned with the public good.'

'I'm *not* concerned with the public good!' Maynard's tone suggested this was an insult. 'I've always found an intellectual satisfaction from work, you know that.'

'But you can have the intellectual side, whatever the Bank of England does. All I mean,' said Duncan, 'is why fret? Anyhow, we're being summoned.'

Sebastian was at the door, peering in at them, floppy hair falling over his forehead. 'Come on, you two. There're nightingales in the orchard and whisky in the bottle!' Two more young men came crowding in behind.

With a flat sensation inside him, like champagne that has been left uncorked too long, Maynard followed Duncan out of the studio.

LYDIA SAT on a bench next to the house, under a mass of overhanging honeysuckle, in the sole company of the gentle, earnest Leonard Woolf. Occasionally reaching out to pluck one of the leaves, she half-listened as he told her all about the Cooperative Movement. Lydia knew nothing about the Cooperative Movement, but she was touched and intrigued by Leonard's enthusiasm, just as she was by Maynard's preoccupations with interest rates and national debt.

'… the fact is, we need to find a way of building a socialism which is not purely confrontational. The Cooperative Movement gets away from class war and, just as important, it is a way of building socialism from the grass roots up … '

Inside the house, somebody lit a lamp and the window next to them, which had been dark, filled with a golden glow. Lydia, still listening to Leonard, gazed almost absently into the room beyond. She could see Duncan, placing the lamp on a table, and beyond him three or four men arranging themselves on sofas and armchairs. After a moment, Lydia spotted Maynard and her expression softened. She liked watching Maynard when he was not aware of her. The way he sprawled like a daddy-long-legs, one arm dangling, with a cigarette held lightly in his fingers; the alert glitter in his eye as he followed a conversation that belied his relaxed manner.

Leonard said, 'And this is why I believe the Cooperative Movement is a more constructive alternative to the violent conflict of Marxism. Who wants to risk a revolution, if we can have peaceful evolution instead?'

'Not me,' said Lydia promptly.

'Yet so many on the left seem almost to welcome the prospect of violent struggle. I find it regrettable.'

'Send them to me,' said Lydia feelingly. 'I tell them.'

'I've written some articles on the subject ...'

A young man had joined Maynard on the sofa. He was looking away from Lydia towards Maynard and she craned her neck, trying to identify him. She felt it might be Sebastian. Certainly, Maynard found his presence agreeable: he was smiling at him, nodding, his eyes large and shining. *His flirting face*, thought Lydia. Further off, Duncan was sitting in an armchair with another young man kneeling at his feet. As Lydia watched, he leaned over and ruffled the young man's hair.

Maynard was doing no ruffling, but he still had that intent, bright gaze. The one that made the beholder feel infinitely interesting. His companion turned his head, laughing at some joke, and she could see his profile at last. It was not Sebastian.

No, she thought, dismayed.

Her attention was reclaimed by Leonard demanding, 'Lydia? *Lydia*? So *would* you like me to send you pamphlets?'

'What?' For a moment she was confused, almost as if she

had forgotten where she was. Then she smiled brightly at him. 'My dear Leonard!'

'Yes?'

'I should love to read your pamphlets!'

'You would? Excellent. I'll make sure to send you some–'

'And Leonard?'

'Yes?'

'You have spider in your hair!'

She detached the creature from just above his ear, then delicately set it free in the honeysuckle. Laughing, she leant forward and kissed the startled Leonard on the nose.

DOWN IN THE ORCHARD, where only the occasional lantern glowed like some strangely coloured glow worm, Virginia and Vanessa were wending their way, arm in arm, among the trees.

Some of the time they kept a companionable, sisterly silence; but when this palled, there was nothing more reinforcing of sisterly bonds than some enjoyably scurrilous gossip. Accordingly Virginia remarked, 'She's trying rather too hard, isn't she, our little sparrow?'

Vanessa sighed. 'She's always like that. Still, I really feel her time is almost up.'

'Haven't I heard that before?'

'But this time – didn't you know? – he's going to Morocco, with Sebastian.'

'No!'

'Yes. Sebastian says so anyhow.'

Virginia turned accusing eyes on her sister. 'Is this your doing?'

'What do you mean? It's nothing to do with me!'

'Oh, nonsense! You campaigned to get her out from under your roof, and now you've engineered this – somehow or other.'

'Absolutely not. Maynard may have mentioned it to me, and I did not dissuade him, but it was already arranged.'

'Well – it's not like Sebastian to assert himself.'

'I think Lytton may have encouraged him. With the very best of intentions, of course. We all want what's best for Maynard.' Vanessa took a sip from the glass of wine she held in the hand that was not clasping her sister's waist.

'Then that will surely be the end of it,' Virginia said vigorously. 'I can hardly believe it's lasted this long. He is all intellect, and she … Though actually, I don't think she's stupid.'

'The poor little thing. She'll be weeping buckets when he goes.' Another sip of wine. 'I'll have to try and avoid her.'

Virginia emitted a low shriek and Vanessa's wine glass tipped and emptied onto the grass, as Lydia leapt out from the darkness. 'Boo!'

The sisters stood staring at her. Lydia gazed back with broad friendliness and declared, 'I'm playing hide-and-seek with the children.'

'Lydia! We were just saying …' Vanessa paused, unpleasantly aware of just what they had been saying.

Virginia finished her sentence: 'How much we will miss Maynard when he's away.'

'Away?' Lydia stared.

'In India,' said Virginia, 'with the Royal Commission on Indian Tariffs. Of course it will be a wonderful experience for him.' Next to her, Vanessa let out her breath.

There was a short, painful pause.

'Of course I love for him to have the good experiences,' said Lydia at last. There was a certain determined bravery in the way she spoke: chin raised, eyes confronting them. *Really, one has to admire her,* thought Virginia. *Such a plucky little thing.*

Vanessa spoke hurriedly. 'I need more wine. And I must see what they are up to in the kitchen–'

'*I* will do it. Give to me.'

Determinedly, Lydia removed their empty glasses and walked off in the direction of the house. As the darkness swallowed her, the two sisters turned and looked at each other.

'That was quick thinking about India.'

Virginia raised an eyebrow. 'Poor little abandoned sparrow!'

22

At the kitchen sink, Grace was washing dishes furiously, her lacy mob cap – for the servants too had adopted fancy dress – falling over her forehead and her face flushed and damp. On the range, a kettle was boiling for more hot water, and she was fast running out of drying space for the clean crocks on the counter next to the sink. The room was full of steam, into which, from time to time, Lottie would appear, bearing a tray loaded with dirty plates and glasses which she would set down with a crash on the kitchen table.

'Give us a hand, won't you, Lottie?'

Hearing the door, Grace had half-turned, wiping the hair back from her forehead and upsetting the mob cap which fell into the sink. 'Oh, pardon me, Miss Loppy.'

Lydia came into the room. 'Mrs Bell wants more wine.' She put the used wine glasses down on the table. 'Whoa! This is not kitchen but Turkish bath.'

She moved for the window. 'It don't open,' called Grace. 'That honeysuckle Mrs Bell's so set on don't let it.'

Lydia tutted. 'No air, not good.' She wrestled with the sash, and after a fierce struggle, the honeysuckle was defeated; a rush of cool air came into the room. Grace hoped that the window was not broken.

'No plant beat me,' pronounced Lydia with satisfaction, wiping off her hands. She looked round. 'You are all alone.'

'Lottie should be here, but she's kept busy fetching and carrying. Seems to take her half an hour to bring a tray. She's most likely gawping at something. Still, she's only young,' added Grace quickly, remembering that Lydia was, if not her employer, still 'upstairs'.

'So let her play.' Lydia picked up a dish towel. '*I* will dry.'

Grace made a half-hearted protest; Lydia ignored her. When Lottie came into the kitchen some time later, much of the steam had dispersed, Grace was washing the last pieces of crockery and Lydia was perched on the kitchen table, humming, while brandishing a plate and a tea towel.

'Oh, Miss Loppy! You shouldn't be doing that.'

'No, *you* should,' said Grace smartly.

'This is chance for me to improve domestic attribute,' Lydia announced. 'Drying plate is my summit, I think. I lack kitchen skill.'

'You don't need it,' Grace said respectfully. 'Not when you dance so well.'

Lottie agreed. Lydia jumped down from the table and curt-sied, with an accompanying flourish of her tea towel, then returned to her perch, where she began to hum again.

'Is that a tune from the ballet, Miss Lopokova?' asked Grace as Lottie started to put away plates.

'*Spectre de la Rose*. I once danced it with Nijinsky—'

'Ooh, madam!'

'— before, unfortunately, he go mad. But not because he dance with me, I hope.'

She laughed, and Grace and Lottie joined in.

'If you don't mind me asking, madam, how did you happen to become a ballerina?'

Lydia swung her legs as she dried. 'I go to Mariinsky Ballet School in St Petersburg when I was just a little child. First, day girl, then boarding. It was very strict. We practise many hours each day.'

'Did you miss your family?'

'Yes, although my brother and sister went to the same school. Also, my father drink.'

Grace nodded understandingly. Lottie asked, 'Did you ever see Lenin, Madam Loppy? And all them Bolshies?'

'I left already. I went with Diaghilev to Paris when I was nineteen. I dance with Ballets Russes. Then I go to America.'

Grace said, 'And you never went back? To Russia, I mean.'

'No. I plan to, but always too difficult.' Lydia turned a glass round and round in her hands. When she next spoke it was so quietly they almost missed it. 'But I should like to see my mother again.'

Grace looked up quickly, then back to the sink. Lottie said eagerly, 'I grew up in an orphanage, miss, but we learnt to be maids, not ballet dancers.'

'Miss Lopokova don't want to know about your orphanage–'

'Yes, yes, I want know everything. Sometimes, I think I can't dance. The work is too hard. But for me to be maid, is no good. And now, I don't dance so much, and that no good either.' She sighed gustily. 'Now, I never know when is the next show.'

'It won't be long, Miss Loppy. You're the most popular ballerina in London. It says so, in the paper. I read it myself.'

'And when you do, we're coming to watch. I've been saving up. We'll both go, won't we, Grace?'

Grace nodded. Lydia was touched. 'Yes, you come, but you don't pay. I get tickets especially for you.'

'Oh, miss!'

'Do you want I show you some dancing now?'

Lydia jumped down from the table and began to move gracefully around the floor. 'It was like *this* I dance with Nijinsky. Now *this*, it is called the *grand jeté*–'

Unnoticed, Maynard stood at the kitchen door. He had been searching the grounds for Lydia and unable to find her. Now, totally charmed, he watched as Lydia attempted to instruct Lottie and Grace in how to turn a pirouette.

'That is right, with the arms. If you can, the head move last. The feet should be like this. Very good … It is not easy. Many times I practise. After this we will do the big jump …'

Turning as perfectly as a spinning top, Lydia caught sight of Maynard. Instantly, her posture changed: her arms and shoulders stiff; her expression veiled.

'Oh, there you are, Maynard.' There was a distinct lack of enthusiasm in her voice.

Lottie and Grace returned to the dishes. Maynard held out his hands. 'Bravo! I've been looking for you everywhere.'

Lydia ignored his open arms, picked up her damp tea towel and shook it out, then hung it with unusual care near the stove. Finally, she went to join Maynard. 'Here I am.'

STROLLING TOWARDS THE HOUSE, Virginia and Vanessa were startled to see Maynard and Lydia emerge from the front door, apparently in the grips of an almighty quarrel. Lydia crossed the gravel drive at a run, while Maynard, following, seemed to be protesting or placating. Either way, his remarks fell on deaf ears: Lydia just stood near the gate, arms crossed, and refused to look at him. Virginia and Vanessa had stopped, uncertain, and while they were still hesitating, Maynard and Lydia suddenly shot back across the gravel towards a long, low-slung sedan car. Maynard opened the passenger door, and

Lydia, refusing to look at him, climbed in. He went round to the driver's side, the door slammed, and a moment later they heard the sound of the engine.

'Isn't that Bunny's car?' asked Virginia at length.

Vanessa said that it was.

'I didn't know Maynard *could* drive,' was Virginia's next observation.

Vanessa said nothing. The car was now proceeding bumpily down the lane, between the scattered revellers.

'Well, Nessa, we shall just have to hope that Maynard doesn't crush any of your guests on his way out.'

INSIDE THE CAR, Maynard said, 'How can I be expected to understand what's upsetting you if you won't tell me what's going on?'

'And you always tell *me* what's going on?'

Maynard licked his lips. The car came to a temporary halt at the bottom of the lane. Somebody who looked rather like Lytton waved at them from a grassy bank. They did not wave back.

'Anyhow, you don't understand anything,' Lydia continued. 'Big books full of gobbledegook, you understand – interest rates and stock market – but the rest: nothing!'

Maynard was contemplating the road ahead. It was impossible to see anything on either side, due to the encroaching foliage. Eventually he took the plunge and pulled out and they began to roll forward through a dark and leafy tunnel.

'I understand you're annoyed.'

Lydia bounced round to face him. 'Today the servants ask me about Russia. They want to know.'

'I've often asked you about Russia!'

'Yes, you are interested in everything. But your friends – the *Bloomsberries* – have they ever asked *one thing* – one little thing! – about where I grow up, my family, Mariinsky, St Petersburg? No! Sometimes they explain to me how ballet should be – they, who have never taken one *step* upon a stage.'

'They can be a bit insular. It's their way.'

'And what is *your* way?'

'What do you mean?'

'What of India?' Her voice shook. 'When were you going to tell me about *that*?' She was breathing heavily, her chest heaving.

'About what exactly?'

'That you are leaving me! For *months*! To go among temples and snakes and dancing girls!'

'Are you talking about the Royal Commission on Indian Tariffs?'

'All I know is you leave me!' She leant over, almost across the steering wheel, trying to see his expression. 'And if I ask you to refuse it, will you?'

'Absolutely not.'

'No! You see? Turn here!'

They were approaching a crossroads, where their lane was bisected by a broader road, free of trees, with a crooked signpost. Lydia was urgently signalling left.

Maynard brought the car to a halt.

'Why that way?'

'It's where my friends live.'

'I thought we were going back to London?'

'No. I don't break up the oh-so-lovely house party. *You* go back. I have a good time with *my* friends.'

Exasperated, he turned the car in the direction she wanted. It lurched about, took the bend too sharp, ground its inner workings in loud complaint, lurched again and came to a halt. Maynard tried to get it started and failed.

'Why you stop?'

'Because we're in the ditch.'

'Oh.'

'Hopefully nothing's broken.'

There was a pause.

'Whose car is this anyway?' Lydia enquired.

'Bunny's. Or maybe Leonard's. I didn't actually ask.'

'So we run away in a stolen car?'

Maynard turned and faced her. 'Listen to me. I'm not going to turn down India–'

'Hah!'

'Because I cancelled it long ago. I didn't want to spend so long away from you.'

'Oh.' She sat for a moment, clasping and unclasping her hands. Then, turning to him a tragic face, she wailed: 'But how will Indian tariffs manage without you? Maynard, you think I want to interfere with your work? You think *I* would ever turn down tour of America for you?'

Before he could reply, she had forced open the door and stumbled out of the car.

Maynard shouted, 'Wait!' but Lydia did not wait. He swore, and tried to open his own door, but it was wedged shut by the ditch. Awkwardly, he clambered over the seats and out of the passenger side. Lydia was marching up the grass verge of the lane, much hindered by her long dress. He shouted, 'I don't understand you!'

Lydia swung round. 'But I understand you! You think you can have everything. Journalist and Government and Cambridge and … and everything! Me and … I *saw* you flirting tonight.'

Panting, Maynard drew level with her.

'I flirt with everyone. It's my way. Someone once accused me of flirting with Lloyd George.'

'All right, but still – you cannot take biscuit and eat it!'

'I don't follow.'

'Or maybe cake.'

'Can we leave the baked goods to one side?'

'Or maybe young man.' Her eyes met his. 'Sometimes you have to *choose*, Maynard.'

Whatever he might have said shivered away into silence. At last he managed: 'Vanessa and Duncan ...'

'We are not Vanessa and Duncan.'

'I know. All the same ... there is something I'd been meaning to tell you. I mean, discuss with you. Perhaps you'd already heard that ... well, Sebastian asked me to go on holiday with him. To Morocco. I suppose he's been feeling rather ... abandoned. I said no, but he reminded me that I'd promised him and ... it's true. I *did* say once we'd go to North Africa and now I feel rather bad that–'

'No, Maynard.'

'But–'

'No. Sebastian is good friend. I like him. He come to tea whenever he like. That is very nice. But nothing more. No holiday. Not with him or ... anyone else. You understand me?'

Another pause, during which he wished there was more light to read her expression. It was a bright summer night, but still he could not tell what she was thinking. Nevertheless, her posture was plain enough. Despite her lack of height, she was implacable, remorseless, like a goddess presenting the choice to her victim, no negotiation possible.

'I always thought ... you have never condemned ... and you have your own friends, Sam ...'

'*Friends*, yes. But I choose friends to be friends *only*, whatever they may wish. So now it is your choice to make.'

Leaves rustled in the ditch next to the hedge: some night creature hunting, or perhaps a humble hedgehog in search of its supper. More distantly, an owl called.

'Damn it!' Maynard said. 'I want you. Everything else can go hang.'

As he spoke, he felt the most enormous relief, as if a great weight had been lifted from him. As if, after all, he was sacrificing nothing and gaining ... what? Everything. At the same moment, Lydia launched herself forward. She held him tight and pressed her face into the front of his jacket. He thought she was weeping.

THE MOON FLOATED FURTHER over the hill side, and a cow mooed in a nearby field. They shifted, eased numbed or aching muscles, realigned. 'I have never before spend night in ditch,' said Lydia, with satisfaction. She picked a long thorn out of his hair. 'I never before make love there. And you, Maynard? Have you ever done such a thing?'

'No,' he said, thinking, *I've had other encounters, in places even more uncomfortable and more risky of discovery, but never a ditch.* 'You see, I've always been more of a town-dweller.'

'Me too.' Lydia wound her arms around his neck. Maynard held her, thinking how strange it was that he had once thought he could never successfully make love to a woman. The idea had always seemed preposterous – and yet now, it felt absolutely right. For a while they dozed. Then the cow mooed again and Lydia woke up, much to Maynard's relief, for he was already awake and trying to ignore the cramp in his shoulders and neck. Crawling out of the ditch, they wiped off the grass and grime as best they could, and Maynard went back to the car, while Lydia hopped up and down to warm up, then did ballet stretches, holding on to the wall that ran at right angles to the ditch. Maynard returned a few minutes later, triumphantly bearing not only a travel rug but a bottle of whisky and a thermos. 'Evidently Bunny fears being stranded in the middle of nowhere,' he remarked. 'Good man.'

'Is it right we drink his whisky?'

'Given that we've already run off with his motor car, I don't see why not. Actually, my head won't take any spirits. I'm hoping this thermos holds strong coffee.'

It didn't, but they shared tepid tea while sitting aloft the stile that surmounted the wall. It was just a shame, Maynard remarked, that Bunny had not seen fit to lay in a stock of sandwiches or Bath Oliver biscuits. The tea finished, they lit cigarettes and watched the dawn transform the Downs from a looming darkness into a gilded vista of rolling hills.

After a while Maynard said, reverting to a thought from the night before, 'You know, you don't interfere with my work. In fact, I've been astonishingly productive since I met you.'

'Truly?'

'Truly. Maybe because you actually think it's worthwhile too.'

'But India–'

'Would just have been a distraction. Sometimes, I work so hard to avoid the work I truly need to do.'

Lydia was intrigued. 'What is that?'

Maynard sat for a while, staring at the landscape. *England*, he thought, *at its most bucolic. It could be a Constable … no, in this light, a Turner.* It was hard to believe in any threat or disturbance in this timeless scene. And yet …

He took a pull on his cigarette. 'We're in a new era. Since the war, everything's changed. But the Establishment still holds to the old mantras: the gold standard; free markets; laissez-faire. Grit your teeth in the bad times and wait for the booms. But how far can you push people? Until they rise up and throw the government down?'

He wasn't sure if she'd understand, but after a while she said, 'So you want to save the world?'

'Yes, I suppose that's it.' He began to laugh.

'What is it?'

'You. Somehow you … see everything. And always surprise me.'

'Of course. How will you do it?'

'Through economics. But that's got to change too. It won't fit with this new world. My old teacher, Alfred Marshall – one of the founding fathers if you like – he wrote it all down, all the theory, and taught me what he knew. He was my master, my Cecchetti if you like. But somehow we've got to move on, tear up the old theory and start again. I'm beginning to feel the way … but this is boring for you.'

'No, you're wrong. I like economics. I like the funny pictures.'

'You mean the diagrams?'

'The curves remind me of ballet. Here. Get down now.'

He climbed down from the stile, expecting her to follow. Instead, she passed him her cigarette, then wriggled out of her dress and stood up on top of the stile. There, wearing only a brief silk petticoat, she proceeded to do an arabesque, one arm extended in front and one above her head, one leg supporting her and one stretched out behind. Maynard called out: 'Interest rates against volume of money!'

She laughed. She looked extraordinarily right and beautiful – however incongruous – perched there like some living statue, a breathing, smiling Degas figurine, in the middle of the quintessentially English countryside.

Around them the dawn chorus rose, echoing from hedgerow and copse. Maynard shouted: 'You delight me.'

'It beautiful here. I always live in cities. Always. But …'

'Yes. It feels right.'

She changed her stance then, smoothly realigning herself into an equally beautiful stance, feet in first position, arms above her head. Maynard said thoughtfully, 'You know, you are how economic theory says the world *should* be. A living, breathing embodiment of the neoclassical model.'

She misunderstood him. 'Oh no, Maynard, I am very modern ballerina. Karsavina, Pavlova, they are the classical idea, not me. I have piglet nose and short legs and laugh too much.'

'But you move so smoothly, so efficiently. No fits and starts. Adjusting without strain to reach a new equilibrium. That's how economists think the world *is* – or should be. Always in balance.'

'And is it?'

'No. It's more like that wretched car we stole: the gears jam, the brakes stick. It judders from side to side. You've got to allow for its glitches, or else the damn thing lands us in the ditch.'

'With you driving, maybe land there anyway.'

He laughed, acknowledging the truth of this, but still pleased with his analogy. He held out his arms. Lydia launched herself from the stile and Maynard caught her, staggered and just managed not to fall over. Lydia observed, unruffled, 'Nijinsky has stronger arms than you.'

'I'm sure he does.' Maynard lowered her to the ground. They wandered back towards the car, hand in hand. As he opened the car door, Maynard asked solemnly, '*Would* you give up a tour of America for me?'

'Of course.' She smiled wickedly. 'I've already been to America.' She looked away and the smile faded. 'Russia on the other hand ...'

'What! You would leave me?'

'I haven't seen my family in fifteen years. But don't worry.' She bent her head and climbed into the car. 'It is impossible to go to Russia.'

MUCH OF THE pleasure in a good party lies in dissecting it afterwards. Vanessa and Virginia, in the garden of Virginia's country home of Rodmell, had already enjoyably relived much of the evening – costumes, food, conversations, the manners of the guests – until finally Virginia remarked, a little surprised that her sister had not mentioned it herself, 'And of course Maynard and his little friend, what was the outcome of their *contretemps*?'

A pause. Vanessa's face was stony. Virginia leaned forward to stir her tea, hiding her smile, both pleased and guilty that she had hit upon a sensitive point. 'They came back next morning,' Vanessa said.

'Next *morning*?'

'Around eight. Presumably they'd been making up their quarrel in a haystack. Making it up *somewhere* anyhow. They were all over each other. Billing and cooing like two birds in a nest.'

'How beastly.'

'Yes.'

'And they're still at Charleston?'

'Oh no. They left to catch the London train.'

'Well, thank goodness for that.'

'Actually, I was hoping to get a chance to really *talk* with Maynard, like the old days. So that I could *speak sense* into him. But no, she stuck to him like a barnacle, and then they were gone.'

'What about Bunny's car?'

'It's got a terrible scratch down one side. Apparently it went into a ditch and Maynard and Lydia pushed it out again. I expect *she* did the pushing. She's strong as a carthorse.'

'And certainly *pushy*.' Virginia laughed at the feebleness of her own joke; Vanessa did not smile.

'It's appalling behaviour to run off with other people's property, and they weren't even apologetic.'

Virginia considered, reaching for a cigarette case. 'Well, to be fair, Nessa, none of us approve of possessiveness of *people*, so why should we approve of it with *cars*?'

'Oh, don't be ridiculous! People are people, and cars are ... well ... objects.'

'If you will freely lend your lover, or for that matter, your wife or husband, then why not your car? What did Bunny say?'

'He hardly cared. So exasperating! He's been all over Maynard, ever since Maynard wrote that book; before that he used to say Maynard was a warmonger. Now he says he owes him for getting him out of the draft all those years ago, when really that was just Maynard's blood money.'

'Nessa,' said Virginia, after a pause, 'you must be careful. You are beginning to sound ... *bitter*.'

The distant sound of the river running.

'And worse than that,' Virginia continued, '*irrational*.'

ONCE SEATED in their train compartment, his briefcase open beside him and his writing board on his lap, Maynard's thoughts moved naturally to London and matters awaiting him there. He began at once to write an article for *The Nation*, condemning the recent rise in interest rates; his resurgent anger channeled into a rapid, lucid prose.

'I shall have to go straight to the offices of the *Economic Journal*,' he told Lydia, in the brief interlude between reaching the end of one page and starting the next. 'Editorial meeting.'

'I drop you on way to Gordon Square.'

She was staring out of the window. There was a softness in her expression which caught Maynard's attention.

'What are you thinking?'

'That I didn't expect to like countryside so much.'

Maynard's thoughts were diverted from the outrage of interest rates back to the rolling fields and dawn-touched hills of Sussex. Briefly, he recalled the stile, the warmth of Lydia leaning against him, the birdsong and the distant lowing of cows. With what seemed to him an entirely natural logic, he said: 'Why don't we get married? It's foolish this thing of separate rooms.'

Lydia emerged from her reverie. She gave him an assessing look. 'You mean, like Vanessa and Clive ... and Duncan?'

'No. Like you and me.'

Lydia considered. 'All right.'

They smiled at each other. Then Maynard, humming, returned to his article and Lydia to her contemplation of the landscape. Opposite them, the young businessman whose ears had been turning ever redder during this exchange, retreated even further behind his newspaper. Really, it was not what you expected on your morning commuter train.

So most certainly war had been declared, thought Maynard, as he corrected the final paragraph of his article. Terrible, and yet in some strange way also a relief, to have the uncertainty concluded, to see clearly who one's enemies were: except that to win this war he must not declare them enemies. But still, he knew his objectives, he knew the wishes of those who opposed him, and he knew what was at stake. The battlefields would be committee tables, the airless meeting rooms of government ministries, perhaps even the great fortress of the Bank itself. No swords would be unsheathed, only wit, intelligence and all the powers of persuasion. But what depended on it, however dull and dry the machinery must seem to the uninitiated, was still the stuff of human life: happiness or misery for thousands (maybe millions) of people; and, beyond that, the very fabric of civil society itself. Raising interest rates had been only the opening move in the game. 'They'll bring down a bloody revolution,' he muttered. 'Well, not if I can stop it.'

Girded for battle, he hardly thought of the conflict he had just lost, closer to home; in fact, he did not see it as defeat. He had already scribbled a note to Sebastian, which he would post from London. 'I'm afraid Morocco won't work out. I will be holidaying with Lydia.' He had no doubt that Sebastian, so sensible, so intelligent, so well-mannered, would immediately see what this meant. He would still come to tea with Lydia at Gordon Square, to eat toasted muffins and be perfectly agreeable; there would be no difficulty if Maynard ever met him at High Table; why they might even go horse-riding sometimes on Saturday afternoons. Lydia would not object. She was not vindictive; she would be gracious in victory. She would likely make Sebastian a friend.

It was even a source of strength to know that, as he prepared for this new conflict, the other had been dealt with: that his rear flank, so to speak, was secured. His eyes rested on Lydia. There was still something reserved about her – strange, in a woman who seemed the very embodiment of *un*reserve – but there were depths he had yet to penetrate. She withheld something of herself: not as a game, but perhaps because there were losses she could hardly bear to share with anybody. She could be laughing one minute and the next a thousand miles away; it was part of her fascination, that she had her own hinterland.

Her eyes met his. She smiled briefly and looked away.

23

————

1 924
Gowns flapping like a flock of windblown crows, the dons made their ungainly way from the Provost's Lodge along the walkway towards the Hall. It was a mild evening, and the snapdragons were in full, flushed, flower against the walls. There were distant shouts from the river, where high-spirited undergraduates were punting on the Cam; their more conscientious contemporaries, who had tried to find a quiet, outdoor spot in which to revise, had long given up, as the breeze kept whipping their notes away from them.

The dons were walking fairly straight: they had enjoyed their drinks with the Provost, but only in moderation, remembering that there would be several wines served at dinner and port to follow. They were pacing themselves.

Jack Sheppard found himself next to the new philosophy fellow, Frank Ramsey.

'Lettice well, is she?' Having been assured that she was, he went on jovially, 'I hope we won't see any cutting back tonight, under our new Bursar. A feast is a feast, you know, and needs to live up to its name.'

'I don't think he's one for cutting back.'

'I hope not, unless it's forced on him.'

'Why should it be? Is there a problem with the college investments?' His energies taken up with philosophy and his wife-to-be, Ramsey had little knowledge of the College's financial affairs.

'No, he's done well so far. But that's not to say he couldn't easily get his fingers burnt. There's something of the gambler in him.'

'Well, you should know.'

Ramsey kept a straight-face, but the corner of his mouth twitched. Jack twinkled through his spectacles.

'Indeed I should. I'm stony broke since Monte Carlo. That's why I rely on College feasts, you see, to fatten me up. *I* lost everything: our new Bursar just lost *a great deal*. Let's hope he's more circumspect with the College's investments. Now he's Senior Bursar there's nothing to hold him back.'

Ramsey looked ahead to where Maynard was deep in conversation with one of the College guests, stooping to catch what they said. He did not think Jack really feared Maynard losing King's money, though it was true that Maynard was something of a risk-taker, in all walks of life, compared to most Cambridge fellows, who tended to prefer a quiet, backwater existence. In any case, the truth was that Maynard had been in charge of the College's investments for years; the promotion from Junior to Senior Bursar was little more than an acknowledgement of the status quo.

'What's bothering him?' he asked. 'Looks like he's seen Banquo's ghost.' For Maynard had stopped suddenly, right in the middle of the path, entirely oblivious to his companions.

Jack Sheppard chuckled.

'Look who's coming towards him.'

Ramsey directed his gaze towards the other side of the

court and saw a thickset old man, with a mass of white hair, clad in non-academic evening dress. He looked vaguely familiar.

'Who is it?'

Jack tutted. 'Talk about inhabiting ivory towers. *That*, m'boy, is David Lloyd George.'

Ramsey felt mildly abashed. As the figure grew closer, he could see that it was, indeed, the former Prime Minister and distinguished Liberal politician, with the Vice Provost bobbing at his side. 'I didn't know *he'd* been invited. I thought someone said Churchill–'

'Winston turned us down, so we got the Old Goat instead. But the Provost thought it would be a good joke not to let Maynard know.' *And so did you, you old so-and-so*, thought Frank, noting the gleeful look on Jack's face. But Maynard seemed to have recovered his poise. He approached Lloyd George and they shook hands with every appearance of great warmth, before walking onwards in the direction of the Hall.

Frank whispered, 'But I thought Maynard hated Lloyd George, and everyone knew it.'

'What makes you say that?'

'Well, the things he's written about him, beginning with all that stuff in *Economic Consequences*. Maynard said he was weak, vain, duplicitous – a moral void.'

Jack laughed. 'Lloyd George is a politician. He probably took it as a compliment. Anyway you should have read the earlier drafts. They were a *lot* more insulting, I can tell you.' He leaned towards Ramsey confidentially. 'It was *I* that made Maynard take out the comparison with Neolithic Man.'

'I really don't see how they can bear to greet each other.'

'That's the trouble with you philosophers, you lack prag-matism. Why treat someone as your enemy, simply because they called you a moral void? Or because you think they *are* a moral void? Maynard and Lloyd George have much in common: they are both Liberals, remember. Both prominent in the party. How much more agreeable to be friends?'

'It may be Christian to forgive–'

'And the Old Goat professes himself a Christian, even if Maynard does not.'

'– but to overlook such differences seems to me completely hypocritical.'

Jack tutted again. 'I daresay, after his initial surprise, Maynard and the Goat will enjoy this chance to converse. Did you happen to notice that he was published in *The Nation* last month?'

'Maynard is always publishing in *The Nation*.'

'Not Maynard – the Goat. Come along.'

As they filed into the dimmed Hall and found their seats at the long tables, Ramsey watched Maynard and Lloyd George, something that it was easy to do for they were seated close to each other at High Table, and it was undoubtedly true that they revealed no ill will. Maynard was nodding agreeably, Lloyd George smiling as he spoke, and their discussion ceased only when the Latin Grace was said, after which the Vice Provost monopolized Lloyd George's attention, and Maynard turned his conversational powers to his own guest. Frank himself had plenty of time to reflect, sitting between an elderly fellow who had little conversation except the soup, and a classicist who was deep in ill-tempered debate with the theologian on his other side about the Oxford Movement. He watched the candlelight flickering against the darkness of wood-panelled walls, from which be-ruffled, seventeenth-century provosts peered in tight-lipped inscrutability, and thought fondly of Lettice, and how it might be to be married to her; and of that strange chap Ludwig Wittgenstein, and whether they would ever be able to entice him back to Cambridge from that village where he had buried himself in Austria. Maynard was being very helpful with that. He had known Wittgenstein in the old days, and was determined that he should return, and when Maynard was determined on a thing, and prepared to devote his time and energy to it, then it usually happened, sooner or later. And he continued pondering about Maynard and Lloyd George. Maynard had thought Lloyd George a warmonger, that was the truth of it; and as a fellow Liberal, he had felt more betrayed by Lloyd George's patriotic posturing and jingoistic talk and, worst of all, endorsement of conscription than he ever had by the same talk from a Conservative politician. What had finally provoked him into print was Lloyd George's behaviour at Versailles. Caught between the promise he had rashly made the British public – that the Germans should pay the entire costs of the war – and what was practically and morally possible, Lloyd George had almost inevitably been forced to adopt the subterfuge and double-dealing that Maynard subsequently condemned so publicly.

It was interesting, mused Frank, that although Maynard often claimed to have elevated himself beyond morality, by which he meant the traditional constraints of Victorian Christianity, he had still been completely outraged on discovering that a statesman like Lloyd George had acted with less than total honesty and integrity. Of course he, Frank, a determined atheist, might well have felt the same ...

This train of thought was terminated by the classicist next to him, who turned to Frank and declared waspishly, 'I am sure *you* are familiar with Cardinal Newman's views on the apostolical succession and can adjudicate,' and he was forced to give his attention elsewhere.

At High Table, Maynard was deep in conversation with his guest, Foxy Falk. 'And how is the delightful Lydia?' Foxy had enquired, and Maynard had explained that she was performing in Paris, having accepted the principal role in a new ballet company, bankrolled by a French Count, which hoped to rival the Ballets Russes.

'I have every hope of a transfer to London,' Maynard said, 'and so I urged her to accept, even though the money fell short of what she deserves. It's a real opportunity. She has been experimenting with managing and choreographing her own ballets, but she has not quite the temperament for it.' *This* was a considerable understatement: somebody who struggled to keep track of their own weekly expenses was not ideally placed to juggle those of even a very small production, and Maynard had inevitably become involved, not only in the day-to-day administration of the Lopokova Ballet Company, but in bankrolling the expenses of the productions, and locking horns with Vera Bowen over dividing up the proceeds. Not that this really mattered, for Maynard had inexhaustible energy when it came to financial administration and disputatious correspondence; he also had deep pockets. What *did* matter was that Lydia herself had become anxious and strained. Far better for her to concentrate on what she did best: performing on the stage. And that being so, it must be better for Lydia to make use of her talents in Paris than to sit in Gordon Square, distracted only by the occasional dance engagement, and wondering why, at the very height of her powers, nobody wanted to employ her. It was an example of the scandal of unused resources, thought Maynard crossly, which even more than hardship itself, was the blight of their age: this endless, sluggish economic mire they were stuck in, oozing along like a barely moving river, with a small current propelling things along at the centre, and barely moving pools of semi-stagnant water on either side.

He did not say all this to Foxy, instead remarking lightly: 'Her life in Paris seems to be a whirl of activity. I'm surprised she can fit in any dancing, what with gorging on lobster and visiting the races and buying ridiculous, fashionable clothes. She seems to be running some kind of salon. All her friends have gone out to visit her – Vera, Sam Courtauld and his wife, even Vanessa and Duncan.' This last had given Maynard particular pleasure, though he himself had been unable to join them. According to Lydia, the three of them had got delight- fully tipsy one night and explored various insalubrious neigh- bourhoods, and the following day had been to meet Picasso. He hoped the rapprochement would continue on Lydia's return to London. *If only there were a permanent British ballet company,* thought Maynard. *A full-size, properly funded, profes- sionally run outfit, with headquarters in London. Really, it's ridicu- lous that there isn't.*

This thought he shared with Foxy, who agreed with him. 'Maybe you should found one,' he said, rather mischievously. 'After all, you are the undisputed Bursar of King's, and in charge of all that lovely money.' Then, alarmed by Maynard's expression, he tapped him on the hand with a spoon. 'I'm not serious!'

'I think,' said Maynard after careful consideration, 'it would be beyond what King's could manage at present. We are about to begin a programme of building works. Also, I'm not sure that a male institution would think a ballet company an entirely appropriate project. If we had any dancers among our undergraduates it might be different. We do have talented musicians and actors, but ballet? No.'

'Well, I'm sure you're quite right, though I'd love to be a fly on the wall at the College Council if you *did* suggest it.'

'I'm having enough problems over the building works.'

'Why, what are you proposing to do? Knock down the Chapel?'

'Very funny. No, on the contrary, I want us to choose some- thing worthy of it, but that hopefully won't take three hundred years to build, either. But there are some very backward-looking elements.'

Maynard would have his way, thought Foxy. He had the energy and the conviction, and in the end, however stubborn dons could be, they would fall into line. He thought they had shown good sense, as well as an acceptance of the inevitable, in making Maynard Senior Bursar. Maynard's own investments had done extraordinarily well over these last few years. From the brink of bankruptcy, he had built them steadily to the extent that he was now a rich man. Indeed, in a way, Foxy's presence that evening was a direct result of that achievement. They had met in the City, as usual, to review their portfolios, and Foxy had concluded, 'Well, Maynard, I congratulate you. You wanted wealth and you have achieved it. Short of a crash,' he laughed at the thought, 'I think you are now secure.'

And Maynard had said, 'There's a feast coming up. Come to Cambridge as my guest. We'll toast our success with the College's best burgundy.'

Foxy was fairly certain someone must have dropped out – it was not like Maynard to leave choosing a guest until the last moment – but that didn't alter his pleasure, and he accepted. The wine was every bit as good as he had anticipated, and he had high expectations for the port.

He wondered a bit about Lydia and her trip to Paris. He guessed there must be some problem, but he did not push for information. He felt his suspicions confirmed, however, by the brooding expression on Maynard's face, whenever her name was mentioned. Maynard was not generally a brooder.

Nevertheless, he was brooding now. He had hardly touched his duck, and whether the subject of his ruminations was Lydia, the new building works or the presence of Lloyd George – Foxy did not think Maynard was as at ease about his presence as he appeared – he knew the one subject guaranteed to distract him. 'This matter of gold ...'

Immediately, Maynard was alert. 'What about it?'

'There's a new committee been appointed to look into it, chaired by Austen Chamberlain.'

'Yes, I heard that too.'

'Before that, I'd been thinking they might forget the whole thing. It had all gone so quiet.'

'Only because sterling dipped. They know they can't move while we're still so far from par against the dollar, but as soon as sterling edges upwards once more, the cry will go out: Back to gold! And of course, the more it seems likely to happen, the more the speculators will send sterling higher on the expectation. And then the gold bugs will claim it's near enough par, and back we go, onto gold – even though its level in the exchanges means nothing about its true value. A self-fulfilling prophesy.'

'But this Committee may not agree.'

'I suspect they just want a rubber stamp.'

'Still, they will ask you to give evidence.'

'Yes, and I will put up a fight! But I suspect I'll be the only one.'

Foxy pointed a fork at him. 'If you do it, Maynard, and oppose them openly as your usual rude, arrogant self, you risk being cast out forever.'

Maynard snorted. 'I seem to have heard that before.'

'Well, if you don't care about that, reflect that more flies are caught with honey than vinegar.'

'Meaning what?'

'That you *flatten* people, when you should *flatter* them instead. Maybe you will have to meet them partway. Be strategic. Don't argue *against* the gold standard, just say that this is not the time, that the proposed level against the dollar is wrong. It's worth a try anyway.'

'That's rich! *You* are considered one of the most outspoken men in the City, I'll have you know.'

'Only since I made enough money that I don't need to care.'

Foxy turned back to his duck. Maynard was still meditating on his words, when Lloyd George turned to him and said, in a genial manner: 'So, Keynes, I hear you did good work for the party in the General Election.'

'Ah, the election.' It seemed a surprisingly long time ago, although it had only been last December. He had not stood himself, but had spent many days campaigning for the Liberals, travelling north to speak at large public meetings in Lancashire and Cumbria. 'I'm afraid I hate the sound of my own voice. Other than that, I enjoyed it. I liked meeting the working people, especially in Barrow. They are having a rough deal and are so passionate about politics. But of course, in the end it did no good.'

'The result can't be laid at your door. And now we have a Labour Government, even if without a majority. The first ever; a historic moment. It will be interesting to watch.'

'At least the forces of Conservatism are on the run. And' – Maynard was ever the optimist – 'we shall do better next time.'

'Don't be so sure.' Foxy leant over to join the conversation. 'Yes, Labour are stronger, not surprising when you gave so many working men the vote in 1918. But much of the electorate are frightened, not least by this election result. They'll run to safety: to the Church, the Union, the Monarchy, all the old order. The rich man in his castle, the poor man at his gate. Even the working classes … many of them are deeply conservative at heart, afraid of change, and if this new Government is not a success – well, they too, like the rich and the professional classes, will retreat into safety, and that doesn't mean the Liberals. To be honest, I understand how they feel.'

'But the problems of our times demand radical ideas.' Maynard tapped his finger against the table for emphasis. 'Only the Liberals have that tradition. And only the Liberals can bridge the class divide. I'm predicting a Liberal victory next time

'I agree with Keynes,' Lloyd George said, smiling. 'Of course, I would. I think the Liberals can forge ahead, but we will need to be bold to succeed.'

'Remember too–'

Remember too, they'll look at Germany, Foxy had been going to say: Germany, where in the last year hyperinflation of an extraordinary and unprecedented kind had destroyed the middle classes, decimating pensions and bond yields, turning professors into porters, and their respectable wives and daughters into prostitutes, while ordinary German were forced to transport their wages in wheelbarrows. What better example to scare the British people away from economic experiment? But Maynard would be sure to reply that it was the continuing burden of reparations that had caused Germany to inflate away its debt: in other words, that the blame lay in the Treaty of Versailles. And that was hardly a bone that should be disinterred in the presence of Lloyd George, for risk of sparking off a dog-fight.

So Foxy coughed, drank some water, and took the excuse of a word from his other neighbour to turn away.

Lloyd George looked hard at Maynard. 'I heard that during the election campaign you actually warned the "Gentlemen of the City and High Finance" that they must listen to the voices of reform, if their world is not to be swept away. That was bold.'

'I felt it had to be said.' Maynard was uncertain where this was going.

To his surprise, Lloyd George said emphatically, 'It did. Most definitely it did. Well done. I'm surprised you don't go into politics.'

'Like I said, I hate the sound of my own voice. Giving lectures is bad enough.'

'A silent politician might be just the ticket.' Lloyd George's humour was a little ponderous.

'No, I think I just have to recognize that others have the rhetorical gift and applaud them.'

Lloyd George, widely considered the orator of his generation, nodded his head in acknowledgement of the compliment. Then he appeared to change tack. 'I received a copy of your book, for which I thank you.'

'Ah, I'm glad.'

'Remind me of its title.'

'*A Tract on Monetary Reform*. It's some ideas I've been working on since–'

'A challenging read for a mere politician, I'm afraid. Not that I didn't prefer it to *some* books you've written.' Maynard, who had been about to embark on an explanation of *A Tract's* contents, was silenced. 'Still, I congratulate you, Keynes. We desperately need new ideas. We need to try something different.'

'I agree.' Maynard spoke wholeheartedly. 'What frustrates me more than anything is that so few are prepared to look past the mantras of the nineteenth century.'

'But it will surely take more than jiggling around with bank rate …'

Lloyd George paused, as one of the serving staff bent over his shoulder to remove his empty plate, and in this interlude Jack Sheppard, opposite, leant forward to ask if the Liberal Summer School would be at Oxford or Cambridge that year, and so the conversation moved onto a new track.

The dinner took its stately course, eventually concluding with Sauternes and crème brulée, an address by the Provost, and the chanting of the Latin grace. As one, they rose to leave the Hall. The candles flickered in wavering lines as they processed past the tables; the scholars of earlier centuries gazed down from the walls and kept their opinions to themselves. Outside, it had grown colder and dark. Frank Ramsey made his farewells and set off towards the gate, in search of his Lettice. Jack Sheppard, rather the worse for wear, stumbled against the edge of the path and steadied himself against the indignant Provost. Maynard and Foxy were part of the group that headed towards the winding staircase that led to the Fellows' Combination Room.

In these more intimate surroundings, they sat beneath panelled walls, passing port, snuff and cigars anticlockwise around the mahogany table. Ties were loosened, jackets sagged and academic gowns trailed lopsidedly. The Vice Provost left after one round of the port, the Provost had retired after the dinner, but Lloyd George elected to stay. For a while, the College building works were the subject, and the other King's men teased Maynard, accusing him of visions of grandeur, of wanting to erect gorgeous palaces while the rest of the country was struggling, its postwar dreams vanishing like smoke.

'Considering you come from Nonconformist stock,' Jack Sheppard declared, 'it has to be said that thrift, Maynard, is not your watchword. Saving is an entirely alien concept to you.'

'He's written entire articles on saving!' protested Arthur Pigou. He was the University's Professor of Economics, a tall, athletic, upright figure, and also a fellow of King's. 'And just look at his new *Tract on Monetary Reform* – which I'm very much looking forward to reading,' he added as an afterthought.

'All entirely theoretical,' Jack insisted. 'I doubt Maynard even had a piggy bank as a child. If he did, it was empty.'

Maynard smiled. 'Thrift is overrated, in my opinion. But you slander the Nonconformists. They were prepared to spend their money on all manner of things.'

'Chapels, you mean.'

'And colleges, libraries, meeting halls, entire industries

even. It's easy to forget, living in the south, but when I went north for the election, it brought it home to me.'

'Well said,' commented Lloyd George. 'You might say the same of Wales.' Jack flushed a little at his gaffe, for Lloyd George famously had his roots in the Nonconformist chapels of Wales, as Jack would surely have remembered, had he not been in his cups.

Maynard, intent on his own train of thought, continued: 'The Nonconformists were not savers. They were investors.'

Jack seized gratefully on the remark. 'Surely, it's the same thing.'

'Not at all. Saving is a sock full of coins under the mattress. Investment is taking those coins and making something with them. For all its perceived virtue, saving may do no good at all. It may even do harm ... if that sock stays where it is.'

'Oh, come.'

'Yes, because it is taking money out of the system – money that could be put to productive use.'

'But, old boy,' intervened Foxy, between puffs on his cigar, 'most people don't put their money under the mattress.'

'Not literally. But this assumption that saving is the same thing as investment ... increasingly, I feel that it's a big mistake. Money squirrelled away will do nothing if it is not put to work: if it is all invested in government bonds, say, or goes overseas, or if it is put in the bank but the bank does not advance credit for productive purposes and it ends up languishing, then it is worse than useless.'

Lloyd George had got up to walk about the room, perhaps to ease a stiff back. Now he sat down again, just as Arthur Pigou exploded with an angry huff: 'But, Maynard, that's quite ridiculous! The interest rate operates to equate savings and investment ... just as the price of any commodity operates to equate demand and supply. That is its role.'

'That's what we've always taught. But what if savings *keep* rising – because of hard times, say, and because people expect them to get still harder – and yet businessmen see no reason to invest? As indeed, they often don't, in hard times. Because what's the point in paying for new plant, when you can hardly sell what you already make?'

Foxy, cigar in hand, nodded, but Pigou was only irritated. 'That's ridiculous. It ignores the adjustment mechanism of interest rates. In the situation you describe, they will fall, with the result that people are inclined to save less – because they get less return on their money – whereas businessmen will invest more, as the costs of doing so have fallen, until finally, savings and investment come into equilibrium again.'

And what if the interest rate is deliberately kept high, thought Maynard, *because the sterling exchange rate is given priority over investment levels – as it is for those who want to return to gold?* But this was not the primary point he wished to make.

'Ah, yes, equilibrium. In the same way, I suppose, that wages, being the price of labour, always adjust, until the demand and supply of labour are in perfect balance, which happens instantaneously, more or less, meaning that unemployment is quite impossible. Meaning at present we are all of us subject to a mass hallucination, and have been for several years.'

'But if you're going to question equilibrium, then you might as well just throw out economic theory – all of Marshall's work! I'm sure Dennis Robertson doesn't agree with you. Have you spoken with him? Or with Alfred Marshall himself? He was your *teacher*, Maynard!'

Before Maynard could reply, Lloyd George intervened – and all fell into a respectful silence.

'I have heard a great deal about your building works, Keynes.'

Maynard, like everyone else present, was startled by the

change of tack. 'Not *my* building works: the College's. That is, if we can find plans we all agree on.'

'But you are the driving force. A lot of people are tightening their belts at present, but you believe in pressing on.'

'That's so.' Maynard was still bemused.

'Investing not saving; following your own philosophy. I wonder if that means you agree with what I wrote recently in *The Nation*? I know we have not always seen eye to eye' – he smiled – 'but this time we seem to be singing from the same hymn sheet.'

Several of those present who had not read Lloyd George's article, but did not like to admit it, looked blank; it was Foxy Falk who remarked helpfully, 'You are referring to your proposal for a programme of public works.'

'Exactly! We need to get the unemployed masses back to work; men who fought nobly in the war, now left discarded, like worn-out old machinery. It is time for the Government to step in.'

'*My* attitude–' Maynard began, but was overridden, as Pigou on the other side of the table erupted into speech.

'And this proposal is coming from someone who claims to be a Liberal! Excuse me, I mean no offence, and your intention is compassionate, but you are going about it wrong. Let's talk about wages, which Maynard mentioned earlier. Now, were it not for rigidities in the system, then wages would do their job. In this time of unemployment, they would fall, reducing the costs of employment, and so employers would be prepared to take on more workers. Unemployment *would* be eliminated. *Why* does this not happen – or not any longer? Because whereas once a man had to go out and work for what he could, *now* he need not; he draws the dole instead. As a result, wages *cannot* fall beyond a certain level. And see what happens? Having introduced one defect, one rigidity, into the system, then inevitably, we try and introduce another, to solve the problem of the first by introducing a second – by which I mean your suggested programme of public works! However well-intentioned, any investment from the public purse will *not* create new jobs, but only serve to crowd out private investment! What will your response be *then*, I wonder? What further new experiment? Nationalize the banks?'

It was not the way a former Prime Minister expected to be addressed. Lloyd George replied, however, with good humour, 'My National Insurance Act being the original defect, according to your argument? For that is what established what is commonly known as "the dole" for the unemployed. Yet I remain proud of it and would hate to see it swept away. I think it an important part of my legacy.'

'Do you really believe what you say?' Oswald Falk addressed Pigou, genuinely curious. 'What happens when wages drop so far that a man cannot eat?'

'That's ridiculous. A man must eat to be productive.'

'But that is the only constraint in your scheme of things?' Lloyd George was shaking his head. 'It's my Nonconformist background, I daresay, but I see a man as something more than a beast of burden. He has more dignity than that. He is no mere unit of labour and must be treated accordingly.'

Maynard said, 'As an economist, I've been struggling for some years with an inherited body of theory which may be as internally consistent and elegant as the theorems of Euclid, yet which increasingly seems in no way to relate to the realities around us. Arthur, you can't force the world to fit an outdated theory.'

'Have you told Alfred Marshall you find his theories outdated?'

Maynard said nothing.

'Of course not. And you can't, for you have no new theory which can explain anything any better.' Pigou's voice was accusing.

'I was under the impression I had just published a book–'

'Of *monetary* theory. Not one that explains the labour market. Not one that overturns the theory of market equilibrium. These wild notions you put forward ... there is nothing *rigorous* behind them. You just like to play devil's advocate, as you always have. Of course, when politicians write,' he nodded towards Lloyd George, 'you don't expect rigour, but from economists you should.'

'I thought you said you hadn't read my book–'

'Gentlemen, gentlemen!' Jack was alarmed: he was the most senior fellow present and discussions over port were supposed to be kept good-tempered; debate was not supposed to tip into acrimony. In particular, eminent guests such as former Prime Ministers were not there to be insulted. Arthur Pigou, perhaps remembering this also, rose to take leave, his manner towards Lloyd George apologetic, even if his attitude to Maynard was not. Jack determinedly led the conversation into less controversial channels.

It was well after midnight when they left the Combination Room. As they emerged from the stair, Maynard remarked to Lloyd George, 'I didn't get a chance to say so, but I do agree with you about public works. I think it is something that must be tried.'

'I thought as much. *The Nation* is more or less your concern, isn't it?'

'Oh, I wouldn't say that–'

'Oh come. I could detect your involvement from the start. But as for public works – well, it won't be easy. We Liberals have always stood for free markets.'

'But with limits. We must not be bound by dogma. But the whole idea needs exploring, fleshing out a little; some hard figures. How much investment is required? I suspect we are talking about a figure of some £100 million per annum ...'

Lloyd George smiled, as if at the fruition of some scheme of his own. 'You are the one to work it up, Keynes, wouldn't you say? If it can be done before the next election …'

'I'll look into it.'

Lloyd George pressed his arm, then departed. Falk, waiting at a distance with a cigarette, said to Maynard, 'You and the Goat, eh?'

'I know. Whoever thought to see the day? But – he is saying what needs to be said. And nobody else in politics is prepared to say it.'

'He isn't even the leader of the Liberal Party, remember.'

'I know. And Asquith would be furious to think I was conspiring with Lloyd George behind his back.' Maynard smiled ruefully. 'You know, I think he may have planned all this deliberately. He wanted to hook me into working on this scheme.'

'I wouldn't be surprised. But you don't have to fall in with him.'

'No, but he's right about public works, I've felt it for a long time. And somebody needs to do the work to assemble a convincing case. It can't do any harm, even if he is the prime mover. Hopefully Asquith and the rest will see the strength of it.'

A bat swooped across the open sky near the Chapel. They turned their back on it and began ambling across the court in the direction of Maynard's rooms.

'What surprised me,' said Foxy after a pause, 'was the hostility of your colleague.'

'Yes,' said Maynard, after a pause. 'Of course he's a bit of an old stick, Arthur; not much imagination; all muscular Christianity and of course he supports gold … I don't think that Alfred or Dennis …' But Maynard's tone was uncertain. 'Of course, Dennis is a parson's son. He believes in thrift, the Victorian mentality, all that. I suppose it's possible he won't see things my way. I hope not; we've done so much work together.'

'It seems to me it's not just the bankers and the mandarins lined up against you; it will be your own profession too, if you keep to the course you are taking.'

Maynard said nothing.

'It's a good thing you never fear a fight.' Foxy grinned and blew smoke into the night air.

24

Sunday morning. Maynard woke late and remained in bed at King's, there being no need to rise and bid farewell to Foxy, who had been leaving early for his golf. He read Lydia's latest letter, read the newspaper, munched toast and drank tea, then rose, wrapped himself in his old wool dressing gown with the fraying cuffs and went through to his study. The church clocks were chiming across the town and early sunlight flooded his desk. He felt that sense of calm that he only ever had on Sunday mornings in Cambridge: for the next few hours, nothing was asked of him, nothing expected; there would be no interruptions; he could devote himself to whatever task he wished. He wanted to write an article on domestic investment, for *The Nation*. The ideas had been shifting about in his head for some time, and while they were still half-formed, he had resisted putting them down on paper. His conversation with Lloyd George had spurred him on. He would make a start now.

Three hours later he laid down his pen, flexed his aching hand and got up to take his bath. Refreshed, clean and shaved, he put on his light suit, gathered up a couple of articles that he had put to one side specially, plus a pot of flowers he had bought yesterday in the market, and set off for Harvey Road.

It was a pleasant walk and one he knew so well that he hardly noticed the surroundings as he headed across King's Parade, then into the market square and past the Corn Exchange. The streets were quiet, with that indefinable Sunday feeling; just a few people here and there, like him, heading towards their roast dinners. He came out opposite Emmanuel College – he'd known a beautiful youth from Emmanuel once, he suddenly remembered, in his second year: whatever had happened to him? At least he had never seen his name in the wartime obituaries – and turned right onto Regent Street. He wondered if his parents would have guests. He hoped not. In fact, he'd hinted that he would rather like it to be just immediate family, Geoffrey and Margaret and their broods if they happened to be down from London (which was unlikely), but not the usual bevy of aunts and extended relatives. Well, he would see.

It wasn't how he had hoped to break the news. But he really didn't have much choice, unless he planned to let Geoffrey do the job for him: Geoffrey was hopeless with secrets, although so far their parents had remained deliberately or inadvertently obtuse. He would have preferred Lydia to have been there too, even if there were certain embarrassments. Still. What must be must be.

Continuing to walk along Regent Street, his mind went back to the moment when it first became clear that their prospective marriage was not going to be straightforward.

He had been dressing for a meeting of Montagu's dining club; Lydia, who had no plans for the evening, was lying prone across his bed, wearing the men's pyjamas he found so appealing on her and stretching various parts of her agile dancer's anatomy. Adjusting his bow tie, his mind mainly on the topic of the evening ahead – 'Wholesale prices as a guide to underlying currency values' – he had remarked absently, 'By the way, now that we are getting married, you must meet my parents.'

She went still for a moment. 'On that matter–' she looked across at him, her hands curved around her left foot–

'Yes?'

'– there may be problem.'

'What's that?'

'I am already married.'

'What!' Wholesale prices were wiped completely from his mind.

'Yes, to Barrocchi. You *knew* about Barrocchi.'

'I knew, but I thought you were divorced!'

Lydia shook her head. Her gaze resembled that of a mournful dog. 'Not divorced. Only separated. But,' she added hopefully, 'it may be I am not married *really*. You see, we married in America.'

'That still counts!'

'But also, when we marry, I think he is already married to someone else.'

'Ah. That's different.' Maynard, the first surprise subsiding, considered the matter, his practical intelligence already chewing away at the subject. Barrocchi, Diaghilev's former business manager, had left England before the opening of *The Sleeping Princess,* and Maynard had neither met him nor given him much thought. He looked at Lydia, who was sitting watching him with her chin on her knees. 'Where is Barrocchi now?'

'Italy … I think.'

'And this first wife of his?'

Lydia shrugged her most Russian shrug. 'I don't know, but she was American, so maybe … America?'

She met his gaze squarely. Maynard contemplated her.

'So,' he said at last, 'a bigamous marriage over two continents, and involving two parties of unknown address.' He rubbed his forehead and his mouth twitched. 'I suppose this is what lawyers are for. I always knew they must be good for *something.*'

So far, however, the lawyers had failed to extricate Lydia from her marital entanglement, or even to run to earth the other parties, although they were certainly not reticent in billing Maynard for their efforts. Maynard, as the months passed, had refused to be discouraged or at least to give any sign of it to Lydia, who was easily engulfed by despair. And although he would ideally have preferred a logical, tidy progression of events – in which bigamous partner was identified, divorce proceedings initiated, new marriage plans announced – he had finally decided that they should no longer have their actions dictated by the vagaries of matrimonial law. Today he intended to put this into effect.

He was greeted warmly, as ever, by his parents, and evidently his mother had registered his hints, for it was just the three of them. Florence took the flowers and placed them in water, sherries were poured, the latest news of Geoffrey and Margaret, their spouses and children, discussed. Maynard passed over the articles he had saved for them, and his mother reciprocated with a piece on unemployment; Neville showed Maynard a new butterfly he had added to his collection. Lunch was served, and once Gladys had left the room, and Neville had finished carving the beef, Maynard remarked, 'There is someone I want you to meet.'

His parents barely reacted. Florence reached for the roast potatoes, as she replied, 'You know we are always delighted to meet your friends.'

'This is a rather different kind of friendship. I am intending to marry.'

Florence dropped the serving fork with a clang. 'My goodness!' Neville expressed his astonishment by taking off his glasses and polishing them on his tie.

'Who is this young lady?' Florence enquired.

'Her name is Lydia Lopokova. You've probably heard of her. She is a Russian ballerina.'

Florence and Neville gazed at him, dumbfounded. Whatever hints Geoffrey had dropped, clearly they had not registered with his parents. 'Russian,' murmured Neville at last, 'ballerina.' But Florence was equal to the occasion.

'I am delighted for you, Maynard. I've always hoped you would find a partner in life, and I've always felt that it must be somebody … a little out of the common mould.'

Maynard smiled. 'She is certainly not made to any pattern but her own.'

'When can we meet her?'

'Soon. I hope as soon as she gets back from Paris. She is performing in a new production there.'

'A dancer,' Neville began. 'My parents–' and perhaps in fear of where he was going with this, Florence interrupted: 'You know I have always admired women of independence who pursue their own careers.'

'Your mother has been asked to stand for Parliament again,' Neville said, diverted from his original chain of thought.

'If one can be useful, one should be useful.' Florence had recovered her aplomb. She started serving the food again. 'When do you plan to marry?' They both looked at their son expectantly.

Maynard picked up his fork. 'It's a little tricky as she has to get divorced first. And that's proving rather complicated. You see, the marriage was probably bigamous and the first wife has gone missing.'

He leant forward to help himself to the gravy jug, while Florence and Neville struggled to conceal their horror. The only sound was the ticking of the clock on the mantelpiece.

'Still, it will provide time for us to get to know her,' remarked Florence valiantly, at last.

Then, a most unusual proceeding, she got up from her place, regardless of the food cooling on her plate, and came round the table to embrace Maynard. He saw to his surprise that there were tears in her eyes, and after a few moments decided, with relief, that they were tears of joy. His father, unimpressed by this demonstrative behaviour, was applying himself to his dinner; but he would follow his wife's lead on the issue, of that Maynard had no doubt.

Before the roast beef was finished, they were already making plans for when and where their first meeting with Lydia might take place.

THERE WERE children playing in the gardens of Gordon Square. The late afternoon sunlight filtered through the leaves of the plane trees, and the railings sent their shadows across the grass. Two small boys were throwing grass and twigs at each other, in the way of small boys since the beginning of time, while another was squatting by a puddle, pointing out something to his little sister, who was steadily ignoring him as she prodded some poor slug with a fat finger. Three girls in pinafores were making something out of leaves and sticks in the middle of the lawn, and a baby sat very upright in a perambulator, watching all these activities with alert interest, while its nurse knitted and chatted to the other nurse upon the bench next to her.

Maynard, emerging from Number 46, registered all this with approval. It might almost have been Julian and Quentin, he thought with unusual nostalgia, but they were too old for such childish things. Then he proceeded across the pavement to his waiting cab and dismissed the scene from his conscious mind, but his spirits had lifted several notches, all the same.

As the vehicle left Gordon Square his thoughts turned to the meeting ahead. A summons really. He had had to squeeze it in after a day full to bursting with meetings. He hadn't even, he now realised, had time for lunch. Still, it was good to be busy. Gordon Square felt empty without Lydia there.

Last night, after one too many whiskies, he had actually confided his feelings to Vanessa. As had once been her habit, she had tried to console him. 'Poor Maynard! You should eat with us in the evening. We never meant separate dining to apply when Lydia *wasn't*–' She stopped short, abashed, and he'd felt divided: on the one hand, it would be more pleasant, more companionable, to eat with Vanessa, Duncan and the children (Clive, too, if he happened to be around) than by himself; on the other, it was Vanessa who had insisted on separate dining rooms in the first place – Maynard and Lydia to be served in state by the Harlands, while the Bells and Duncan were waited on by Grace. It seemed almost disloyal to Lydia to join the others, although of course it would make life easier for the servants, and most likely Lydia would not mind: she had plenty of company in Paris.

Vanessa then offered to organize a party for Maynard at Gordon Square: a quintessential Bloomsbury party, with dressing-up and acting and dances and rude games. Which was kind, but somehow not really what he wanted. What he *wanted* was Lydia back, and some good news about this damned divorce.

'Perhaps it's no bad thing, Maynard … after all, it gives you time,' Vanessa had said last night, when he had confided his frustration about the continued elusiveness of the former Mrs Barrocchi, aka Mary Hargreaves. 'Time for *what*, exactly?' he had retorted, and she had flushed but continued, unrepentant, 'Time to consider if it's what you *want*,' to which he had replied, 'Dammit! I think we've had too *much* time. At this rate we'll be getting hitched just in time to pick out our beds in some nursing home.' Vanessa had winced at 'hitched', which she obviously thought vulgar – she only liked vulgarities of her own choice – and Maynard had added ruthlessly, 'Anyhow, what about children? We're not getting any younger,' and Vanessa had winced again, and Maynard had allowed himself briefly to feel disappointed in her.

Sometimes recently he'd wondered if his friends actually *wanted* his happiness. But then he reminded himself that lasting friendship was one of those things worth living for and smothered the unworthy thought.

Maynard shifted uncomfortably in the back of the taxi. He had a pile that was irritating him. It was the kind of thing he could have told Lydia about: she had a voracious interest in all physical ailments, her own and his, and no embarrassment in discussing them. When he read her letters, they were full of news about her blisters, her periods and whether or not she could still fit into her costume after gorging on cream cakes. If you were a dancer then you were always intimately aware of your own body: you relied on it for your living, there was no part you could afford to forget or ignore. By contrast, his Bloomsbury friends affected openness, but would have been horrified if he had tried to ask their advice about his pile – just as as they had been when Lydia on a country-house weekend had famously thrown her used sanitary pads into an open fire. Maynard sighed.

I must write to her this evening, he thought, remembering suddenly that he owed her a letter, after two days crammed with appointments.

'Down this way, guv?' asked the taxi driver, and Maynard leant forward and said, 'Yes, that's right.' He shifted his briefcase against his knees.

They entered Horse Guards Parade and drove past the Foreign Office and the India Office. Maynard found he was drumming his fingers. He wondered why Otto Niemeyer had requested the meeting at his office, rather than at a club or restaurant. It seemed very formal somehow. *Maybe he's going to offer you a job*, he thought facetiously and grinned, remembering a long-ago autumn morning in Cambridge, and a hasty motorcycle ride to London in answer to a desperate summons at the start of the war. He tried to imagine Otto saying, 'We need your help, Maynard. You must start at once. Things can't go on like this. We need a new approach and you're the man for that.' He smiled at himself and shook his head.

The taxi came to a halt. Maynard paid his fare, then stood for a moment looking up at the building where he had worked almost every day of the war: His Majesty's Treasury. Ten minutes later he was being shown into Otto Niemeyer's office on the second floor.

Otto rose, shook his hand, asked if he would like tea, then sat himself down again behind his desk, with much fidgeting around with papers and repositioning of his chair. Behind him was a long window, but not much sunlight penetrated the nets and the sombre, Civil-Service-issue curtains. There was a distant drone of traffic from the street.

'A trip down Memory Lane, I suppose,' said Niemeyer, with an attempt at humour. 'I mean for you, coming here.'

'Yes, indeed. Back to the war years.'

'Although I have been here much longer. As I recall, we did the Civil Service entrance exams together in '06. But you went to the India Office, of course.' *Because I came top of the pass list, and you were only second*, was the subtext to that. Maynard was amused.

'A *very* long time ago,' he said pointedly.

Otto huffed a little, fetched out his glasses, polished them on his handkerchief, put them back in his pocket. 'Have you ever regretted …? No, let's put it another way: have you ever thought you might like to work at the Treasury again?'

'My word, Otto. You know, on my way here, I actually

thought *perhaps he's planning to offer me a job*, but I never believed it for a moment. Do you mean I was right all along?'

Otto huffed some more. 'Offer you a job – no, really – but still, it never serves to rule anything out. After all, you do have admirers. I've always been very impressed by the fertility of your mind, your nimbleness in an argument. An institution such as ours, for all its strength, may become hidebound in its thinking.'

You don't say, thought Maynard, in a phoney American drawl. Aloud, he replied, 'I enjoyed my time at the Treasury. Or perhaps *enjoyed* is not the right word, in the circumstances – certainly, towards the end, it was almost more strain than I could stand. But it was stimulating and important work and I was glad to contribute.'

'But not now, in the workaday world of peace?'

'I'm not sure I'm the best person to work within Government. I'd be very constrained in what I could say or do.'

'You might have greater influence however.'

'I doubt it,' said Maynard frankly. 'What are you suggesting, Otto? That if I was a Treasury official then the Chancellor might listen to me about gold? That Montagu Norman would decide I was right about interest rates after all?'

'Chancellors are unpredictable animals. Who knows? Who are they more likely to trust than their own officials? Surely not a Cambridge don with a sideline in writing for the press. *When* he can get published. I've heard you had to resort to buying your own magazine. But my point is rather different.' He coughed, then said, speaking very deliberately: 'Which *is*, that if you go on the way you are going, then the possibility is gone forever. That all credibility will be lost.'

Maynard considered this, the tips of his fingers pressed together, in a stance familiar to Niemeyer from numerous economic discussions.

'So, hypothetically were I to want a job–?'

'It's nothing to do with *jobs*. As you know, the Treasury rarely appoints outsiders in any case.'

'I'm a bit mystified as to what you *are* saying then.'

Niemeyer coughed again, straightened his shoulders. 'When you resigned from the Treasury and wrote that book, it ruffled feathers. Of course you know that. Most civil servants do not resign their job and immediately recount their experiences in the form of a polemical invective, condemning their political masters. This is a profession, above all others, where trust and confidence are paramount.'

'I take your point, Otto, but it was not lightly done. And I was co-opted into the Civil Service because of the war, not by my own career choice.'

'All the same, there was a certain amount of anger and resentment. However, time passes. You have continued to play a role in public life. I won't deny that your contributions are valuable, especially at our monthly Dining Club, which is, after all, designed to be an interchange of ideas from men of all walks of life, prominent in their respective fields and institutions. Even if sometimes you play the role of devil's advocate – or perhaps I should say *enfant terrible* – that, in its way, has value.'

Maynard leant back in his chair. How pompous Otto was! Was this what happened to a man after nearly twenty years at the Treasury? Or was it Otto's inherent pomposity that made the Treasury the perfect fit?

'I say what I think,' Maynard said bluntly. 'I'm not saying I know more than you, or Montagu, or anyone. But institutions have their own biases. So does every profession. Montagu, in particular, spends a lot of time among bankers – dammit, he can't escape them – he probably takes in their prejudices almost by osmosis.'

'But *you* alone remain impartial?'

'No, but I'm an academic, so I'm somewhat outside the

usual interest groups. And my journalism has allowed me to
have an independent voice.'

'Ah, yes, your journalism.' Niemeyer reached into his desk
and brought out a copy of *The Nation*. It was folded back to a
particular page. '*Unemployment: Does it Need a Drastic Remedy?*'
he read aloud. '*By J.M. Keynes*. You argue here for a
programme of massive public investment directed at bringing
down unemployment rates.'

'Yes.'

'So you are choosing to adopt the tenets of socialism, and
want the state to take over the economy purely for the sake
of it.'

'Lloyd George called for the same thing not long ago. He's
no socialist.'

'Some would disagree.'

'Yes, the most hardened, prejudiced Tory or the most dyed-
in-the-wool supporter of laissez-faire.' Maynard tipped back
his chair and surveyed Otto. 'Anyway, as a disinterested
servant of the elected Government, don't you have to temper
your views a little? Isn't our present Government socialist?'

'The Chancellor, I am glad to say, has a thorough respect for
the tenets of orthodox finance. Mr Snowden attaches the
greatest importance to balanced budgets and sound money.'

I'll bet he does, thought Maynard crossly. He had a low
opinion of the Chancellor of the Exchequer, Philip Snowden, a
Victorian Methodist through-and-through, who idolized thrift
and had an innate horror of any kind of debt; surely the kind
of Nonconformist that (contrary to Maynard's own remarks to
Jack Sheppard on the subject) would never have built a college
or a meeting place – or not if it required borrowing a penny to
do so.

'You make my point for me,' he said aloud to Otto, 'that
this is not about political ideology. You can be of any political
persuasion and still be unsure about what is the best solution

to what is, ultimately, an economic problem. We have unemployment that is stuck at about one million. The evidence is surely overwhelming that the free market alone will not solve the unemployment problem.'

'Keynes, you know perfectly well if the State steps in and invests money in public works, all that will happen is that it will crowd out equivalent investment by the private sector. The country will be deprived of business investment and prosperity, and the recipient of a lot of dubious "make work" schemes.'

'I know that has always been the Treasury view.' *And sadly that of many Cambridge economists*, he thought, but did not say. 'But this whole notion of "crowding out" is based on false premises. It assumes capital and labour are already fully employed. We are looking *now* at a situation where resources are *unemployed* – underutilized – both labour and capital. Public investment need not *crowd out* anything. It will simply take the unemployed and put them to work.'

'Eliminating unemployment payments would achieve the same end.'

'Firstly, we don't know that. I don't think the problems we are seeing at the moment are due solely to the dole. Secondly, we *can't* abolish the dole without risking the most enormous social upheaval. For God's sake,' he added, crashing his chair down with a thump, 'some of these men fought in the trenches. Now they have no jobs and yet you plan to tell them that you will take away their dole as a way of solving the mess we've put them in?'

'We haven't put them in a mess.'

'The war created the mess, and you and I were part of the government machinery that conducted the war. It destroyed the financial and trading systems that preceded it. It almost bankrupted this country and plunged Europe into chaos and now we have to find something new that works. That's our job.

Or the socialists really will take over,' he added. 'Or possibly something a lot worse.'

The two men confronted each other: Maynard with arms folded, his moustache bristling in indignation; Niemeyer, hands clasped neatly in his lap, back ramrod straight, mouth pursed. *You old school mistress, you,* thought Maynard.

'Listen,' he said, more pacifically, 'we are both the same really. We're not ideologues: we're technicians. It's our job to keep the bus on the road. It's not our job to preach some kind of Utopia, whether that's socialism or some lost Golden Age.'

'But you *are* political, Keynes. You need not deny it. You're an active member of the Liberal Party. You are conniving with Lloyd George. I even hear you will be standing for Parliament for Cambridge in the event of another election.'

'That's quite untrue.'

'I have been told definitively that Keynes will be on the ballot!'

'That'll be my mother, Mrs Florence Keynes.'

'Ah … well … ahem, a misunderstanding obviously. But you campaign for them in elections, you speak at their Summer Schools, you dine with their leaders–'

'And bet on their victories,' interjected Maynard cheerfully. 'A very expensive habit when they will insist on losing.'

'And yet you claim to be unaligned.'

'No, I said I'm not an ideologue. I'm interested in making things work. I've always been a Liberal, true, but that's an accidental allegiance. I suppose you could even call it a matter of birth – or class.'

Because the Labour Party is committed to a class war I do not think necessary. And because I detest the Tory Party and its hidebound loyalty to the past, its pig-headed championing of the prejudices of the Church, its suppression of women and homosexuals. But those are not things I am about to discuss with you.

Niemeyer said stubbornly, 'The Liberal Party does have an

ideology, however, Keynes, and one that you seem intent on betraying. It was founded on free markets, free trade, limited government.'

'I know. But we adapt with the times.'

'When you worked here, you were not impressed with politicians. But now you don't, you have forgotten what they are like.' He paused delicately. 'As with your new friendship with Lloyd George.'

That's really getting under his skin, thought Maynard, amused. *I wonder why?*

Aloud he said, 'I have more trust in officials than politicians. We need less ideology and more expertise. I told you … we need technicians.'

'I don't think of myself as a technician.'

'But you surely don't think of yourself as an ideologue? You are a public servant. I'm not arguing for anything ideological; it's merely a matter of polishing up the engine and making it work.'

'Methinks you do protest too much. Whatever you may claim, you are advocating fundamental change. *Dangerous* change. And if you are so happy to give more power to officials–' he stopped short.

'What is it?'

'Nothing.' But Niemeyer was smiling, a secretive look on his face, as if he had realized something in his favour. Maynard felt uneasy. The old devil had come first in those exams for a reason, after all. He was no fool (or, if he was, then he was a clever fool). He had something up his sleeve.

Niemeyer rose to his feet. 'Where is that tea? I shall ask my secretary.' He went to the door, while Maynard continued to regard him suspiciously, still pondering their last exchange. 'Miss Chilperic, we need tea for two, if you please. And biscuits; the *lemon* ones,' he added, with the air of man pushing the boat out. Then he turned back towards his desk, announcing as he did so, 'I want to discuss the Empire.'

'The *Empire*!' Maynard was knocked sideways. He watched Niemeyer sit down, hitching his trouser legs carefully as he did so, then polishing his glasses once more.

'You see the relevance?'

'No, frankly.'

'But you are a defender of the interests of the British Empire? You care what happens to the Dominions? They are close to your heart?'

'Otto, what are you on about? The last time I checked there was still a whole lot of pink on the map. But actually I'm not that concerned about the Dominions, not if that means letting the City invest all our capital overseas, for example. I'd far rather the Empire got on with its business and let us get on with ours.'

'An odd view for a man who once worked in the India Office.'

'The most I ever achieved at the India Office was to arrange an export license for a rare breed of bull. "Th'expense of spirit in a waste of shame." Who said that?'

'Shakespeare. But it's not very apt, in my opinion—'

'The point *is*, I was more than happy to see the back of the India Office.'

'The point *is*, Keynes, the Empire's business is *our* business. Its preservation is a fundamental interest. It cannot just be left to *get on* with things, as you put it.'

'But what's it to do with anything – unless you're talking about some kind of Imperial preference scheme? But you've just been telling me you support free trade.'

'I'm talking about *gold*. The good of the Empire is intimately tied up with the future of the financial trading system. And that all hangs on the gold standard.'

Maynard thought: *It had to be this.* The door opened behind him and Niemeyer's secretary appeared, bearing a tray of tea and biscuits. She glided in, silent and austere as a nun, placed the tray on the desk, then glided out again with never a look at Maynard.

Fussily, Niemeyer poured the tea. 'Of course you will have strong views on tea from your India Office days. I'm fond of Darjeeling. Earl Grey is too perfumed for my taste … lemon or milk?'

'What? Oh, milk is fine. Listen, Otto, I don't see how it helps the Empire to let British industry go hang, and I don't see why the gold standard is such a great thing for it anyway.'

'The Dominions are clamouring to go back on gold.'

'So let them clamour. The point is–'

'We need to show leadership.'

'We need to do the sensible thing. If they want to go back on gold regardless, then let them.'

Niemeyer shook his head slowly. 'You have no conception of the realities,' he said at last. 'The *political* realities.'

'I wish the Dominions no ill, but I would not see British workers sacrificed on a crucifix of gold. To borrow the phrase of … well, some American, I forget who.'

'An *American*,' said Niemeyer distastefully.

'Yes, William Jennings Bryan, I remember now. An interesting man.' *Like Snowden, another supposed radical who failed to see things through.* 'Anyway, I don't think this is about the Dominions. I think it's about the City of London. They would rather invest anywhere but their own country, about which they seem to know less than nothing, and they think gold will facilitate that. Believe me, I've spoken to them,' he added bitterly.

Niemeyer pushed a plate of biscuits across the desk. 'Help yourself. They're from Fortnum's.'

Absently, Maynard put a biscuit in his mouth and crunched it. 'If you want to restore a stable, managed currency system, then I agree; it's in the interests of everyone. But the gold standard is unduly rigid, there's no room for adjustment, the Yanks own all the gold anyhow, and above all else' – he swallowed the biscuit and picked up another – 'if we rejoin at the pre-war dollar par we invite disaster. That's far too high a level for sterling.'

'*Disaster* is a strong word.'

'Yes, but sometimes appropriate. Like, for example, when I pointed out at the Treasury during the war that we were only two days away from national bankruptcy, and that something must be done. It was true, and fortunately, we did. Anyway, *you* just described *me* as dangerous – or implied it. So you can't complain about strong language.' He spoke through a shower of crumbs.

'It is how you are being perceived, and not just by me: dangerous and radical. And I would like to point out that your ideas may be harmful to *you*, Maynard.' For the first time, he used his Christian name. 'I know you are fortunate enough to have a fellowship at King's, but still, you are active in the City, are you not? You have directorships? Emoluments? You serve on government commissions? Even your journalism depends upon your status as a man who moves in high circles.'

Maynard stared at Niemeyer, as the implications slowly sank in. Then: – *Blackmail!* he thought, astonished. And from Niemeyer of all people. He was refusing to meet Maynard's eye, his left hand fidgeting with his tie, his right hovering over the biscuits, as if selecting one from an identical plateful was a major intellectual exercise. There was a mottled flush on his neck. Who had put him up to it?

As if reading his thoughts, Niemeyer added, 'I might say that Montagu Norman knows about this conversation, indeed he even suggested that I speak to you. We think of it … well, as a friendly warning.'

Maynard did not feel it friendly in the least. Ostracism! By

Government and the City, at least in so far as Niemeyer and Norman could effect it. With a sensation of relief, Maynard considered the health of his equity portfolio: at least he need not fear financial ruin. But still, shares could fall as well as rise, he had been wiped out before, and he did not want to be thrown back on his Cambridge fellowship, not with – or so he hoped – a wife and family soon to support. Besides, he had plans: Lydia's career might prove expensive, so might *The Nation*; Vanessa and Duncan needed assistance. Still, he was confident he could always make money. Much more important was the threatened loss of influence.

He crunched two more biscuits, thinking, while Niemeyer shuffled papers on his desk. At length he said, 'I'm not sure why you are so disturbed, Otto. The decision about gold is not mine.'

'What we are *most* concerned about is the Chamberlain Committee. You will be called. It would be immensely helpful if everyone was singing the same tune.'

'Why?'

'Anything else will be … confusing … for the Chancellor.'

'I was under the fond impression that the point of such committees was to consider *all* the arguments.'

'Just think on what I've said. You are the isolated voice on this: is there really any point going out on a limb?' It was a strictly rhetorical question; Niemeyer rose abruptly. 'Did you like the biscuits?' He gazed reproachfully at the empty plate.

Maynard allowed himself to be escorted to the door. As he turned at the threshold, he said, 'It's no good really, Otto. But maybe we can still try to find a way through if we–'

'Think things over. I'm glad you enjoyed the biscuits.'

Maynard found himself on the other side of the door, which shut firmly in his face. He glared at it; then he began to laugh. *Well, at least I ate all your damned biscuits*, he thought.

25

I am the subject of an attempted blackmail, Maynard imagined himself writing to Lydia, as he flagged down a cab to take him out of Whitehall. *By Little Otto at the Treasury, of all people.* A balloon of laughter rose inside him, making him snort, and causing the driver to peer around at him.

As they drew closer to Bloomsbury, his mood subsided. He stopped recalling Niemeyer's face as he issued his threat – like a Victorian maiden aunt about to have a fit of the vapours – and the ludicrous discussion about the British Empire. Instead he recalled Niemeyer's words: *You are the isolated voice on this.* He really had thought better of the Treasury. He might be a gadfly, but that they would try and suppress his independence ...

The cab stopped at Gordon Square. The children had all left the gardens; there was no sign of life.

Maynard heaved himself out of the back – *I'm getting middle-aged,* he thought, *and fatter too* – paid the driver and made his way to the front door. He stood for a moment in the hall, hoping to hear someone, anyone, but all was still.

Then, somewhere above him, a door opened and shut.

Lydia. He almost called out her name, but she was in Paris; he had received a letter from her only that morning. Still, surely that had been his study door? Of course, it could be one of the servants ...

Sebastian's head appeared over the banisters.

'Maynard? That you?' He grinned wickedly.

'Sebastian! What are you doing here?'

'A series of disasters.' Sebastian set off down the stairs, relating the details as he came: a dinner cancelled at the last moment; his host for the evening called away; an unfortunate and complicated misunderstanding about keys. 'So I'm seeking shelter. Lottie let me in. She says Lydia is in Paris and she didn't know when you'd be home, and everyone else is out or away, so I've been sitting here wondering when on earth anyone would turn up or if I should just take the opportunity to rob the silver cabinet. Of course I *could* get the Cambridge train, but I need to be in town again tomorrow and I hoped–'

'It's good to see you.' The warmth in Maynard's voice was genuine and Sebastian flushed with pleasure and surprise. 'This has been ... what a day. Drinks are called for. There is some quite good sherry in the drawing room and I've got some decent Bordeaux stashed in the cellar, if Lydia hasn't used it all up entertaining her crazy Russians. And of course we'll find you a bed. Lottie can make one up.'

While speaking, Maynard had divested himself of his coat and dumped his briefcase on the floor. He picked up the late post from the hall table and began to flick though it.

Sebastian, standing next to him, thought he looked tired. There were bags under his eyes. Missing Lydia? Or just weary of being alone?

'There's no real need to make up a bed ... not if everyone's away. It's a pity to inconvenience the servants.' Sebastian's tone was delicately playful, suggestive. 'After all, when you think about old times–'

Maynard did not hear him. He was staring in a fixed way at one particular envelope. Sebastian, taking a sidelong glance, decided it could not be from Lydia: it was typewritten, and had a neat and official look.

Maynard ripped open the envelope.

'So sherry, then dinner?' Sebastian suggested. 'We could go out, like I said, no need to trouble the servants. Somewhere simple: a good pub maybe. Beer and a pie, that would suit me. Then home to a quiet evening just the two of us–'

'Excellent!' Maynard looked up from the letter, his eyes gleaming. It was as if a torch had been switched on; he glowed with energy and vitality. 'God bless Mary Hargreaves!'

'Who?'

'Sorry, I can't say. Nothing personal, but I must tell Lydia first.'

'Oh, well then, shall we celebrate with a glass of something?'

'No time.' Maynard was reaching for his briefcase. 'I'm off to Paris.'

'What!'

'Yes. I'll pack a bag and get the night train. Will you call for a taxi?' Maynard made for the stairs. Halfway up the first flight, he turned and looked back at Sebastian. 'And of course, do stay here, if it suits you. You can have my dinner. And my bed. But don't trouble with the silver. There's nothing worth stealing.'

'But Maynard – what if you miss the train? Wouldn't it be more sensible to–'

'I won't. But if there's a problem then I'll book into a hotel and get the first train in the morning.' Maynard disappeared upstairs, whistling.

Sebastian went in search of the drinks cabinet.

· · ·

LYDIA STOOD STARING at her reflection in the mirror. She was wearing a navy-blue, sombre suit, conservatively cut with broad shoulders and clean lines, enlivened only by white lapels. She had about her the air of a child dressing up in adult clothing, an impression reinforced by the fact that the suit was slightly too big. Her mouth was pursed up, undecided. Behind her, Vera and the assistant hovered, both with bright smiles fixed on their faces.

'I look like Mrs Prime Minister, or perhaps lady ambassador,' said Lydia at last.

'You look marvellous,' said Vera. 'Of course it's slightly loose at the waist, but that can be adjusted.'

Behind her, the assistant murmured that the suit was '*très chic, très élégant*'.

'But Maynard say he like me best as peasant, in smock or shawl.'

'Lydochka, you are a famous dancer, a woman of society. You need to think more about your appearance. This is very groomed, very refined.'

'But groomed, is that me?'

'It could be,' said Vera firmly, 'if you worked at it. A regular manicure, a good hairdresser, decent shoes–'

Lydia heaved a sigh. 'I feel like I to a funeral go–'

Their attendant smoothly intervened. '*Madame préfère peut-être ...?*' And she proffered another suit, this one a rich wine colour, with a more fitted jacket and lower cut neck. Lydia brightened. Vera considered, head on one side, then shrugged and nodded. Lydia, with her usual disregard for modesty, began at once to undo her clothes and drop them on the floor.

Twenty minutes later the wine-coloured suit had been approved and ordered, and the two women left the shop, both well satisfied: Vera, that she had persuaded her friend to buy an elegant Parisian outfit, albeit not her first choice; Lydia that she had been saved from the garb of an *ambassadress*. Lydia almost skipped onto the street, and her eye falling on the shop opposite, she declared delightedly in Russian, 'Oah, hats!'

'Absolutely not,' replied Vera firmly, also in Russian. 'That's enough shopping!' Although she hated buying clothes, Lydia adored hats, and in Vera's view, already owned far too many of them, mostly unsuitable. She took hold of Lydia's elbow and steered her firmly past the shop, but only to fall prey to a new temptation: 'Cake!'

The two women gazed hungrily through the windows of the *salon de thé*, at the exquisite cakes and the equally exquisite women eating them. 'Well ...' began Vera, stomach rumbling.

'I like best the little tarts with the strawberries,' said Lydia yearningly. 'But I eat too much; too many fancy restaurants. Big Serge says I am getting fat. I do not want him to think I wobble when he comes to watch me dance.'

She set off down the street and rather reluctantly, Vera followed her. Lydia was right, of course, but those little gateaux with the nuts ... 'I don't think you need be *so* concerned about Diaghilev's opinion,' she said, this time in English. 'He's not employing you anymore.'

Lydia said nothing but her expression spoke volumes. How ludicrous to suggest that Big Serge's opinion could ever be considered irrelevant by any of his dancers, whether past or present!

The two women walked on arm in arm. In a more conciliatory voice, Vera said, 'Tell me about rehearsals. I know you're not happy with the count, but are you happier with the dances?'

'I like *Gigue*. It's a ballet set to Bach. Very nice. But the dance at the Lido ...' Lydia clicked her tongue against her teeth.

'What's the matter with it?'

'It is a *love triangle*.' Lydia rolled the words disgustedly on her tongue. 'There are three of us sunbathing, all in bathing costume. I am the married lady, Massine is my husband, but ... guess what ... he likes beautiful young man. So I am to act jealous. But,' she added, 'I don't. I can't. It's not in my nature.'

'I would have thought it a very natural response.' Vera's eyes were hooded.

Lydia shrugged. 'For me, I should ask him to choose. And then, whatever happen, one must act well. No hostility.'

'That's very generous.'

'It is the only way.'

Vera considered this. 'It sounds a rather sensationalist piece anyhow,' she said at last. 'Trying too hard to be modern.'

'Yes, it's always the way now. Shock, shock, shock. I crave something else for the ballet.'

Vera could have pointed out that the Ballets Russes had once made its name (and Lydia's) through shocking its audience. But then it had always done far more than merely shock, whereas Lydia's current performances, under the direction of the self-indulgent count ... She sighed. Poor Lydia!

'Have you heard from Maynard?' she asked, as they stood waiting to cross the street.

'Ah, Maynard!' Lydia gazed into the distance, her expression mournful. Vera watched her warily. 'Sometimes I think we never marry,' said Lydia at last. 'No news on divorce and his friends still do not like me.'

'You aren't marrying his friends.'

'No.' Lydia's mood was sombre, as they began walking up a row of eighteenth-century shops. 'But Maynard's friends are almost like family to him. Still, soon I meet his real family.' She sighed again. 'What if they hate me too?'

They were passing another *salon de thé*. Vera reached a sudden decision. 'For God's sake, let's have something to eat. You don't have to eat anything fattening.'

Lydia nodded. 'But I must leave for my rehearsal by three.' They went in and were seated towards the back of the room.

Nobody was very close and Lydia and Vera had no fear of being overheard, especially as they were speaking English, the language of their adopted country.

'You miss him, don't you?' Vera asked. 'Maynard, I mean.'

'Yes, I miss him. I wonder if he misses me?'

'But he writes every day.'

'No letter yesterday, no letter this morning. That never happen before. And Vanessa and Duncan – who knows what they've said to him? That I was looking fat, and drink too much.' Lydia looked so woebegone that Vera felt compelled to shore her up.

'It is *your* choice if you marry him. You mustn't think that it all depends on him. It is whether *he* pleases *you*.'

They were interrupted by the waitress pushing a trolley of cakes. Lydia eyed the selection of patisserie greedily. 'You could just have a plain biscuit,' Vera suggested, at the same moment that Lydia pointed at the most decadent of the offerings, a concoction of chocolate and nuts, and announced, '*Je voudrais celui-là, s'il vous plaît.*' Vera clicked her tongue, decided she might as well order the same and said, 'I hope you can dance after that. You won't have much time to digest it.'

Lydia was not listening. She ate half her gateau greedily, then gazed pensively over Vera's ear. 'In New York, they paid me $2,000 a week,' she said at last. 'What happen? Now I lose money even dancing for the count. Yes, unless it switches to London, I will be poorer. And I no longer think it will switch to London. If it were not for Maynard ...'

'What are you saying?' Vera's eyes narrowed. 'That if you were rich you would be able to leave him?'

'No. Just that everything I eat, drink, the clothes I wear, depend on him. This evening, I must write to tell him about new suit.' She sighed again.

'And will he object?'

'No, just send money. But *I* mind. Once I had plenty of money of my own.'

Vera frowned, but having been wealthy all her life, not with much understanding. She took a forkful of cake. Lydia, perhaps made confiding by so much sugar, continued: 'Every dancer fears getting old. How do we support ourselves? Our fortune is in our feet, our legs, our arms, which grow weak. And in our face, which grows wrinkly. Even forty is old for a dancer.'

'You're not forty yet!'

'No, but it's on the way.' Lydia licked chocolate from her spoon. 'When I was young I hoped to be actress. I loved to act. I was good at it, and I took lessons in New York. Once I even went on Broadway. Reviews were terrible though.' She made a face. 'If only I were actress, it would be easier. You can act when you are old. But ...' She shrugged.

'Regardless, one should never marry for money,' said Vera, with the conviction of one who would never face that choice. 'Anyhow, Maynard is not the only possibility. There are other men, after all. I think Sam loves you. The other night at dinner ... And God knows, he's rich.'

'Sam has wife.'

'Well, yes, that is true.'

'Anyhow, Sam has not the beautiful soul.'

Vera looked at her in astonishment. 'You are saying Maynard has?'

'Maynard writes such beautiful things. It is not always necessary for me to understand them to know that. He is given up to a higher cause. Like a monk or a holy man. All the time he works for a better world.'

Vera eyed Lydia suspiciously, but Lydia gave no sign that she was joking. 'Well, Sam is benevolent too. He's ... well, he's given a very generous sum to the National Gallery.'

'Yes, but he does not soar. Maynard is the lark that climbs in the sky; Sam the fat partridge hopping on the ground.'

'Maynard is nothing like a lark.' Still, Vera was moved. She laid her hand over Lydia's. 'Don't give up.'

'I don't. But even if I get divorce, am I the wife for him? Am I the right person for grand dinner? For entertaining Cambridge friend? For talking the clever talk with Bloomsbury?'

'It's just polish,' said Vera, rather weakly. 'And I certainly wouldn't worry about *Bloomsberry*,' she added, with more conviction. 'They are nothing like as clever as they think they are.'

'Maybe not, but–' Lydia gave a squeak. 'But I have to go! I will be late!'

Vera turned at once to summon the waitress for the bill. When it came to the theatre both women were consummate professionals who took rehearsals seriously. 'Why don't you go on?' she suggested, as the waitress was intercepted by another customer, and Lydia fidgeted, visibly impatient. 'I'll settle this.'

'Thank you, dear Vera!'

Lydia leapt up and was gone. Vera looked after her tolerantly, then fetched out her purse. She was getting up to leave when she saw that Lydia had left behind her a canvas bag containing, upon inspection, a pair of ballet shoes, several packets of Russian cigarettes and a bottle of vodka. Vera raised her eyebrows at the vodka but was troubled by the shoes. Perhaps she would need them for the rehearsal; it was no great trouble for Vera to drop them at the theatre.

Vera was rather surprised, on reaching the theatre, to find no rehearsal in progress and no sign of Lydia anywhere.

LYDIA, on leaving the *salon de thé*, walked briskly up the street and around the corner. Then she stopped, looked in her purse and checked that she had plenty of franc notes. It was at this point that she noticed the missing bag. She cursed, turned around, then changed her mind and continued on her way, in the opposite direction to the theatre.

Several times she consulted a piece of paper, on which were scribbled directions in pencil, and despite the directions, more than once she had to reverse her steps. She had entered a warren of streets in a shabby neighbourhood, and navigation was difficult. Twice she asked passers-by for help in her Russian-accented French; one of them replied to her in Russian. Once she hesitated on the steps of a shop that sold alcohol, and again at the window of a florist's shop, but both times she went on without entering.

At last she stopped at a door with flaking paint in a nondescript side street and studied the list of names at the side. Ten minutes later, she was standing outside the entrance to the attic apartment: a great many steps up, even for Lydia's dancer's legs. The door opened and a tiny woman, dressed in a full pleated skirt, shawl and colourful headscarf, with huge eyes in a wrinkled face, peered out at her. 'Ah, little Lydia!' she cried, coming forward to kiss her.

'Irina!'

They both wept.

As Lydia followed her into the apartment, and could not help noticing that the woman she had last seen gliding across the stage at the Mariinsky now had a limp, and that her home had a stale, fetid smell.

Inside the tiny space, they sat, drank sweet, black tea and reminisced about St Petersburg: about dancing in *Prince Igor* and *The Fairy Doll*, about private performances at the Hermitage for the Tsar and his family, about the Grand Dukes and their scandalous affairs with the principal ballerinas ('You were far too young to hear anything about that, of course.' 'Oh no,' Lydia replied, 'we knew how they came by those furs and diamonds') about travelling back and forth to the theatre by coach with the strict governesses in attendance ('The toads – how they bullied us') and about their teachers, especially the beloved Enrico Cecchetti.

They grew warmer, more intimate, as they talked, laughing and joking, forgetting their initial awkwardness, and that they had not, after all, known each other well, Lydia being still a child when Irina entered the corps de ballet. Later, their paths diverged: Lydia left Russia with Diaghilev never to return; Irina stayed on and escaped only after the Revolution. Lydia spoke readily of subsequent years, but Irina did not reciprocate and Lydia did not question her. The poverty of her home and appearance told their own story: although less than ten years older than Lydia, she looked much older.

Lydia rose to go. 'I had presents for you, but I am so sorry, I left them behind. But please, have this.' She pressed the wad of francs into her companion's hand; Irina protested, but half-heartedly and Lydia laughed, tweaked her cheek and did her best to turn the whole thing into a joke. Then they embraced and Lydia departed, aware of the slight figure watching from the top of the stairs, and wondering how she ever managed, with her lame leg, to get up and down. She was thankful now that she had forgotten the ballet shoes. They had once belonged to Pavlova, and had seemed like a charming reminder of old times; now she winced at the thought.

Once on the street she wasted no time, but ran for the theatre.

26

L ater that evening, sitting at her dressing table, Lydia remembered her conversation with Vera, and regretted it. So many of her friends were richer than she was. She must not remind them of her poverty, or seem to be asking for pity (or worse still, hinting for handouts). Nor would she remind anyone, including herself, that she was getting older. Youth, even more than talent, was essential to a dancer. Lydia, at the behest of various publicists and managers, had been knocking years off her age for as long as she could remember, but there were limits: *Facts are facts*, she thought grimly. She thought fleetingly of her mother, now in her sixties and struggling to make ends meet, painfully grateful for everything Lydia could send her. It was not how things should be. How much pleasanter to be Vera, and say, 'Money does not matter'. That, truly, was a luxury only money could buy.

Certainly she would never tell Vera about her visit to Irina.

Maynard would be interested and sympathize, which was a good thing, as he would have to foot the bill for her generosity to her former compatriot. But he did not truly know how it felt to be a dancer growing old, because it was too far from his own experience, and she did not wish him to know. Momentarily she thought of New York and her former independence. Then she recalled herself to the here and now.

Her rather haphazard preparations completed – make-up applied, hair coiled up in a high bun – she made her way to the wings, where she peered out at the large number of empty seats, and the less-than-enraptured expressions of the audience. She was right, she concluded, this show would never transfer to London. *Oah!* The simple truth was for all his faults Big Serge was a genius and Count Beaumont was not, and so everything lacked the crucial spark, even though the talented Massine was the choreographer and the dancers, including her, were more than adequate. But what could she do? What choices did she have once this production folded? Go back to England, and the dribs and drabs of only half-satisfying work? Revive the small company she had tried to run with Vera? But she had hated running a company with Vera. Or try and wheedle her way back into the Ballets Russes? She had managed it before more than once, but she had the feeling Big Serge would be less welcoming now. There were other ballerinas, younger and thinner than her. And even if she did succeed, then she would have to go wherever Big Serge took the company, touring the world maybe. Almost certainly, she would have to leave London: which meant leaving Maynard. *I want London and Maynard and Ballets Russes*, thought Lydia. *Also, to be rich woman and famous actress.* She snorted a bit. *You don't want much, do you? Maybe also turn back clock, and get rid of Revolution while you're at it, or else magic whole family out of Russia on flying carpet.* She was more grounded than Vera though; she knew some things could never be.

And then she was dancing, and had no time to think of anything except the steps that propelled her across the stage.

In the interval, she sat in her dressing room, bandaging her foot in an attempt to cushion a blister that would not heal. She glanced at the photo of Maynard on her dressing table. He, like Vera, had lived a golden life. He was generous, but he did not understand that it was humiliating to survive on handouts. Although strangely, thought Lydia, it would not be humiliating to be supported as a wife. Why? Where was the difference? She could not say. She doubted Vera would understand or any of the Bloomsberries – they also had the casual attitude to money of those who had never been short of it. But it was so. *I should like to support myself even as wife*, she thought. *But if I cannot, I cannot. Anything would be better than this.*

She tucked in the end of the bandage and caressed her painful toes. *I should like to give present to Maynard for once. And to know he does not give me money because he is sorry for me.*

Suddenly, it all felt unbearable: she was swept away by a wave of melancholy. Her dressing room felt desolate. Her face, gazing back from the mirror, seemed too wide, too exposed. She began to slap on the greasepaint, more than usual, and as she did so remembered that she had received no letter from Maynard that morning, nor the day before, nor the day before that. Maybe, in this long absence, she was vanishing for him, like footprints swallowed in wet sand. In a fraction of a second, she made up her mind: it would be better to be like Irina than suffer like this; it was time to leave him.

Meanwhile, it was time to earn her wage, however pitiful: dressed as a doll, she must toddle onto the stage and perform her pert little number with Massine. Wondering briefly how many dolls she had impersonated in her life – and puppets, did they count? – she smiled brightly at the stage manager who had arrived to summon her and rose to return to the stage. Nobody, watching her chirpy brightness, would have guessed at the anguish beneath.

It was the final ballet of the evening. She entered from the wings, running across the stage *en pointe*, the audience gasping at her speed; was lifted into Massine's arms; smiled and descended; jumped and jumped again (the audience enraptured, for her jumps had always been her great strength) and almost mid-jump, changed her mind. No. She would *not* give up on Maynard. However hopeless it seemed, this time she would *not* run away. She leapt again, and her heart leapt too. That was the miracle of dance, that however dismal one felt, it could transform one's mood. Regardless of the too small audience, the ache in her shoulders and the niggling blister on her toe, Lydia felt light as thistledown.

Coming out of the wings after the last curtain call, onto the stair that led to the dressing room, she walked smack into Maynard. She blinked up at him, still befuddled by the dimness after the bright lit stage.

'But you did not tell me–'

'There wasn't time. You look wonderful, Lydochka.'

'You see performance?'

'Yes, it was marvellous. I've been searching for you all day, but you were nowhere to be found, and I did not want to tell you just before the show. The most wonderful news.' She could see his face clearly now: he was beaming. He fetched out a letter from his jacket and brandished it at her. 'She's been found. Mary Hargreaves.'

'Barrocchi's wife?'

'Of course.'

Lydia started to tremble. She took the letter, her hands shaking.

'They have evidence of the marriage and also witnesses who can swear that she was alive when you married Barrocchi. That's enough. We can ask to dissolve your marriage.' He blinked down at her. 'But what is it, Lydochka? Why, you're weeping.'

· · ·

ONCE MAYNARD HAD LEFT Gordon Square in a flurry of raincoat and suitcase and evening paper, Sebastian soon recovered his equanimity. After all, he had pretty much given up on Maynard as a prospect, and there was something rather touching in his eagerness to get to Paris and see Lydia. Hopefully he would make the train. Like a true Stoic, Sebastian decided to make the best of things: he told Lottie, who was passing through the hall, that he was going out for dinner, put a bunch of door keys in his pocket and set out for the pub. He found a place to his liking, thick with smoke and Irish brogue, moved on eventually to another even darker and dingier (this one full of handsome lads from the docks), and returned to Gordon Square after midnight, where he climbed the stairs in unsteady fashion and went into Maynard's bedroom. He collapsed, fully clothed, onto the bed, and remembered nothing more.

At four he awoke with a raging thirst. He stumbled to the bathroom, drank down some cold water, relieved himself, and returned to the bedroom, where this time he pulled down the sheets and blankets and removed his clothing before climbing into bed. He lay for a moment staring up at the ceiling, breathing in the pub smell of stale beer and cigarette smoke (if there were any lingering undertones of Maynard it was impossible to detect them). Then, like a stone dropped into a well, he plunged back into dreamless sleep.

Eventually he woke again, and drifted slowly towards consciousness, watching the birds fluttering outside the window (he had not troubled to draw the curtains). The need for more water drove him out of bed, and he wrapped himself in a dressing gown of Maynard's. On the landing he encountered Gates bearing a coal scuttle.

'Good morning, sir.' Gates's frog-like eyes fastened on his with a peculiarly avid quality, then flickered towards the bedroom door behind him. 'It's Mr Sprott, isn't it?'

'Yes. You're …?'

'Gates, sir.'

'Right,' said Sebastian, vaguely resenting the encounter.

'We haven't seen you so often lately, Mr Sprott.'

'I don't recall seeing you at all,' said Sebastian bluntly, and walked past Gates into the bathroom.

He would have forgotten the exchange, except that on returning to Maynard's bedroom he noticed that the door, which he was fairly sure he'd left standing open, was now closed. He looked to see if anybody had brought up tea, a newspaper, or laid a fire, but there was no sign of anything changed in the room. (So where had Gates been carrying that coal scuttle?) He checked to make sure his wallet was in his jacket pocket: it was, and if lighter than he might have hoped, this was most likely due to his own evening activities, of which he had only the haziest memories.

He put it out of his mind, until later the same day, sitting on top of a London bus, he wondered suddenly if that man had thought … if he'd assumed … and if so, whether he planned to tell Lydia. Given that less than a year before Sebastian had considered her his rival, it was strange how much he disliked this idea. But what could he do? It would hardly help if he, Sebastian, were to write her a note of explanation. *Appearances to the contrary, I was not fornicating with your beloved in your absence, I simply needed a place to sleep. When shall we next have tea?* Nor did he fancy going to discuss the matter with Gates. Anyway, most likely he was imagining the whole thing, and jumping to the most far-fetched conclusions.

He stared out through the grimy window, his thoughts coiling uneasily like smoke.

THE WELL-DRESSED and prosperous stockbroker Oswald Falk was not often these days in Whitehall, and felt rather out of place when he did venture there. Waiting outside the meeting room of the Chamberlain Committee, he was glad when the doors opened and a throng of sombre-suited gentlemen poured out into the lobby. He had no trouble picking out Maynard, who always made a striking figure due to his height, and who was today unusually grim-faced. He stubbed out his cigarette and rose, raising a hand so that Maynard would spot him.

Maynard, who had been loping towards the exit, veered around to greet him.

'Foxy!'

'You look very impatient to be gone. Had you forgotten our lunch?'

'No, no – let's just get the hell out of Whitehall.'

Foxy raised his eyebrows, looked beyond Maynard towards where Otto Niemeyer, flanked by others of the great and good, was emerging into the lobby – he recognised Arthur Pigou and John Bradbury, the former Permanent Secretary to the Treasury, among them. He pulled a face. 'Right-oh. Let's find a cab.'

Making their way to the street, he wondered what had upset Maynard; it was unusual for him to be so rattled. Certainly he wouldn't have thought that a hearing of the Chamberlain Committee could do it. But he bided his time, keeping up a light chatter about the current state of the markets, until they were actually sitting with their plates of dover sole and their glasses of white wine at a restaurant near Lincoln's Inn patronized mainly by the legal fraternity. ('I'm actually feeling quite kindly towards lawyers at the moment,' Maynard said.)

'So? How did it go?' Foxy asked. 'I take it they didn't fall on your neck and declare "This blasted gold standard! The scales have fallen from my eyes. A pox upon it and all its children!"'

Maynard barely smiled. 'No.'

'They were hostile?'

'No more really than I expected ... given who the panel are.'

'I saw Niemeyer – Pigou – Bradbury. They wanted to make sure, didn't they? Or rather, Montagu Norman did.'

'Oh yes. They know the result they want. No surprise there. But I think I made a mistake, Foxy. I tried to trim and to meet them halfway, when I should have stood firm. And then ...' He looked grim and speared a piece of fish with his fork.

'You wanted to find a consensus. It's the only way. To find a solution everyone can accept.'

'Yes, but this time it made me look weak, or that's my fear. Of course, I said all my usual stuff about the need for a constant price level and not being constrained by sterling; how my book shows it's better to target internal domestic prices and we need to set interest rates to that end. Talked about unemployment. Talked about deflation, and the inflationary risks, too, imported from America if American prices rise–'

'Very clever.'

'Too clever by half, you mean. They don't take it seriously as a threat. In their minds, all it suggests is that sterling is likely to rise naturally towards par, as American prices rise. That's as far as they see. Hence, no reason to wait–'

'Did you mention gold licensing?'

'Yes, but that was a mistake too. It's a detail, a distraction.' Maynard chopped up his fish savagely. 'I should have stood four square – stressed, and *kept* stressing, the damage deflation will do; talked about lower wages, unemployment, injustice, workers on the street – a bloody revolution.'

'We know they don't give a damn about those things.'

'True. They are afraid of course, but their only idea is to crush dissent. In fact, as unemployment makes the bargaining position of the unions weaker, I'm not sure they don't even welcome it. A mass of unemployed, disorganized, apathetic, undernourished humanity, out of sight in the northern towns and cities ... that suits them very well. Just as a shambolic, weakened Germany, lurching from crisis to the next, also suits them. But it's hardly a strategy is it? For the long term? Or maybe it is, I don't know.'

'You sound unusually cynical.'

'Sometimes I think of myself as Cassandra in the Trojan War – the only one who can see disaster bearing down, desperately crying out her prophecies of doom, only to be laughed at and ignored. Even my friends seem to think I'm a bit of a bore.'

'Not all your friends.'

'No. Not you and not Lydia either. Of course, Lydia is one of the few among us who has experienced true disaster.'

'Still, you may have done more good today than you realised.'

'No, all I've done today is muddy the waters. I can't think why I tried to soft-soap them–'

'Actually, I was the one that suggested it.'

'– but all I've done is concede ground.'

There was a melancholy pause, during which Foxy had time to register as a consoling fact that the fish was excellent, as was the Bordeaux. He doubted Maynard had tasted any of it. 'Is there more to it?' he asked. 'You seem more shook up than seems warranted.'

Maynard snorted. 'Niemeyer sandbagged me.'

Foxy raised an eyebrow. Maynard continued, 'Oh, he got Austen Chamberlain to do his dirty work, but Otto was behind it. They raised the whole issue of credibility. According to *my* scheme of things, who would control credit, they asked? *Somebody* has to, if there is no gold standard to do it for us. *I* said the Bank of England. Really, they said? A *private* institution? I said the Bank was so much more than that: *heaven-sent* I think I called it–'

Foxy laughed.

'I know, I thought I'd try flattery. Yes, that *was* your advice, wasn't it–'

'Mea culpa.'

'Only flattery doesn't come naturally. I think they thought I was joking, although actually I was deadly serious. I *do* think the Bank should do the job. Well, someone has to. Anyhow, then Austen develops the theme and says, how would I stop a Chancellor of Exchequer running up the deficit indefinitely, without the discipline of gold? To which I say there is no way to stop a really wicked Chancellor of the Exchequer – that is precisely why we need an electorate so they can kick him out.'

'I doubt they liked that.'

'No, so I made a few more grovelling remarks about the Treasury and the Bank containing many fine and upstanding gentlemen who could well look after our credit supply–'

'It *is* a point, though, Maynard. Without gold, the politicians *do* hold more sway. Or their officials.'

'Of course they do, but you have to choose. *Who will guard the guardians?* I forget the Latin–'

'*Quis custodiet ipsos custodes,*' said Foxy obligingly.

'I should have used that on Otto: he loves a Latin tag. But Latin was never my strong point. Anyway, it's always a problem. But at the end of the day, you can't automate the entire world. Not if you need to retain some flexibility. And you certainly shouldn't tie yourself to a completely arbitrary, pointless, immovable object, by which I mean the bloody gold standard, just because it *is* immovable.' Maynard lapsed into a brooding silence.

'Why blame it on Niemeyer,' Foxy asked, 'if it was Chamberlain asked the question?'

'Oh, I think I was there when he got the idea. That time he hauled me into the Treasury. I don't think I told you about that, did I? "Are you happy to give power to officials?" he said then, or something like that, and it was as if some little light bulb lit up in his head. I could see him mentally rubbing his hands. He put together the whole ambush, I'd put money on it. I came back at them but, as you say, in the end it *is* almost unanswerable. If you have a Governor of the Bank of England or a Chancellor of the Exchequer hell-bent on ruining the country, you probably *are* better off on gold – or *anything* that limits their power of action. But the truth is, at the end of the day, they *do* have power, lots of it, and they can ruin the country anyway. So what can you do?'

'It's since the Labour party started winning seats en masse that they all got so worried,' Foxy observed. 'Sooner or later we'll get a Labour majority, no Liberals needed, and then we may see *real* socialists in charge. I don't much like the idea myself.'

'I thought you were predicting a Tory resurgence?'

'I think the Tories will benefit from fears of socialism, and the socialists will benefit from fear of the Tories, and it's the Liberals in the middle who will be squeezed.'

'What a charming prospect. Anyhow, that's why we need a strong Bank and strong Treasury officials. They transcend politics.'

'Except that you *do* think the Bank and the Treasury are getting it all wrong at the moment. They're the Unholy Alliance pushing us back on gold, more so than the politicians.'

'Yes, that's the paradox.' Maynard gave the glimmer of a smile. 'That's why cunning Otto has been so clever. It makes me look foolish when I try and argue that they are our natural enforcers. Damn it! We do need them, pig-headed though they are – but we need them to listen to sense!'

'To listen to *you*.'

'That would do,' Maynard agreed. 'Not that I *always* get things right–'

'Oh, come, *now* you're being modest–'

'But I *do* know we shouldn't rejoin the gold standard at the rate of $4.86 to the pound.'

The waiter appeared to remove their empty plates. Refusing dessert, they sat back and lit their cigarettes.

'I'm surprised you're on my side on this, Foxy,' said Maynard, in a reflective tone.

'What do you mean?'

'Well, virtually everyone who works in the City thinks the opposite – they take the Montagu and Niemeyer line–'

'Not quite everyone.'

'– and you can pay a big price for being thought unorthodox.'

'Oh, as to that, I've got as many directorships as I want, and as for the rest, it all depends on whether or not you make money, that's all. If I call the markets right, then I'm all right, don't you know, and they'll do business with me, even if I do hang around with such disreputable types as Mr J.M. Keynes.'

Maynard laughed, then said more seriously, 'You make light of it, but Otto Niemeyer tried to terrorize me, you know.'

'What? Little Otto? He couldn't terrorize his own aunt!'

'I know it sounds ridiculous, and I wouldn't say he was much good at it, but he kept hinting at dire outcomes.'

'Like what?'

'Like my name being mud at the Treasury and that I'd never be able to work there again. That all the City financiers would turn against me and I'd lose my directorships. That my reputation would be blackened and I wouldn't want to live off only my fellowship, now *would* I?'

After a pause, Foxy remarked, 'He obviously hasn't seen your share portfolio.'

'I did think of that. It was comforting.'

'D'you really think he meant it?'

'Afterwards I couldn't help remembering how my journalism seemed to dry up overnight – at least when it was anything criticising official policy, and especially on gold. The editors just stopped returning my calls.'

'I can't see Otto nobbling Fleet Street ... but Montagu ...'

'Could have had a word.'

They fell into a sombre silence. Around them, the restaurant was quiet, most of the legal types having now departed. Both of them felt an unease that neither felt able to put into words.

Foxy recovered his spirits first. 'If it's so, then Monty must have been furious when you bought *The Nation*! After all his trouble!'

'I daresay ... but listen, Foxy. I know you're friends with Montagu.'

'Oh, as to that' – Foxy turned to summon the waiter – 'a joint interest in opera only goes so far.'

The waiter poured them coffee and departed. Maynard stubbed out his cigarette. 'Well, I'm not giving up. I've still got the patriotic line to try: if we do join the gold standard, we'll be in perpetual thrall to the Americans. I thought I'd use it with the House of Commons, if they call me. What do you think?'

'Sounds about their level.'

'The way Otto tells it gold is all about Empire and patriotism. So let's try a bit of bombast.'

'Can't hurt. *Nobody* likes the Americans, so far as I'm aware. Except Winston, of course.'

'But for my main attack, I'll take to print once more. And this time, no messing about. I'll spell it out in words of two syllables. If we want yet more unemployed, I'll say, then go ahead–'

'*Unemployed* has three syllables.'

'Well, but what do you think?'

Foxy pursed his lips thoughtfully. 'You know, Maynard, how about appealing direct to the politicians themselves? Not the backbenchers, the ones who count. They're not frightened of Evil Chancellors. Dammit, they *are* the Evil Chancellors. They don't *want* to be curbed, just because Little Otto and his like think they should be. And more to the point – they'll decide. The Chancellor makes the decision about gold, not the Bank.'

'It's worth thinking about.' Maynard was nodding. 'It's just a pity Snowden is so hidebound.'

'Write your piece and we'll just have to make sure it gets under the right noses.' They downed their coffee and prepared to leave. 'And how is the divine Lydia?' asked Foxy, getting up, and watched Maynard's face brighten. *He really is in love*, he thought.

'Very well. Back from France, and looking forward to our summer holiday. Though I wish the divorce hearing hadn't been postponed. Not that it really matters; we've incontrovertible evidence. But still, it makes Lydia twitchy and,' he added frankly, 'me too sometimes. She's got to give evidence in court, and you know what she's like. If she lets slip that *I* exist, or starts calling the judge names – tells him he's an impudent beetle …'

Foxy laughed, though it was no laughing matter. Then he thought of saying that so long as Montagu Norman had no friends on the bench, all would be well. Instead, he nodded towards the door.

'Look. It's Winston.'

He was coming straight towards them, Mr Winston Churchill MP, his head sunk tortoise-like in the folds of his neck, heading towards a group of diners on the far side of the room. Drawing close, he paused, narrowed his eyes, muttered, 'G'day Keynes,' at Maynard, nodded at Foxy, and moved on.

'Wouldn't have thought this was his kind of place,' Foxy murmured *sotto voce*.

'Why not, eh? Damn good crab.'

Foxy turned, startled, to see Churchill staring at him piercingly out of beady eyes before, with a flourish of his stick, he went on into the restaurant. Foxy laughed. 'I'll try the crab next time.'

AS MIDNIGHT STRUCK on the hall clock in 46 Gordon Square, Gates took out a pad of plain paper and laid it on the table of the empty kitchen. Then he took up the pencil Mrs Harland used for the laundry and grocery lists and began to write in careful, square block capitals.

He did not sign his letter. Instead, he folded it carefully and put it into a plain envelope he had taken from Clive's study. He then took a small piece of paper from his pocket and uncrumpled it. There was a name there, recorded as part of a telephone message left for Mr Keynes. Gates copied it onto the envelope in block capitals then wrote the address: HM TREASURY.

He turned back to his writing pad. He had one more letter to write.

27

Maynard rang the doorbell of a solidly built detached house on the outskirts of Cambridge and listened as its chimes echoed faintly from inside. It was a mild day, and there was a wonderful scent from the old roses growing against the fence. Nevertheless, he felt oppressed by the house: its tiled steps and elaborate, stained-glass porch, surrounded by dark-leaved laurel bushes; the patterned brick in the walls; the square bay windows and the peaked roof with a turret at the top. It was so archetypally Victorian. Of course, so was 6 Harvey Road, his parents' home, but there the nineteenth century was undoubtedly in retreat, and in any case, he was too used to Harvey Road to see it.

The door opened and a woman in her sixties stood smiling at him. 'Maynard!'

'Dear Mary, I came when I got your message.'

'He'll be so glad to see you.' She spoke stoutly, as if with more hope than certainty, but added firmly, 'And I *certainly* am.'

She turned and led the way inside, responding to Maynard's murmured enquiry with: 'He's very weak. But he's fairly content. He will remember you, I hope, but his short-term memory is fading. Would you like some tea? No? Then I'll take you upstairs and we'll have tea afterwards.'

She had turned to face him as she spoke, standing next to the newel post, in a hall that, like the exterior of the house, was also deeply Victorian: the tiles in diagonal patterns on the floor; a pot of ferns in front of a brass fire screen; a heavy, ornate sideboard made, like the banisters, from dark oak. She was somewhat Victorian in appearance too, with grey hair pulled back into a low bun and a high-necked blouse, and yet Maynard looked on her with straightforward affection. Her gaze was intelligent, serious and direct; her blue eyes unassuming.

'I'd like that, Mary. I hope you aren't having too bad a time?'

'Oh my goodness, no! He does like to tell us off – I mean, the nurse and me; insists that we women are foolish creatures. Fortunately, he takes more notice of the doctor.' She hesitated, then said, 'I hope he's not too hard on you.'

Without waiting to explain her meaning, she led the way upstairs and across the landing. Lying in a vast bed, propped up on pillows, her husband looked shrivelled and small, with a long, old-fashioned nightgown and a nightcap on his head: *a bit like Wee Willie Winkie*, thought Maynard, mentally describing the scene for Lydia. *Do you know that nursery rhyme, Lydochka?* Sunlight filtered in through a gap in the heavy drapes. A nurse sat in a corner, knitting, but she rose when they entered and got ready to leave.

'It's Maynard Keynes to see you, Alfred. I'll let the two of you talk together.'

Mary patted his hand, smiled at Maynard and followed the nurse out of the room.

Maynard sat down on the high-backed wooden chair next to the bed. For a while he just watched the old man, who blinked back sleepily at him: Alfred Marshall, former Professor of Political Economy at Cambridge, and the reason Maynard had become an economist. One of the founding fathers of the subject in its modern form – his book, *Economic Principles,* its defining text – and the man who had lobbied and harassed the University until finally they had created a School of Economics and Politics, so that the subject had a degree of its own. He had devoted his entire life into making Economics a respected, rigorous, academic discipline.

I owe him everything, I suppose, thought Maynard surprised, then amended this: *or at least a good deal.*

'It's me, Keynes,' he said.

'Keynes? Maynard? Not Neville?'

'My father sends his regards. I'm sure he will visit soon.'

Marshall snuffled a bit. 'Wanted him to take the Oxford job, you know. Lectureship. Had it all arranged. He wouldn't have it. Still don't understand it.'

'No.' Maynard thought briefly of his father and his long decades working in the University's administration – hard to believe now that he had ever been thought of as a potential academic. Marshall had lost that battle.

'One of the best students I ever had, you know.'

'Yes.'

'But something stopped him: fussy, nervous sort of mind. Lacked boldness. Bit like a woman.'

'Actually my mother *would* have gone to Oxford, I'm sure, under the same circumstances.'

The old man ignored this. 'Thought you were going the same way: chucking it all in for the India Office. A clerk … a pen-pusher.'

'Yes, but then I chucked *that* in to come back here, thanks to you.'

'Knew you'd be good, even though you only did – what was it, a term? – before heading off to London.'

'I'd spent most of my life in Cambridge. I needed to go to London and get it out of my system.'

Maynard looked back on those years, as if through the wrong end of a telescope: the degree in mathematics that had never fully engaged him, although the rest of student life most certainly had; the first-class result, followed by a couple of months studying economics with Marshall. But by then all his friends had left, Cambridge felt stale and he'd been itching to try something new.

The new had not really been the Civil Service: it had been life with Duncan Grant. Not that he was about to explain that to the Victorian Alfred Marshall.

'Needed good men here,' Marshall said. 'Vital for the future. Knew you were good. Like your father but more ... more ... That was the trouble at first. We couldn't get good men. It's better now.'

'All thanks to you,' said Maynard obligingly. Marshall was drooling slightly, he noticed. He wondered if he should wipe the old man's face or simply ignore it.

'But now you're never here. Spend all your time in London – or up north. Campaigning about unemployment.'

Maynard was taken aback. 'I am in Cambridge a good deal.'

'Can't be. Always writing in the papers–'

'I didn't know you read *The Nation*.'

'Mary reads it to me. She tries to keep me amused.'

More drool. Maynard reached a decision, and reached over and gently wiped the old man's chin with his handkerchief. 'You know, my College has no complaints. And I've just published an academic book, my *Tract on Monetary Reform*–'

'Yes, yes–' The old man flicked his hand impatiently. 'But even you only have so much energy. Politics, journalism, the City ...' (His voice died away – had he also said "young men"?) 'It's all distraction. But economics ... choose the premises carefully and you can build a world. And then it's watertight, invulnerable. They can't destroy it.'

Maynard stared at him. That was what *Economic Principles* aimed to be, he thought. Watertight, invulnerable. Like Euclid's Geometry. Start with a few premises and build from there, with elegant demonstrations and beautiful diagrams. Marshall had synthesized the subject, had laid out the basis of economic equilibrium; never set out so fully or explicitly before. The fundamental beauty of free markets, expressed with abstract logic: immutable proof.

Or was it simply an abstract, beautiful, inflexible sterility?

In either case, Marshall was the High Priest, leading the worship at the altar of the twin deities of Supply and Demand. And he, Maynard: was he still the acolyte?

'I'm fighting a battle at the moment,' he said. 'Like at Paris. Against rank stupidity and – if the powerful get their way – suffering and waste. I can't throw in the towel. I need to make them listen, and I can't do that with an article in the *Economic Journal*.'

'Do you really think they'll let you win?' There was pity in the old man's tone. 'But the other – they can't defeat.' Having concluded this speech, Marshall seemed to fall into a doze. Maynard sat watching him, prey to disturbing and conflicting thoughts.

'Goodbye,' said Marshall suddenly, making Maynard start. 'Keep the flame burning.' His pale eyes were moist and watering.

'Don't worry.' Maynard pressed the old man's hand. He sought for something comforting to say, aware that this was probably their last meeting. 'Your achievements won't be forgotten.' He winced mentally at the gaucheness of this, but Marshall seemed satisfied, judging from the closed eyes, the faint smile on his lips. Maynard made for the door, surprised by the prickling in his eyes.

'Don't be like your father,' said Marshall. 'Don't give up.'

'I can assure you,' said Maynard, with some asperity, 'that I have never had the slightest urge to give up.'

The old man chuckled. Maynard went out onto the landing, and the nurse, who had been sitting there knitting, rose to move past him into the room. Maynard paused and blew his nose loudly. Then he went in search of Mary.

'HERE.' Mary Marshall finished pouring and gently pushed the tea cup towards him.

'Thank you.' Maynard helped himself to sugar. They were sitting in the back garden which seemed, in contrast to the house, delightfully light, airy and not at all Victorian. 'He's still very sharp.'

'I'm afraid he will soon forget you've been here. But it will have given him pleasure. He's always thought so highly of you, and was so pleased that he could entice you back to Cambridge.'

'He seemed to want to pass on the torch, so to speak.'

'I daresay. Nothing has meant more to him than economics. And you were his best student.'

Unless it was you, thought Maynard. *Plenty of people still wonder how much of* Economic Principles *was your work.* But if she had contributed and gone unacknowledged, she did not seem to care, any more than she cared that her husband, years after marrying one of the first females to attend the University, should have decided that having women at Cambridge was a mistake, and spoken sternly against the granting to them of full degrees. For Mary, like Alfred, work was the thing. His books had been cherished as their joint progeny, regardless of the name on the cover.

'Maynard, you seem troubled.' Startled, he looked up from his tea and into gentle, blue eyes. 'Don't be. He's not suffering.'

'I know. I suppose, I feel he wants me to carry on the same tradition. That I will always build on his foundations.' He ground to a halt.

'You are bound to go your own direction.' Mary's expression was quite serene. 'You don't have to worry. Who was it who said, *It does not repay a teacher to remain always a pupil*?'

'Nietzsche, I think.'

'Oh!' Mary's composure was briefly shaken. 'I thought it was John Stuart Mill. Anyway, it's still true, regardless. You shouldn't feel constrained, Maynard, certainly not by gratitude. Alfred would have no time for that.'

She smiled at him, her face open and innocent. *Perhaps she doesn't think anything I do will ever really undermine Alfred's legacy. She's certain the fortress can never be stormed. Maybe she's right.*

'You haven't had any cake.' She pushed the plate towards him. 'It's a bit old, I'm afraid, but they say fruitcake improves with time, develops a richer flavour; more depth and complexity.' She watched as Maynard took a slice. 'They say it's the young who are the natural revolutionaries but it's not always true. You were rather a conventional young man.'

Maynard was so taken aback he spluttered crumbs across the table.

'What do you mean?' he demanded when he'd recovered.

'I'm not trying to offend you. And of course, I can't comment on your private life. But you were a very conventional young economist.'

'What about *Economic Consequences of the Peace*?'

(*Conventional, indeed! A disciple of Moore! A member of Bloomsbury! Surely it wasn't so!*)

'Oh well, that caused a great stir, but it wasn't groundbreaking in an intellectual sense. Then there was your *Treatise on Probability*–'

'Years of labour, and young Frank Ramsey demolished the central premise almost as soon as it was published!'

'That is the risk with all research. Dear Frank seems very happy with Lettice, by the way–'

'I said then I'd never attempt anything on the same scale again.'

'But you didn't give up.'

'No, and of course now there is my *Tract on Monetary Reform*–'

'But nothing you've done academically, it seems to me, is truly *radical*, compared to the policies you advocate in the press.'

Maynard stared at her, this decorously dressed, elderly lady, urging him on to … to what, exactly?

She helped herself to more fruitcake. Two pigeons cooed in the chestnut tree, where the sprays of rambling rector hung heavily from the branches, covered with abundant white blooms.

'The thing is,' said Maynard after a pause, 'I grasp things intuitively when I think about policy issues. It is as if I can see what neoclassical theory leaves out: the importance of expectations in markets, of psychology, the contagious nature of beliefs. And the– the *stickiness* of the real economy. That it does not all adapt smoothly like a perfectly oiled machine. But to turn that into coherent theory …' He paused. 'Well, I'd have to pull away the foundations.' *Alfred Marshall's foundations.*

'Then that's what you will have to do,' said Mary Marshall serenely.

Maynard said nothing. For a while they sat and drank their tea.

'Alfred's been very lucky,' he said at last.

'*You* should marry, Maynard.'

'I am doing my best.'

'It's so hard to find the right person?'

'Oh, I've found her. There are … obstacles, that's all. But hopefully nothing that can't be overcome.'

'Oh, I'm so pleased!' She beamed at him. 'I should so much like to meet her, when … when …'

'You shall. We'll look forward to it.'

28

Maynard, sitting very still on the sofa at Gordon Square, a letter in his hand, became aware of Lydia looking up at him from the floor, her face quizzical. 'It's my old master,' he said, running a thread of her hair through his fingers. 'He's died.'

'Ah! I am sorry. He was your Cecchetti. My Cecchetti has flown like seagull to Milan.' She rubbed Maynard's foot consolingly.

Maynard was reading the letter again. 'I must introduce you to his wife. You'll like her. She's a very intelligent woman.'

Lydia patted his foot and did not remark that there were some of Maynard's intelligent women friends that she could have done without. Instead she turned back to studying the score that she had laid out on the rug.

'Maybe we'll invite her to visit us this summer.'

Lydia looked up from the score. She pondered, and after a long pause enquired, '*Where* shall we invite her, Maynard?'

'To Sussex, of course.'

Lydia scrunched up her eyes and considered him. He was still reading the letter and seemed unaware of her scrutiny.

There were two things she wanted to ask: the first was how they could invite anyone to Charleston, when Charleston was primarily Vanessa's; the second was why Maynard even thought they themselves could visit Charleston, when Vanessa had expressly forbidden Maynard from setting foot there if he brought Lydia too. Unless Vanessa and Duncan were going to France ... But no, she had heard Grace discussing arrangements with Mrs Harland only the other day. She hoped Maynard did not have some idea of installing her at an outlying cottage; she was not prepared, at this point, to be a satellite planet in the Bloomsbury solar system.

Of course, the simplest thing was to ask Maynard what he meant, but this she could not do, without revealing that she had heard Maynard and Vanessa quarrelling, and this would be too painful. Lydia did not feel vindictive towards Vanessa, but she felt hurt. And confused. She had known for some time that Vanessa did not love her, but she had not guessed the depth of her contempt until she heard Vanessa shout, 'I just can't bear it, Maynard; she will *ruin* Charleston for me!' What had she ever done to invite such dislike?

'I have a surprise for you.' Maynard was looking at her.

'For me? What is it?'

'Wait and see.'

Maynard smiled mysteriously, turned back to his pile of post and selected another envelope. Lydia wrestled with this new information. The surprise could not be that they were going to Charleston, because Maynard had as good as said that they were going already. And anyway, Maynard did not know that *she* did not know she wasn't welcome there. On the other hand, if Maynard *had* persuaded Vanessa to change her mind, this could not be the surprise, because Lydia was not supposed to know that Vanessa had banned her in the first place. The convolutions made her head ache.

'Might as well be talking to Mr Wittgenstein,' she muttered.

'Or Frank.'

'What's that, Lydochka?'

'Nothing. Just that I am not philosopher.'

'Oh, but you are. Not an Aristotle, but certainly a Socrates—'

'Is the surprise my divorce?' she interrupted with sudden hopefulness.

'No. But do not worry, my Lydochka; even though judicial time sometimes seems to approach geological time, you *will* get your divorce.'

'It makes me feel like grasshoppers in stomach. Can't you come to court with me?'

'We've discussed this before. You mustn't even say a word about me.'

'But you are eminent man.'

'That's nothing to do with it. If you hint that there is anybody involved, besides the errant Barrocchi, it would compromise your case and they might not grant your divorce. In fact, best to say nothing at all.'

'Staying quiet not easy for me.'

'Then pretend you are the Sleeping Princess, *before* she wakes up.'

Lydia laughed. 'I will pretend I am being presented to the Tsar, as I was many times in St Petersburg.'

'If that makes you quiet and respectful, then it will do very well.'

'And with your mother, when I go for tea at Geoffrey's tomorrow, must I be the same?'

'Oh heavens, no! Say to my mother what you like.'

And in fact, whatever nerves there might have been on all sides, the meeting went off extremely well and soon after she visited at Harvey Road with equal success. Florence and Neville might hitherto have known little of Russians or of dancers, but they took to Lydia and she to them. 'It is because we all think *you* so marvellous,' she told Maynard afterwards, only half-joking. 'You are our complete god.' Nobody was so tactless as to mention Barrocchi or upcoming court cases.

And still nothing direct was said about Charleston. Vanessa, Duncan and the children had departed to Sussex some time ago, their servants likewise; August was advancing; and Maynard seemed to be taking it for granted that at some point soon they would be going too. The discussion was not of *where* but only *when*, and of the lengthy tribute to Alfred Marshall that Maynard intended to write while he was there. 'I'm more tired than I'd realized,' Maynard told Lydia. 'My hand keeps seizing up.' He flexed his writing hand to demonstrate. Lydia suggested that perhaps a real rest was what was needed – 'Lie in sun, ride horse, breath country air.' But Maynard responded breezily that writing about Marshall would be just what he needed; a complete break from the rigours of his new book, and besides, he had promised Mary Marshall.

Lydia said nothing. The prospect of Maynard shut up in his study, leaving her to make small talk with Vanessa – a Vanessa who had only been persuaded to accept her presence under duress – was daunting.

It was a bright, sunlit morning when Harland, puffing rather, carried down Maynard's cases. Gates had already brought Lydia's luggage round and it was waiting in the hall, as was Mrs Harland. The other servants had already left for Sussex. 'I just wanted to say goodbye, miss,' said Mrs Harland, and Lydia reached out and shook her hand vigorously, much to Mrs Harland's surprise. Heading out of the front door, Lydia said to Maynard, 'Wouldn't it be wonderful if we had our own place, with our own servants?' but Maynard said nothing. Lydia followed him into the street, wondering if Vanessa would insist on separate dining arrangements at Charleston too.

She emerged from her thoughts to find herself standing on

the pavement and Maynard regarding her.

'Well?'

'Well, what, Maynard?'

'My surprise!'

She blinked, and finally realized: parked at the kerb was not a taxi cab, but a Rolls Royce, a rather familiar looking Rolls … 'That is Sam's car.'

'I've bought it from him.' Maynard polished the side of the bonnet with his sleeve. 'He said you'd always liked it. I'm going to drive us to Sussex.'

Lydia gurgled, and when he demanded to know why, replied, 'I remember last time you drive us in country, we end in ditch.'

'And look how well that turned out,' replied Maynard with aplomb, opening the passenger door. She allowed him to hand her in, and settling back into the familiar leather seats, tried to ignore the jerks and jolts as Maynard negotiated his way out of Gordon Square, or the grinding of gears every time they came to a junction. As urban streets were gradually replaced by suburban villas, she wondered if now that he could afford a Rolls, he might also be able to afford a chauffeur to drive it.

SHE MUST HAVE DRIFTED OFF, for when she next peered out of the window they were passing between tall hedges. She rubbed her eyes, sat up, glanced at Maynard, who was gripping the steering wheel with an intent expression, and then looked out of the window again, in time to recognize the very same crossroads where she and Maynard had quarrelled – and made up – after that fateful party. *So we are going to Charleston.*

The car started up the familiar lane. 'Maynard,' said Lydia, a little desperately, wondering how at this late stage to broach the matter – *you see, the truth is, Vanessa does not like me, and we must respect her feeling on that –*

But he said, 'Just a moment.' And then, with a brief, side-ways smile at her: 'I must admit, I'm remembering now why I love trains so much.' The car lurched around the corner.

And now she could see the familiar building, the red roof and surrounding trees ... but it was only a glimpse. They were past and for a moment she thought he had missed the turn. But the car was turning into a different lane – past some farm buildings – and then they were drawing up in front of a house: white, with simple, plain proportions, nestling in its own trees in a dip beneath the Downs, with Firle Beacon gently rising against the sky behind. Lydia turned enquiring eyes towards him as he ground the car to a halt. He wiped his forehead. 'Well, what do you think?'

'What is this, Maynard?'

'Tilton Farmhouse. I've rented it for the summer from Lord Gage.'

'It is for us? *Just* us?'

'That's the plan.' His face dropped. 'Damn it, you're not *still* insisting on a chaperone?'

'Too late now. I am hitched to your star, like – like donkey to post.'

'Very romantic! Well, then, little donkey – give me a kiss.'

She obliged. A while later they disentangled themselves and he beamed at her. 'It does feel almost like honeymoon, doesn't it?'

Lydia might have responded that few husbands planned to spend their honeymoon writing a twenty thousand word tribute to their former economics professor. But she didn't, because, in fact, she was perfectly happy: indeed, as the weeks passed, she thought to herself with some surprise, happier than she had ever been in her life. Every morning, while Maynard was shut up in his study with Alfred Marshall, Lydia did her exercises, picked fruit from the orchard or kitchen garden or lay in the sun reading, sometimes, to the scandal of the hired help, with nothing on. *It turns out I am complete peasant,* she wrote to Vera. *I love the country life.* In the afternoons, Maynard emerged and they walked on the Downs, inspected the farm's livestock – 'Have you ever thought of pig-breeding as a sideline?' Maynard asked her, quite seriously – and entertained the guests who occasionally came to interrupt their solitude. Among these was Mary Marshall, who arrived by train, clutching a box of Alfred's papers for Maynard to consult, and who was met in the – by now rather mud-spattered – Rolls.

As it turned out, Lydia did like Mary very much, and her liking was reciprocated. It seemed that an elderly academic widow and clergyman's daughter could get along perfectly well with the still-not-yet-divorced Russian ballerina who was also the live-in mistress and unofficial fiancée of her late husband's one-time protégé. This greatly pleased Maynard, just as the extent of his parents' liking for Lydia had also surprised and delighted him. If only Vanessa had been so easily won over! (But perhaps, thought Maynard, ever the optimist, there was yet time.)

The *Life of Alfred Marshall* appeared in the *Economic Journal* to an overwhelmingly favourable reception. Mary pronounced herself greatly moved by it, and even Lytton Strachey, Bloomsbury's pre-eminent biographer, writing to Maynard, was fulsome in his praise.

If Maynard himself had lingering doubts, he did not share them with anyone. Writing about Marshall, he had found strange thoughts stirring below the surface of his mind. In writing about the death of an economist, was he also writing about the demise of a certain kind of economics? Was he paying tribute to an intellectual framework which was, he now suspected, deeply flawed? Hardly was the ink dry, than he was scribbling down notes for a lecture to be given at Oxford later in the year. Its title – 'The End of Laissez-Faire'.

Although Tilton was barely yards from Charleston, they

saw little of Vanessa and Duncan. Sometimes the young people – most often Quentin – appeared, to explore the grounds or dance with Lydia in the drawing room. Their parents waved cordially from the footpath that passed the boundary of Tilton, or from the other side of the street when encountered shopping in Lewes, but did not seem eager to engage in more than pleasantries. Maybe, thought Maynard, they too sensed the honeymoon nature of this particular summer. But when he voiced this thought to Lydia, she did not reply.

Long after the summer was over, Maynard found images from those weeks arriving at unlikely moments. Sitting in a College committee, he pictured Lydia sunbathing in the vegetable patch; in the midst of a Board Meeting of National Mutual Insurance, he would see again the view from Firle Beacon. And in the middle of an editorial meeting of the *Economic Journal*, he was suddenly visited by a vision of twilight over the Downs and heard again the rattle and rummage of rooks in the beech trees as he and Lydia sat curled up together, watching from the window.

FOXY SPENT his summer on a range of diversions, one of which was an opera evening at a friend's country house. Among the guests was Montagu Norman, and although relations between the two men had been slightly strained since they had aligned themselves on different sides in what Foxy thought of as the Battle of the Gold Standard, they greeted each other with civility and sat next to each other for the recital. Foxy was not hopeful that Montagu was about to change his mind, but it was possible. And as Maynard said, until the cause was lost, they must maintain relations and exercise every power of persuasion.

During the interval, they drifted onto the terrace with their glasses of champagne, both in agreement that in the duet from

Le nozze di Figaro, Susanna had been excellent, but the soprano singing the Countess had perhaps not brought quite enough lightness to the part.

Mellowed by the discussion, they stood easily together, gazing out at the eighteenth-century landscape: Capability Brown all the way, as Foxy remarked, even down to the tumbledown folly, the eccentric whim of some long-dead aristocrat.

Montagu Norman said, 'Our friend, Mr Keynes, is a little eccentric in some respects.'

'Maynard? Well, yes, I suppose so.'

'Have you ever heard there was anything *vicious* in his tastes?'

'No, I have not,' said Foxy emphatically. *What a way to put it,* he thought. *And from Montagu, for heaven's sake.* Inwardly, Foxy was reeling, even as he casually sipped his champagne.

'Ah. I just wondered. You see, I received a communication.'

'As it happens,' said Foxy, 'I can tell you that Keynes, at this moment, is ensconced in the country with a lady who nobody doubts, once her divorce comes through, will become his wife. The divorce makes it a rather delicate matter – I trust you won't repeat it.'

'Of course not. And you won't mention the other thing to him. I felt I should ask,' he added, after a pause. 'It is a serious accusation. The law is the law. But I personally don't feel we should pry into others' lives.'

I'm not surprised, thought Foxy. *Who knows what we would find in yours?*

Montagu turned the conversation neatly then, to his forthcoming trip to America to meet with Ben Strong of the Federal Reserve and his hope to take in some opera at the Met when he was there. Foxy was left to wonder whether Montagu had been convinced, and if he had seriously been thinking – was *still* thinking – to use such accusations against Maynard.

29

1925

In the pale, January light, Vanessa and Duncan were dabbing paint on the drawing room walls at 46 Gordon Square. It was Vanessa who had decided that the murals needed touching up. Duncan suspected that she was using the exercise as a way of laying claim to the territory – like a cat spraying – asserting herself in a space that was increasingly under threat of a Lydia Invasion. *But you can't put paint on Maynard*, thought Duncan. *I did warn you.* He had another warning to deliver also, but he had been putting it off until the right moment. *She won't like it*, he thought. *But maybe she'll have to lump it.*

Vanessa, from the top of a stepladder, was brightening a Bacchante's hem. Pausing to admire her handiwork, she remarked, 'I still like this, even though I might do the figures slightly differently now. I sometimes think though that Maynard doesn't care for it.'

Duncan grunted.

'Actually I've never felt he *really* likes my work; he only accepts this because you painted it too. I mean, look at my portrait of Lydia that he refused to buy.'

Because you made her look like she was made from dough, Duncan thought. Out loud he said, 'I'm afraid Maynard doesn't have the best aesthetic sensibilities. We all know that.'

'I suppose so. But I did feel there was hope for him, if only …'

She petered out, in the face of his discouraging silence.

Duncan applied a purple sheen to a bunch of grapes. The whole enterprise felt pointless to him. However, he always liked to paint, and it was a small price to pay if it made her … well, more receptive to his plans.

'I was thinking,' she said, 'if we work on this evening, we might even finish by tomorrow.'

'The light won't be very good.'

'Oh, I quite like lamplight.'

'Also, I'm going out.'

'Not *again*?'

There was a brief, charged silence, during which Duncan said nothing and Vanessa did not ask where he was going, or with whom. But her expression, as she bent over her patch of wall, was one of mute endurance.

Duncan realized there was no point in delaying his bad news; it might even serve as a distraction. 'Maynard spoke to me last night … after you went to bed.'

'What, going over the election again? Or gold? I'm tired of both.'

'You're not going to like this, but I don't think there's much we can do. Certainly nothing *you* should do.' Vanessa fixed her eyes upon him. 'He's taking a permanent lease on Tilton.'

'Oh no, Duncan!'

'It is rather a blow, I admit. But maybe they will grow tired of the place.'

'Or else they'll have a brood of children and we'll be plagued by lots of little Keyneses tumbling about Charleston.' Duncan laughed. 'No really, imagine if they are as air-headed as their mother, and as clumsy as their father. And the parents will be constantly invading us. I think,' she added desperately, 'it may be time for us to *abandon* Charleston. I've heard that Norfolk ...'

'Is very flat,' Duncan finished for her. 'Let's not do anything sudden, I implore you, Nessa. Above all, say nothing to Maynard. After all, we hardly saw them this summer, or only really when *you* insisted.' Vanessa, he thought, was like somebody who couldn't resist picking at a scab.

Vanessa burst out, 'Do you think, if it *does* happen, and they do marry, they will want *this* house to themselves?'

'No. Why should they? Maynard loves communal living. Anyway, it might never happen.'

'They found that Mary Hargreaves.'

'True, but it's January now and still it drags on. Maynard is so good at pulling strings. Don't you think if he were really so terribly keen on the idea, he'd have found some way to hurry up the divorce?'

'That's true.' Vanessa was comforted. 'I hadn't thought of it like that. Still, if the worst comes to the worst– I'm going to suggest they look at Kensington.'

'Might as well suggest Birmingham. Don't *fret*, Nessa. Put it out of your mind.'

Vanessa had ten minutes to reflect that, after all, he might be right, while Duncan pondered regretfully on Maynard's betrayal – when Maynard had been more available, Vanessa had been much less resentful of Duncan's adventures. Then, from somewhere in the house, they became aware of a flurry of movement: raised voices, a loud screech (Lottie?) and banging doors. Vanessa looked at Duncan, eyebrows raised. 'What–?' There was the sound of footsteps on the stairs, then a high-pitched shriek of 'Vanessa!' in an unmistakable Russian accent.

Duncan put down his paintbrush and moved towards the door; Vanessa began to descend from the stepladder, but before they could get any further Lydia burst in on them. Maynard followed a couple of steps behind.

Lydia was glowing, ecstatic. 'It is done!' she proclaimed. 'We can marry! The judge say so. We need only *degree nix*.'

'Decree *nisi*,' said Maynard, beaming. He reached out and shook Duncan's hand.

Duncan said heartily, 'Well done.' And in a warning tone of voice: '*Vanessa*.'

Vanessa said, 'Congratulations, both of you. I know you wanted this.' She submitted to Lydia's embrace.

'No more hiding about!' declared Lydia with satisfaction. 'Now everything honest and open.'

Vanessa went to kiss Maynard. 'Why didn't you tell us you had a court hearing?'

'I suppose I was worried about a last-minute hitch. I felt superstitious.' Maynard laughed at himself, half-embarrassed. He turned to Duncan. 'Will you be my best man?'

'My goodness,' Vanessa said quickly. 'Big weddings are not really our thing.'

'It's not going to be big.'

'It's going to be teeny-tiny.' Lydia was bouncing on her toes from excitement. 'What matters wedding? We just want to be together. Like hen and rooster.' She took Maynard's arm and beamed at Vanessa.

'Oh yes, and I daresay you'll want larger quarters now. I wonder,' Vanessa took a deep breath, 'have you considered Kensington?'

Lydia and Maynard burst into laughter. Vanessa felt her cheeks grow hot.

'But you are funny, Vanessa.' Lydia reached out to squeeze her arm. 'Of course, we will live here.'

'I see.'

'I'm going to have a library at last.' Maynard was glancing around the room as if, Vanessa thought resentfully, he were already planning bookcases. 'And plenty of space to entertain.'

'Well, we'll have to discuss it.'

'Of course there's lots of room for you next door.' Maynard, for the first time, seemed aware that his friends might resent his plans.

'I'm sure we can settle things before Duncan and I go down to Charleston.'

'Ah, Charleston.' Lydia clasped her hands together like a delighted child. 'Vanessa, you have heard? We are to be neighbours!'

'So I gather.'

'I am to be happy peasant, pootling in mud. And Maynard has lots of plans.'

'That's right. I'm going to get the architect who did the work at King's to build me a library. And I'm planning to breed pigs.'

'Fascinating.' Duncan's tone was deadpan.

'Yes, I think it will be. I've been looking into traditional breeds. If it goes well, I might try cattle too.'

'We shall all to market go!' Lydia flung open her arms. 'Here! Come share our happiness!' She was about to envelope them in what would have been, on Vanessa and Duncan's part, a most unwanted embrace, when she was prevented by the arrival of Lottie, bearing a parcel.

'Excuse me. It's for Mr Keynes.'

Maynard, still beaming, ripped open the envelope and extracted a thick document, and then – it was as if somebody had flicked a switch, thought Vanessa wonderingly, as he stared at it, intent and grim-faced. What could possibly make him look like that? With a fluttering of butterflies in her stomach, she suddenly thought the stock market; their investments that Maynard was managing – Maynard said that the stock market had done wonderfully since the General Election, the fall of Labour and the advent of a Conservative Government. But he had also made it plain that he had no confidence in the economic competence of the new Government, and maybe, Vanessa thought, the markets might have come to the same conclusion. If they really had to move, this would be the worst time to lose money …

'What is it?'

He looked up and scowled. 'It's a draft copy of the Chamberlain Committee Report.'

'That is about gold standard,' said Lydia helpfully, as Vanessa and Duncan both looked blank, but they were not much enlightened by her explanation.

'Entirely predictable, of course.' Maynard was still studying the document. He sounded angry. 'Pigou has done the drafting. I recognize his style: "the clear conclusion", "the overwhelming consensus", "the time is ripe". *Huh*! Well, there was never much hope, I suppose. Excuse me. I must make a telephone call.'

He turned and left the room. Lydia shook her head and gazed mournfully after him. 'This is grievous news,' she told the puzzled Duncan and Vanessa.

'MONTAGU THINKS he has me licked. Well, he can think again.' Maynard was in his study, speaking into the telephone. He had lit a cigarette, which he kept forgetting to smoke. 'I'm not signing off on it. That's what they want: unanimous agreement to put to the Chancellor. Well, the Bank and the Treasury may agree. I don't.'

'But you're not on the committee,' said Foxy. 'You can't sign off on anything.'

'No, I know that obviously. The Report is a lost cause.'

'You've heard that Montagu Norman is in New York? I'm

told that he keeps writing back to the Bank saying we must go back onto gold.'

'The Americans are twisting his arm.'

'I doubt it needs much twisting. But yes. The Fed say they've been helping sterling higher and now it's time for us to jump aboard. Of course, it's partly speculation that's driving up the pound. Knowing that the Chamberlain Committee are looking at it and what they are likely to say; knowing that Norman is in America; knowing that the Federal Reserve is working on Norman; hearing all the rumours–'

'Expectations at work, you see: the foreign-exchange dealers expect something to happen, and so they bet on it, and because they bet on it, it makes the very thing they bet on more likely. Expectations are a very neglected factor in economics.' Maynard stubbed out his cigarette.

'I suppose that's true. Funny world, isn't it? Hardly fair.'

'No indeed. The speculators will win out twice over, and the industrial workers will lose out twice over, because they have no money to gamble.'

'Unless the speculators get their fingers burnt. It's not over until the fat lady sings, you know – or rather, until the Chancellor signs the papers, which means Winston. So spell it out in words of four letters, stick it in *The Nation* and this time make sure Winston reads it.'

Maynard lit another cigarette. 'I suppose I had better get started.'

LYDIA'S DECREE nisi was celebrated with a dinner at Gordon Square, and anyone who might be feeling less than celebratory at the prospect of the approaching Keynes–Lopokova nuptials found it easier to at least simulate the appearance of happiness by the liberal imbibing of champagne. Vanessa and Duncan became *very* tipsy. Clive and his mistress stopped by to give their hearty congratulations, and several glasses later were still giving it. Bunny appeared. Lytton telephoned. Jack Sheppard, up from Cambridge, was effusively, loquaciously delighted. Vera and her husband came for dessert, as did several other of Lydia's Russian friends, while Sam and Lil Courtauld, who were in America, sent an enormous bouquet of roses. At times, the various factions eyed each other a little doubtfully over their wine glasses, but any awkwardness was dissipated with yet more champagne.

Halfway through the evening, people began to dance. Maynard, lounging on a sofa, cigarette in hand, watched as Lydia revolved with Duncan. Their intrinsic grace and beauty moved him. Duncan was middle-aged, but he hadn't really changed (Maynard fingered his own paunch doubtfully, but then reminded himself he had never had any beauty to boast of anyway). Duncan moved with rippling ease like a panther, and Lydia ... well, Lydia might be snub-nosed and dressed as unconventionally as ever in a satin dress with a woollen cardigan on top, but she was a dancer from her toes to her finger tips. Against the background of the newly brightened Bacchus mural, it was like watching a nymph and satyr in some forest glade. His reverie was interrupted by Vanessa, who asked him to dance; he shook his head – 'I would just stand on your feet, Nessa' – and fell back into contemplation.

Later, taxis were summoned to take the guests home, or else to further revelry at the Savoy. Maynard was not among them: he saw Lydia installed in a taxi with Duncan and Vanessa, told her not to drink too much – by which he really meant to keep an eye on Vanessa, who was looking the worse for wear – and, jestingly, not to dance with too many handsome young men. Then he went to his study, where his gentle, tender mood was immediately replaced by a sense of serious purpose.

No holds barred, he thought, as he uncapped his fountain

pen like a weapon and launched himself into a condemnation of the Chamberlain Committee.

Flexing his hands rather stiffly two hours later, he contemplated ruefully the ashtray of half-smoked cigarettes and, with more satisfaction, the handwritten sheets. His eyes went to a framed photo of Lydia and he reached out and patted it affectionately.

He stretched his shoulders, then turning over the sheets, began to read the introductory paragraphs again.

He glanced up as the door opened, expecting Lydia. Instead, Gates entered the room.

'What is it?' he asked, rather irritably, turning back to his papers. 'And do knock.'

The man came further into the room. He was breathing heavily.

'There's too much goes on behind closed doors in this house,' he said.

Maynard looked up, suddenly alert. Gates's face had a dead, clay-like quality and there was a sheen of sweat on his forehead.

'What's the matter with you, man? Have you been drinking?'

'No. I never touch it.'

'Then what do you mean? And what are you doing here now?'

'No need to cut up nasty. We're men of business, Mr Keynes.'

'What are you getting at?'

Gates shuffled his feet. The corner of his mouth was working. 'I heard as you and Miss Lopokova was getting married.'

'So? Are you saying you've come to congratulate me?'

'No. I'm saying as there's things you might not want her to know.'

Maynard laid down the page he was holding. He placed

the fountain pen neatly on the top, like a paperweight. Then he got to his feet. 'I don't know what you're talking about.'

'Oh, don't you?' Gates was clenching and unclenching his hands. 'I know all about your *friend.* Mr Sprott.'

'What about him?'

'Don't make me laugh! I'd heard the rumours. But it was all over, or meant to be. More likely, I thought, they've just got more careful. And then I saw him last summer coming out of your bedroom when she was away in France. I thought, no need to upset Miss Loppy, not yet. Didn't breathe a word. But now I hear as you're getting *married.* She might cut up if she hears – throw your plans right out. Even tell the police. That has to be worth something, doesn't it?'

'So this is an attempt at blackmail? That's a crime, let me remind you.'

'So's the other. Though *you* might think you're above the law.'

Something in the way he said it, the ferocity in his voice, startled Maynard. He stared at the pale face and the anger etched upon it. No, not anger: hate. Why? Was the man simply a bigot? A religious fanatic, say? Or just someone who was revolted by the very idea of sodomy? God knows, there were plenty of them. But if so, then what the hell was he doing working for Bloomsbury?

He said abruptly, 'A law that is most often ignored,' and even as he said it, with a lurch of his stomach, remembered Peter. He had first met him at Eton. A Cambridge graduate, an apparently happily married man, but once of a different persuasion; intelligent, artistic, civilized; a stockbroker and City gent, but one of the humane ones, like Oswald Falk. One morning he had been found with a bullet through his head. Was it really depression, as the Coroner said? Or was it, as the whispers had it, that Peter had been found out? A hook-up that had gone wrong, a set-up in a bath house or public toilet?

Or even that Peter was being blackmailed by someone like Gates?

How ironic, thought Maynard, if after all this time, and so many reckless encounters in alleys and parks and under bridges, it should be now, *now* when he had left all that behind, that he was dragged into the mire. For a moment he contemplated a possible future of court cases, newspaper reports, social and professional ruin. Then he thrust it aside.

'There's nothing in it,' he said. 'You've no evidence because there *is* no evidence. And, my God, Gates, what are you about? Are you going around the denizens of Bloomsbury with your lists of accusations? It won't work.'

'Maybe not with them. But you've got a reputation. You're Mr High and Mighty, goes to dinner with the nobs, your name always in the paper. You get telephone messages from the Governor of the Bank of England and Lord this and Lady that. You've a lot to lose.'

This was undeniably true.

'What evidence do you think you have?'

'I told you. He was coming out of your bedroom. When Miss Loppy was in France. Lottie and the Harlands would swear he was here, if they was under oath, I reckon. And I found *this*,' triumphantly, he produced a grubby and crumpled handkerchief, 'next to the bed. It's even got his initials on.'

Maynard looked at it, then began to laugh.

'What's so bloody funny?' A red flush rose up Gates's neck. 'And don't tell me it was the only time neither. I wasn't born yesterday!'

'But I wasn't here. I was on my way to Paris. I just let him use my bed for the night.'

'Don't expect me to believe that shit! I *know*!'

'I don't care what you think you know. I'm not going to pay off your sleazy blackmail threat, and you can tell Lydia what you want. She won't care.'

Gates recoiled as if he had been hit. There was silence. 'You get away with things because you're rich,' he said at last, in a voice silted with emotion. 'You didn't serve in the war neither. You think you can do what the hell you like, with never a price to pay. You're - *filth*.'

The word hung in the air. Then Gates looked straight at him – a look of pure, undiluted rage – and turned and lurched from the room. Somewhat shaken, Maynard sat down. *Even Montagu Norman never looked at me so murderously*, he imagined telling Foxy, though of course, this was something he would never tell Foxy. Perhaps he would never tell anyone ... except that he had to warn his friends, Duncan for example, who might be vulnerable. And what on earth should he do about Gates? Sack him, without references? But then what would happen to him?

Maynard abandoned the question as a waste of energy: he refused to waste his time wrestling with scruples about Gates. In any case, he reminded himself, there was bound to be a shake-up now in the domestic arrangements of Gordon Square, and Gates's departure would be less obvious.

What had disturbed him most in the encounter was remembering Peter. Disgrace and ruin were never far away, even at the height of success. But they weren't worth brooding about, either. He uncapped his fountain pen and turned back to his article.

FOXY FALK LURKED in the foyer of the House of Commons, with a large envelope tucked under his arm, thinking how much he disliked the world of party politics and politicians. Jesters, the lot of them. Looking at the faces of the passing MPs, they reminded him of the bankers and stockbrokers that he watched swarming down Cornhill on the way to the underground each day: complacent, hidebound, despising anything beyond their own experience or interests. And at least the inhabitants of the City of London did not pretend that they had special status simply because a few thousand ignorant members of the electorate had put a cross next to their name on the ballot paper.

'You're getting cynical,' Maynard had chided him, when he had recently expounded these views over dinner. 'If you think this way now, what will you be like at sixty? You have to save up some rancour for your old age. Anyway, what political system would you prefer? A tyranny in which the tyrant is one Oswald Falk, Esquire?' prompting Foxy to retort, 'I'm not greedy – we'll be joint tyrants, like Hippias and Hipparchus.' Maynard replied, 'As long as I'm not Hipparchus,' and Foxy reflected, with some amusement, that for all his intellectual brilliance the classics were not Maynard's strong point.

Foxy felt that the last election, in October, proved his case. Whichever party you preferred, what had really changed, now that the Conservatives had power? To take a matter of great interest to both Foxy and Maynard, the Chancellor of the Exchequer was no longer Philip Snowden, a man both considered a dangerously conventional idiot, but Winston Churchill. Foxy conceded that Churchill was not entirely an idiot, but he hadn't the foggiest about anything to do with economics: a disadvantage when his job was to take charge of the country's finances. Furthermore he was notoriously reckless and headstrong ('so are you,' Maynard said, but Foxy ignored him) and so capable of doing anything, but it did not follow from this that he was likely to do anything sensible. Maynard had disagreed: 'at least Winston *knows* he knows nothing. That's something. It gives us a chance. Snowden was convinced he knew everything. It was like trying to move – well, Snowdon'.

Nevertheless, Foxy had no great hopes for his present venture. He pulled out the envelope, and read the superscription again: *The Rt Hon Winston Churchill, MP*, written in

Maynard's writing. He had been carrying the damned thing around for three days now. This was Foxy's last chance.

'If Little Otto's minions nobble you afterwards it doesn't matter, so long as you've got it into Winston's hand,' Maynard had exhorted him on the telephone from Cambridge. 'There's no point my trying – I'm *persona non grata* at the Treasury. Besides, I've got College Council and a lecture to give.' Maynard had, of course, sent an earlier copy by post to Winston, along with a letter imploring him to appreciate the seriousness of the issue – but Maynard and Foxy reckoned both were heading straight for Otto's wastepaper basket. What was really needed was a direct approach. But so far Foxy had been rebuffed when he had called at the Treasury; had failed to persuade mutual friends to set up a meeting ('Absolutely not,' said Lady Violet Asquith, 'not now that wretch Keynes is cosying up to Lloyd George,'); and had drawn a blank at Winston's club.

There was a humorous side to it, Foxy had to admit: preparing to accost a Cabinet minister, shadowing his movements like some kind of Daring Dan, or the hero of a John Buchan novel. *Foxy Falk, Undercover Agent.* He broke off from his reverie to glower at what looked like Ramsay MacDonald's back disappearing into the gents – *Damned socialist!* – then became aware of a flurry and a bustle. A small group was emerging from the deeper recesses of Parliament, in its centre the unmistakable figure of Winston Churchill.

Foxy prepared to lunge.

From the opposite side of the foyer, somebody hailed Winston. He veered around, his protective horseshoe of officials turning in rotation with him. Foxy, swearing inwardly, prepared to muscle his way through, then came to an abrupt halt, recognizing Winston's companion. Even he, Foxy Special Agent Falk, was not prepared to elbow aside the Prime Minister.

Heads close together, Winston Churchill and Stanley Baldwin left the building, and remained deep in conversation until the Chancellor reached his car. From a distance Foxy was forced to watch as he was driven away.

HE TOOK REFUGE IN A RESTAURANT: the same place he had lunched with Maynard after the hearing of the Chamberlain Committee. He glanced around dutifully, but with no real hope: he could see only well-fed lawyers chomping oysters; there was no sign of Winston. To the head waiter he remarked, rather despondently, 'I suppose Mr Churchill isn't dining here today?' The man just shook his head.

He ordered the crab anyway, as a tribute to his elusive prey. *It tasted like ashes in my mouth,* he imagined telling Maynard, although in fact it was light and succulent. He chewed slowly, wondering why he had agreed to all this anyway. What made Maynard so persuasive? Was it his optimism, as much as his brilliance? Although Maynard, like Foxy, was often infuriated by the stupidities of the world, he was seldom downhearted or discouraged, or not for long. His hopes were not always borne out – witness the current dire state of the Liberal Party – but he never, ever gave up.

Finishing his crab, Foxy was suddenly transfixed by the sight of Winston Churchill heading past the open door of the dining room, and presumably down the corridor beyond.

Foxy dropped his fork with a clang. In one easy motion, he slid from his seat and sprinted for the corridor, dodging waiters with commendable agility. There was no sign of Winston.

'Damn, damn, damn!'

He stood for a moment staring around the corridor, and then opened the nearest door and found himself looking in on a private dining room. Sleek men in suits gazed back at him, mildly indignant. Muttering apologies, he withdrew, considered a moment, then plunged into the gents opposite.

There was a back turned to him, with humped shoulders and a balding head.

'Mr Churchill–? Oswald Falk, you may remember – I've something for you – My friend Mr Keynes is most keen that you should read it.'

Winston turned slowly, fumbling with his flies. He was glowering. 'Can't a man relieve himself in peaceful solitude?'

'What's that? Oh, yes, I do apologize, but it's rather important.' For a brief, horrified moment he thought he had left the envelope on the table, then he found it in his jacket pocket and drew it forth with a flourish. Winston made no move to take it, and Foxy thought it best to open the envelope and extract *The Nation,* turned back to the page of Maynard's article. 'This was published last week. I know you are very busy, with many calls on your time, but Mr Keynes would most appreciate it if you were to–'

Winston's cheeks puffed out like an indignant pug. 'I don't want the damned thing.'

'But–'

'Don't want it. Won't take it. I've already read his article.' He scowled at Foxy from under beetling brows. 'I always read 'em.' And he walked past Foxy into the corridor.

Well, I'll be damned, thought Foxy, with a sudden inclination to engage in half-hysterical laughter.

Shortly afterwards, Maynard received an invitation to a dinner party, to be held at Number 11, Downing Street: his host, the Chancellor of the Exchequer, the Rt Hon Winston Churchill MP; the subject for discussion, Britain's proposed return to the gold standard.

30

In the kitchen at Number 46, the trays were laid out ready on the table, the kettle was boiling and Mrs Harland and Lottie were scurrying back and forth with muffins and teacups. Grace was sitting in the armchair by the range with her feet on the fender and her lap full of mending; Vanessa, Duncan and Clive were all out, which meant that she could watch the rest with a clear conscience. Ruby, Lydia's new personal maid, was sitting at the table, giving the cutlery an extra wipe. She was a slim, hare-eyed girl from Norfolk, still in awe of her employers and the metropolis, and choosing to lay low, look and learn.

'I'll be glad when it's all settled,' Mrs Harland was saying as she arranged the tray cloths neatly. 'I've said it before and I'll say it again. Like musical chairs it is round here, sometimes. You never know where you'll end up.'

'I don't want to go to a new place,' said Lottie. Her lip wobbled. Gordon Square was what she knew, other than the orphanage, and she had no wish to go back there.

'Dearie, if we do move, it would only be across the Square.

They don't go far. They just shuffle around, house to house. Why they can't stay put, I don't know.'

'Grace says there's talk of *Mayfair*.' From Lottie's voice, Mayfair might as well have been a different country rather than a different part of London.

Mrs Harland shot Grace an accusing look. Grace flushed and said, 'There's talk. There always is. You know that as well as I do. But it's only Mrs Bell keeps on about it. She reckons Miss Loppy is more Mayfair than Bloomsbury. Don't mean it will come to anything – not on her say-so.'

'I heard *her* say …' Mrs Harland began.

'Her?'

'Miss Loppy. She said to *him* as she don't want to move. She likes it here and she don't want to live among the smart people in Mayfair, like the Asquiths, she says, meaning him that was Prime Minister. She feels comfortable *here*, she says, among friends, and of course he agrees.'

'She wants to hear what Mrs Bell says when she's not there,' Grace said darkly. 'She might not feel so comfortable then. Of course, she has been much nicer to them lately.'

'What *does* she say?' Lottie turned around from the range.

'Never you mind. Well … Mrs Bell, she don't care much for Miss Loppy. We all know that.'

They shared conspiratorial glances, expressive of their feelings about upstairs. If the servants could get on in their cramped quarters, why couldn't their employers rub along together?

'What about *him*?' asked Mrs Harland. 'What does he think?'

'D'you mean Mr Bell?' asked Grace. 'Or Mr Keynes?'

'I mean Mr Grant.'

'Oh, well, he tries to keep the peace. He always does. But he says to her he will lose out when they marry. I don't know what that means.' Grace's brow crinkled. 'And they're planning to paint the ceilings. They've finished the walls, they say, so why not the ceiling? Starting with the drawing room.'

Mrs Harland sniffed. 'A nice distemper, cream or powder-blue, or a striped wallpaper, that's what *I* should like to see. And proper drapes.'

'Miss Lopokova will most likely have it done over like a Russian palace, whatever that's like,' Grace observed, and they looked at each other again, slightly awed at the prospect.

'I never thought I should be working for a foreigner,' said Mrs Harland at last, and Lottie immediately protested: 'You can't call Miss Loppy *foreign*,' as if Mrs Harland had offered a deadly insult.

'No, well, but she *is*, Lottie,' Mrs Harland replied. 'I'm not saying anything against her. I speak as I find, and she's a good-hearted lady. And her Russki friends are nice enough.' Mrs Harland had not, initially, thought much of Lydia's Russian Sunday lunches, held for a mixture of expatriate, theatrical and society friends: lunches which seemed to go on and on and needed a great deal of cleaning-up afterwards. However, she had since decided that many of Lydia's friends, though odd (like their hostess) were also (like her) very charming. Besides, they tipped.

'But they won't let me go, will they?' Lottie voiced the fear that had been preying on her mind ever since she had learnt the news of the impending nuptials. She felt that Lydia liked her – and Maynard did not seem to dislike her, whenever he actually noticed her. But she was painfully aware of her record of burnt toast and smashed cups, stewed tea and smoking fires.

'Don't speak nonsense, child. Mind you, I'll dismiss you myself if you slop any more milk over that tray!'

Lottie put down the milk jug, but she was not to be diverted. 'After all, they got rid of Mr Gates.'

'Gates left.' Mrs Harland sponged up milk vigorously. 'We don't know as he was dismissed.'

'But why else–?'

'Mr Keynes was surprised he left, that I do know. Asked me where he was.'

'Upset, was he?' asked Grace.

'No, I shouldn't say that. He seemed quite pleased. *That fellow Gates*, he called him. And *I* say as he's no loss either,' said Mrs Harland bluntly. 'A listener at doors; something sly about him.' Her tone was the slightest bit defiant. Mr Harland was disappointed that Gates had gone; he missed having another man around, both to do some of the work, and as a fellow male in an otherwise feminine basement. But in Mrs Harland's mind, it was definitely a case of 'Good Riddance.'

'Don't know what will happen to him,' put in Grace. 'Jobs aren't easy to come by.'

'That's his problem. And you need to get that tray upstairs, Lottie. It's late. At this rate, we'll be starting on dinner before they've finished tea. Anyhow, it's only her this evening. He's going out – *Downing Street*.' Her voice took on a satisfied quality, all cat with cream. Grace's employers, the Bells and Duncan Grant, had surely never been invited to such a place.

Grace yawned: a less than satisfying response. She had perhaps picked up from the Bells this unfortunate lack of respect for social hierarchy. As Lottie disappeared through the door, clutching her tray, her apron strings coming undone as usual, Grace turned back to her sewing.

FOXY FALK HAD ARRIVED UNEXPECTEDLY for tea, and while Lottie struggled with cups and teapot, and Lydia seized muffins for toasting on the fire, Foxy took the chance to stare about him with the curiosity that he had been trying, for the sake of politeness, to conceal ever since he had arrived. He rarely visited Gordon Square and could not get over the notion that it was an odd place for Maynard to live. Of course, Maynard had many sides to him – *Many masks*, Foxy thought – but while some, such as a love of Russian ballet, and Russian ballerinas, were wholly understandable, Gordon Square with its murals that were now even encroaching on the ceiling, seemed simply eccentric. What did they think it was, the Sistine Chapel? Foxy put it down to misplaced loyalty. Maynard never gave up on a friend and moreover, liked to think of himself as a patron of the arts. No doubt he would be living with the daubings of his allegedly artistic friends (Foxy had his own opinion of their talents) forever.

'So tonight is the night,' Foxy said.

'It would seem so,' Maynard agreed, leaning back in his chair.

'What will you try this time? Sounding off about the Americans again?'

'No, I think I'll give Winston more credit. Anyway, he's half-American.'

'But a real, patriotic British bulldog.'

'Even so. I'll just have to get a feel for it; see what his questions are. Use my instincts.' Maynard looked gloomy. 'It didn't go well with the Commons. They're just desperate to rejoin gold before the rest of the Empire does. They think, once on gold, it will be back to the good old days again.'

'It's always the same story. Only you and I, who served in the Treasury, and saw first-hand how we almost went over the cliff, know how truly bankrupt we are. The good old days are gone for good. Still,' he added, 'you've been gaining some traction, you know.'

'Oh?' Maynard stirred his tea.

'Yes. Charles Addis at the Treasury has been defending your line – McKenna too. Even Little Otto had his moment of doubt, although he got over it.'

'I don't believe it. I mean, that he ever doubted.'

'A little bird told me.'

'What little bird?'

'I have my sources, Maynard. Remember, *I* worked at the Treasury too.'

Lydia came hopping towards them, bearing a plate of muffins which only her excellent balance prevented from landing on the rug. 'See, I too am little bird. I bring gifts for you. Eat, eat and do not fret about foolish metals, Treasury satsumas and other bad things.'

Foxy smiled and accepted a muffin he did not really want. Lydia served Maynard a muffin also, then went to eat her own on the window seat, where she sat cross-legged, her plate balanced on her knees and her head bent over a letter that she had picked up from the cushion beside her.

'Something else I heard, about the Treasury,' said Foxy.

'What's that?' Maynard was eating his muffin enthusiastically, the butter dripping down his chin.

'Winston wrote a memo. He wants Otto and his merry men to explain just why it is all the bad things you say in *The Nation* about going back on gold won't ever come to pass.'

'Really?' Maynard paused mid-bite and peered at Foxy over his plate. 'So he *did* read it.'

'Yes and with attention.'

'So there is hope after all.'

After Foxy had left, Maynard sat scribbling down thoughts in a small notebook that he had taken from his jacket pocket. *Don't underestimate Winston,* he wrote finally. *He is not a trained intelligence, but he has intelligence.* He replaced the notebook and looked towards Lydia. Earlier she had exchanged lively opinions with Foxy on Chopin's nocturnes and Rachmaninoff and the latest season of the Ballets Russes. But now the sparkle was gone and she sat gazing out of the window, completely still, everything about her expressive of melancholy. Such a vivacious creature, and yet sometimes a shadow fell and she vanished to a darker place. He noticed the sheets of paper in her lap. Of course! Today, she had heard from her family. She had read him extracts at breakfast. It was always the same: the initial joy at receiving news only served to remind her of the aching gap of space and time.

I wonder ... Then he rose and went to kiss her.

'I'd better dress for this famous dinner.'

She looked up, and her mood altering in an instant, flashed him a radiant smile. 'You must put everything right.'

'Yes,' said Maynard modestly, 'I suppose I must.'

THE LAMPS GLEAMED in a foggy Downing Street. Maynard, crossing the wet pavement, glanced up at Number 10 and wondered what Mr Baldwin might be up to: most likely bridge rather than work, if accounts of his habits were true. He made his way to the entrance of Number 11 where his coat was taken with a kind of hushed solemnity and he was ushered upstairs to a long dining room. At one end a small group was having drinks; he immediately recognized Reginald McKenna, Otto Niemeyer and Winston, who came to greet him.

'Ah, Keynes, good to see you. Was very struck by that last piece you wrote in *The Nation*.' (So Foxy was right so far.)

He was given champagne, which he sipped cautiously, and he struck up a conversation with McKenna. At some point he became aware of Otto Niemeyer scowling at him. He caught his eye and Otto's expression turned to a sickly smile. They nodded at each other.

'Let's be at it,' said Winston at last, and they sat down at the dining table and were served oysters.

'Montagu's not here,' observed Maynard conversationally to Niemeyer, who was sitting across from him. 'Well, I suppose he doesn't need to be.'

Otto flushed slightly. 'I'm sure Winston is fully confident he understands the position of the Bank.' Which was, it went unspoken, exactly the same as the position of the Treasury. Maynard ate another oyster.

The topic of the evening arrived with the saddle of lamb. Winston waved a loaded glass.

'Gentlemen. I think you know why we're here. I've got to make a decision on this issue of gold. You all know the background. This matter has been hanging over us for years, ever since the Cunliffe Report, but sterling and the dollar haven't been close enough to par. Now I'm being told it's the right moment at last, and no time to waste. We've had the Chamberlain Report, or should I say Bradbury Report, come down in favour.' He nodded at Sir John Bradbury, who had taken over as Chairman, sitting at the table. 'And I've heard plenty from the Bank and the Treasury and the City. But there are those, like Keynes here, who say it's all a mistake. So that's why I've invited you gentlemen to try and thrash this out once and for all.' He took a swig of wine.

Otto coughed and when Winston nodded at him, at once launched into a summary of the Treasury view. Maynard laced his fingers and let the familiar phrases wash over him.

'Last few months … Substantial appreciation in sterling … Now approaching the pre-war exchange rate with the dollar … The discrepancy no longer significant … Need to seize the moment … Gold the bedrock of free markets … Gold the foundation of capitalism … Gold the pillar of the world trading system … The Empire expects … The Americans expect … The City of London expects …'

Next to Winston, his Private Secretary, Mr Griggs, a grey, reserved, expressionless man, was scribbling down the notes that would later form an official record of the meeting. Winston yawned. McKenna was shaking his head slightly, and Maynard felt hope kindle.

Otto ground to a halt at last. Maynard said, 'As for the sterling-dollar exchange rate, I don't think the recent appreciation is a real appreciation. I think it is driven by speculation. My estimate is that the difference between American and British prices is still more like ten per cent, and so this is the extent of the adjustment that will be called for; a significant adjustment that will inevitably take the form of rising unemployment.'

He continued, assisted sometimes by McKenna, to state as forcibly as he could the painful likely effects of fixing sterling at the wrong level. The arguments were by now so well-rehearsed that they flowed seamlessly. 'And then we must consider the future,' he concluded. 'There is already a disparity, but what if economic changes in America further alter the economic fundamentals? The result would surely be a most damaging deflation–'

'I suppose you would prefer inflation,' Otto burst out. 'Like the Germans, who you admire so much. Instead of inflation you would have us transporting our cash in wheelbarrows, every time we want to buy a loaf of bread. That is the result of financial indiscipline!'

'That's ridiculous. We don't need to choose either extreme. We certainly don't need to impoverish our coal miners, just because Germany chose to bankrupt their bondholders–'

Winston held up a hand. He also, with a look, silenced Niemeyer, who was clearly bursting to respond.

'What strikes me most,' said Winston after a pause, 'is what Mr Keynes has highlighted in his articles; what he calls 'the paradox of unemployment amidst dearth'. *That* is what I increasingly feel the Treasury needs to address. Do you agree, Mr Keynes?'

'Absolutely.' Maynard felt an agreeable sense of surprise. Of course, he reminded himself, Churchill used to be a Liberal; at one time a close confederate of Lloyd George. 'It is the unique problem of our times. Never before have we seen such sustained high levels of unemployment, and I have no confidence they will decline of their own accord any time soon. Much of the Treasury view is based on the idea that wages and other prices can adjust seamlessly to any change, including a change in the exchange rate, if we go back onto gold. But if this were so, then we would not see the level of unemployment that we do now. Rather than prices – including wages – adjusting, it is likely that a return to gold will simply lead to yet higher unemployment.'

'But I'm told it will be good for the City.' Winston was still looking at Maynard.

'Who do not seem to care that the main impact will be to make our exports significantly more expensive in foreign markets, and that the only way for our exporters to respond, will be to lower production costs through lower wages. This will inevitably be resisted by workers and the process of forcing wages downwards will not be easy or comfortable. I would expect increased unemployment, strikes and industrial unrest, plus a permanent contraction of our manufacturing industry.'

No harm in spelling it out once again, he thought. Winston was not really interested in economic detail. He was interested in the politics.

Winston said, 'But we need a flourishing City of London too.'

'The City is not England, Chancellor. It is not Britain. The gold standard may indeed be desired by the City of London, but there are more coal miners than stockbrokers.' *Even if they don't vote for you.* Still, Winston surely did not wish to preside over large-scale strikes, or the decimation of the coal industry.

And indeed, it was with real warmth that Winston replied, 'That is a point, Mr Keynes: I am loathe to sacrifice industry to the captains of finance.'

Otto said quickly, 'If some manufacturers find the climate

harsher, that is no bad thing. A cold shower is bracing – better than living in a fool's paradise of easy credit.'

'We already have unemployment of one million.' Maynard was determined to keep coming back to that. 'Your cold shower may result in us drowning in a cold sea.'

'It is the certainty of the gold standard that is its strength.' This was Bradbury, speaking for the first time. 'Everyone knows where they are; there is no room for meddling. It cannot be rigged; it is entirely knave-proof.'

'And after all, what is the alternative?' Otto leant forward eagerly. 'Mr Keynes,' he turned to Winston, 'says that the Bank of England should manage the exchange rate – that he would hand discretion to the Bank of England, who is entirely at the mercy of the Government!' He glared at Maynard. 'You would hand power to a load of politicians!'

Winston raised his eyebrows. 'Mr Niemeyer, you seem to have forgotten, *I* am one of those contemptible politicians.'

'But you must acknowledge there are many flavours of politician. Who knows what kind of government we may see in years hence?'

Winston grunted: this time in acknowledgement of a point taken.

Maynard said, 'The truth is you can't eliminate politics entirely; it's a political decision. If we go back on gold you are putting one class's interests ahead of another. You are selling out workers in the heavy industries, who have already suffered enormously since the war, for the sake of financiers and the owners of capital. If there is such a thing as a social contract, you are breaking it, and those workers will feel betrayed.'

'I understand there must be an adjustment, but if every-one's wages fall ... if we all take our medicine together ...

'But that is not how it will be. There *is* no mechanism for ensuring a general fall of wages across the country. Instead, each group, each industry, will have to fight it out with their employers. You will unleash a bitter series of struggles, during which some will come out worse, through no fault of their own. And then they will be stuck. I would remind you that a coal miner whose wage is cut cannot simply go out and seek a higher wage in some other occupation – not in today's world. There are no opportunities at hand and no housing for him elsewhere, even if there was work to go to.'

From across the table, Niemeyer muttered something about 'socialism'. Maynard ignored him and continued, 'Surely it's the primary duty of any political party, any government, to try and maintain some kind of balance between the different parts of the population, based not on equality necessarily, but on a basic sense of fairness. That's part of Conservatism too. I'm not a Conservative, as you know, but I've always been an admirer of Edmund Burke. The structure of society must be respected, change must be evolutionary. What you're suggesting here, by contrast, is a damaging, radical dislocation, justified only by economic cant. By its writ everything – every social relation, every sense of fairness and compassion – will be crushed beneath the economic juggernaut.'

How on earth did I get onto Burke? he wondered, even as he listened to his own words – and made a mental note to save 'economic juggernaut' as an apt phrase for a future article. *I suppose because I've made all the other arguments so many times already, and also because Winston, whatever he is, is no economist. He's a very new Conservative and I've got to try and speak to that.*

Winston's forehead crinkled. It was hard to tell what he was thinking.

'Also, in these volatile times there *needs* to be room for adjustment. We must not tie our hands behind our back. That is why I should like to see day-to-day management of the exchanges under officials' control, but retaining the possibility of political oversight in the vital national interest.'

A little flattery, he thought hopefully, could not go amiss.

Winston was nodding. Otto was desperate to speak, but Winston turned to McKenna.

'What is your opinion?'

Was it Maynard's imagination, or was McKenna avoiding his eye?

McKenna coughed. 'There are good points on both sides. Mr Niemeyer and Sir John are right, however, that with the gold standard there is a level of certainty for everyone that is not the case if the exchange rate is left to the mercy of officials or politicians. However, as Mr Keynes says, we operate in an environment of unprecedented and extraordinary levels of unemployment. That is crucial to remember. I think he is right to say that there is a risk of imposing an economic contraction, particularly on an export sector which is not robust. On the other hand, the creditworthiness of our financial system is no negligible matter either, whatever Mr Keynes might say.'

And to think I dared hope McKenna would fight my side! It seemed to Maynard that he had seldom heard a more classic piece of fence-sitting in his life. Winston, however, thanked McKenna warmly. There was a brief interlude while the remains of the lamb were carried out and the desserts brought in. Mr Griggs polished his spectacles. A Sauternes was poured, its mellow sweetness at odds with the asperity of the debate.

The servants gone, Otto Niemeyer took the stage once more, leaning forward and jabbing with his finger to emphasize his points.

'Mr Keynes has introduced a philosophical tone to our proceedings. I am not going to continue with his thought-provoking examination of Edmund Burke. Mr Keynes often says, in his speeches and writings, that we must find a philosophy fit for our *own* age and not constantly be harking back; however, if he wishes to reference a writer inspired by the French Revolution, then that is up to him.' The rest of the company laughed; Maynard laughed obligingly too. 'However,

I *will* say that for all great political thinkers, including Burke, there is something that trumps any issues of fairness between mere groups, and that is the national interest. Many countries are now lining up to rejoin the gold standard. We need to rejoin now, to show ourselves a leader, and not come late to the table. Imagine if other parts of the Empire join before us? Hesitate too long and we will indeed be seen as subordinate to the Americans.'

Maynard could not disguise his impatience. 'National status and national vanity should be the last criteria for making an economic decision!'

'Some of us wish to keep Britain at the top table.'

'But–'

Winston held up a hand. He signified to Otto to continue.

'Mr Keynes is insightful, but he is narrow.' Otto was breathing deeply. 'He looks at the issue of distribution between worker and financier, when in reality it is the health of the whole international trading system that is at stake. Get that right and everyone will benefit - eventually. *That* is what he overlooks. Mr Keynes says in his latest work, "in the long run, we are all dead". That is a most un-English way of thinking. It is the responsibility of those in government to look to the longer horizon. There may be short-term pain, I do not deny it,' he smiled, a pious smile, like a kindly old headmaster, 'but it will be in the long-term interest of establishing a stable, workable, dependable international trading system, from which ultimately all will benefit.'

'So you say,' Maynard shot back. 'Or it may turn out to be nothing but a pipe dream. If the economic fundamentals are wrong, it can't hold. And don't dismiss Burke,' he added. 'He witnessed a revolution. He knew what was at stake.'

The door opened and the butler entered to serve the port.

31

After dinner, coffee was served in the library. Winston disappeared; Otto Niemeyer talked determinedly to Griggs; and Maynard addressed himself to McKenna, trying to strike the right tone between outright reproach and letting him off the hook entirely. His aim, if it were not too late, was to put a bit of backbone into him – to screw his courage to the sticking-place – but it was an effort of persuasion that strained even Maynard's rhetorical powers, and he was glad when a lackey appeared and asked him to come to Mr Churchill's study for a moment.

Winston was sitting at his desk, blowing smoke clouds into the air. 'Ah, good. Come here, Keynes.' He waved Maynard to a chair. 'Care for a cigar?' Maynard declined. Churchill leant forward. 'Thing is, it concerns me what you say. I don't want to sell out our manufacturers for the sake of the City boys.'

'And the working men; they will suffer most.'

'Yes, yes. I have a copy of your book here.' He picked it up and contemplated it. '*Tract on Monetary Reform.* Don't understand a bloody word of it.'

'It was written with a more technical audience in mind.

That's why I also write in *The Nation*, for the less specialist reader.'

'Trouble is, Keynes, you're a clever man, a very clever man, but all the others are telling me the exact opposite from you – that we must go back onto gold. So what am I to do?'

'You've never been one to follow the crowd. The rest of them are clinging to old dogmas. And they're ignoring the social and political situation.'

'You foresee bloody revolution, eh?'

'I know this much. The Bolsheviks argue that capitalism is flawed and will fail. I say, we can save it and make it work. It is not working now.'

'But then what's the answer? Socialism?'

'No. But we must experiment a little, find a new way. Returning to gold is not the answer.'

'Hmm.' Winston took a deep drag on his cigar. Then, very drawn-out: '*Hmmmm.*' The smoke curled its way from his nostrils towards the ceiling.

'If we could–'

'But it's since the war everything's gone to pot, is it not? If we go back onto gold ...' Winston left the rest of the sentence hanging in the air.

'It's a fallacy. You can't restore one part of the system and expect it to work as before, if everything else is broken. Before the war we dominated international trade. But we lost our foreign markets during the war – textiles, for example, or ship-building. Other countries moved in and we haven't been able to win those markets back. If you go back on gold, you'll just do more damage; you'll be kicking them when they're down.'

'Hmmm,' said Winston again. He took a swig of whisky. There was a bottle at his elbow, Maynard observed, impressed that Winston managed to remain lucid, or even walk straight, on the quantities he put away. Of course, Geoffrey said that the body adjusted, but even so ...

'They hate me you know, in Tonypandy and Llanelli,' said Winston, startling Maynard out of his reverie. And then, seeing Maynard's puzzlement, 'You talk a great deal about the miners … it brings it to my mind.'

Of course, thought Maynard. The strikes of – when was it, 1910? – when Winston, then Home Secretary, sent in the troops against the miners of South Wales. His mother's housemaid was from Llanelli. Nobody in the Keynes household was ignorant of what Gladys felt about the matter. People had died, he believed; there had been riots, court cases.

Only, what did it mean now? That Winston reckoned he was damned with the miners anyway? Or that he wished to learn from past mistakes? Should Maynard pursue the point or evade it altogether?

Putting words to his dilemma, Winston said, 'So what do you think of that then, eh, Keynes?'

'I think it's unfortunate.'

Winston looked at him out of small eyes, uncomfortably reminiscent of a pig that Lydia and Maynard had viewed at a livestock market near Tilton; a magnificent creature, but its eyes said *keep your distance*. Then he began to chuckle.

'Unfortunate … that's one way of putting it!'

'Once you have to decide whether or not to send in the army, it's already too late. You want to avoid having to make those decisions. So you need to get the economics right.'

'The underlying conditions? … You sound like a Marxist.'

'Well, in that if nothing else, Marx was right. Revolution doesn't happen just because somebody picks up a copy of *The Communist Manifesto.*'

Winston chuckled again. 'Damned right. As I said, you're a clever man, Keynes. A very clever man.'

. . .

THE GATHERING RECONVENED SOON AFTER, Winston once more took opinions, and this time McKenna came out in favour of the gold standard. It would hurt like hell, he said, but it must be done. Maynard tried to suppress the sad suspicion that McKenna's view would carry more weight, simply from McKenna having sat on the fence all evening, giving him an appearance of judicious consideration that he did not deserve. The fact remained, however, that Maynard was now isolated. Otto Niemeyer, to rub the point home, gave a little speech listing the many prominent figures, domestic and international, who also supported an immediate return to gold, and to rub salt in the wound, stated that he had no doubt that the previous Chancellor of the Exchequer, Philip Snowden, would not have hesitated for a moment. And, Otto continued, in sanctimonious tones, Snowden was from the very party that claimed to represent the working man, but *he* did not fear their anger: he was prepared to put their long-term interests first. To which there was little Maynard could say except to point out that being a member of the Labour party did not prevent someone being a bloody fool, as he was sure they would all agree. He felt though, as the talk continued, that he was battling not only those around him, or even those cited by Niemeyer, but an army of ghosts: dead officials, Victorian bankers, above all, perhaps, dead economists; all of them guardians of a cherished orthodoxy that still held their descendants in its grip.

It was approaching one o'clock when Maynard left Number 11, walking out into the night with Niemeyer. Unlike McKenna, who showed an inclination to scuttle off, head down, as if to avoid Maynard's eye, Niemeyer was now in a thoroughly agreeable mood and not averse to chat.

'So, well, Winston will sleep on it. He is never entirely predictable. Things may yet go your way.'

Maynard grunted; he was tired and eager to be home.

'Of course, neither of us knows what the future holds,' Niemeyer went on. 'A few weeks ago, I was even coming around to your opinion, but in the end ... Events may yet prove one or other of us right or wrong, but only time will show.'

'That's true, of course.' Maynard was polite at what seemed to him a mere platitude.

Niemeyer paused a moment. 'I had a rather odd communication about you. I was not sure whether to mention it or not. It suggested ... well, it was offering to sell information about you; personal information. Implying that your tastes were ... not as they should be. Someone trying to make something out of your bachelor status, I daresay. Of course, I gave it no credence. I had heard that you were engaged.'

Maynard made a sound somewhere between a harrumph and a cough. Niemeyer was already moving on. About to climb into his car, he stopped and regarded Maynard for a moment, his eyes bright and bird-like in the light from the street lamp.

'You are nimble in an argument, Maynard. But it is not sound. None of what you say is sound.'

MAYNARD, entering Number 46, was startled to come across a small figure sitting on the stairs. In the dimness – he had not lit the hall light – he almost fell over her. 'Who's that? Why, it's you, Lottie. Whatever are you doing there?'

Lottie, arms hugging knees, gazed up at him with the forlorn expression of a Victorian street child.

'Excuse me, Mr Keynes, but it's been preying on my mind, and you're always that busy, I never have a chance to ask ...'

'That's all right, Lottie. What is it?'

'You see, when I bring breakfast you're always on the phone, or at your work, and I don't like to interrupt, and you're so busy the rest of the time, and I should have asked Miss Loppy, but she's got her own maid now, and I don't want to presume ...'

'What is it, Lottie? Go on, spit it out.'

'It's just there's all these changes, and Mrs Bell moving out, and you may not need so many servants no more ...'

'You're saying you would like to go with Mrs Bell? I understand, Lottie, you mustn't feel bad.'

'Oh, no, I want to stay with you!' Lottie's eyes were beseeching, spaniel-like. 'I don't want to move out, and I could come to the country too and help you and Miss Loppy, if only you'd have me. And I know yesterday I dropped the coal scuttle and the toast–'

'Lottie.' Maynard laid a hand on her arm. 'Do not exercise yourself. I haven't had a chance to speak to Lydia, but I know she would say the same as I do: you are welcome to stay with us. I'm only sorry that I hadn't realized it was on your mind.'

'Oh, thank you!' She was weeping, he saw. He continued to pat her arm in a perfunctory way, very conscious of the strange contrasts of existence. Through her sobs, she continued to thank him, and to apologize in a garbled manner for a litany of domestic disasters, which she pledged not to repeat.

'What is a slice of burnt toast here and there?' Maynard asked. 'Charcoal is excellent for the digestion.' He reached into his jacket, drew out his wallet, and extracted a note. 'Now, Lottie, here is something to cheer you up and to show our appreciation. But I give it to you on one strict condition.'

'What's that?' Lottie spoke in tone of hushed reverence, her eyes fixed upon the money.

'That you go out at once and spend it.'

'What, *now*?' asked Lottie amazed.

'Well no, not this actual moment, but I mean there is to be no squirrelling it away under the mattress or anything like that. Spend and enjoy. Our lords and masters won't see sense,

Lottie – they have pledged us to a hair-shirt policy of depriva-
tion and endless belt-tightening – so it is up to us to do what
little we can to counteract them. I'm sure there are plenty of
things you want!'

'Oh yes!' Lottie's round eyes appeared almost hypnotized.

'Then indulge yourself.' He patted her arm one more time
and got up. Looking down at her shining face he observed,
'Really, I'm grateful to you. At least I've achieved something
this evening.'

He climbed slowly up the stairs. Passing his open study
door, he was aware of a shadow moving. 'Duncan?'

Looking sheepish, Duncan emerged onto the landing with
something tucked beneath his arm. 'Hello, Maynard.'

'What's going on? I just fell over Lottie on the stairs …
now here's you, burgling my study … you don't need to look
so guilty … do you mean you actually *are* burgling my
study?'

Shamefaced, Duncan produced a framed picture from
beneath his arm: a portrait that Vanessa had painted of him
years before. 'Vanessa says it's hers but you won't agree. So she
asked me to … umm …'

'Pinch it? Oh take it, I don't care. Let's not fall out over
trifles.' He looked from the picture to the original. 'Duncan …
that fellow Gates …'

'What about him?'

'Why was he working here?'

'Because the Stracheys were going away.'

'But why did they employ him to start with? … No, don't
worry, no reason for you to know.'

'I do know actually. It's because he was chucked out of the
army for being a sodomite. So of course, we wanted to help
him out.' And as Maynard stared at him, astonished: 'Didn't
you know? Well, I suppose you've never noticed Harland
drinking the whisky, either.'

'But – Gates tried to blackmail me. Threatened to ruin my career.'

'*Really?* I suppose it was too tempting to make some extra.'

'It was more than that. There was real hate. He … he used the word "filth".'

Duncan considered. Eventually he said, 'Well, no wonder. We did with impunity what he ended up in clink for doing. And we were never sent to the front. I spent the war buggering Bunny and picking fruit.' He smiled at the still bewildered Maynard. 'You're good at reading diagrams, not always good at reading men.'

'No,' Maynard admitted.

'Don't worry,' and Duncan laid a hand on his arm in passing, 'you have Lydia to do that for you.' And he went off to his own quarters, taking the picture with him.

AT THE END OF APRIL, Winston Churchill announced in the House of Commons that he was returning Britain to the gold standard. With the rest of the British Empire lining up to rejoin, he claimed, Britain had little choice, unless it wished the gold standard to be 'a gold standard of the dollar'. Maynard allowed himself half a day of rage and despair, cosseted and comforted by a patient Lydia, then took out his feelings in a series of excoriating articles in the *Evening Standard,* republished soon after as a small book by the Woolfs' Hogarth Press, under the title *The Economic Consequences of Mr Churchill.* He drew particular attention to the plight of the coal miners. They were, he wrote, 'the victims of the economic juggernaut', sacrificed by the Treasury and the Bank of England to satisfy the interests of the City. He predicted widespread industrial unrest. 'Will there be a revolution?' asked an apprehensive Lydia, and Maynard shrugged.

Winston Churchill penned Maynard a note of thanks for

sending him a personal copy of the book and nominated him for membership of his private dining club.

LATE THAT SUMMER, various friends and acquaintances of Maynard's, picking up their newspaper, were startled to be confronted with the headline: FAMOUS ECONOMIST WEDS BALLE-RINA. In the photograph underneath, Maynard and Lydia, emerging from a London registry office, looked happy if bewildered by the crowds and flashing cameras.

Virginia went to Charleston to comfort her sister, who was taking it hard. 'I knew it was going to happen,' Vanessa complained, 'but somehow I thought something would intervene; that the scales would fall from his eyes. But that's all over now. We've lost him.' Virginia made soothing noises. In her own mind, she thought they had lost Maynard long ago: to Mayfair, Whitehall, the City of London, and all they represented, even if the new Mr and Mrs Keynes – to Vanessa's intense annoyance – were determined to keep their residence in Bloomsbury.

'At least you weren't there to see it,' she pointed out.

'No, and Duncan will tell me the ghastly details anyway.' Duncan had been Maynard's best man. 'We shall just have to face up to the awfulness. I will throw them a party to celebrate, here at Charleston, of course.'

Virginia, who was aware that Duncan was – or had been – Maynard's heir, wondered how he felt about the wedding. After all, Maynard was surely now a wealthy man, and even someone as unworldly as Duncan must feel the pain of being supplanted in this, as in other realms. For that matter, Virginia had long suspected that many of Vanessa and Duncan's expenses, both at Charleston and Gordon Square, were covered by Maynard, who was always ready to buy a painting, subsidize the costs of an exhibition or pay more than his share of the rent. Still, Virginia thought, so long as they don't have *too* many children *too* quickly, there will surely be plenty to spare.

If Duncan was bitter, he gave no sign of it at the wedding ceremony. Indeed, it would have been hard for anyone not to be touched by the sight of Lydia, so pale and ardent, as she signed the documents. 'She really is a dear,' Florence observed to her daughter Margaret, as they left the registry office, to return to Gordon Square, where tea and wedding cake were waiting. 'I could never picture what Maynard's wife might be like and I certainly never imagined someone like Lydia, but I do feel more and more that I am extremely fond of her.'

Margaret might have replied that she had, for a long time, never pictured Maynard with a wife at all, but instead she just patted her mother's arm and ushered her to the waiting taxi.

Florence was not the only one delighted. Jack Sheppard and Mary Marshall, meeting unexpectedly on King's Parade, agreed that it was the perfect match. Lytton Strachey was less warm. Having taken in the headline, he pushed the newspaper across the table, without comment. Sebastian sent the married couple a present (a book on Marxist theory) and a note saying he was looking forward to enjoying crumpets at the fireside with Mr and Mrs Keynes.

Climbing into the back of the Rolls Royce for the drive to Sussex, Lydia gripped Maynard's hand so hard he yelped.

'Oh, Maynarochka!' she cried, immediately contrite. 'It is just that I don't want to lose you.'

'There's no danger of that. I'm officially yours. All signed and sealed.' Maynard was cheerful and matter of fact. Lydia stared at him almost with anguish, her lost puppy-dog look, then she smiled too. She put her hand to his cheek.

'Soon, soon, I believe it.'

The car, driven by a new chauffeur (Lydia's innovation) pulled out into the road. Watching as Gordon Square receded, he said, 'I wanted to ask you something. Do you think I should give up now? I mean, on … on my desperate crusades? So much energy, so little result. Duncan and Vanessa think I'm wasting my time – they've said as much. And, well, it's not just me I've to consider now.'

She turned around to face him, her mouth an 'O' of astonishment. 'Are you mad?' she asked simply.

'Oh, good,' said Maynard, relieved, 'that's what I think too.'

The car crossed the river at Waterloo Bridge. To the left, lay the City of London, clustered around the dome of St Paul's, to the right, Westminster and the rooftops of the Houses of Parliament. For a moment it was all spread out around them, glittering in the summer sun, and then it receded, was left behind. He pressed her hand and said, 'I've something to tell you. A surprise.'

Lydia regarded him suspiciously. 'Tilton was enough surprise.'

'This is a trip abroad.'

'To work?'

'Well, there is a conference but–'

'Oh, Maynard!' Lydia could not suppress a wail. 'I don't want to go abroad! I thought now we spend time *here*, together. Where is this conference?'

'I thought you might see it as a wedding present–'

'To sit in hotel? To talk with boring economists? *Tilton* was my wedding present.'

'I hope you don't find *all* economists boring. But, you see, there had to be a conference. It was the only way. It's not easy, otherwise, to organize a trip to Russia.'

Lydia stared at him, completely motionless.

'Do say something,' he said at last. 'I'm not used to your silence. It unnerves me. Where is my Lady Talky?'

'It true?' she asked in a low voice. 'We are going to Russia?'

'Yes, in just a few weeks. To Moscow and what they now call Leningrad – St Petersburg.'

Lydia did not say anything, but her eyes filled with tears. As the car moved through London, she was still silent, the silver streams running down her cheeks. Finally, using the mime gestures of classical ballet, she brought her crossed arms towards her chest, then held out her hands, offering him her heart.

Please sign up at www.EJBarnesAuthor.com to find out about the sequel to Mr Keynes' Revolution.

If you have enjoyed this book, please consider leaving a review or recommendation on Amazon or another review site.

AUTHOR'S NOTE

I came upon Keynes by accident while researching an entirely different project, a possible book about domestic service. I was reading a lot about early twentieth century maids and governesses, and at some point stumbled upon Alison Light's book, *Mrs Woolf and the Servants*.

This led me on to the Bloomsbury Group, in which I'd previously taken little interest. I'm not a particular fan of Virginia Woolf's novels, had never been to Charleston, and didn't even know that John Maynard Keynes was a member of the group. In fact, I didn't known much about Keynes as a person at all. I did know about his work, because I had studied economics at Cambridge University where there was a big Keynesian tradition. However, although I knew something about his ideas, I knew nothing about the life of the man who had tried to save capitalism from disaster.

The more I read about Keynes and the events of the 1920s and 30s, the more fascinated I became. It was extraordinary to me that while Bloomsbury's literary and artistic members had often been fictionalized and dramatized, sometimes over and over again, the life of John Maynard Keynes – who had the greatest impact on history, and to my mind was the most intriguing – had been strangely neglected. Eventually I decided to take the plunge and try and fill that gap.

Writing a novel set in a historical time period, especially one based largely on real characters, obviously poses questions about historical accuracy. There are various approaches the writer can take, according to the nature of their particular project. One is to aim for absolute accuracy – so any diversion from the historical record (in so far as that can be established) will be the result of author error. Another is to allow some diversion when the needs of the story seem to require it. Yet another is to play completely fast and loose with the historical record, on the grounds that a work of fiction is, at the end of the day, just that: fiction.

In the case of *Mr Keynes' Revolution* I initially wrote the story as a film script. This brought into sharp relief some of the issues involved, because it is impossible to distill any real life story successfully into a two hour script, without taking some liberties with what actually happened. In the case of Maynard's story, there would simply have been too many characters, too many events, too many meetings and conversations, too much diverse, muddled, nuanced, bitty "stuff", and the storyline would have become cluttered (and interminably long). It was necessary to compress; to combine certain characters; to take something that might have happened gradually, in a back and forth way, through letters, telephone calls and other encounters, and distill it into just a few dramatic scenes. It was actually helpful to realise this at an early stage, because it immediately focused my mind on what I was trying to achieve, and what essential "truths" I was trying to convey about the characters and period.

A novel presents more lee-way; it is less compressed. Yet ultimately the same constraints remain. The requirements of storyline and drama require a pruning of messy reality. It is best to accept this, and think hard about what one is trying to achieve. I would argue that those historical novelists who aim for complete accuracy can do so because there is relatively little source material about their subject – so they have the creative space in which to craft their story, to decide on the key scenes, to fill in the gaps. John Maynard Keynes, by contrast, has a life which is incredibly well documented, as do most of his associates. They wrote to each other incessantly, they kept diaries, they were reported upon by others: one could possibly construct some kind of timeline accounting for pretty much every day of their lives (I have not attempted to do this). Dramatizing their story with complete respect for every detail would be impossible: one would end up creating an elaborate and cluttered approximation of reality – but that is not what successful fiction is.

I would suggest that anyone who wants a strictly factual account should consult one of the many biographies, bearing in mind that even so, a biography will be a selective account.

Although I have not aimed for complete accuracy, I do care about history. What I have attempted to do is to build up a picture of who these people were, what mattered to them, and how they related to the world around them. I haven't tried to introduce much that is new or exotic, or to exaggerate events: the reality is colourful enough, that is why I wrote the story. John Maynard Keynes really was an economist of genius; he really did live through turbulent times; and he really did try to find an answer for what struck him, and many of his contemporaries, as looming economic and political disaster. Arguably he found that answer. He was an apparently gay man who fell deeply, passionately and lastingly in love with a ballerina (the deep and real nature of their relationship is evident from their letters and the accounts of those who knew them).

Lydia really was a celebrity, a gifted dancer, a member of the Ballets Russes and an exile of the Russian Revolution; her life did indeed include an entanglement with a famous composer and an exiled Russian general, a bigamous marriage and several mysterious disappearances. She was famously eccentric and there are many accounts of her warmth, wit and idiosyncratic way of speaking. She was despised by much of Bloomsbury, although held in great affection by many others who knew her.

I have attempted to remain true to my idea of them; nevertheless my version must inevitably be just that, a version, and one that undoubtedly reflects, if unconsciously, my own concerns and outlook, and those of the time I live in.

Useful Sources

The following is a selective list.

There are several biographies of Keynes, and my greatest debt is to the three volume biography by Robert Skidelsky, *John Maynard Keynes*, which not only chronicles Keynes' life in detail but also the wider cultural and intellectual context. I also owe much to the first biography I read, *Universal Man: The Seven Lives of John Maynard Keynes* by Richard Davenport-Hines. Lydia's life story is expertly told in Judith Mackrell's *Bloomsbury Ballerina: Lydia Lopokova, Imperial Dancer and Mrs John Maynard Keynes*, and some of Maynard and Lydia's correspondence is collected in *Lydia and Maynard: The Letters of Lydia Lopokova and John Maynard Keynes*, edited by Polly Hill and Richard Keynes. Finally, Zachary Carter's *The Price of Peace: Money, Democracy and the Life of John Maynard Keynes* has only just been published as I write this, but looks to be a fascinating treatment both of Keynes' life and his intellectual legacy.

For the history of twentieth century economics and economists and Keynes' place within it, Sylvia Nassar's *Grand Pursuit: The Story of the People Who Made Modern Economics* is a recent overview. *Keynes Hayek: The Clash that Defined Modern*

Economics by Nicholas Wapshott looks at the lives and work of Keynes and Hayek as exemplars of two competing traditions in modern economics. *Lords of Finance* by Liaquat Ahamed focuses on the role of central bankers during this period. A full account of the Paris Peace Conference and the Versailles Treaty is provided by *Peacemakers: Six Months that Changed The World* by Margaret MacMillan.

For those wishing to delve into Keynes' own writings, *The Economic Consequences of the Peace* is highly readable and has never been out of print. Many of his more journalistic and accessible writings were collected by him in *Essays in Persuasion*. Among these, *Why I Am A Liberal, The End of Laissez-faire* and *Economic Possibilities for our Grandchildren* provide insights into his broad political philosophy. An overlapping collection, with a valuable editorial overview, is *The Essential Keynes*, edited by Robert Skidelsky. Keynes' magnum opus within the academic subject of economics is *The General Theory of Employment, Interest and Money*, which spear-headed the subsequent Keynesian Revolution, but which was written after the time frame of this book.

There is a vast literature on the Bloomsbury Group and its individual members which I won't list here. Alison Light's *Mrs Woolf and the Servants* shines a light on those who worked for Bloomsbury, and so helped inform the characters of the servants in this novel. Quentin Bell's *A Cezanne in the Hedge*, and Angelica Garnett's *Deceived with Kindness* provide first hand accounts of life at Charleston. More generally, and because it is an enormously enjoyable read, I have to mention EM Delafield's *Diary of a Provincial Lady* and sequels: Delafield was acquainted with Virginia Woolf, and it is tempting to see some of her portrayals of literary society as lampoons of Bloomsbury.

ACKNOWLEDGEMENTS

The books I have used are listed separately, but I'd like to thank Stella Butler, the Librarian of Leeds University, for showing me material relating to Maynard, Lydia and Blooms-bury in the University's collection; and Michael Proctor, the Provost of King's College, Cambridge, who showed me the murals that Vanessa Bell and Duncan Grant painted for Keynes' college room. I owe a debt to those who taught me economics, beginning with Mr Philip Hall of the Edinburgh Academy, who taught me the basics of Keynesian macroeco-nomics, which I then explored later at the University of Cambridge. Thanks to the staff of the Leeds Library where I conducted some of the research.

This novel was firstly a film script. At that stage I received invaluable feedback and encouragement, above all from Charlie Bury whom I met at the London Screenwriter's Festival and who provided great insight. I'm grateful to Lucy Juckes who encouraged me to follow my heart into a new project. I am grateful to Gale Winskill for editing the book, and for additional editorial input from Jane Wickenden. Thank you to Sarah Coulson for various support, especially assistance with cover images. The cover was the work of Andrew and Rebecca at Design for Writers. Thanks to Evy Kersalé for help with the French. I'd also like to thank everyone who offered good advice on the Alliance for Independent Authors forum.

I am lucky enough to have some good writer and non-writer friends. Thank you to Teresa Flavin for encouragement and for the time and expertise you brought to the creation of the Keynes "deck". Thank you, fellow Flatcappers – Karen Bush, Penny Dolan, Joan Lennon, Susan Price, Sue Purkiss and Linda Strachan – for your invaluable support and feedback, and to Paul Harker for chats about scriptwriting. I'd also like to thank Neera Johnson, Rajni Sharma, Jay Williams, Gillian Holding and Rebecca Lansdowne; my parents Pam and Barry, my sister Rosy and my daughter Abby, for so much encouragement; and my husband Steve for being first reader, for trudging around Charleston and the Downs, and for his belief in this project.